A DANCE OF GHOSTS

"That's the way this world works, Muzien. It's the best of us who die before their time, the ones who the world gives cruel jokes and ignoble deaths."

"If that is true, then why do I still live?"

Ridley winked.

"Because you're *not* the best of us. You're the worst of us, Muzien, the very worst."

At that, the Darkhand had to smile. He looked to the sleeping city that, despite the fire he set, would not dare come to put it out, not while so many of his guild walked the streets in all directions, ordering men and women to return to their beds should they poke their heads out their doors. The city was alive, Muzien knew, a living, breathing conglomerate of beings, and like any being, it could be made to fear, and fear him it would.

But there was still one man out there who wouldn't fear him, who could be a great asset to his plan, or its most terrible threat.

"Where have you gone, my student?" Muzien asked with a breathless whisper that was carried away by the night wind along with the smoke, ash, and all else that remained of the Hawk Guild.

By David Dalglish

A DANCE OF GHOSTS

SHADOWDANCE: BOOK 5

DAVID DALGLISH

orbit

www.orbitbooks.net

ORBIT

First published in Great Britain in 2014 by Orbit

5 7 9 11 12 10 8 6 4

A CIP catalogue record for this book
is available from the British Library.

ISBN 978-0-356-50282-3

Printed and bound by CPI Group (UK) Ltd, Croydon, CR0 4YY

Papers used by Orbit are from well-managed forests
and other responsible sources.

MIX
Paper from
responsible sources
FSC® C104740

Orbit
An imprint of
Little, Brown Book Group
Carmelite House
50 Victoria Embankment
London EC4Y 0DZ

An Hachette UK Company
www.hachette.co.uk

www.orbitbooks.net

To Rob, for keeping me from ever losing my confidence, and Krista, for answering every medieval question I could come up with

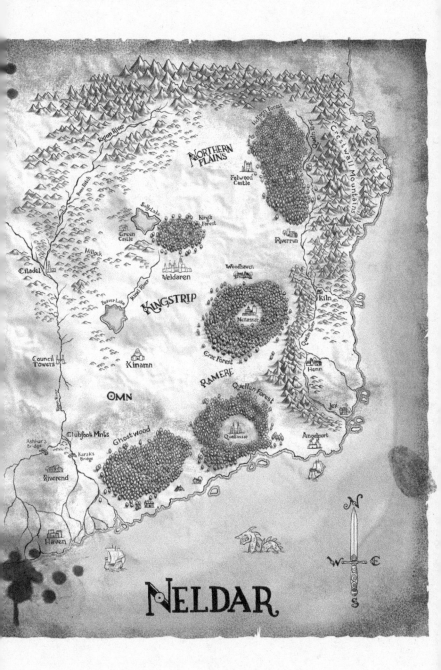

NELDAR

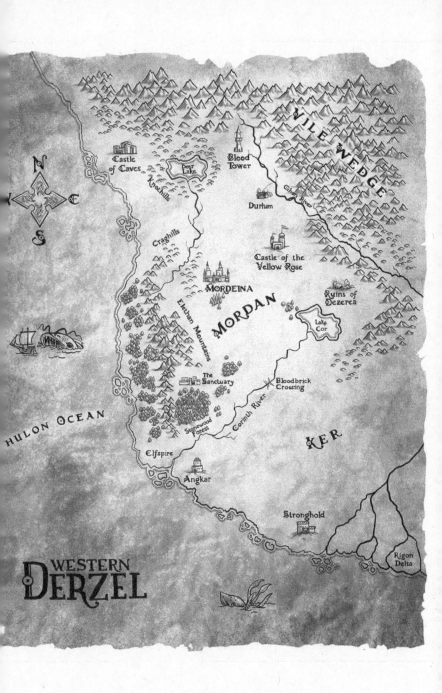

PROLOGUE

Kadish Fel wore a rut into the dirt floor as he paced in the center of the large warehouse. The smell of dust overwhelmed his nose, and he sneezed often. All around were giant squares of hay stacked to the ceiling, hay Kadish would sell to the outlying farms come winter. He kept his hands clasped behind his back, for it was the only way to keep himself from drawing his swords and twirling them as a nervous tic. But drawn weapons wouldn't do, not when he needed his ambush to succeed.

"Not sure I've ever seen you so nervous," said Carlisle, a squat man who helped Kadish with the more brutal affairs of his Hawk Guild. "You really think Darkhand will be that frightening in person?"

Kadish stopped his pacing, just for a moment.

"You know his reputation," he said, running a hand through his auburn hair.

"Aye, I do," laughed Carlisle. "But I also know people love telling tales, and that the tales get larger with the telling. This guy lives three kingdoms away, and every story making its way here probably went through many tellings before ever reaching us."

Carlisle reached into his pocket, taking out a pinch of snuff and snorting it.

"Besides," he continued, rubbing his eyes as they watered. "I don't care if this guy's the biggest shit in all of Mordeina; he's still coming into our city. Our *home*. That arrogant prick dies tonight."

Kadish looked to the rafters, to the tops of the mountains of hay. Hidden above were nearly twenty members of his Hawk Guild, every last one armed with crossbow bolts tipped with poison. On the ground were ten more, their daggers ready. In but a moment, Kadish could bring the wrath of his entire guild upon the man he was soon to meet for the first time. Yet he still felt he was the one in danger.

Muzien the Darkhand, no matter how bloated his reputation, no matter how far he was from home, was still a man to fear.

"Perhaps he won't show," Kadish said as the minutes crawled, midnight passing and the truly late hours arriving. "He might have anticipated our ambush."

Carlisle sat down on a single bundle of hay, grunting and shifting at its lack of comfort. He took another hit of snuff, then shook his head.

"Or maybe he's abandoned coming into Veldaren altogether. That Victor fellow, how long ago was it, three weeks..."

"Five," said Kadish.

"Five, right. Whatever. Victor's men thrashed the Sun Guild, drove 'em out of the city like they were rats on a ship. Fuck, even the fabled Grayson Lightborn got his ass killed. Perhaps Muzien took one look at our city and decided he didn't want to share his right-hand man's fate?"

"Then why set up this meeting if he was just going to turn tail and slither back to Mordeina?"

Carlisle spit.

"He's an elf. Who says he has to make sense?"

Kadish shrugged. Well, Carlisle did have a point there. Still, the reputation the Darkhand carried...

"No," Kadish said. "The Sun Guild isn't finished with our city just yet. He's here, in Veldaren. And he'll be here for our meeting, even if he makes us wait a few hours."

"What makes you so certain?"

Kadish crossed his arms and leaned against one of the nine support beams throughout the middle of the building. The wood was rough and splintered, but his long brown cloak kept him safe from its discomfort. His brow furrowed, and he let his voice drop in hopes that only Carlisle, and not the rest of his hidden men, would hear.

"Because a man with a reputation like Muzien's doesn't get it through accident," he said. "He gets it by working his ass off for it and making sure nothing tarnishes it. He's like Thren in that regard, except even better if we're to believe the stories. By Karak, I think every child alive has heard the tale of Muzien's Red Wine."

Carlisle snickered.

"Well," he said. "Make sure you don't drink anything that elf offers you, then, eh?"

"Indeed. But my point is, calling us here for a meeting and then flaking... all it takes are a few whispers by me and everyone hears of his cowardice, his unreliability. He won't allow it, no matter how petty. He wants us afraid, every single one of us. I have a feeling we're not the first he'll talk to tonight."

"Perhaps," said Carlisle. "But we'll sure as shit be the *last* he talks to."

"I pray we are."

With a sudden bang, the worn door blocking the only entrance to the building smacked open. Despite the many hours of waiting, despite his fear of the unknown guildmaster of the Suns, Kadish felt relief that the time had finally come. In through the door walked two hard-looking men dressed in dark grays and tightly fitted clothing. Daggers gleamed from their belts. They wore no cloaks, instead bearing the four-pointed star sewn just above their hearts. From what Kadish had learned, the rings in their ears signified solo kills, and each man had at least a dozen hoops and studs. They strode in without pause, their eyes scanning every corner of the room. Kadish swallowed, trusting his men to be adequately hidden.

And then in stepped the Darkhand. He was tall, and despite the long dark coat he wore, it was striking how slender an elf Muzien was. That slenderness belied a smooth strength, for each step he took was carefully weighted, every twitch of his muscles like that of a feline predator. His hair was a dark umber, the front of which was hooked into two braids and tied behind his head. From his hips swayed two swords, mimicking him in length and slenderness. Upon entering the building, Muzien glanced about the place, seeing the tall stacks of hay, and smirked. That done, he brought his attention to Kadish as he moved to join his two acquaintances. The moment those cool blue eyes settled on Kadish, he felt his scrotum tighten, felt the air around him thicken. Kadish had met hard men, had spent decades among those who viewed life as something to trade and fuck and cut short without a second thought.

He'd not seen eyes quite like Muzien's. Beneath that gaze, Kadish felt like an insect seeking an audience with the boot about to crush him beneath its heel.

"Wel...welcome to Veldaren," Kadish said, gathering his

senses. He expected better of himself, and he used his wounded pride to find the strength to stand a little taller, and let a bit of mockery enter his voice. "I pray you won't be staying long?"

Muzien stood several feet opposite Kadish, with his bodyguards on either side. His long, pale fingers slowly twirled a gold band on the index finger of his left hand, which, true to his name, appeared to have been crafted out of coals instead of flesh.

"I'll stay until my task here is done," he said, openly staring at Kadish. Disliking the cryptic answer, Kadish felt himself snap.

"Not sure that's wise," he said. "Your kind ain't wanted here, Muzien. You think your little trick with your ears fools anybody?"

Muzien tilted his head slightly to one side, as if amused. The tops of his ears, where there should have been the distinctive upturned curve of his race, were instead two mutilated scars.

"What was done to my ears was not done for you, nor the wretches who fill this city," the elf said. His voice was deep and aged. "Nor do I care if I am unwanted. That did not stop my Sun Guild in Mordeina, and it shall not stop us here. Now please, I've come to hear your answer, not your pathetic attempts at insult."

"To get an answer, you need to ask a question," Carlisle said, earning himself a glare from Muzien. "So far, I don't think me and my guildmaster here have heard one yet."

"Is this toad yours?" Muzien asked. "I guess I should take comfort in knowing that mankind shows no greater patience here than it has anywhere else in our world."

"He only speaks my mind, if a bit hastily," Kadish said. He wasn't happy with Carlisle's outburst either, but he would still defend his own over the accusations of some foreign elf guildmaster. "You asked to meet me, so here I am. You said you have questions, and I'm here to answer. Ask away, and I'll do my best to play the good host."

Kadish put his hands behind his back and tried to look relaxed. In truth, he was preparing to dive aside the second any of the three drew their blades. The moment he shouted out, his guild would reveal its ambush, but until then he wanted to learn what he could about the Sun Guild's intentions, just in case someone else took up Muzien's mantle after his death.

"I have but two questions," said Muzien. "First... where is Thren Felhorn?"

Kadish was honestly surprised.

"Thren?" he asked. "Why do you care?"

At Muzien's glare, Kadish shrugged.

"Fine, then; don't tell me," he said. "But Thren's gone missing ever since he disbanded his Spider Guild. Rumors on the street claim your right hand Grayson killed him, but others said he got away only to be killed by Lord Victor Kane."

"So he is dead?" Muzien asked. "Has anyone seen his body?"

Again Kadish shrugged.

"Not that I know of."

"Then he isn't dead."

It was spoken so simply, with such finality, Kadish didn't bother to argue. What did it matter if the legendary Thren Felhorn was dead? His guild had been disbanded, his territory swallowed up by the remaining guilds. He was a nonentity now, a relic of the past in an underworld willing to move on and forget within the blink of an eye.

"Well, there's question one," Kadish said. "What's your second, so we can get this over with and I can go find myself a bed and a pair of tits?"

Still Muzien twisted the ring on his finger, as if it was nothing more than a nervous tic of his own. But it seemed strange to think that...seemed strange to even consider a man with those cold blue eyes ever being nervous about anything. The gold of the band appeared ludicrous when contrasted against the dark flesh beneath it.

"I offer you and your guild the same chance I will offer the Wolves, the Serpents, the Ash, and all the rest," said the elf. "Despite whatever setbacks you think I have suffered, be assured our takeover of Veldaren is inevitable. The Sun Guild rises, and all who stand against us shall fall."

"Big words," Kadish mumbled. "You think we've not heard the same a hundred times before? There's always a new challenger on the streets."

Muzien smiled.

"You've not had a challenger like me. Listen well, Kadish Fel, for it is your only chance to survive this night unharmed. Toss aside your cloaks and accept the four-pointed star. There will be a place for everyone in my guild, for I will need strong hands and sharp minds to shape the future of Veldaren. You will have a station of honor, one worthy of the position you once held. All others will be given roles suited to their talents. No blood will be spilled. No wars fought between guilds. My victory is inevitable, so let us not waste the time, nor end lives unnecessarily."

Kadish could hardly believe what he was hearing, and despite the deep pit of fear in his belly, he laughed.

"Is that so?" he asked. "Inevitable? You are truly something special, Muzien, but I fear you've let your pride overwhelm your common sense. *Hawks, now!*"

From the hay sprang his men, slipping out from behind bales, falling down from the rafters onto piles, dark sheets meant to hide them during their long wait discarded. Before the two bodyguards could draw their blades, a half dozen arrows plunged into each of their bodies, dropping them. Blood pooled at Muzien's feet as he stood there, still twirling his ring. He'd not even blinked at the sudden ambush.

Kadish drew his own sword, took a step closer to Muzien.

"Not everyone here is as cowardly as you'd believe," he said. "Now tell me why you've come to Veldaren, and why now."

"Or what?" asked Muzien. "You'll kill me?"

"Look around you," Kadish said. "My guild is here and ready. However many you brought with you, it doesn't matter. My arrows have you sighted. My swords are ready to plunge into your heart and lungs. You walked right into my home, you egotistical elf, so do you really think I wouldn't be ready for an intruder like you?"

Slowly Muzien shook his head.

"Ready with an ambush, yes," he said. "But for you to be stupid enough to spring it? No. No, I did not."

The door to the warehouse slammed shut with a heavy thud.

"You and your guild fail to realize how far out of your depth you really are," Muzien said as the rest of the Hawk Guild turned to the door, unsure of what was about to transpire. "You cannot see Veldaren's fate even though it is as clear and unde-niable as the rising sun. Your whores, your drug trades of leafs and powders, your *territory* as you would call it, will be swept into my arms. You could have continued on under my care. You could have had your place."

A few of Kadish's men pushed the doors, lightly at first, then with their entire bodies flung against it. The wood rattled but would not move.

"You could have lived," said Muzien.

Kadish turned to the archers still in place.

"Kill him!" he shouted.

The arrows flew, but Muzien never moved. His body became a blur, the sight of it somehow hurting Kadish's head. And then the arrows thudded into the dirt, leaving Muzien standing there, not a drop bleeding from his untouched form. The pit of fear in Kadish's stomach turned to full-blown terror. As if lost in a dream he stepped closer to the elf and raised his sword. Muzien only stared at him with an expression that was equal parts pity and condescension. Still his swords remained buckled at his sides. Taking in a deep breath, Kadish plunged his weapon forward.

It disappeared into Muzien's stomach without a hint of resistance, all the way up to Kadish's hand. He felt nothing, only air. When he pulled the blade back, he knew his life was over.

"Do not resist," said Muzien. "Let the smoke take you. Your death will be more peaceful that way."

Kadish dropped his sword as the elf ceased the turning of his ring. Muzien's image flickered, then faded away until it was as if he'd never been there at all.

All around him he heard screams, banging at the doors, people begging to be let out. Others were swearing they would change allegiance and join the Sun Guild. Kadish glanced to the door, saw even Carlisle was one of the ones willing to turn. It should have disappointed him, but it didn't. Kadish was willing to toss aside his own cloak now, but he knew it was beyond that. He'd seen the look in Muzien's eye. He knew his place now, what he meant to the Darkhand. They were but vermin to be destroyed.

From the very walls came the first hints of smoke, followed by the flickering tongues of fire.

Muzien watched as the building burned, twelve members of his Sun Guild forming a perfect circle surrounding it and holding torches aloft in silent ritual. The screams from within took several minutes to stop, and it wasn't until they did that he spoke.

"He said he doesn't know where Thren is hiding."

Beside him stood his new right hand, a stocky man named Ridley with a pockmarked face.

"Did he at least offer an idea to explain the absence?"

Muzien nodded.

"He did. He said he believed Thren to be dead, though no proof of it has surfaced."

Ridley took a step forward and tossed his own torch onto the burning wreckage. A large crack followed, one of the support beams having weakened so much it broke under the strain of the roof, which crumbled inward along with it.

"Of your students, who was the better, Grayson or Thren?" asked Ridley.

"Grayson."

"Easy enough. Thren is still alive."

Muzien cocked his head at that.

"How so?" he asked. "If the stronger and the more skilled has perished, why then should Thren have also survived?"

Ridley gave him a crooked smile.

"Because that's the way this world works, Muzien. It's the best of us who die before their time, the ones who the world gives cruel jokes and ignoble deaths."

"If that is true, then why do I still live?"

Ridley winked.

"Because you're *not* the best of us. You're the worst of us, Muzien, the very worst."

At that, the Darkhand had to smile. He looked to the sleeping city, which, despite the fire he set, would not dare come to put it out, not while so many of his guild walked the streets in all directions, ordering men and women to return to their beds should they poke their heads out their doors. The city was alive, Muzien knew, a living, breathing conglomerate of beings, and like any being, it could be made to fear, and fear him it would.

But there was still one man out there who wouldn't fear him, who could be a great asset to his plan, or its most terrible threat.

"Where have you gone, my student?" Muzien asked with a breathless whisper that was carried away by the night wind along with the smoke, ash, and all else that remained of the Hawk Guild.

CHAPTER

 1

The wagons, all three of them full of men and women laughing and calling to one another, rumbled along on wooden wheels down the road that split the forest. So far, it seemed none realized they were being watched.

"I don't see why we must hide," Thren whispered beside Haern as they crouched together against the trunks of trees fifteen feet out from the road.

"Caution over haste," Haern said. He gestured to the dark gray clothes and long cloak each of them wore. "Besides, neither of us is inconspicuous."

As Thren shrugged, Haern returned his attention to the three wagons, particularly the men and women visible at the front or walking alongside. They'd passed so many already, yet if there were even more…

"They're with the Sun Guild," Thren said, his voice slowly growing louder as the wagons continued. "If that is what you're searching for, then stop bothering. Their earrings mark them clearly as such."

"Damn," Haern muttered, thudding his forehead against the rough bark of the tree, feeling it scratch his skin. "How many will he move into our city? A thousand? Ten?"

"A hundred thousand if need be," Thren said, drawing his two short swords and calmly walking toward the road. "That's how Muzien works. The idea of failing doesn't even enter his head."

Haern reached out to grab his arm, hesitated just before. Thren paused and looked his way, and there was a fire in his glare at the very idea that Haern might try to stop him.

"What is it?" Thren asked, pulling his gray hood up over his blond hair. "Since when are you one to shy away from bloodshed?"

"We have no reason to fight."

Thren laughed.

"Those wagons are full of killers and thieves that will make life miserable for everyone in your precious little city. We're doing the world a favor. Now either stay and watch, or take the east flank. Your choice."

Haern watched his father break out into a sprint, racing just outside the limits of the road so the trees still blocked sight of him with their low branches and their wide green leaves. Despite his speed, he was still a whisper compared to the cheer coming from the wagons. Haern estimated at least twenty total in the group, perhaps more if anyone were inside wagons and hidden by the sun-bleached tarps. Twenty dead, and all for what? Wearing the wrong earrings?

They're not innocent, Haern told himself as he drew his own swords and dashed to the other side of the road, rushing through the trees while eyeing the rapidly approaching wagons. The people in the Sun Guild were flooding into his city, taking over the various drug trades, demanding protection money from every street they controlled. They were threatening the peace he'd bled for. That was what he told himself as he watched his father come leaping out of the woods, spearing a raven-haired woman through the neck as she walked alongside one of the horses. That was what he repeated in his head as the driver of the wagon fell, intestines spilling out beneath him before he hit the dirt.

Not innocent.

From the other side, Haern emerged, his sabers feeling heavy in his hands. The party was letting out confused cries, many making mad dashes for wherever it was they'd stashed their weaponry. Haern knew the early period was when they'd need to score the most kills. If the survivors could band together, form a perimeter...

One saber cut through the heel of a fleeing man, and his other lashed out, opening the neck of a man who'd come rushing in with his own sword raised. A turn, a step, and the wounded man on the ground died with his lungs pierced through the back. As the blood flowed, Haern let out a grim chuckle.

Who was he kidding? The combined wrath of the Watcher and Thren Felhorn had descended upon the Sun guildmembers. There would be no survivors.

"Fall back!" a man yelled, heavyset and with dirty hair hanging over his face. He seemed to be the only one aware of what was going on, and Haern set his sights immediately upon him. His foe wielded a long blade in his left hand, his other ushering people toward the third wagon. Two more had joined his side by the time Haern came crashing in, whose haste nearly cost him dearly. The two others, each holding a short sword, tried to rush him simultaneously, their blades slashing. Haern skidded to a stop out of reach, and he flung himself to the right, smashing away the pathetic attacks to create an opening. The third man, however, had far more skill than the other two and anticipated the maneuver. Out lashed his sword with his long reach, its aim for Haern's chest.

Fighting off panic, Haern whirled the saber in his right hand about, and he let his weight drop unsupported. The thrusting blade batted upward, and Haern fell, tilting his head back and watching the blade stab mere inches above him. Landing hard on his knees, he rolled once to put his feet beneath him, then lunged. His skilled foe was already pulling back, but the other two were not so lucky. Haern struck down the first, rammed his knee into the second, disarming him with a slash to the wrist, and then cutting him down as well.

"You'll die for this," the dirty-haired man said, still retreating toward the back of the wagon. "You're messing with the Sun Guild; don't you get that?"

The threat had only the opposite effect on Haern. Instead of frightening him, he felt relief. They had made no mistake when guessing their allegiance.

"You're about to be dead men, and you waste your last words on empty threats?" Haern asked.

The man grinned, and from around the corner stepped two women, each armed with small crossbows. Before the man could even open his mouth to give the order to fire, Haern was already flinging his cloak into the air to obfuscate his movements. Instead of dodging to either side, he rushed low and straight at them, and when he heard the surprised cries of the three, he dropped into a roll. He heard the twang of crossbow strings, and he tensed on instinct, waiting for the piercing pain of a bolt. None came. He pulled out of the roll, and then his sabers did their work. The man died, having survived for only three exchanges of their blades. One of the women dropped her crossbow to draw a dagger, the other still frantically trying to reload.

"Drop your weapons," Haern told them.

They had no chance to respond. Blades pierced both their chests, and they gasped before they fell. Thren Felhorn stood behind them, his swords and clothes caked with blood.

"Drop your weapons?" Thren asked, swinging his short swords in a futile attempt to fling the blood off them. "Did you plan on taking prisoners?"

Haern looked around for any more to fight, but the three wagons had been abandoned.

"Does it matter?" he asked.

"You hesitate to kill women," Thren said, shaking his head. "The ones immersed in the lives we live are just as dangerous as any man. You'll get yourself killed someday if you let such a weakness linger."

"Perhaps." He sheathed his blades. "Did you kill the rest?"

Thren gestured north, toward the forest.

"About five or six managed to flee. I'm sure they'll come back for the wagon in a day or two, see what's left of it. We have nothing to fear from those cowards."

Haern was less ready to be so dismissive, but he did not argue the point. Instead, he stood and stared at the bodies bleeding out before him as his father walked over to the nearest covered wagon and tossed aside one of the flaps. One of the women was not yet dead, but her eyes were glassy, her breath coming in rapid, shallow gasps. Her fingers were near her face, digging into the loose earth as her hands convulsed at random intervals.

"We needed to refresh our supplies, so meeting them was

fortunate," Thren said, and Haern heard rattling as he pushed aside unseen things to search through the wagon's contents.

"Aye," Haern said, kneeling down before the woman. He reached into his belt, withdrew a dagger he kept for emergencies. The woman continued to gasp, slower now. Feeling like he'd swallowed a rock, Haern forced her eyelids closed with his left hand, then stabbed with his right. Unlike his father's strike, his pierced the heart directly. He left the blade in there, not wishing to increase the pain any further, and instead watched and waited. The woman let out a gasp, but it sounded more surprised than anything. And then the breath leaked out of her, the movement of her chest stopped, and her fingers curled in tight and moved no more.

Haern pulled free the dagger and stood. As he cleaned it on the bottom of his cloak, he glanced over his shoulder, caught his father watching him.

"That wasn't necessary," said Thren.

"I disagree. Did you find anything useful?"

Thren gestured for him to come closer and look for himself.

"Plenty of food and drink," Thren said as Haern glanced inside. "But it looks like it was only for the crew manning the wagons. I thought there'd be some crimleaf in here, maybe some wines laced with Violet, but instead we have only these..."

He pushed aside the lid to a crate, reached inside, and lifted out a thick stone slab. It was roughly the size of his chest, and by the strain on his muscles, it was clearly heavy. Thren dropped it down on the wood, and at sight of the mark carved onto the front, he turned and spit.

"Egotistical bastards," Thren said. "They can't mark territory like any other guild. They have to carve it into the very stone of the walls and street."

Haern reached down, his fingers tracing the four-pointed star of the Sun Guild, deeply cut into the tile with a skilled hand and then painted a soft yellow. The sight of it grew a pit in the center of Haern's stomach as he wondered what all transpired in Veldaren during his absence. He'd hoped that after they drove out the first wave of members, plus killed the priest, Laerek, who'd been helping the Sun Guild move into the city, they would have earned a respite. Apparently, that was not the case.

"How many are there?" Haern asked, looking further into the wagon.

"Ten in this wagon alone," Thren said. "The Darkhand plans on taking over the entire city, by the looks of it. These stones will signify their territory, and I have a feeling that in a few months, it will be impossible to cross a single street without seeing one."

"Darkhand?" Haern asked.

Thren shook his head.

"Leader of the Sun Guild. Don't worry about him for now. We have our own matters to attend. There's cheese wrapped up near the front, plus some butter and lard. Grab your pack and get to it while I load up on whatever oats they had. If we're to have a city left waiting for us by the time we're done, we need to reach Luther and the Sanctuary as soon as possible."

With their supplies now refilled, the two walked until nightfall, then found a spot safely far enough from the road to build a fire and eat the small portion of smoked pork they'd taken. Haern sat opposite his father, trying to do his best to relax and forget the previous hours of the day. He'd gone through far worse during his scouring of Veldaren. Why should a simple caravan bother him so much now?

Thren, meanwhile, looked the happiest he'd been since their

trip began. Cleaning a bit of pork from his teeth, he tossed a scrap too burnt and hard to eat into the fire and stared at Haern, who shivered, feeling as cold as ever beneath that gaze. Haern shifted side to side, trying to find a way to make the carpet of leaves beneath him into something more comfortable.

"That hood," Thren said, breaking a silence that had lasted more than an hour. "Who did you get it from?"

Haern tugged once on its side, and he huddled closer to the fire.

"What does it matter?" he asked. "It's only a hood."

Thren shook his head, clearly disappointed.

"I'm no fool. No matter the time of day, there's always a shadow that falls across your face. Sometimes I can see your eyes; sometimes I can't. And your voice, it's not like it should be. It sounds more like you're whispering, except it's loud as you need it to be for me to hear even if I'm five feet away or five hundred. There's magic in it, and you're not the kind of man who wields a wand or a staff, Watcher. You deal in steel, which means the magic came from someone else. I'm only curious as to who. It's an effective trick, albeit a simple one."

Haern drummed his fingers on the hilts of his sabers, pondered over how to answer.

"I took it from a man I killed," he said at last.

"Do I know him?"

He shook his head.

"An elf from afar. He thought to control a city with his blades. I showed him otherwise."

Thren let out a chuckle, and he lay back against one of the trees that surrounded their camp, with the hope that their trunks and leaves might hide the light of the fire from travelers.

"So you took it as a trophy?"

"Not a trophy," Haern said harsher than he meant. "A warning, for myself."

"And what kind of warning might that be? Not to be weaker than your opponent?"

Haern let out a sigh, and he stared into the fire instead of answering. How could he explain to his father that the reason he'd taken the hood was as a reminder to never believe as the elf, Graeven, had believed? To feel he was a god among mortals, controller of all their fates?

"A warning against what I might become," Haern said. "I'd rather not discuss it."

"Of course, of course," said Thren. He pulled his own hood back, used it as a cushion between the harsh bark of the tree and his head. "The perfect, noble Watcher. Never a man who could bribe him, never a whore who could seduce him. The way my men describe you would make you a god of death and shadows. Fear is a weapon you wield with skill, so spare me vague sentimentalism about warnings and reminders. You wear it to frighten your prey; just admit as much. It's sad to see someone living a lie."

Haern stood, and his hands fell to his sabers. He had no intention to draw them, but he wanted to deny the casual dismissal, to say or do something to somehow show his father the seriousness in which he took his words. Instead, Thren ignored him completely, closing his eyes as if to sleep.

"You're not going to wear that hood the whole trip, are you?" Thren asked.

Haern froze.

"I might," he said.

"It's been three weeks, and I've never once seen you pull it down. Do you fear me seeing your face, Watcher? And must I call you by such a stupid title?"

"You wish to know my face and name?" Haern asked. "What makes you think I'd be foolish enough to give either?"

Thren opened an eye.

"You freely travel with me, rely on my skills in combat to keep you alive, and sleep opposite of me by a fire. If I wanted to kill you, I'd have done so already. If *you* thought I would kill you, you'd have already tried to kill me, or at least run off to infiltrate the Stronghold on your own. So, please, let's drop at least a little of the suspicion, hrm? Besides, you don't have to give me your true name. Any other name would be preferable to 'Watcher.'"

Haern took a step back at the rebuke, then glanced around. So many times he'd endured such rants while growing up, and it did to him now what it always did to him then: made him feel like a complete fool. His fears were naïve, his wisdom unfounded. And sure enough, he'd hidden his face all during their travel southwest, down through the green lands of the Kingstrip and past the hills of Omn as they made their way toward the Gods' Bridges.

He sat back down, taking meager comfort that his father could not see the way his face blushed or how frustrated he was. Of course, Thren would still sense it, read it from the way he sat, the gestures his hands made, the tiniest of inflections in his voice. But at least it'd be somewhat less obvious. He thought to give a false name but decided keeping such a thing straight in his head was pointless. Haern was a common enough name, and already it was a disguise, a burial of the Aaron he had been.

"Haern," he said, crossing his arms. "For now, call me Haern."

"Very well, Haern. Care to tell me how you really obtained that magical hood?"

Haern tried to think of where to start, where was appropriate. In the distance, a coyote sounded, and the noise emphasized to Haern just how far from home he was, how distant the walls of

Veldaren. Where he sat, there were only the woods, the animals, and Thren Felhorn... and his father more closely resembled the animals than any fellow human he'd normally associate with. The howl continued but was not taken up by any other animals, and that made it seem all the more lonely. When it stopped, Haern began.

"I went south to Angelport at the request of a friend," he said. "An elf was using my old mark as a way to mock his victims as well as pay homage to my own reputation in Veldaren. This elf was killing anyone he needed to bring the entire city crumbling down. He thought war would purge the evil from it, a desperately needed cleansing at the hands of his race. The reason I took that hood was to remind myself to never, ever believe as he did. My skills, my blades, they can shape the future, but it is never my place to do so as if I were a god."

He fell silent, and in the center of his chest, he felt a pressure growing, a strange anxiety. He knew what it was, but that just made it all the stranger. He wanted to know what his father thought of it. Why, he could not say. The man was a monster, he knew that, he truly believed that. But for some reason, that didn't seem to matter.

While Haern had thought Thren would immediately mock him, instead, his father stayed relaxed by the fire, leaning against his tree. His left hand slowly picked at a leaf beside him, systematically stripping it so only the stem remained.

"Humility is rarely a virtue I practice," Thren said when the leaf was naked. "I'll admit there are times when accepting your own limitations can save your life, as well as lead to necessary growth in skill, but you taking that hood for such reasons is nothing more than a self-serving lie."

Haern opened his mouth to ask why, then closed it. Thren would tell him why, of course. He always did. Better to remain silent, hide behind the shadowed mask so his father would not see just how deeply his words stung.

But for once, Thren did not continue. His own face had grown distant, his gaze elsewhere.

"Why?" Haern asked when it was clear he would not continue.

Thren looked up, and there was something hidden in his face, something...proud.

"Because you *are* a god among the people of Veldaren," Thren said. "You command the fear and loyalty of so many, it makes a mockery of our own king. With your blades, you have shaped Veldaren's future more than any other man and woman alive. Yet that power scares you, doesn't it, Haern? Better to tell yourself you aren't that powerful. Better to tell yourself it isn't your *place* to make such decisions over the lives of others. You're a giant stooping down to pretend to be a man. You convince no one but yourself."

"You would call me a fool?"

"No. I merely question the man who is afraid to be everything he was meant to be."

The comment stung far worse than it should have. Haern knew who his father had intended him to be. He'd wanted a perfect killer, denied friends, starved of affection, left without faith or family. Only the skills to take a life, and the ruthless training to lead his father's guild. Haern was never meant to be anything other than an echo of Thren living on after his father's death.

"Who are you to decide what I was meant to be?" Haern asked him, unable to keep the bite from his voice.

"Just a man slowly getting older," Thren said, laying down and closing his eyes to sleep. "But I know denial when I see it. All I said was that you are a god among the people of Veldaren. Never once did I say how you should wield that power."

The darkness was deepening, the sound of the cicadas growing loud enough to overwhelm. In that midnight cacophony, Haern pulled his knees to his chest, crossed his arms over them, and stared at the man that had been his father.

"Why did you never kill me?" he asked, softly enough he wasn't even sure if Thren would hear. But he did hear, and after a moment, he answered.

"My men whisper that I couldn't even if I tried. Your reputation has surpassed mine, or have you not noticed?"

Haern swallowed, and he felt naked as he spoke.

"For years, I struck at your guild, killing those loyal to the Spider. I ended your war with the Trifect, effectively putting all thief guilds on a leash, and no matter what Deathmask tells me I know it was against your wishes. Yet night after night, I prowl, and never once have you tried to bring me down. No ambushes. No plots. Tonight, you ask me for my name...have you not once searched for it? You ask of my face...have you never looked for those who have seen it? I know you, Thren. I know you were never afraid of me, so why was I left alone? Why did you not crush me when you had the chance?"

On and on droned the cicadas.

"Your inaction can only be two things," Haern whispered. "Either I meant something to you...or nothing at all."

A lengthy silence, followed by a sigh.

"You presume much," Thren said without ever opening his eyes. "You want to know why I never did? Because I didn't want to."

"That's not a reason."

"You're right," Thren said, rolling over and putting his back to Haern. "It's not *a* reason. It is *the* reason for all we mere mortals do, and it is the only one I've ever needed in my life. Perhaps you'd best learn that yourself."

Haern rose from the fire and stalked off into the forest. He'd done it before when they first traveled, needing space, needing a winding path between him and the fire so he might sleep feeling safe. The following morning, he'd find Thren waiting for him on the road west, tired and in a sour mood. He always did.

Picking a tree at random, he put his back against it, wrapped his cloak about himself, and tried to sleep. Sleep didn't come easily, and it wasn't that much of a surprise. Instead, he heard his father's voice echoing in his ear, again and again.

You convince no one but yourself.

…no one but yourself…

…no one…

At last he slept, and his dreams were of Robert Haern, teaching him in the darkness.

CHAPTER

2

Alyssa lay on a padded couch braced against a large oval window that opened out into a garden, not that she could see it. The colors of the petals were but memories now since Stephen Connington took her eyes. Sunlight shone upon her, the warmth comforting. Eyes closed, she did her best to absorb it, to remember brighter times. Before the loss of her sight. Before the dooming of her family line.

The door opened, and she heard footsteps of someone entering.

"Lady Gemcroft?" Victor asked after clearing his throat.

Alyssa held back a sigh as she tilted her face so that her glass eyes would be gazing in his approximate direction. A practiced smile twisted her lips. For a moment, she wondered if Victor had ever seen an honest smile from her. If not, would he ever know the difference? She doubted the glass eyes would ever help, either. Her servants insisted they were expertly crafted, pale blue with hints of veins in the corners, but she knew that whenever she wore them, people always sounded the slightest bit unnerved. Or perhaps that was only due to them not knowing how to appropriately behave in the presence of a blind woman who still wielded incredible influence and power. If she were a beggar on the street, she had a feeling every last one of her guests would know exactly how to treat her.

"Victor," she said. "Have you come to see me again already? I daresay any spare time of mine I find quickly occupied by your arrival."

She tried to keep the bite out of her words, but could tell she failed. Part of her had wanted to ask why he bothered coming to her so recently after his last visit. All of them, no matter how kind or earnest he behaved, always came down to the same purpose: he desired her wealth and her mercenaries to use in his ill-conceived scheme to clean up the streets of Veldaren.

"I hope you don't find the time ill spent," Victor said, and Alyssa chuckled.

"Ill spent? Of course not."

Her smile said otherwise.

"Is it all right if I sit?" Victor asked, and at her gesture he sat down in a chair opposite her. He made sure to make plenty of noise so that she might follow him, but she didn't bother. Instead, she turned back to the window, closing her eyes and placing her face back into the streaming sunlight. The warmth of the sun ... if it hit her face just right, she could pretend to see its golden glow through her eyelids.

"Your beauty is radiant today," Victor said after a lengthy pause.

"So my servants tell me," she said. "Their word is all I have to go on now, and I must say, it makes the process of their powders and perfumes all the more tiresome."

"Even if you were to forgo it, you would still steal the breath of any man in this city."

Alyssa smirked, and her fingers idly tapped against the glass of the window.

"I doubt you've come just to flatter me," she said, refusing to look his way. "It's the Sun Guild again, isn't it?"

"It is," Victor said. "Their rapid expansion cannot be ignored any longer."

"You and the Ash Guild chased them out, I thought?" she said. She knew the answer, of course, but she felt it prudent to remind him of how he had already failed once in his goals. Maybe with enough attempts, some wisdom might break through that thick skull of his.

"It was only temporary," Victor said. "Muzien the Darkhand came soon after, and he brought a second wave of guildmembers that Veldaren's soldiers cannot, or will not, stop from overwhelming the remaining thief guilds."

"Fascinating," Alyssa said. "But I've ceased caring about what these wretched criminals do to one another."

"But you must care," Victor said. "If Muzien succeeds in taking total control of Veldaren's underworld, I fear even the power of the Trifect will crumble. The Spider Guild hurt you, but this elf is different somehow. The guilds fear him in a way they never feared Thren. Thren was one of them, better than them perhaps, but still one of their own. Muzien...he's a beast, a ghost, a demon in gray. No one will be safe once he brings his attention to those beyond the poor hovels and back alleys."

Alyssa turned away from the window, and she leveled her glass eyes at him. Though she kept her face an emotionless mask, beneath her temper began to flare.

"No one will be safe?" she asked. "Do you mean *me*, Victor?"

"I do," he said, and she was stunned by his audacity. "Muzien will kill you, your family, your son..."

"Shut your mouth," she said, interrupting him. Rising to her feet, she took a step toward him, then reached out until her hand brushed his chest. That located, she grabbed his shoulder and used her other hand to clutch at the top of his tunic. Leaning down, she put her glass eyes mere inches from his own. Let him stare into those lifeless orbs, she thought. Let him see all she had endured before his ever coming into her life.

"Do you think I am blind to the world around me?" she asked. "My family, my legacy, teeters above a ravine filled with lions. I fear Nathaniel will never live past his tenth birthday, let alone inherit the fortune that is rightfully his. But you...you would dare come in here and throw that fear in my face, and for what? What is it you want, Victor? Is it money? Soldiers? Validation for your failed crusade? Tell me, so I can deny it and banish you from my life forever."

Victor stood, and he grabbed each of her wrists and freed himself of her grasp. When he refused to let go, she pulled back, just once, but he held her there. Alyssa's heart began to pound, and she wondered if she had pushed him too far. Still, she was not alone with Victor. If the man made another move, a single wrong word...

"For once, open your ears and listen," Victor said. "Do you think I am as callous and cruel as others you've known? I see the soldiers positioned at every door, and it's not your crest they wear on their chest. I can *help* you, Alyssa, and believe it or not, I'll do it because I feel it is the right thing to do, not just for you, not just for me, but for this *whole damn city*. Too many are ready to let it burn so long as they get theirs first, but I want to build something. I want to inspire, to salvage a golden coin lodged deep in the center of a pile of shit. It's not my fault if you can't see that!"

Alyssa jerked against his grip, his words infuriating her. He let go as suddenly as he'd grabbed her, and with her hands now free, she raked her nails across his face. Victor stumbled backward, most likely into the couch just behind him.

"I may be blind," Alyssa said, pointing a finger at him, "but I can see what you can't. Your attempts at fixing Veldaren are the hopeless, pathetic excuses of a little boy pretending at power. Your parents died in the riots years ago, and now you think you can come in like a god among us and wipe away every crime, every black heart. Gods forgive me, I was even foolish enough to believe for a moment you could do it. But no more. I won't endure your hollow attempts at flattery. I won't entertain your madness. You are not welcome in my home; now go."

"No."

She tensed when he said it. Ahead of her, she heard the floor groan from him taking a step.

"I said leave," she repeated.

"And I said . . . no."

His hands took hers. She tensed, a knife-edge away from screaming for her guards. Not yet, though. If she were in danger, Zusa would have already sprung into action from her hiding place.

"My flattery is not hollow," Victor said, and there was a change in his tone. This wasn't prepared. This wasn't practiced banter and honeyed lies to win her over. "You are a beautiful woman, your wealth legendary, your personality a mixture of fire and diamonds. I do not love you, Alyssa, but I would protect you as fiercely as any man has protected a woman in all the kingdoms. Your family line teeters on death. Nathaniel's legitimacy will never be accepted; you know that. Not unless another vouches for him and adopts him as his own."

He pulled her closer, pressed his forehead against hers.

"You are one of the very few people who have stood before the scum of this city and vowed to take no more," he said, his voice growing soft. "I would be proud to have you at my side, and proud to raise an intelligent boy like Nathaniel. What we could accomplish together would shake the world. But if there is to be a future for us, for any of us, then Veldaren needs to be tamed. We cannot build a castle upon a foundation of rot. You say you once believed I could succeed. Believe in me again."

With a shaking hand, she pushed him back, and he allowed her to do so. Her chest felt hollow. He wanted to ignite hope in her, she knew, and the pleading honesty in his voice tore at her worse than anything he'd said before. What he asked of her…five years ago she might have leaped at the chance. But now…now she couldn't. She didn't feel the strength left in her to challenge the might of the city. Every time she dared hope, every time she tried for happiness, there was always a man or woman waiting with a dagger. Sometimes, it was her enemies. More often, it seemed it was those she should have been able to trust most. Why couldn't they let her raise her son in peace? Why couldn't Nathaniel grow up happy and beautiful and loved, instead of with vultures circling above their household and hungry eyes staring from all sides?

"Leave," she said. "Please, just leave."

Victor stood and stepped away, footsteps leading toward the room's exit.

"You're afraid," he said. "And you have every right to be. The pointed star marks over half the streets of Veldaren, and soon Muzien will seek to paint it across your doorstep. But don't let that fear deny you hope. You are capable of great things, Alyssa, both you and your son. And at my side, we can reach them still, reach higher than you have ever dreamed. These setbacks have not shaken my confidence, nor my desires. They have only forced me to raise my ambition even higher."

"I could never trust you," Alyssa said. "Too many have betrayed me already, and you would only be the next."

He laughed from the other side of the room, the sound both amused and terribly sad.

"My dear Alyssa," he said. "Of all the men in Veldaren, I am the last who would ever betray you. For good or ill, I am a man of my word, and if I say I would die for you, I mean it. If you wish to seek out those who would turn against you, begin looking closer to home."

With that, the door opened and shut, and with him gone, she turned and swung her fist toward the glass of her window. It struck, she heard a crack, and letting out a gasp of frustration, she dropped down into the couch, holding her bruised hand to her chest. Tears began to grow along the edges of her glass eyes, and she hated herself for it.

"He should not speak to you in such a way," said her closest friend. Strange as it might seem to someone else, it was no surprise to Alyssa that the voice came from the high corner of the room. No doubt Zusa had hidden there the entire encounter, daggers drawn and eager to carve an extra smile or two into Victor's face.

"He was just being honest," Alyssa said.

"Honest or not, he disrespected you. To do so in your house, no matter how highly born the bastard is, should never be allowed."

Zusa was at her side now, and Alyssa shifted so the woman could join her on the couch. The woman did so, a wrapped hand sliding around her shoulders. Alyssa accepted the comfort, and she wiped away the few tears that had grown.

"Forget him," she said. "What he said...what did he mean about the crests on the chests of my soldiers?"

Zusa hesitated the slightest moment, fingers on her shoulder clutching tighter.

"John Gandrem's soldiers outnumber your house guards," she said. "He seeks to fill you with doubt; that is all."

Alyssa shook her head.

"Doubt that may be well-founded."

"John would never turn on you and Nathaniel. He's too honorable, too dedicated to tradition and law."

"And what of Melody? How strong is his dedication to her?"

At that, Zusa gave no answer. Alyssa thought of the way John had spoken with her mother, Melody, of how close the two had grown ever since the loss of her eyes. John had assumed many responsibilities, particularly those he felt were too difficult or mature for Nathaniel to handle. But helping him at every turn was Melody Gemcroft, always eager, always offering advice.

Melody...the woman from the grave. The woman Stephen Connington had professed his love for, just before taking out Alyssa's eyes.

"If my mother plans something..." Alyssa began.

"If she does, she plans only her suicide," Zusa said, holding her tight. "I am here. I am with you. Trust me to keep you and your family safe, my love. I let myself be distracted, and I failed you, but never again."

Alyssa put a hand atop Zusa's. At least, she had someone she could trust to the very end. Someone who would never betray her. She wished she knew how to say it, but the words always seemed awkward when she tried.

"Thank you," she said, accepting another embrace from Zusa. "I know you'll always be there, no matter what happens. No matter who may turn on me. But I need you to keep your eyes open and watch where I cannot, and in the shadows listen for what I cannot hear. Someone will make a move against us, and if not from within, then without."

"You mean Muzien," Zusa said.

"I do," Alyssa said.

"Do you fear him?"

"No," she whispered. "There's only one person I fear. Watch her closest, Zusa. If Melody turns on me, strike her dead. If she would come back from the grave to betray me, send her right back to the grave. Damn the courts. Damn the consequences."

"Consider this my word," Zusa said, rising from the couch. "If you fear Melody, then Melody should quake in fear of me. While I live, you live. While I live, your enemies will perish."

Alyssa let herself smile, and she prayed it was far more authentic than the one she'd given Victor.

"You can't save me from the whole world," she said.

Zusa laughed.

"No," she said. "But I can damn well try."

CHAPTER

3

Are you sure you must do this yourself?" asked the withered old man escorting her down the dark stairs. The air was cold as it blew across her skin, but that was not why she shivered.

"I must," said Melody Gemcroft, wishing she had her own torch, wanting its light to be under her control. With every step downward, she felt herself slipping back into a world where only her beloved Karak could save her … and even then, it had taken years.

"This particular prisoner has proven very stubborn," the old man continued, slowly working his way down the steps without any sign of hurry. "I understand the use he might be to you, but I must confess I doubt he will listen to any request you have. He is too dangerous, too narrow-minded."

"And that is why it must be me," Melody said. She put a hand on the stone wall beside her, but the stones were clammy, and when she pulled back, dirty water was on her fingertips.

The old man, Warsh, continued on as if not realizing she had paused.

"If you insist," Warsh said. The hand not holding aloft the torch scratched at his balding pate. "I wonder at what magic you think you have to make him listen."

"Not magic," Melody said, continuing once more to follow. Her right hand clutched tighter at the jar wrapped in cloth she held. "Just a song and a gift."

"I'd more suggest offering freedom, but I doubt he'd stay loyal to you the moment he stepped into the open air. Impressive, really. Usually, after a few years with the gentle touchers, a man would willingly obey."

"I am well aware of the sick things the gentle touchers might do to a man," Melody said. "Or a woman."

The venom in her voice caused the old man to stop and turn.

"The gentle touchers have served the Conningtons since the earliest days of the Gods' War," Warsh said, staring at her with his red, weepy eyes. "Kings and thieves, peasants and princes, they've all had their time in these cells. There is an art to what we do, a gift that involves a lifetime of sacrifice and study. I understand your anger for what my fellows have done to you, but I assure you none of it was ever done with malice. You were like a painting, Melody, a beautiful painting, and you endured greater than most any I have seen descend these stairs. When Leon died, and Stephen granted you your freedom, I was so very happy for you. So, please, remember that you are a guest here now, not a prisoner, nor a queen, so treat us gentle touchers with the respect we deserve."

Melody bit back her retort. Instead, she dipped her head and gestured for Warsh to continue.

At the bottom of the stairs deep beneath the Connington mansion, closed in on either side by stone walls, there was a single door. Melody felt her breath catch at the very sight of it. She had seen that door only twice. The first was when she'd been dragged there by the bulbous Leon himself. The second had been when Leon's son, Stephen, had granted her her freedom...nine years later. The wood was aged and thick, blackened steel strips and bolts holding it together. On the other side would be the rows of cells, having never once been touched by the light of the sun. After all those years, all her suffering and torture, she was to return, and guided back by one of her torturers, no less.

"I would understand," Warsh said, seeing her hesitance. There was pity in his old eyes, and for some reason it made her angry.

"Open it," she said.

Stepping into the dungeon filled her heart with terror, but she choked it down. The darkness closed in on her, and the distant dripping of water in the prison's lone well brought back countless nights of passing the time counting those little plinks. She pushed it away. Keeping her head high, keeping her eyes on Warsh's torch, she followed him along the path. They passed the cells to either side of her, the fronts barred but the sides built of thick stone, preventing any one prisoner from seeing another. Nearly all of them were empty. Stephen had cleared out most upon his ascension to control of the Connington fortune, but a few he'd left alive, the few with special purpose, or those the gentle touchers had asked to leave under their care for political or social reasons. Sometimes, even kings wanted someone to disappear, after all.

Step after step, she felt her breath tightening, and at last she stopped before the cell that had been hers. She put her hands upon the cold bars, leaned in close. It'd been more than a year since her stay within, but still she remembered every last crack and scrape upon the stone. She saw the marks she'd made to signify the months and years, scratched with another piece of stone she'd managed to pry loose from the ground. So many times she'd thought to use that stone to slit her throat but never did. It'd have been a sin to die in such a way, and she would not kneel before her beloved Karak only for him to rebuke her for her rejecting the life he'd given her. So, instead, she'd sung her songs, flooding the darkness with the only worthwhile thing she had left to offer.

Warsh said nothing, only stayed behind her, torch held high to help her. He seemed to understand her curiosity at seeing it, her need to be before the place of her lengthy torture. There on the floor she saw the pillow they'd given her, still in the corner where she'd left it. There on the wall were the chains Leon would put her in when he came down for his perverted pleasure. And everywhere, just faded spots on the stone, were the dried markings of her blood.

"Where are the other touchers?" she asked, her voice faint even to her own ears.

"They are away," Warsh said. "I was the only one to never lay a hand upon you, and that is why they felt it best I be the one to accommodate your request."

"Are they afraid of me?" she asked.

Warsh shrugged.

"You're a woman of power now. They are not unreasonable in their fear."

Melody felt a bitter smile stretch across her face.

"The gentle touchers are the ones afraid of *me*," she said. "I guess I should find humor in that. But they're right to hide. Should I have seen them . . . I might not have been forgiving."

Closing her eyes, Melody prayed to Karak once more for the strength to continue, for wisdom to influence the words she was to speak. And then she continued on to the next cell, and to the man she'd come to find.

He was chained to the wall on his knees, his arms spread wide and clamped down with iron. His skin was dark as obsidian, and when he stared out at her with his brown eyes, the whites seemed to nearly glow in the gloom. His stare followed her as she walked alone to the door, much like a panther might watch its prey. He was naked from the waist up, revealing several brutal scars running across his chest. Dirty hair was matted to his face, and an uneven beard grew from his chin. Even on his knees, she could tell he was a giant of a man. His body was obviously malnourished, yet he still had enough muscle to overpower any ordinary man.

Without a word, Warsh ambled forward, unlocked the door, and then gestured for her to enter.

"Do you have a name?" Melody asked as she stepped inside. She glanced back once, involuntarily. No matter how hard she berated herself, she could not shake the fear that she'd be locked into one of the cells, this time to stay forever.

"I once had many names," said the prisoner.

"Tell me your real name."

The man chuckled as if terribly amused.

"I do not know it anymore," he said. "The gentle touchers here have pricked me, beaten me, burned flesh, and dislocated joints, yet I have no one to blame for that particular loss beyond my own wretched self."

Melody crossed her arms, studying the man further. He spoke eloquently enough, and despite the years she knew he'd been imprisoned, he acted fairly controlled and aware of his surroundings.

"I was told you were once a skilled killer," she said.

"I was," said the man. "One of the very best there ever was."

"Until the Watcher defeated you."

At the name, the prisoner tensed, and his smile faded away.

"I let my guard down; that is all. I was better. I should have won."

Melody could tell he believed it. She shifted the cloth package she held from one hand to the other, trying to decide how best to broach her request.

"I have need of you," she said at last.

"And I have need of many things, but you're fooling yourself if you think I'm going to let you debase me any further than you already have. I won't be your slave just because you've thrown me into a prison and left me to rot, Melody."

She took a step back, surprised he knew her name.

"Oh, yes, I've been told all about you," he said, seeing her reaction. "You're some highborn whore of the Trifect whose very presence should leave me in awe." He glared at Warsh. "They wanted me to behave."

Melody walked over and slapped him across the face.

"I am not some highborn whore," she said. "I was the wife of Maynard Gemcroft. Soon, the entire wealth of the Gemcroft family will be in my hands, and I assure you, I have earned every single gold coin that will touch my fingers."

"Forgive me," said the man. "My years down here have stolen from me my usual courtesy, but you're convincing no one but yourself that you *earned* the pile of wealth you either married or were born into. Look around you, woman. Do you think you could even comprehend the suffering I've endured?"

Despite his anger, his naked hatred, she stepped even closer, falling to her knees before him, not caring that it would sully her dress. The floor was cold, shivers worked their way up her spine, but it had to be done.

And then she began to sing.

"I was born beneath a darkened sky," she sang. *"Screaming out a false name. I was born while the Lion roared, yet I could not hear him, could not hear him..."*

At her words, a change came over him, and for the first time since stepping before his cell, she saw him let down his guard.

"You," he whispered when she fell silent, her song over. "The woman beside me, the one who sang..."

Melody rose from her knees.

"Stephen freed me a year ago," she said. "Nursed me back to health before revealing me to the world. You remember my voice, don't you? Remember my sorrow? Would you still mock my suffering, my understanding of your world? You've been here for four years, yet I suffered for nine in this cruel place."

"I thought they killed you," the man said. "When they took away everyone else, when they emptied out this horrible place, I thought they killed you. Your voice, I've missed it. Melody? Your name is Melody..."

Even the lowliest of criminals will cling to order when lost in darkness, but only if you offer it to them, thought Melody, mirroring the words she'd learned from Luther's tutelage of Karak's way. She stepped closer, slowly, carefully letting her hand brush the side of his face. It was warm and slick with sweat, but unlike with the stone beside the stairs, she did not pull away in revulsion.

"I've come to free you," she said. "All I ask is that you kill those who are a danger to my ascension. Because of them, they put our entire city at risk of destruction and fire."

"Who are they?" he asked.

"A woman named Zusa," Melody said. "She used to be one of Karak's faceless women, and now protects my daughter with a disturbing zeal. Her very existence threatens my own, and she must be dealt with swiftly. You'll find her skulking about our mansion, acting like the loyal watchdog she is."

"Who else?" he asked.

"The Eschaton Mercenaries continue to interfere with my plans. Do you know of them?"

The man nodded.

"I do. Is that all?"

"No," she said. One name left, the one she'd felt certain would earn his cooperation no matter how stubborn he might be.

"The Watcher," she said. "He's gone into hiding, but you can find him, can't you? Bring him to justice?"

The man fell silent for a long moment, then nodded.

"For three long years, the beauty of your voice helped me endure the darkness," he said. "For that, I owe you greatly. Release me."

Melody stepped away, and she gestured for Warsh. The old man hobbled forward, a set of keys jangling in his wrinkled hands. Off came one lock, then the other. With a groan, the dark-skinned man stretched and leaned forward, letting out gasps of pain as his back popped. Warsh exited the cell, and he cast a strange look at Melody as he did. Not caring what it meant, Melody at last unfurled the cloth from around the small box she'd brought with her.

"I've been told of your certain . . . peculiarities," she said. "So, I brought this with me. I thought it might help remind you of who you were and who you truly are."

She put the box down before him, and he reached over for it and removed the top. Within was an expensive white powder, and it clung to his fingers when he dipped his hand inside. With practiced efficiency, he bathed in the powder, covering the skin of his face, even rubbing it into the uneven growth on his chin. That done, he put aside the box and rose to his feet. There was something truly terrifying about him then, the contrast of the paint on his skin, the way he towered over her, rising up as if from a grave. He smiled at her, and for the first time, it seemed as if he were truly alive.

"I once had many names, but Ghost was the one I carried the longest," he said. "And after four years in this death pit, I daresay I've earned the damned title."

He stretched out his hand and she took it. His fingers were puffy and speckled with scars, the results of the gentle touchers' needles.

"The Watcher, the Eschaton, and the faceless woman," said Ghost. "I'll kill them all but the Watcher. Him I get to drag down these stairs and make suffer just as I suffered. After that, I make my own life."

There was a nobleness to him, a sincerity to his promise. Above all, he doubted not a single word he spoke. The deaths of her enemies, the interlopers to Karak's great plan, would die by Ghost's hands.

Melody smiled.

"Then we have a deal."

CHAPTER

4

Haern did not consider himself a skilled tracker when it came to the wilderness, but it didn't take much to know a successful ambush when he saw one.

"Impressive," Thren muttered as they looked upon the carnage.

It'd only been three days since they had overrun the Sun Guild wagons, and they'd traveled through light forest for all three, following the well-worn path toward the Gods' Bridges. Not long after dawn, they'd traversed a brief stretch of hills, rising up like warts on the land amid the forest. At the top of the third hill, they'd come upon the bloodied remnants of what had once been men and women. Blood soaked much of the road, and at the crest of the hill was a great pit where there'd been a fire. Haern tried to count the bodies, but they were all cut to pieces and strewn about as if they were but playthings for their murderers. Crows had already descended upon the various pieces, and they shrieked out their annoyance at Haern and Thren's arrival.

"Should we proceed?" Haern asked as he drew his swords. "Whoever did this might still be near."

Thren shook his head, walking nonchalantly into the midst of the gore.

"If there was an ambush planned, it'd already be sprung on us," he said, glancing about as if looking for something. "These butchers have already moved on."

Haern followed his father, and he winced at the smell. From what he could tell, the deaths were recent, perhaps only the day before. He stepped over a severed hand, kicked at a crow pecking at a face, and then searched the ground for any sort of belongings, finding none.

"Bandits?" he asked.

"It seems as such," Thren said, kneeling down before a mutilated head, half a spine still connected at the base. He brushed aside stiff, dark hair to reveal an ear torn in multiple places.

"The last of the Sun Guild who fled," Haern said, guessing at what his father was inferring. "Whoever killed them ripped out the earrings."

"That would be my guess," Thren said, standing up and giving a disapproving glare about the hill. "Though whoever did it has rather poor taste."

Haern took a step closer to the large fire pit, and he pulled his cloak over his face, unable to stand the stench. Leaning over, he saw a crude spit and, within the fire, a collection of bones. Hoping he was wrong, but deep down knowing he was not, he reached inside and pulled out what could only be the bones of a man or woman's arm.

"Poor taste?" he said, tossing them back down and looking to Thren. "They massacred them all and then ate one for dinner. Poor taste doesn't begin to describe what happened here."

Thren crossed his arms.

"The more savage outlaws are known to have cruel tastes. It may still be bandits."

"If they are, I hope they decide to move against us next," Haern said, breaking the spit with his heel. "I'd love the chance to remove their scum from this world."

Thren laughed.

"Ever the hero," he said. "But you may just have your chance. Whatever group did this made no attempt to hide their movements. Their footsteps lead on ahead of us, and if they had such fun with their last ambush, I suspect they'll do it again. Let us see just what kind of men we are dealing with."

They continued on down the hill toward the next, taking time while they had the height to search for any possible sign of bandits, smoke from a fire, or movement on the road. So far, none, but their eyes were open, their ears alert.

"Perhaps we should leave the road," Haern suggested after half an hour.

"Extra care here is probably justified," Thren said. "I have no intention of being some sick bastard's meal."

Their speed dropped immensely doing so, but Haern felt better. Despite fighting against the brush and constantly ducking at the grasshoppers and beetles that zipped about as if angry at their trespassing, he preferred knowing no one would easily spot their approach. Haern led the way as Thren followed, head down, arms crossed. They kept the road to their right, always ensuring it was just within sight.

After the fourth hill, the land evened out, and the trees grew farther and farther apart, the thick shade from the canopy above growing spotty, the sun peeking through with ever increasing regularity. Less than half a mile from the forest's edge, Haern heard the first unnatural sound of the entire day.

It came from the direction of the road, and he froze, lifting a hand to order Thren to do the same.

"You certain?" Thren whispered, and Haern nodded. Slowly, each stepped toward the nearest tree, leaning against the thin, pale trunks so they could better hide. Peering around, Haern watched the road, listening for what he'd heard before: laughter.

A minute crawled by. Worried he'd been imagining things, Haern kept his head low and crouch-walked to the next tree, shrinking the distance between him and the road. The grass rustled beneath him as his weight settled atop it, and not for the first time, he wished he could have had training in dealing with the natural world. But Thren had only wanted him to rule a criminal empire in the city; why would travel in the wildlands ever matter?

He was just about to stand and declare he'd only been tired and hearing ghosts when a loud, guttural roar sounded throughout the forest.

"Fuck it, Gremm; we're going back."

Haern pressed closer against the tree, and from his vantage point, he watched as over thirty men emerged from hiding amid the forest on the opposite side of the road. A spark of panic flickered in Haern's chest as he realized how unaware he'd been of their existence, how different their luck might have been if they'd been traveling on the other side.

As the men stepped out, all brandishing crude weapons specked with rust, Haern frowned at their strange appearance. Something about them was wrong, and while he couldn't place it immediately, it nearly screamed at him from his gut. From behind him, Thren ducked low and made his way near, crouching and looking around the other side of the tree so together they could watch the bandits gather into a crowd in the center of the road.

"Get back here, you pig cunt," one of the bigger men shouted as a group of seven began heading the way Thren and Haern had come from.

"I don't believe it," Thren whispered as the seven sent back rude gestures without hardly missing a step. "We were wrong. Not men. Orcs."

Orcs? Haern leaned out closer, closely scanning the faces of the men. Their skin was sickly looking, nearly gray in color. Their hair was long, unkempt, and clearly uncared-for. Many had tattoos and ritual scars cut into their skin, and their ears were long like those of an elf, except instead of curling upward like Graeven's had, they drooped downward. All of the orcs were tall, their chests broad and their arms and legs thick with muscle.

"No one's coming for miles!" one of the seven orcs shouted as they marched along the road. "I ain't sitting here doing shit. We go back, wait for more to come. Deeper in the forest we stay, the better."

"What are they doing out here?" Haern asked as several more of the larger pack followed after the rest, clearly in agreement with the sentiment. "Shouldn't they be trapped in the Vile Wedge?"

"They must have crossed one of the rivers," Thren whispered. "The paladins of the Citadel used to patrol the lower reaches of the Rigon and the Gihon, but with its fall, I doubt anyone has taken up the responsibility."

"Come on, Gremm," one of the lingering orcs said to a particularly large orc bedecked in brown leather armor and carrying a massive ax over one shoulder. "No harm in checking back. These roads go both ways, after all."

"Stubborn jackasses," Gremm growled. "Go on, then, but next time you all ignore me like that, my ax starts swinging."

Haern and Thren watched as the last of them trudged down the road, calling out insults and shouting for the orcs farther ahead to wait up. As Gremm left, Haern caught sight of a sack slung over his shoulder, the bottom of it stained red, a limp hand hanging over its side.

"We have to stop them," Haern said, rising to his feet.

"There's thirty of them," Thren said, frowning at him. "And I fail to see any reason why we *have* to do anything."

"We nearly stumbled upon them ourselves. Whoever follows after us will do the same. We can't let another group of travelers suffer the fate of the Sun guildmembers."

"We can," Thren said. "And we will. It isn't your job to protect the world, Haern, nor play the savior for every damn stupid person who walks the land. We have a task at hand, and that is what matters right now. If someone travels this road unaware of the dangers, that is their own fault, not ours. We avoided their ambush, so let whoever follows us do the same."

"You'll disregard their suffering so easily?" Haern asked.

Thren stepped closer, and he spread his arms wide and gestured to the wilderness filled only with flittering beetles and grasshoppers.

"Whose suffering?" he asked. "You'd have me weep for men and women who may not even exist? The next party those orcs attack may be well-armed men transporting goods for the Gemcrofts, and they'll butcher every single one of the gray-skinned brutes. You don't know, do you? What you do know is that you've seen someone bad, and now you want to stop them. Gods, you're like a child."

"These aren't even bandits," Haern insisted. "You saw what they did. The mutilation. The cook fire."

A beetle landed on Haern's cloak, and when he tried to brush it away, its spindly black legs remained hooked on the cloth. Frustrated, Haern swatted at it again, hard enough that it struck a tree beside him and crushed its glittering green shell. Thren saw it and smirked.

"Will you kill all the beetles in the world, too?" he asked. "We'll never even make it out of this forest."

Haern looked once more to the northeast and the path the orcs had taken. It felt wrong to leave them be, but they were already pressed for time...

"They are but thirty," Thren said, as if able to read his mind. "And by finding Luther and discovering his plans for our city, we may spare the lives of thousands. Don't be foolish, and learn to control your emotions. The goal must always be weighed against the cost, and right now, those orcs mean little more than shit to you."

Haern clenched his jaw, and with a sickening feeling in his stomach, he turned away and resumed their travel. He said nothing, and with his decision obvious, Thren let the matter drop. They continued on, an hour passing by as the midday sun began its slow descent. With every step, Haern felt worse. If he'd been on his own, he'd have avoided the orcs no differently from how he had with Thren. But something about using Thren's reasoning made him uncomfortable. In some ways, he agreed with it. The people of Veldaren were more important, the risks to the city far greater than what a few wretched remnants of an ancient war between the gods could do.

But still it bothered him, and when he glanced back and saw the fire, he froze.

"What is it?" Thren asked, and then he too saw the trail of smoke rising above the forest. "That fire may only be the orcs setting up camp."

Haern stared at it. It was a campfire, all right, and several miles behind them on the path.

"What if it's not?" he asked.

Thren shrugged.

"Then we're too late. They'll have to fend for themselves."

"No," Haern said, and this time Thren's answer would not suffice. "No, they won't."

Boots thudding upon the packed dirt, he raced along the road. After a moment, his sprint settled into a jog, and he focused on keeping his breathing steady. He kept his eyes straight ahead, staring at the smoke, trying a hundred times to decide its meaning. Was it just a campfire? A message? Was it only the orcs and he was acting like a fool?

He looked back only once, and when he did, he saw his father following.

Thren caught up to him after the first mile. Both of them were winded, but Haern pushed on, knowing if the camp was not yet under attack, it would be soon. The sun continued to set, and in his gut he knew that if the orcs were to attack, they'd do so after nightfall, perhaps several hours after to ensure all were asleep. Assuming whoever built the campfire wasn't alone and easy prey.

Damn it, thought Haern. *Too much I don't know. We should have taken them out when we had the chance!*

"You're going to get yourself killed trying to save everyone," Thren said as they climbed their way up one of the hills.

"Thought weakness was what would kill me?"

Thren let out a laugh.

"They're the same thing, you fool. Now run harder, or must an old man show up a youngster?"

And then he was ahead of Haern, pushing himself on, and to Haern's shock, there was a smile on his face. Sucking in breaths, cloaks billowing behind them, they both chased the smoke in the distance as the sun settled down behind the trees, and out came the stars. As they neared, Haern realized the smoke came from the same hill as the first ambush, and for a moment, he felt relief. Perhaps it was only the orcs, camping where they had before, and no one was in danger. He mentioned the idea to Thren, who chuckled.

"We'll still kill them," he said. "I didn't run all this way *not* to get blood on my blades."

Haern slowed to a walk, and Thren did the same. They were at the base of the hill, and as they climbed, they both needed to recover their breath. His sides were cramping, his legs sore, but Haern knew he could push himself harder if he needed to. There was no limit to his body he'd not been trained to break.

Halfway up the hill, they heard the first shouts over the din of the cicadas. It was the orcs, there was no doubt to that, and they sounded in a jovial mood. Haern drew his sabers, his father his short swords, and together they veered into the trees to ensure no one spotted their approach. Amidst all the hooting and hollering, Haern knew their stomping through the brush would go unnoticed, and he quickened his lead, until at last they reached the crest.

He'd expected the orcs to be feasting, perhaps wrestling and fighting or doing whatever it was they did, but instead he saw two wagons and a fire burning between them. The orcs had formed a circle surrounding the camp, their weapons held up into the air as they mocked those inside. Haern crept closer, baffled.

"Why don't they attack?" he asked, slipping even closer.

"They have," Thren said, crouched beside him as together they moved through the trees. He pushed aside a low branch, then pointed. "Look there, by the left wagon."

Sure enough, he saw two orc bodies crumpled at the entrance. It was odd, for they were clearly dead, yet there were no marks on their skin, no blood pooled beneath them. Haern tried to see if he could spot any survivors, but they were no doubt cowering hidden behind the thick white canvas that covered the wagons.

"Something's spooked the orcs," Thren said. "Looks like they might be doing a bit of yelling and screaming to prepare themselves for another charge."

Haern took another step, putting him almost to the edge of the clearing. To his left and right were two orcs, both holding large axes above their heads and screaming out profane things they planned to do to the bodies of whoever was inside the wagons. He put his blades to the ground, felt the cold grass bunch beneath his knuckles.

"If we hit hard, we can scatter them before they know we're here," he said.

"Better to kill them all now and leave no chance for them to escape," Thren said. "I'll sneak over to the other side, find where they seem most careless. Once there, I'll wait for your signal."

"My signal?" Haern asked. "I thought you said all this was folly?"

"It is," Thren said. "And it's your folly, so you can choose when we strike. I trust you to know when the time is right."

Haern opened his mouth, closed it, then remained crouched beneath one of the low-hanging branches as his father hurried away, fading into a gray blur in the night.

Later, he told himself, turning his attention back to the clearing. The circle around the two wagons was slowly tightening, the shouting intensifying. Haern spotted their leader, Gremm, near the middle of the path, clanging together two swords above his head in a bid to gain their attention.

"No devil magic will keep us back!" Gremm hollered. "No pitiful human trickery will keep us from dragging you screaming from those wagons! We'll cook you over your own fire, won't we? Won't we!"

The orcs cheered in affirmative.

"Come on out," Gremm continued. "Fall down on your knees, and we'll make all you die quick instead of slow. Quick now, or slow later. I'll make you watch us eat you, I fucking swear it by the spirit of the Scorpion!"

Haern saw movement from one of the wagons, and he rose to his feet knowing he had to strike before anyone threw away their lives. He looked to the orc on his left, then right, to decide who he would strike first, and that's when the blinding white light hit. It came from the wagon, a great flash that burned into his eyes and made it seem like the brightest of days had descended upon the hill. Turning away and jamming his eyes shut, Haern let out a cry from the pain.

A priest of Ashhur? he wondered. That explained why they were not yet overrun. He opened his eyes, saw spots swimming in his vision, but he knew the orcs would be suffering far worse than he. Already one of them fell dead, a golden sword materializing in the air and slashing through his body. The others groaned, stumbling and crying out their fury. Haern took in a breath, gripped his sabers tight. The time to attack was now.

He gave no war cry, no challenge to frighten the orcs, nor a signal to alert his father. Their deaths would be enough to send Thren into action. He sprang to his feet, leaping toward the orc on his right. His right arm extended, thrusting the tip of his blade through the side of the orc's neck, and then he turned to the left, yanking free his sword so that blood and gore flew through the air. Both weapons, one clean, one smeared red, crashed down atop the orc's back and shoulder, catching him in mid-turn after hearing the first's gargled cry of pain.

As the orc fell, Haern looked to the far side of the camp, and he saw two more drop, his father appearing behind them like a specter. Meanwhile, the rest let out cries of fury, and Gremm led the charge toward the two wagons. Haern caught Thren's eye for only the briefest moment, but he saw his nod and the implied strategy. Thren would guard the wagon nearest him, while Haern would go for the one where the flash originated. Breaking into a run, Haern charged after the battle-raging orcs, needing to kill more before they could realize his arrival and turn. The first one he caught he sliced through the hamstring, then danced over the body as it rolled. The second he came up alongside, then leaped into the air, twirling as he did. His sabers sliced cleanly through the orc's throat, and then Haern landed on the opposite side, still running.

Their cries of pain were enough to alert the others, though, and several turned to face him, bringing their weapons to bear. Outnumbered four to one, Haern never even slowed. As their crude swords and axes swung, he leaped into the air, extending his legs to slam his heels into the chest of the leftmost orc. His momentum carried both to the ground, and despite the jarring hit to his knees, Haern immediately dashed away, cloak spread wide to disguise his movement. An ax failed to hit Haern, instead burying itself in the chest of the fallen orc and ceasing his angry protests. Upon landing, Haern tucked his shoulder and rolled once, then exploded back out in a flurry of slashes. The first two batted out wide an orc's sword, the third slipped between his ribs and into a lung, and the fourth cut across the jugular vein in his throat for good measure.

"Stop him!" one of the orcs screamed, and Haern knew he had to up his pace. Instead of avoiding the remaining two orcs, Haern charged right at them, getting in closer despite their superior strength. One chopped with an ax, and as he sidestepped it, the other thrust with his sword. Twisting again, Haern found himself between the two, each overextended and unable to defend themselves. Spreading his arms out wide, he spun, cutting one orc across the eyes and giving the other a gash across the shoulder that seemed to only infuriate his opponent.

His spin ended with him facing them both, and as one clutched at his eyes, Haern kicked him in the groin, parried a second thrust from the sword, and then finished off the first with a stab that went through the orc's fingers and into his already wounded eyes.

"I said stop him already!" shouted the same orc, and Haern realized it was Gremm. Heart pounding in his chest, he turned to face a mad rush of five orcs, with Gremm watching behind them with his weapons crossed above his head and banging together. A quick glance at the wagon showed that those within were being completely ignored, and Haern felt relief. They'd stolen away their attention. Now he just had to live.

Just before the orcs reached him, he spun, flinging the intersecting parts of his cloak into a bewildering array. There'd be no way for them to predict his movements, and that was exactly what he was counting on. Two more steps and he dashed straight at them, even though the last they'd seen of him, he'd made it appear he was preparing to retreat.

Each of his swords stabbed the chest of an orc, and he drove them both to the ground while they screamed in pain. His left hand released, and he rolled while yanking out the right. Coming out of the roll, he slammed the saber into the knee of the orc beside him, then sliced upward as he turned and ran four steps. The distance was all he needed, for when he spun, he caught one orc chasing him ahead of the others, ax raised to the sky. Haern cut his throat, kicked his dying body into the way of the others, and then grabbed the fallen ax.

"Come die," Haern told them, readying both weapons. The ax was heavy, but he had no intention of using it for long. Only two remained to attack him, and one of them was limping from the cut across his leg and knee. Haern faded to his left as they hacked at him, blocking a downward slash with his sword and shoving the orc's sword out of position, freeing up an easy hit with his ax. He buried it in the shoulder, snapping the orc's collarbone and splattering blood across his chest. Leaving the ax there, Haern turned on his final foe, who screamed at the top of his lungs in a vain attempt to intimidate.

Haern clutched his sword with both hands, blocked two simple swings, and then finished off his opponent with a riposte that ended with the blade of his saber deep in the orc's belly. When he yanked it free, he kicked the orc across the face to send him to the ground to die.

His lone saber dangling from his hand, Haern approached Gremm, who stared at him with a mixture of hatred and abject horror.

"What are you?" Gremm asked, lifting his swords and preparing to fight. "Why attack us?"

Haern yanked his other saber free from a corpse as he walked past, not even slowing his walk.

"Because I wanted to," Haern said, and he grinned as he realized he was parroting his father's words. "That reason not good enough?"

Gremm swung both his swords in a dual chop, and when Haern blocked, he realized how much smarter it'd have been to just dodge. The orc was incredibly strong, and his swords connected with his sabers in a ringing clang that jarred his arms and hurt his elbows. Gremm took a step closer, trying to ram him with his shoulder while their weapons were interlocked, but Haern was the faster. Instead of avoiding, he slammed his shoulder right back into Gremm, and as they hit, Haern rolled along his body, spinning as fast as his feet could allow. Coming out of the turn, he slashed for Gremm's neck, but the orc was quicker than the others. Around went his swords, parrying away Haern's finishing hit.

"You're fast," Gremm said, slashing again. Haern, never one to consider himself a slow learner, hopped back and out of the way. "But I am strong. Stronger than you!"

"Perhaps," Haern said, catching movement from the corner of his eye at the wagon. "But I have better friends."

He closed his eyes as another brilliant flash surged across the battlefield. As Gremm screamed, Haern slipped both his sabers between the orc's defenses, then jammed them upward through his chest and into his neck. The orc lifted his swords to strike, but the blood was draining out of him fast, and his legs gave way before he could swing. The weapons hit the ground with a thud, followed by the orc and a much heavier thud. Haern stepped back, shook blood from his sabers. A quick look to the other wagon showed Thren finishing off the last of the orcs, chasing down two that had turned to flee.

"Well, then," Haern said, walking toward the wagon he'd defended. "I daresay you all owe me a..."

He froze as a woman hopped out from the back of the wagon, red hair falling down past her neck and a smile on her lips.

"I was wondering if you'd show up," said Delysia, and as the rest of the survivors piled out of the wagon, relieved men and women in plain clothes and dresses, she flung her arms around his neck and kissed his cheek.

"...thank you?" Haern said, and as the rest surrounded him, eager to offer their thanks, he glanced back to the other wagon in search of his father, found him at the edge of the clearing, arms crossed over his chest, bloody swords leaning against a tree.

Strangely enough, he was still smiling.

CHAPTER

5

It was the pins that were the worst of it. Ghost had endured stabbings before, broken bones, and brutal beatings. Those he'd always known how to black out in his mind, to ignore as if they were happening to someone else. But the gentle touchers were too clever and too patient. As he wandered down the street, his entire body wrapped in a thick robe with a heavy hood, he could still hear the sick words of the man first sent to torture him after he'd been found dying in Leon Connington's room.

"You're a big man," the gentle toucher had said. In all four years, Ghost had never learned his name. His face had been withered, his nose thin and scarred, his skin paler than the moon. "A big man, and you might be responsible for the death of our lord. So, I'm going to break you with the tiniest of things; do you hear me?"

The first pin slid into the flesh of his forefinger.

"The very...tiniest..."

Every hour, that man had come and inserted another pin. Underneath his fingernails, into his fingertips, his toes, his toenails. If the man slept, he didn't for long, because for three weeks straight, the man had come, always cheerfully telling him the hour as well as the pin's number.

"It's just after midnight," he'd say, grinning, stabbing a pin just left of Ghost's eyelid. "And this is your seventieth. I'll see you for seventy-one."

At the three hundredth pin, the last sixty of which had been focused on his groin, Ghost had finally relented and begged for death. But death hadn't come.

Only more pins.

"One day," Ghost muttered, shivering despite himself. "One day, I'll return as the one holding the pins."

The hour was dark, which suited Ghost fine. He kept his hood pulled down across his face, hiding the white paint. Now was not the time for attention. The pins had done their work, and while the gentle toucher had removed them over the years, the ones in his fingertips had remained the longest. Even now they were puffy, scarred, and ached at the slightest pressure. The idea of holding a sword and wielding it in combat was preposterous. At least, without aid...

Ghost stopped before cracked white steps he recognized well. In what felt like a previous lifetime, he'd fought on those steps, keeping back a mad horde of mercenaries bent on desecrating the temple of Ashhur in their attempt to slaughter more of the thieves that infested the city. Doing so had earned him the help of a certain priest, a priest Ghost hoped would still be living within. He climbed the stairs, grunting at the pain in his feet. At least the gentle touchers considered themselves artists above the more basic forms of torture. If they'd resorted to breaking bones and hacking off limbs, he'd have been hobbling up the steps like a toothless cripple. Perhaps that was the real secret to their art as well as their longevity. They could drag the truth out of kings and lowborn alike, yet still send them back to their lives without significant damage. What person of power wouldn't have the occasional need for such a tool?

Torches hung from the marble columns atop the steps, keeping the double doors well lit. Up to them Ghost went, rapping twice on the door. After a moment, he heard a creak followed by the door opening a crack. A young boy, twelve, maybe thirteen, peered out at him. His eyes widened at the size of him, the deep color of his skin, the paint on his face.

"The...the temple is closed," the boy said. "If you need succor, you may sleep on the steps until..."

"I will not stay out here until dawn like a beggar," Ghost interrupted. He put a hand out on the door, let his massive weight keep it from shutting. "Wake the priest named Calan. I demand an audience with him."

The request certainly didn't help the boy's composure.

"The high priest is not to be disturbed after his evening prayers."

Ghost chuckled.

"Either you disturb him, or I will. Which would you prefer?"

It felt good to know that despite all he'd suffered, he still could be an intimidating presence. The danger in his deep voice had not vanished amid those four torturous years.

"And who should I say is asking?"

"Tell him what I look like," Ghost said. "Tell him it's a ghost. He'll remember me."

"A moment; just give me one moment," the boy said, looking as baffled as he sounded. "I need to ask first. Stay here, please."

"If you insist," Ghost said, giving him a grand smile.

When the door shut, Ghost's humor quickly fled. He leaned against the temple, letting out a heavy breath. Simply clutching the door with his right hand had flooded it with pain, and his feet were beginning to swell from his barefoot walk to the temple. The feeling of light-headedness was helping none, either. Food had never been consistent in the dungeons, and despite his exit, he'd not had much to eat. It felt like his stomach was forever tied into a knot, and he knew it might take weeks before his normal appetite returned. It seemed almost laughable what he'd promised Melody he'd accomplish. Kill the Watcher? Ghost closed his eyes and felt the cold of the marble against his cheek. As he was now, he had a better chance of beating down the temple with his bare fists than killing someone like him. Someone whose rage had seemed endless, whose speed and skill, already brilliant, became something otherworldly upon witnessing the death of his friend, Senke. But a promise was a promise, and he'd not go back on it now.

The door opened fully, and an older man with a waist-long beard stepped out.

"Follow me," he said. There was no hiding his distaste at the white paint across Ghost's face. "Calan said he'd meet with you, though only Ashhur knows why."

The man led him through the entryway, and the crimson carpet beneath Ghost's feet felt divine. Once within the grand worship hall, they veered right, up to a single door that was partially ajar. Without waiting for permission, Ghost yanked it open and stepped inside.

An older man waited for him, in a room sparsely furnished but for a large bookshelf, a desk, and the simple bed he sat upon. His round head was bald, his face cleanly shaven. His beady green eyes seemed to light up at Ghost's entrance, though there was no doubt plenty of hesitance as well.

"Most sick and feeble have the decency to wait until morning for me to pray at their sides," Calan said, slowly rising from his bed.

"I am not most sick and feeble," Ghost said.

"You're exactly like them, just with more pride. Have a seat, if you'd prefer. At my desk is fine."

Ghost settled into the wooden chair, and he pulled the hood from his face. In the candlelight, he knew he must look quite a sight, and hoping to blunt away any questions, he extended his hands.

"I am in need of healing," he said. "And I do not know of any other who might be better at the art."

"I think it safe to say I'm the only one of my ilk you know," Calan said, staring at Ghost's hands. "Which makes your praise rather . . . unimpressive."

The priest took a step closer, and slowly he took Ghost's hands. Finger by finger he scanned them, the lines on his brow deepening.

"I've seen marks like this before," he whispered. "But only twice in all my years. You've been at the mercy of a gentle toucher, haven't you?"

Ghost was impressed at how fast he discerned it, and he felt a glimmer of hope that he still might be made well.

"I have," he said.

"How long?"

He swallowed.

"Four years."

Calan looked up from his hands, his eyes wide.

"Four years? By Ashhur, you poor soul. Consider yourself blessed you're even alive and of sound mind."

"How do you know I'm of sound mind?" Ghost asked as Calan sat down before him.

"You have a charisma about you," Calan said, inspecting

Ghost's feet as he had his hands. "If you'd come in here shouting and ranting, or perhaps groveling, then I might be more uncertain."

"I've never been one to grovel," Ghost said, and immediately his memories reminded him of the lie it was, the way he'd begged for the gentle touchers to put an end to his suffering. It'd only been once, just that once, but still he felt the shame of it haunting him. Calan seemed to notice his unease, but he said nothing of it, only stood and tapped his lips with his fingers.

"They were careful with you," he said. "That, plus Ashhur's power, gives you hope. Close your eyes, Ghost, and give me your hands."

Ghost swallowed, and he felt a tightening in his chest. He did as he was told, and he reached out, felt the older man's thinner, wrinkled hands press upon his. The contact sent a brief spike of pain up his arm, and he gritted his teeth against it.

"This won't be easy," Calan said. "And forgive me, but this will hurt."

Bony fingers clamped down tight, and Ghost clenched his teeth harder. Despite his self-control, he let out a gasp of pain. The whisperings of a prayer reached his ears, but the words were soft, and he could not focus on them. He felt a tearing, the pressure tightening, the fluid in his fingers dripping down his arms as Calan lifted all four of their hands to the ceiling. The words of the prayer quickened, its intensity growing. A sound, like that of a distant ringing, flooded his mind. Ghost had been healed before of a sickness in his knee, but something about this time differed. Was it the age of the injuries, or the sheer amount across his fingers? He didn't know, and he felt strangely uncomfortable in asking.

He looked only once, and the blinding white light shining from Calan's hands as it enveloped his own was enough to make him close his eyes and leave them shut until the prayer ended and Calan let him go.

"Was it enough?" he heard Calan ask, and so he opened his eyes.

Where once his fingers had been swollen, they were now back to their original size. The many scars remained, white fleshy dots across his obsidian skin, but they no longer caused him pain. His fingertips, always the worst, were now slick with blood and pus, and he asked for a rag so he might clean them off.

"They feel better," Ghost said as he accepted a square of white cloth from the priest. He gingerly applied it to his fingertips and was surprised at how he felt no pain at all at its touch. It was strange, like stepping backward to a time before the gentle touchers, the needles, and the permanent care he'd had to take in handling even the smallest of objects.

"Not done yet," Calan said, sounding out of breath. "Your feet now."

Ghost leaned back in his chair, heels resting on the soft carpet, and then closed his eyes when the priest wrapped his fingers around the tips of his toes. Again came the pressure, this time broader, more evenly spread out across the entirety of his foot. Again, he felt liquid running down to his heel and then dripping to the floor, and it was shockingly cold. The words of the prayer came and went, the light faded, the ethereal hum died, and at last Ghost opened his eyes.

"Amazing," Ghost said as he wiped the blood and pus from his feet. Calan took the rag from him, cleaned off what he could not see, then wiped it across the carpet, even though it clearly would not remove the stain.

"What is amazing is that I did not make you wait until morning," said the priest, rising to a stand. "Falling asleep has slowly gotten more difficult over the years, and interrupted rest does not tend to improve matters."

Ghost ignored him, instead flexing his hands and taking several careful steps back and forth. The priest watched him, his mood turning somber.

"What is it you plan on doing with those hands?" Calan asked. "Will you hurt and kill, as you once did?"

Everyone knew priests of Ashhur could sense a lie as easily as a normal man could feel the wind blowing on his skin. So instead, Ghost avoided it altogether.

"If I say yes, would you have still healed me?" he asked.

The priest chuckled, and he lay back down on his bed and groaned in pleasure as he settled underneath the covers.

"I would have healed you anyway, yes," he said.

"Then why ask, if it changes nothing?"

The priest shrugged.

"Was hoping you'd put my mind at ease, is all. But I would rather help all I can instead of helping no one for fear of aiding a man with evil in his heart."

"Seems naïve," said Ghost. "There are some men that should receive no blessings, for there is nothing good left within them."

Calan looked over at him, let a smile crack his face.

"I remember you, Ghost. You're not one people tend to forget, and more than anything, I remember feeling there was a speck of hope buried down deep, perhaps lost along with your original name. Naïve or not, I will be here if you need me. You endured a long time in darkness in our cruel, cold world, and if there is anything this cruel, cold world hates most, it is letting go."

"I'll keep it in mind. Is it all right if I see myself out?"

"Shut the door behind you," Calan said, rolling over and putting his back to him. "And snuff out the candles, if you wouldn't mind."

*   *   *

The temple was only the first of Ghost's many stops he had planned for that night. Gaining the strength back in his hands and feet was an important one, and relied solely on the mystical arts Ashhur's priests were known for. His next step, however, was one far more firmly rooted in the material realm. He hurried to the main road running north to south through the heart of Veldaren, then turned south. Not far into the district, he took a left, stopping before a squat little cube of a building. It bore no written sign, just a large board above the doorway, marked by an image of an x formed by the crossing of a sword and an ink quill.

Ghost checked the door, found it barred on the other side. He frowned, considered trying to break it down, decided otherwise. He had a feeling such measures would be unnecessary.

"Bill!" he cried, banging on the door with his fists. "Bill Trett, get your ass out of bed and to this door!"

Making such a ruckus at night might normally have unnerved him, but four years under torture had removed much of his caution. What enemies did he have that might come for him? Only one, the Watcher, and if he had not already spotted his white face hurrying through the streets, then hollering at the mercenary guild's headquarters would hurt matters none.

"Bill!" His fist thumped against the wood, and he took considerable pleasure in its rough feel, and more importantly, how it caused no pain to his hand. "I know you're there, Bill; now open the door!"

When he paused to listen, he heard a scuffling, coupled with a veritable barrage of curses, at last followed by a lifting of the bar.

The door flung open, and an old man with a badly scarred face and bushy white unibrow stepped forward, a dagger in hand.

"What the bloody Abyss do you want?" Bill asked. "Answer now, before I stab you in the..."

The man froze, and his watery eyes widened as he caught sight of Ghost in the moonlight.

"Well, I never," he said. "Ghost? Is that really you?"

"Back from the dead," Ghost said. "Now put that toothpick away and let me in."

Bill hobbled away from the door, but he kept ahold of the dagger. The man wore a long night robe, and when Ghost stepped inside the cluttered mess of papers, names, lists of locations and jobs all strewn about the shelves, he was not surprised to see a single cot in the center of the room.

"I thought you might sleep here," Ghost said.

"Not much point in going home," Bill said, stumbling back to his cot. "Only time I ever leave is to get drunk at a bar. It's more interesting than getting drunk here, anyway."

He crossed his arms, looked to sit, then changed his mind. Ghost could tell he wanted to ask dozens of questions but had far too much discipline to do so. Just one of many reasons the man had risen to his position when his time as a mercenary ended.

"I've been away," Ghost said. "And not taking other jobs, either, so don't hassle me about my dues. I'm out now, though, and have several kills already lined up."

"An interesting person who'd hire you looking like, well..." Bill gestured to Ghost's ratty clothing, his bare feet, and his clear lack of weaponry. "Like you do now. Did they dig you up out of the ground before offering the job?"

Ghost cracked a smile.

"You're closer than you think, Bill. But I need coin, swords, and clothing. Given all I did for the guild, I feel I'm due."

Bill frowned.

"You know I don't keep any coin here overnight. Guild policy."

Ghost gave him a look.

"All right, fine. Follow me, you bastard. But if I do this, I want one question answered after it's all said and done. That fair?"

"Fair as this world can be."

Only a third of the building was used to greet wealthy clientele needing to hire escorts outside the city, patrols for their property, or more permanent protection for their various farms, mines, and homes scattered throughout Dezrel. Past a door behind the counter, they entered the rest of the building, which was a single storage room. Two tall windows let in enough moonlight for him to see rows of shelves filling the center, and they were stocked with all kinds of weapons, armor, and clothing. Ghost beamed at the sight.

"Always knew I could count on you," he said.

"Until you vanished, *I* could always count on *you*," Bill said.

Ghost glared at him, and the old man quickly apologized.

"Just take what you need," he said. "I'll write it off as an expense at bringing you back into the fold. A man of your skills could easily find work today, especially given all the insanity we've been seeing in the city lately."

"Anything beyond the usual?" Ghost asked. "Or is Thren's private war finally dying down?"

"Dying down?" Bill asked, and he looked confused. "That ended when the Watcher's truce began. Was about the same time you vanished, Ghost. Most of us just thought you were one of the many casualties of that night."

Watcher's truce?

Ghost realized just how badly behind the times he was. Four years had passed, and in the underworld, such a span could be a lifetime. It wasn't just food and water he'd been starved of by the gentle touchers.

"So, did this Watcher kill him?" Ghost asked as he lifted the lid on one crate to see five or six short swords. None looked in good enough condition for him to use, plus their length would not be sufficient to fully utilize his height and reach. "I don't see Thren Felhorn as one to sign any sort of truce."

"You'd think," Bill said. "But no, Thren's alive, at least last I knew. Things have gotten hectic, what with the Sun Guild's arrival and the Spider Guild's disbandment."

Ghost froze, a plain gray shirt held before him to check its size.

"Disbandment?" he asked. "Bill, if you are trying to amuse me..."

"It's too damn late for jokes," Bill said, crossing his arms and leaning against the doorframe leading into the storage room. "The Sun Guild's come in from Mordeina, and they've hit like a gods-damned thunderstorm. The Hawk Guild has been fully destroyed along with the Spiders, and both the Shadow Guild and the Serpent Guild are serving like the loyal little bitches that they are. As for the Wolf Guild, from what I've been hearing, it should fold within the week. I think the only ones left to fight are the Ash, but honestly, they're fighting a hopeless struggle. Anyone can see that, and I'm sure they do too, hence why they've been lying low."

"So, we trade one rat for another," Ghost said. "Does the difference really matter in the end? Either way, the city remains filled with vermin."

Bill shrugged.

"At least we used to know who the rats were. This Darkhand fellow is a giant mystery to most of us. When you're in the business of killing, mysteries are rarely a good thing."

Ghost removed his old shirt and replaced it with the new one. It was overly tight, but he flexed his arms a few times until it stretched. In the next crate, he found a stack of four breeches, and taking the biggest, he put them on next. Bill crossed his arms and turned away to give him some privacy.

"What can you tell me about the Gemcrofts?" Ghost asked as he tightened its drawstring, then grabbed a pair of boots he'd found during his scavenge.

"Alyssa's still running things there, though not for long." Bill turned back around, and he looked glum as he continued. "That crazy woman's been great to our guild, always kept things interesting, but she's in over her head now. Some sick man took out her eyes, left her blind. Her mother's been steadily taking over responsibility, especially given Nathaniel's age."

"Nathaniel?"

"Her son."

Ghost grunted, finished tying the boots, and then continued with his search for supplies. If Melody Gemcroft was coming to him to kill Alyssa's protector as a way to ensure Melody's ascension, then Bill was right about Alyssa's days being numbered. His role looked to be little more than paving the way for whatever else Melody had planned. He wondered if she would come to him afterward, ask him to deal with Nathaniel or Alyssa herself. The idea put a twist in his stomach, but given the freedom Melody had brought to him, what did a few more killings matter?

"Do you have a mirror?" Ghost asked as he found a weapon rack hanging on the wall, and his eyes lit up at seeing the many swords.

"In here somewhere."

"Help me find it."

Bill began rummaging, and as he did Ghost pulled two

similarly sized swords from the rack, tested their weight. They felt a bit heavy, but he knew his time in the dungeon was more to blame for that than the swords themselves. His arms would grow stronger, their weight less noticeable in time. Beneath the rack was a box with old sword belts, and he grabbed one, looped it around his waist, and slid both sheathed blades into it.

"Here you are," Bill said, coming over from the corner.

Ghost grabbed it, then returned to the front of the guild-house to stand in the light of the candles. When he could see, he drew one of his swords, lifted the mirror, and examined his face. He'd never been capable of growing much hair on his face, and in the four years of capture, his uneven beard was disgusting to behold. Slowly, Ghost scraped the blade's edge along his face, slicing away the growth and congealed bits of white paint. Bill watched in silence, his arms crossed, until Ghost began cutting at his hair.

"If you're going to shave your head, do it right," Bill said, retrieving a small satchel from underneath his desk and tossing it to him. "Use a damn razor like a civilized man."

Ghost flashed him a grin.

"Civilized," he said. "Is that what you think I am?"

Still, the razor was small and sharp, and it cut across his scalp smoothly. It took some time, and he could see how annoyed Bill was at having the dirty hair fall upon his floor, but when he was done, Ghost felt more relieved than he had in ages. He turned side to side, scanning his face in the mirror. There were scars around his neck now, and a thinness to his cheeks that only time and plentiful food would remove. His eyes in particular were sunken inward and rimmed with dark circles. The gaunt look was unnerving, he had to admit.

Taking the box of paint Melody had given him out from his pocket, he dipped his fingers inside and began to smear it across his newly shaven face. Thicker and thicker he spread the paint, whitening him, hiding him. The last thing he wanted his opponents to see was himself, not with how sick and tired he felt. He needed to be the killer again, the brutal hunter no one could escape. With his swords, his clothes, his paint, he was as close to that as he'd been since being thrown into the Connington dungeons, and as the last of the paint spread across his neck, he let out a wide smile.

"How do I look?" he asked, setting down the mirror.

"Like your old self," Bill said.

"And for that, I have you to thank." Ghost dipped his head in respect. "Keep quiet about my return. Once my tasks are over, I plan on traveling far from Veldaren, and if I can, I'd like to ensure no one can follow me."

"Of course," Bill said. "Besides, who would believe me? All they'd think is that an old man saw himself a ghost in his sleep."

He grinned at his own joke, and Ghost slapped the man across the shoulder.

"A shame we never fought side by side," he said. "No doubt you were a fine mercenary."

"Best this sorry guild ever saw."

Before Ghost could leave, Bill returned to the front, used a key from his pocket to unlock a drawer, and then pulled out a small bag tied shut with string.

"Take it," Bill said. "It'll rent you a room for a bit, buy you meals when you must. And find yourself a washbasin. Even for a man of the streets, you reek."

"The guild will not be happy with its disappearance," said Ghost, accepting the offer.

Bill laughed.

"You don't get it, Ghost. That there is a death bag, for families of those who die on the job. You had no family and so we kept it, but now I daresay that coin belongs to you. Wouldn't you agree?"

Ghost flashed him a smile.

"The guild has no idea how lucky it is to have a man like you."

"Perhaps. Before you go . . . you promised me a question."

"I did," Ghost said. "So ask it, and I promise to answer the best I can."

Bill clapped his hands together, clearly nervous. Bobbing his head up and down, almost like an old bird, he finally asked his question.

"Where have you been all this time?"

Ghost thought it over, the years, the tortures, the dungeon cell. It seemed impossible to explain it all, nor did he desire to. So, he kept it simple, and gave the only answer that mattered.

"Darkness."

And with that, he stepped out into the night, and he breathed in the air like a man newly awoken.

"Zusa," he said, testing out the name of his prey. The Watcher and the Eschaton were both formidable opponents, but this woman was unknown to him. He'd take his time, gather his strength before challenging them, but until then, he knew he should find out more about his mystery target. As Bill adeptly put it, in the killing business, mysteries were rarely a good thing. More often than not, they got you killed.

Well, if Zusa was Alyssa's watchdog, then there was only one real place to expect her to be. Ghost followed the street north for a mile, keeping his eyes open for the various thief guilds as he did. At the height of the war between the Trifect and the thief guilds, Ghost knew he could have spotted at least one man or woman keeping watch in practically every road. Now, though, he found himself feeling more and more alone.

Where were the guilds? Where were their watchful eyes? When the Sun Guild destroyed them, did they have no intention of replacing their numbers with their own?

When he turned west down Copper Road, he paused. Nearby was one of many taverns, and dug into the very ground at its entrance he saw a stone tile. Its newness, as well as its stark gray contrast to the worn brown dirt, made it stand out all the more. Carved into the front of it was a four-pointed star.

"You mark your territory with stone," Ghost said, and he chuckled. "No wonder you've crushed Veldaren's weak, hollow guilds so easily."

A scrawny man with a similar emblem sewn onto the front of his vest leaned against the tavern, just shy of the door, and he gestured him closer.

"Leaf, powder, or woman?" the man asked him, and his accent was one Ghost recognized immediately, that of western Mordan, where he himself had grown up.

"Perhaps later, when the night is not so young," Ghost said.

"Out on business, then?" the man asked, and he pulled up his dagger so that the light from the tavern flickered across it. "Make sure it's something we wouldn't mind you doing in our city."

"Your city?" Ghost asked, and he smirked at the dagger. "You'll need more than just that little knife to claim a place like Veldaren."

The scrawny man smirked back.

"You'd be surprised how well these little knives work when wielded in the hands of thousands."

Ghost purposefully put his back to him and marched on. There'd be no conflict between him and the Sun Guild, not unless he started one, but it annoyed him anyway, just hearing the arrogance in the man's voice. If there was ever a city in the world where power was ephemeral, it was Veldaren, and it'd take more than a few stone slabs to change that fact.

Down the street he walked, even more brazen than before. This time, he did see a few men tailing him, and he had little doubt as to what guild they belonged.

At last, he reached the sprawling gates to the Gemcroft mansion. A single man remained on guard at the front, standing there with his sword sheathed and his eyes drooping. Ghost remained in the shadows of the other nearby homes, curling around toward the western side. From there, he had a fine view of the expansive garden and green grass that filled the border between the fence and the mansion proper. Climbing the fence wouldn't have been too difficult, though the sharpened spikes at the top did give him some pause. But entering the complex wasn't necessary for his task.

If Melody needed Ghost to kill this Zusa, and considered her Alyssa's loyal watchdog, then he had a hunch she was someone more like him and less like the bored guard out front. Someone skilled, someone capable of wielding a blade like a living extension of themselves. And someone like that would not take long to notice Ghost lurking just outside the fence, his painted face grinning in the moonlight.

Ghost settled in, arms crossed and legs folded beneath him, but the wait was not long.

"You pick a strange place to sit and rest," said a woman's voice from above the fence top. Ghost looked up, and his jaw dropped. The woman perched atop the bars of the fence, her legs angled as to keep the pointed tops from piercing her flesh...he recognized her. He recognized that tattered cloak, those dark wrappings, and most of all, that beautiful face with the piercing dark brown eyes.

Ghost rose to his feet, and he kept his hands on the hilts of his swords.

"Forgive me," he said. "But I was denied the chance to discover your name before, yet today I think I was gifted such knowledge. Zusa?"

The woman tensed at the mention of her name, and he saw her peering down at him with new understanding. When the realization hit her, it might as well have been his fist.

"I remember you," she said. "You tried to kill me years ago."

"A simple misunderstanding," he said. "I thought you were the Watcher, remember?"

Zusa vaulted off the fence and landed light as a feather in front of Ghost. Her daggers were drawn, and she made no attempt to hide that fact.

"Why are you here?" she asked.

Ghost laughed, and he shook his head, hardly able to believe it. The strange woman he'd had but a single exchange with, the one he'd challenged in a race to find and kill the Watcher... she was Zusa, the one Melody needed killed?

How disappointing.

"Forgive me," Ghost said, "but I do not enjoy this fact any more than you will. I am to kill you, Zusa."

She froze, her whole body going tense. Those brown eyes widened, and Ghost knew a single quick movement on his part would set her tumbling. So instead, he remained calm, the hilts to his swords still comfortably resting in his large palms.

"It's a strange assassin who reveals himself and then his plans," Zusa said, clearly distrusting his statement.

"Look at my face," Ghost said. "Strangeness and I are welcome bedfellows. But I only wished to speak with you, Zusa, and give you warning. You deserve as much, so consider this a token to make up for my earlier rudeness."

"I am not one for games," Zusa said, taking a careful step backward. "If you are to kill me, then draw your swords now and try."

"I said strangeness and I are welcome bedfellows," said Ghost. "Not foolishness. We will fight when *I* am ready, Zusa." His grip on his swords tightened. "Either that, or you can charge me now and die. The choice is yours."

He stared her down, the animal instincts of the killer resurfacing with such clarity and familiarity, he was shocked by their strength. This moment, this calm before the bloodshed, was one he'd always cherished. Never more was he so close to death, yet so alive.

Zusa leaped, but it was backward, a vaulting flip that sent her over the spiked tips and onto the grass behind the fence.

"So full of surprises," Ghost said. "Perhaps you will not be the first to die."

"Stay away from my family," Zusa said. "Stay away from my home."

"I'm only here for you," Ghost said, deciding to toss her a bone. "If you seek threats to your home and family, look elsewhere."

Zusa's eyes narrowed.

"Be gone by morning," she said, then turned and fled back toward the house.

Ghost let go of a blade and saluted her departure. Yes, she was definitely interesting, the strange wrappings, that intense stare...not to mention her ability to leap through the air as if she were but a sparrow on the wind. He would save her for later, perhaps even for after the Watcher's death.

He strolled away from the fence, a bounce to his step. If she was to wait and the Watcher was to be last, then that meant the Eschaton Mercenaries would be the first to die.

CHAPTER

6

There were fifteen men, women, and children in the two wagons, and despite the late hour, the group drove to the following hill rather than staying among the corpses of the orcs. Haern kept to the rear of their formation, uncomfortable with the tearful thanks many gave. Following them all like a shadow was Thren.

When at last a new fire burned and the families lay down for sleep, Haern built his own fire beyond the outer ring of the wagons and waited. Part of him was curious who would arrive first, and in the end, it was Delysia.

"They'll be telling stories of tonight to their children for ages," she said, crossing her legs and sitting down next to him.

"It was just a few dead orcs."

"The Watcher of Veldaren saved them on the road to Ker," she said, nudging him in the side. "Not everyone is lucky enough to have such an experience."

He chuckled.

"I doubt I'd consider them lucky, other than to have had you with them as well. They'd be long dead if you hadn't kept them back."

Delysia inched closer to the fire, and she leaned toward it, her red hair cascading down the side of her face.

"It wasn't easy," she said. "I managed to kill those first two right when they entered the clearing, then blinded the rest. That scared them enough to pull back, and from then on, I kept either blinding or striking the loudest of the brutes to keep them frightened."

She shivered.

"Such horrible creatures," she said. "They're like the elves, only drained of everything good."

"Good in an elf? I think you might have hurt your head in the fight."

She laughed and elbowed him again. When she did, he jerked to the side, and when she leaned further in, he slid his arm around her and held her against him. She didn't seem to mind, her head on his shoulder as they both stared into the crackling fire.

"Why did you follow me?" Haern asked, knowing he'd have to ask and wanting it out of the way now, while they were at peace and his father away.

"I was worried about you," she said.

"Me? Trust me, Del, I can handle myself."

"That's not what worried me. You were to be alone and with him. I know you still bear scars from the way he raised you..."

He squeezed her tight, but it was less a gesture of comfort and more an excuse to say nothing, for he wasn't sure what to say.

"I'm not the little boy I was," he said, trying to explain it. "He's still Thren, but this time, I think...I think I might be the one to reach him. I might be the one to show him a way to build a legacy without cruelty or murder."

She snuggled in closer against him.

"I'm glad you're trying, Haern, but he scares me nonetheless. Just...just don't let him change you, all right? I'd hate to lose the sweet boy I first met all those years ago."

He chuckled.

"You won't lose me. So long as you're here, I will be, too. What *does* surprise me, though, is that Tarlak was willing to let you go off alone."

She pulled away from him, scoffing.

"As if I need his permission," she said, feigning outrage. "But no, he was not pleased, especially knowing where you two are going and that I'd be alone. I only left a day behind you, though, and I caught up with the Bartlets over there, whole family riding west to start a new life in Ker. My hope was to find you when you neared the Stronghold. Needless to say, I didn't expect *you* to find *me* in mid-battle."

"I seem to be quite good at that," Haern said. "Let's see; there was tonight, and there was that first night Alyssa unleashed her mercenaries, where I found you hard-pressed at a fountain. Oh, and when I stumbled upon you and that Ghost fellow having a nice talk..."

"I believe I saved your life that time," she said. "Or has your pride conveniently forgotten my blinding spell right when he was to cut you in half?"

"Well, that taught him to think a little girl like you was no threat," Haern said. He smiled, but the remembrance was tinged with pain, for when he'd come stumbling into the Eschaton home, he'd found Senke badly wounded and leaning against the wall. He'd lived, but that same killer, Ghost, had finished the job during Haern and Senke's combined assault on

Leon Connington's mansion, which had put an end to the thief war that had strangled the city for ten years.

Delysia fell silent as well, and he felt the memory hanging over both of them, stealing away the weightless mood.

"You pick strange company to keep, Watcher," Thren Felhorn said, stepping out from the trees and into the light of the fire.

Haern grinned at his father.

"Of course I do," he said. "You're here, aren't you?"

Thren grunted and took a seat opposite them of the fire. There was no hiding his disapproval of Delysia's presence.

"Your humor is wasted at this hour," he said. "Besides, we have decisions to make. The wagons will only slow us down, though if we share in their food, it might make up for the delay. Given our recent heroics, I'm sure it would be easy enough to take advantage of their gratitude."

"There won't be any need to take advantage of anyone," Delysia interjected. "The Bartlets will share their food willingly, especially after all you've done."

Thren paused, and he stared at Delysia like he would an animal that crawled up to him, opened its mouth, and began speaking.

"These matters do not concern you, woman," Thren said. "I suggest you go join the wagons while we discuss. We have no need of a prostitute."

Haern's eyes spread wide, and he was too stunned to speak. Delysia, however, was not.

"I am a priestess of Ashhur," she said, a hard edge entering her normally soft voice.

"Then you're a whore for the wrong god," Thren said, hardly caring. "At least with gold, you can accomplish something in this world."

She moved to stand but Haern held a tight grip on her wrist, keeping her seated. He met his father's eye, and his tone made his opinions clear.

"Delysia is a guest, and will be staying with us for as long as she pleases," he said.

"Is that so?" Thren asked.

"It is. She's a founding member of the Eschaton Mercenaries, and will prove valuable in our attempt to find Luther."

"Valuable?" Thren asked, turning his attention back to her. "Is that what you are, Delysia Eschaton? Valuable?"

Something about the way he was staring at her, the way he said her name, made Haern suddenly uncomfortable. It was almost as if he recognized her somehow, but from where? Had Tarlak ever tangled with the Spider Guild prior to Haern's joining them, perhaps?

"I will be no burden," Delysia said, but the answer was unsatisfactory for Thren.

"So be it," he said, rising to his feet. "I cannot do this on my own, and if this woman is a requirement for your aid, Haern, then I will endure. I take it we are to travel with the wagons?"

"Until we cross the Gods' Bridges," Delysia said. "After that, they will be continuing west at Umbridge while we head south."

"Of course," Thren said, his look a mixture of acid and condescension. "Good of you to plan our path for us. Perhaps you will be valuable after all."

He wandered back into the forest, and at his departure, Haern felt Delysia relax considerably in his arms.

"How did you stand being alone with him for so long?" she asked, pulling her arms across her body as if cold.

"He's not always like that," Haern said. "Something about you set him off. I don't believe he thinks too highly of Ashhur."

"Of course not," Delysia said. "There's no room for gods in his heart. He already views himself as one."

Haern shook his head, remembering the words he'd been taught.

"'Let them think every breath of theirs is a gift,'" he echoed. "'Not from the gods, but from you.' Thren once taught me that."

Delysia shivered.

"How horrible," she said.

"That's just who he is."

"No, not that," she said, staring off into the woods. "That he'd have you believe it yourself."

Traveling with the families was pleasant enough, and they passed over the Gods' Bridges with relative ease, which was fine for Delysia. The last thing she wanted after the orcs' attack was excitement. Once at Umbridge, the three of them parted from the group and began their trek south. Travel was easy, given the fine weather, at least the physical aspect of it. Being around Thren Felhorn was always awkward, especially given the strange way he behaved when she was near. It was as if he knew a secret she did not, something that made him far more guarded than he had any reason to be.

Over the course of their travel, food had become something of an obsession for Delysia. As their smoked meat and dried grains ran low, dry tack became their food of choice. Boiling it helped a little, but it still hurt Delysia's teeth and made her stomach cramp during their days of walking. Their only real fresh food beyond that was either from hunting (a rare kill should Thren or Haern manage to hurl one of their throwing knives and pierce a rabbit) or, more commonly, foraging for berries.

"It's getting late; stay and help me with the fire," Haern said as he cracked a branch over his knee. High above, the sun was beginning its descent, heading toward the long row of hills that lined the horizon. All around were tall grass plains, dotted by scattered trees and the occasional bump of hill.

"I still have an hour, at least," Delysia said. "I believe I saw a raspberry patch just off the path, and I'd love to have something else to eat tonight."

"Thren might come back with a rabbit or squirrel," Haern said.

"If he does, then we'll make it a feast," she said, grabbing a small basket and taking it with her.

It was clear he didn't like seeing her venture off on her own, but though she'd never say it to his face, she was getting tired of his protective gaze, his constant presence. Even the little things, such as how he always made sure he slept with his bed-roll between her and Thren, added up like tiny needles pressing into her skin. He wanted to keep her safe, she knew, but it also meant he didn't trust her to stay safe on her own.

Delysia glanced to her fingers as she bounced down the hill. A moment's prayer, and a bit of white glimmered on her fingertips. Someday, she might have to remind Haern how capable she actually was. At least he wasn't as bad as her brother. No doubt Tarlak would have eventually cracked and just teleported her back home to Veldaren while she slept. That he hadn't done so already showed how much he trusted Haern, or how busy he was with other events. Given the state of the city when she left, her instincts said it was more the latter than the former.

With a shake of her head, she scattered such thoughts. The weather was fine, the sunset a beautiful mixture of red and yellow, and she would not dwell on such frustrations. When she reached where the path veered right to slice through the center of two adjacent hills, she pushed off the path toward the thick set of bushes she saw several hundred feet away. As she neared, a smile spread across her face. She'd been right. They were raspberries and perfectly ripe. The first bush she reached, she yanked off several, popped them in her mouth, and squeezed out the juices with her tongue.

"You can keep your squirrel," she said, picking several more and filling her mouth. "Nothing is better than this."

After another minute of indulging, as well as staining the tips of her fingers purple, she grabbed the basket she'd brought with her and began to fill it. The berries would only last for a day at most, but as with every time she picked a basketful during their journey, their moods would lighten considerably. She began to hum a song, focusing on picking faster to ensure the basket would be full before the sun could set completely. So focused, in fact, she did not hear the sound of footsteps through the bushes.

"This patch was well hidden by the tall grass," said Thren Felhorn behind her. "I'm surprised you were able to see it."

Delysia tensed on instinct, then quickly recovered. She felt foolish for behaving so, but there was always a seriousness to Thren's tone that made it impossible to feel at ease. Trying not to show how flustered she'd been, she grabbed the basket and turned to face him. He stood with his head cocked to the side, a curious look on his face. In his right hand, he held a rabbit by the legs, blood running down the brown fur and dripping drop after drop from the creature's mouth, which was locked open in death. In Thren's left hand, he held the slender blade that had performed the killing.

"I guess I have an eye for these things," she said.

"I have an eye for things, too," Thren said, and he looked to the rabbit. "Where to hide. How to tell a lie. How to kill."

He only wants to intimidate you, she told herself. As if the blood and knife were nothing, she turned back to the raspberry bush in front of her.

"A shame yours won't keep us fed tonight," she said.

"I disagree, or did you not notice the rabbit?"

She glanced over her shoulder.

"Oh," she said, as if it were new to her. "So you did. Haern should have a fire ready, and he can start cooking it if you bring it to him."

It was a subtle attempt to guide him away from her, to show she was not afraid of his presence but still wanted him gone. Instead, he remained standing there, and the longer he did, the more the bloody dagger occupied her mind. The sounds she made as she gathered, the scraping of her feet on the dirt, the rustle of bushes with their thorns, failed to fill the silence between them as he stared.

"I remember you," Thren said, and Delysia's heart stopped.

"Is that so?" she asked, keeping her back to him.

"Your name is first what felt familiar, has been ever since I learned the Watcher was staying with your mercenaries. But then I saw your face...and now I see your back. You were younger then, when I put an arrow through it. You should be dead, priestess, just like your father."

She put the basket down before her, slowly rose to her feet. She wiped the raspberry juices on the lowest part of her dress, turned to face him. Thren Felhorn stood mere feet away, dagger in one hand, dead thing in the other, and never before had Delysia seen someone so perfectly encapsulated by a single image such as then.

"I'm sorry to disappoint," she said, proud there was no

quiver in her voice. "But someone took me to Ashhur's temple for healing, and it'd have been rude of me to die on them after such a risk."

"You were corrupting my son," Thren said.

"I was saving him."

"The only thing he needed saving from was you."

"I was but a child and had only my words," she said, meeting his cold stare. "Yet still you were frightened of me. But I guess you should know how much power there can be in words."

She felt electricity building in the air around her, felt her power growing in her chest and sliding down into her fingers. Whatever Thren tried, she would be ready. Even if he killed her, she would not die without striking back.

He took another step, bringing him dangerously close. She could smell the blood dripping from the rabbit, almost taste the coppery liquid on her tongue.

"Because of you, I lost my son Aaron forever," he said. "I won't let that happen with the Watcher. Go home, Delysia. Go, and leave him far behind. He's beyond needing your weak morality, your false teachings. I know what he is, and what he can become, far better than you do. It's time to let the beast within go unchained so all of Dezrel may cower before his blades. You cost me a son. Don't cost me an heir, not if you want to live."

"I'm not leaving, Thren," she said, and she prepared for an attack. "I'm staying at his side. I won't let you have him."

Light sparked from her fingertips, but if he was afraid, he showed no sign of it.

"You mistake my kindness," Thren said, leaning in close so his cheek was brushing against hers, so that his lips were whispering into her ear. "Leave now, or pay the price for staying. Don't you see? It won't be by *my* hand that you suffer. Keep that in mind when you make your choice."

And with that he left, casually strolling back toward the road, rabbit swinging in his right hand. As he faded from sight, Delysia dropped to her knees, letting out a breath she never realized she'd been holding. With both hands, she grabbed the basket's handle, and she held it as she tried to regain her composure.

He's a madman, she told herself. *Mad, absolutely mad, and he won't stop until Haern's just like him.*

It seemed the whole world stopped, the soft wind blowing through the field becoming still as the realization hit her like a stone to her chest.

Just like him…

Thren knew. The Watcher wasn't an enigma, a foe, a counter to his Spider Guild. No, he had to know, for why else would he be so defensive? Why else would he fear her influence so powerfully?

You cost me a son… don't cost me an heir.

Delysia grabbed the basket and ran back to their camp, ignoring the cuts against her skin from the thorns. She wasn't sure what she'd say, and part of her feared what Thren would do. But what could he do other than kill her? Even that would be a risk. If he wanted to win Haern over, her death would put an end to their cooperation. Thren needed time; he needed opportunity.

The sun was almost set and she out of breath, by the time she reached the camp. Haern sat before the fire, a crude spit set up to cook the rabbit above it. He smiled when he looked up and saw her and the berries, but he quickly sensed something was amiss.

"Del?" he asked.

Beside him sat Thren, and he glanced at her with a passive expression, as if nothing at all had been said between them only minutes before.

"I need to talk to you," she said. "Alone."

"Whatever needs to be said I'm sure can be said in front of me," Thren said.

"No, it can't," Delysia said, glaring. Haern looked between them, and his hand drifted down to the hilt of his sword.

"I'm sure you won't mind giving us a moment of privacy," Haern said as he stood.

Thren shrugged.

"Go ahead, but I make no promises on the raspberries. If you take too long, and I eat them all, it's on you."

At Delysia's lead, the two wandered away from the camp, until she felt comfortable Thren would not hear. Leaning against one of the few trees nearby, Delysia crossed her arms over her chest and tried to make sense of her thoughts.

"We have to go back," she said.

"What?" asked Haern.

"All of us, we have to go back; we have to stop this. Whatever you're hoping to accomplish, it isn't worth it. We can do more good in Veldaren."

Haern glanced back to the campfire, and a frown came over his face.

"Is that why you came all this way?" he asked. "To tell me to turn back? Because I won't, Delysia. I have to know what is going on, and this is the only way."

She knew it wasn't, but there was no doubt in Haern's voice, no questioning in his eyes. His mind was set, and she felt her stomach sink.

"It's not worth it," she said, voice quieter. "Not for such a risk."

"I can handle a few dark paladins."

"That's not what I meant."

Haern let out a sigh, and he kicked at the tall grass.

"I'm not afraid of him," he said. "He needs me."

"He does," Delysia said. "And that's what I'm afraid of."

She pushed off the tree, took a step toward him. She put her hand on Haern's cheek, guided his eyes to hers. His eyes were so blue, she thought. Like a child's. Like his father's.

"He knows," she whispered. "Who you are. Don't you understand? *He knows.*"

His entire body tensed as if preparing for battle.

"Did he tell you this?" he asked, his own voice softer.

"No," she said. "But I feel it in my gut. After all these years, he views this as a second chance. He wants to bring you back to him, make you as you were. Can't you see that? Thren Felhorn wants his son returned to him. He wants his heir."

"It's impossible," Haern said, shaking his head. "Why wouldn't he have confronted me before now? Why let me live on the streets for so long, working against him? It's not like him; he wouldn't have…"

"He'd do whatever it took to get what he wanted," Delysia said. "And he won't let anyone stand in his way. He told me so while I was in the field."

His face darkened, and she saw the thought go through his mind.

"Did he threaten you?" he asked.

Delysia swallowed. Haern would not return to Veldaren. His mind was set, but if she revealed the threat, she knew what he'd do. He'd send her away, refusing to trust her. That was how Haern worked, and she'd come to accept it. The man would take any risk so long as the consequences were only on himself, but should it be someone else, someone he cared for…

"He never said he would harm me," she said, as close to a lie as she could manage, and still she felt ill by it.

Haern let out a sigh.

"I'll pay more attention, all right?" he asked. "But I refuse to believe he knows I'm his son. He'd have acted far sooner. The moment he knew, he'd have torn Veldaren apart to have me back at his side. Listen, perhaps you're right, and he wants to recruit me in some way. If that is the case, I promise you, I'll never be what Thren wants me to be. I'm stronger than I ever was, smarter, wiser. I can stand against him far better than when I was a child."

The words were like tiny needles to her heart, and she stood on her toes so she could kiss his cheek.

"Don't you see?" she asked him. "It's the child you were that must survive."

With that, she returned to the fire, determined to deny her fear of Thren, to be there no matter the cost. At her arrival, Thren tore off a leg of the rabbit and tossed it her way.

"Dig in," he said as she caught it. "It'll be tougher than it looks, though."

He winked, and she smiled sweetly back as she bit into the flesh, vowing that no matter the cost, she would not let such a horrible man win.

CHAPTER

7

Lord Victor Kane stood before the mirror and adjusted the collar of his shirt for the third time.

"Forget it," he said, yanking off the silken garment. "It's not me, anyway."

Instead, he put on a plain undershirt, followed by his finely woven chain mail shirt. It was heavy, but when he clasped his sword belt to his waist, it helped to distribute some of the weight. That done, he grabbed his sword, pulled a tunic with his family's crest over his head, and then looked once more into the mirror. This time, he looked ready for battle, the rings of his chain mail shining in the light streaming in through his window.

Much better, he thought. Better he be comfortable than pretend to be something he wasn't.

"Milord?" asked a man at the door after a quick set of knocks.

"Come in, Sef," Victor said.

The door opened, and into Victor's small room stepped Sef Battleborn, a heavyset and bearded man whose long brown hair had more than a fair share of gray in it. Sef had been a loyal soldier of his family for decades now, and Victor hoped he'd be around for decades more.

"Going to Alyssa's again?" he asked, looking Victor up and down.

"Hard to woo a woman when you're not at her side."

"The poets say differently."

"The poets write their ballads so that young maidens will throw themselves at their feet afterwards," Victor said, tugging on his chain mail to readjust its weight so it was centered instead of too far on his right shoulder. "And since when do you listen to poets?"

"When I'm off drinking," Sef said. "Something you used to do with me before all this started."

Victor ran a hand through his hair, glanced at Sef.

"Is there a reason you're here, other than to complain about my not getting shit-faced with you at a tavern?"

"Sadly, there is," Sef said, and he sighed. "The mercenary captains have all gathered downstairs. They want to be paid, Victor, and they aren't leaving until they get what they think is theirs."

"How many?" Victor asked Sef, who stood in the doorway to Victor's room looking miserable.

"Fifteen," his old friend said. "If you tally up those under their command, it's nearly six hundred of our mercenaries."

Six hundred of their remaining thousand. Victor slowly stood from his chair, walked over to Sef.

"Fetch me soldiers still loyal to my cause," he said. "Have them outside in case I need them."

"Yes, my lord," Sef said, bowing his head. "Will you come speak with the captains?"

"In a moment," Victor said. "Just...tell them to give me a moment."

When the door closed, Victor walked back to his desk and grabbed his dagger off it. Staring into the edge, he asked himself how far he was willing to go. His parents' death...how far must he go before they were avenged? How much spilled blood was the city of Veldaren truly worth?

"One more drop," he said to his distorted reflection upon the blade. "Every day it seems I say it: just one more drop..."

Was that how rivers began, with just one more drop? He didn't know, but what he did know was that the memory of his parents was worth an ocean; sheathing the dagger on his belt, he flung open the door to his room and marched down the steps into the lower floor of his converted tavern. Sitting in chairs, standing at the bar, by the door, and leaning against the walls were the various mercenary captains. Victor knew them all well, had befriended many of them over the past few years. They'd formed the backbone of his forces required to cleanse the scourge of the underworld from Veldaren. But it'd all been a gamble relying on the king to help shoulder the load of paying them, and as the men had died and the grumbles began, that gamble had failed spectacularly.

"He emerges," said Joras One-Eye, sitting at a table with a large glass in his left hand. A bit of foam from the beer within coated his short beard. "I hope you managed to find a few extra bags of gold underneath your bed while we waited."

Victor walked over to him, and while the others watched, he stole Joras's drink and finished it himself. Feeling the burn going down, he used it to give himself the extra push he needed.

"I see no reason for this farce," he told them. "Time. That is all I ask for. How much coin have I already poured into your open hands? Surely you can trust me to wait a few weeks more..."

"Hard for a dead man to pay his debts," Joras said. "And we all know that's what you are: a dead man walking."

"If you all did your damn jobs, the danger on my life would be irrelevant." He glared at them, then set his glass back down on the table. "Nothing has changed. Come here and threaten as you wish, but it won't get you your gold. If you want to disband and send your men home, then do it. If you won't wait for your payment, then you won't receive it. The truth is that simple."

"Aye, that's simple, all right," said another of the captains, a hefty man with two axes strapped to his belt. "So how's about we make it simple for you, Lord Kane? If we don't get paid, me and my men go find our payment elsewhere. How about in your family lands? I think there's a few extra silvers lost in those golden wheat fields of yours."

"I hear women can go for a pretty handful of silvers in parts of the world, too," a third captain piped up.

"Are you threatening me?" Victor asked.

"I think we are," Joras said, standing. The others mumbled their agreement. "And I think you need to give us a better answer than the one we've had. All of us have bled and died for you, for this wretched city, and while *you* might be a weeping-heart fool, we aren't doing it for the good of our souls."

"Good of our pockets, maybe," someone from the back chimed in.

Victor swallowed hard, and when Sef stepped inside, Victor nodded.

"So be it," he said. "Give me but a moment, and I will see what I can do. Good men as you deserve payment for the work you've done."

He walked to the door, patted Sef on the shoulder, and then together, they stepped outside.

Gathered in loose formation by the door were three hundred soldiers, the ones most loyal to Victor's family. Victor knew he should feel pride at their supporting him, but those three hundred had also been paid. It seemed even the loyal must still be bought.

"Kill them all," he said to Sef. With a quick set of hand motions, Sef sent in several squads of the three hundred. They stormed through the door of the tavern, and shouts of warning quickly sounded from within, followed by the clash of metal and cries of pain.

"Inform the other mercenaries they are to be dismissed," Victor said to Sef. "Tell them they will be paid in time if they are patient, but the moment I hear what I consider dangerous talk, they will be executed on the spot."

"They're not going to be happy about their captains' deaths," Sef said. "They might seek vengeance."

"Then they can get in line."

As the sound of combat from inside began to die down, Victor turned away and walked down the street. Sef hurried to join him and he asked where he intended to go.

"Anywhere," Victor said. "Anywhere but here. I need some fresh air. I need to remind myself why I even bother with this damn city."

Sef hardly looked pleased, but he accepted the answer and walked alongside him. Victor's first thought had been to go to the market, to buy himself a small trinket or perhaps something fine to eat in an attempt to cheer himself up. The coming days would be ugly, for once the various mercenary groups elected new captains and finished with their interpersonal bickering, they'd be back again to demand money...and he doubted those who did would come alone like their former captains had.

As they walked, Victor noticed how quiet the street seemed, how few people milled about. He felt his instincts begin to cry danger, but the moment the group of five stepped out from one of the alleys ahead, he knew it was too late.

"Victor..." Sef said beside him, reaching for his ax, but Victor grabbed his wrist so he would not ready it.

"Stay calm," Victor said. He glanced over his shoulder, saw three more stepping out to block any retreat. One held a drawn dagger, the other two large crossbows. All of them bore the pointed star of the Sun Guild. Bringing his attention back to the front, he braced himself for a potential fight. He'd long known of the Sun Guild's advance, but since their return to Veldaren, he'd yet to strike at them and they at him. Hand settling on the hilt of his sword, he prayed it would remain that way.

Of the five approaching, the one in the center stood out above the rest. He wore a long leather coat that had been stained a dark black, his umber hair tied into braids and pulled back from his face. His long ears were scarred at the top, revealing his elven heritage. Most obvious of all, though, was the blackened hand when he lifted it in greeting, making his following introduction unnecessary.

"Greetings, Lord Victor Kane," said the elf with the scarred ears. "I am Muzien the Darkhand, master of the Sun Guild."

"Shit," muttered Sef.

"Your reputation precedes you," Victor said, louder. "I wondered if you would someday come calling."

Muzien smiled, and he seemed so pleasant, so calm, it made Victor all the more nervous. Only a man of absolute confidence could enter such a meeting in broad daylight and be so relaxed.

"Every man and woman of importance within this city shall have their time before me," Muzien said, and he continued his slow pace, arms clasped behind his back as if he were on a careless midday stroll. "Whether they spend it on their knees or facedown in a pool of their own blood will be up to them."

Again, Sef looked ready to grab his ax, but Victor glared his way, ensuring such a foolish action did not happen.

"Consider me flattered you think of me as a man of importance," Victor said, trying to keep his voice light. The last thing he wanted was to reveal fear before someone such as Muzien. It'd be like throwing bloody meat before a pack of hungry wolves.

"How could I not?" Muzien stopped just outside sword's reach, the remaining four with him lingering behind. The elf crossed his arms before him, and he narrowed his eyes as an amused smile spread across his lips. "After all, are you not the man who was to come into this city and cleanse it to its very core? Were you not here to deny us our shadows, to bring us into the light so we might wither and die? My, how people talk of you. All my ears hear are pomp and pride and an idiocy so stubborn, it must be religious zeal. So, here I am, and here you are, yet you do not act against me. My men live, and trust me when I say this, Victor, they still find plenty of shadows."

"Circumstances change," Victor said, trying not to let his bruised ego dictate his speech. "Surely you can understand that better than most."

"Indeed, I can."

Muzien gestured to his left, to where a stone tile bearing the symbol of the Sun Guild was freshly dug into the earth just before the entrance to a brothel.

"Circumstances *have* changed," the elf said. "And it is not to your advantage, you petty lord of a beggar kingdom. Sell all your lands and all your titles. Bring to me the sum of your wealth and lay it before my feet so I may spit on it as unworthy of the time it'd take to stoop down and take into my hands. I have no desire to deal with you. I don't want to see your men, I don't want to hear word of your inquisitors, your books, or your record keepers. All your systems and courts mean nothing to me. They will not save you, nor will they stop me, so if you wish to live, you will abandon whatever idealistic notions you have and return to your home."

"Things aren't so simple as that," Victor said, and this time it took more effort than he thought he could muster to keep his temper in check. Never before in his life had he been treated as so thoroughly inferior. "I have no intention of leaving, and if you kill me, the other lords of the land will realize how great a threat you are."

"The other lords will see you receiving the fate they all anticipated the moment you marched into this city with your banner held high," Muzien said. "Do not try to play politics with me, human. You're not skilled enough for the dance."

The elf snapped his fingers, and the rest turned to go.

"This city is mine," he said. "Like the sun, from the ground I rise. I control the thief guilds along with the common folk in their slums. The merchants and the lords will soon follow. When kings are in my pocket, you will find yourself alone, and when you do, pray it is far, far from here."

And with that, he marched away. Sef and Victor remained still, both trembling with rage. A glance behind them showed that the Sun Guild rogues with their crossbows and knives had also left.

"That fucking elven bastard," Sef said. "You'd think he has the king's crown jammed up his asshole with how he struts about, acting like he owns everything he sees."

Victor shook his head, thinking of the reports he'd read recently.

"He's not that far off," he said. "Come on, while we still have our dignity."

They continued their walk, Sef mumbling curses, Victor silent with his mind racing. If Muzien was confident enough to openly mock him, then his takeover of the underworld had to be nearly complete. Nearly, but not quite, because at least one guild still resisted him . . . at least, as far as Victor knew. He had to find out for sure. He had to know if his lone ally in the darkness was still willing to be his loyal monster.

"Change of direction," Victor said. "We've a graveyard to visit."

Sef started to ask, realized what it meant, and then shook his head.

"Day keeps getting worse," he muttered.

It took twenty minutes to cut through the weaving rows of homes gathered in the far south of the city, always heading east toward the wall. The farther east they went, the more spacious the homes grew, less crowded together. By the time they hit the wealthiest corner, many were surrounded by tall fences, with a few even sporting a bored mercenary or two keeping watch at the entrance. And then, in the midst of all the grand buildings and obvious wealth, like a mocking reminder to the fate of such owners, was a cemetery. Victor was certain that was the reason Deathmask had chosen to flee there in the first place.

"Wait here," Victor told Sef. The man was never pleased with the order, but every time they'd come, outside he remained, as per Deathmask's orders. Past the opened gate surrounding the cemetery, there were many crypts, each marked by the name of its wealthy family. Some still existed, such as the Gemcrofts, whereas others like the Blackbards and the Garlands were long dead and gone, falling to poverty or extinction. It was to the

Gemcroft one he went, and as he climbed down the cold stone steps, Victor couldn't help but chuckle at the irony. Just as he went to Lady Gemcroft's mansion for money for his mercenaries and prestige to validate his actions, now he went to her family's long-forgotten burial tomb for aid of a far darker sort.

The only light within came from the open entrance, and at its farthest edge, leaning with her back against one of the coffins placed in gaps carved into the stone walls, sat Veliana.

"Well, this is unexpected," said Veliana, amusement twinkling in her right eye. The other was a bloodied red; seeing it made Victor uneasy. If there was anything that made him squeamish, it was having things near his eyes or watching something done to other people's eyes.

"I find that hard to believe," Victor said. "Usually, your group knows of what happens in Veldaren sooner than I do."

"Perhaps," Veliana said. She hopped down from her perch, smoothed out her pants. "But I fear today I am alone in here. Did I miss something fun up top? New developments, clever schemes?"

She stepped closer, pulling her dark gray cloak tighter about her body and smirking up at him.

"Of course not," she said. "It is the Sun Guild, always the Sun, every street, every corner, every plot and lie."

"You sound displeased by this," Victor said.

"And why wouldn't we be?" asked someone from the entrance, his shadow falling over them as its caster blocked the sunlight. Victor turned, felt the corner of his mouth tug.

"I heard how you have always thrived in chaos," Victor told Deathmask as the guildmaster entered the crypt. "Then what greater chaos is this?"

"This isn't chaos," Deathmask said, shaking his head. "It's

a slow, steady conquest. Muzien is the opposite of chaos, Victor, and more like an unstoppable force. By the Abyss, if there's going to be any way we can stop him, it'll be through pure, unchecked chaos."

"A bit simple," Victor said, "but I'm not here to argue. Muzien surrounded me with his men today, and he's threatened my death if I do not leave. During his little bit of bravado, he claimed the underworld was his. I've come to see if that really is the case."

Deathmask walked right past Victor, stopped to kiss Veliana on the cheek, and then stepped into the darkness of the crypt. As he walked, torches hooked to the top of the hall at either side burst to life, burning purple flame that gave off no smoke. At Veliana's beckon, Victor followed. They passed by row after row of the dead, finely crafted stone mimicries of their human bodies sealing in their dusty bones. At last, they reached the end, and upon a great stone wall that marked the crypt's limits was a map of the city stretching from corner to corner, easily twice Victor's size. The detail was impressive, crisscrossing streets, labeled shops, brothels, taverns, even marks to show where prostitutes gathered together when not employed by the brothels. Most important, though, were the colored lines made out of string that portrayed the limits of the various thief guilds.

Lying on the floor were piles of thread, green and red and black and blue. On the map, there were only three colors: a dark gray, a white, and a yellow. The gray and white shared but a small stretch, whereas encircling nearly the entire city from wall to wall were line after line of yellow.

"It's down to just the two of us left to fight," Deathmask said, snapping his fingers so that another torch sprang to life directly above them, giving them more light to view the map. "Cynric's Wolf Guild is holding out best they can, but I'm fairly certain he's received his final ultimatum from the Sun Guild."

"Will Cynric cave in to Muzien's demands?" Victor asked.

Deathmask shook his head.

"Cynric's too much of a warrior. Plenty of his guild will turn on him, but that's to be expected. His core group of men will stay. They all remember the glory days at the start of the thief war, and I daresay Cynric was quite fond of it, too. The other guilds may have built their little empires trading women and wine, but killing has always been what Cynric excelled at best."

Victor crossed his arms, feeling overwhelmed by the sheer size of the map. So much yellow thread...

"Does he have a chance?" he asked.

Veliana laughed at his question.

"If he did," she asked, "don't you think we'd be out there with him? No, he has no chance. He's excellent at hunting down prey, and he'll hurt Muzien before he's done, but this is something beyond his skill and understanding."

"It might even be beyond ours," Deathmask said, shaking his head. "I thought crushing Grayson's advance would have stalled the Sun Guild, at least make them rethink things. Instead, it seems to have only made them more careful."

"We need to act soon," Victor said. "Find out where Muzien is, where he sleeps, where he eats. I know you can discover this, and when he's alone, we can surround him with my soldiers and bring him down. We crushed Grayson, we crushed Thren Felhorn, and we can handle Muzien. Even if we can't kill him, we just have to make it not worth the risk, neither the men we kill nor the coin we take."

Deathmask chuckled, quiet at first, then louder as it seemed a bit of insanity leaked into his mismatched red and brown eyes. Reaching out, he grabbed the thread signifying the Wolf Guild and yanked it to the ground, followed by the dark gray of his own.

"You don't get it, Victor," he said. "The Darkhand *trained* Grayson. He *trained* Thren. At the Council of Mages, we were well aware of those two bastards long before they ever stepped foot into Veldaren to make their mark on the city. They were Muzien's chosen heirs, just in case someone ever managed to sneak a lucky knife into the elf's back. They were to conquer Veldaren, to make it an extension of Muzien's empire in the west. And for a long while they looked to succeed, the Spider Guild a perfect mirror image of the Sun Guild...but then everything collapsed. Nothing Thren built seemed to endure. The guilds continued to war, the Trifect scored its victories, and then the Watcher reared his pretty little head."

"What are you saying?" Victor asked.

Deathmask turned, jammed a finger against Victor's breast-plate.

"What I'm *saying* is that Muzien's come to succeed where his heirs failed. Loss of coin means nothing. Death of his men means nothing. When I said he came here to conquer, I wasn't being snide or melodramatic, because that is exactly what is happening. This is a war, and we fight against one of the greatest minds to ever take up the blade. Muzien might have one day ruled over the Dezren elves as their king, but he was banished for being viewed as too extreme by even those pointy-eared pricks. Muzien sees Veldaren as a foreign city to be conquered in war. The loyalty he inspires in his guild, the careful distribution of power, the aura of fear that accompanies his name, it all puts the guilds here to shame. Only Thren has ever come close, and now he's dead or missing. The priests of Karak hold the king and queen of Mordan in their pockets, and even *they* have been forced to broker deals with Muzien lest they be destroyed. We have no hope here, Victor, not even the tiniest shred."

All the while Victor's hands clenched and unclenched. First

from Muzien's own lips, and now from Deathmask's, he must hear how amazing the Darkhand was, how unbeatable. The sheer worshipfulness of it was infuriating, and at last he could stand no more.

"He's not a god!" he shouted, drawing his sword and slashing through the map of Veldaren. "He can be killed, just like any other. I know you believe that, because why else haven't you surrendered?"

Deathmask grinned, unbothered by the drawing of Victor's sword.

"Do you know why I still fight?" he asked. "Because I cannot stand to lose. Muzien is a legend, but new legends are born in the deaths of the old. We have no hope here, but we had none to begin with. We have insanity. We have chaos. We will need to use the weapons available to us, the weapons that care not for rationality and tactics. We need men willing to kill and burn, coin to bribe and swindle. I need an army unafraid of both the king and the Darkhand. Can you get that for me, Victor?"

Victor swallowed, and he thought of the men he'd executed only hours earlier.

"I need time," he said. "But how do I know you're not using me for your own ends? What makes you a better choice than Muzien?"

"I sought only to use Veldaren as a playground for my amusement," Deathmask said. "Muzien would rule it like a god. Why do you think he let you live? Every subject, from the lowliest of peasants to the greatest of kings, will have their chance to kneel in service. Those who submit will receive their rewards. Those who disobey, he'll thoroughly destroy. If you need assurance, then have it. I will never kneel, not to a god, and certainly not to him."

Victor turned, gestured to the map.

"Then we still do have a chance. One, just one, but it is something. I can get you your army, Deathmask, one bought and paid for. It's already waiting for us, if only I can convince her."

"You speak of Alyssa Gemcroft," said Veliana.

"That's right," Victor said. "Her wealth, her mercenaries... combine your power with that of the Trifect and we can crush this damn elf once and for all. But I have to convince her how dangerous Muzien is, and that won't be easy. Until she trusts me, or her fear of the Darkhand breaks her pride, she'll refuse my advances. Can you buy me time?"

"You need not worry about us," Deathmask said, and he smiled. "We are ghosts when we need to be. It's you who I fear for. Keep your head down and your actions quiet. The moment Muzien thinks you still plot against him, he will crush you with his heel."

Victor shook his head, blood still boiling in his veins.

"If he does," he said, "then Muzien will discover that even in death, some small things can still sting."

CHAPTER 8

I don't see it," Nathaniel said, rubbing his forehead with his only hand as he stared at the scroll unrolled before him on the desk. He sat in John Gandrem's room, and the lord paced behind him, arms locked behind his back, a sign Nathaniel knew meant that John was getting closer and closer to losing his patience. Not that he'd yell or strike him, only give him that disappointed sigh and a condescending answer that always made him feel horrible.

"Think harder," John said. "Look at the map, and remember everything you've learned. Sir Eldon knew he couldn't outrun the enemy on his heels, so where would have been best to meet his foe in battle?"

Nathaniel leaned closer, scanning the colored lines drawn all across the scroll. Before him was a representation of a stretch of land he'd never see, and sketched in along the northern half with triangles, squares, and circles were various units of Sir

Eldon Gemcroft. Giving chase on the southern half were even more triangles and circles of the combined forces of Derrik Blackbard. The battle had taken place hundreds of years ago, and for the life of him, Nathaniel could not figure out why he needed to know *anything* about it.

"Here?" Nathaniel asked, pointing to the only river on the map. It was the best guess he had.

"Why?" John asked, still pacing. Nathaniel let out a sigh. Of course, John had to ask why. No answer was ever good enough. A lucky guess never counted, even if it were correct, if Nathaniel couldn't provide reason for the guess.

"The river would slow down their charge," Nathaniel said. He pointed to the many triangles in Sir Eldon's forces. "Since his army was mostly archers, Sir Eldon could use that advantage to win."

"Good thinking," John said. "But you're wrong."

He tapped a finger on a set of hills nearby.

"That river's barely a foot deep, more of a stream, and Derrik's horses would have thundered right across. No, he went and camped his army on top of this hill here, for reasons similar to what you listed earlier."

Nathaniel frowned.

"But they could just surround him on the hill instead of charging up it. Why not wait them out?"

John beamed at the question.

"Now you're beginning to think like a lord," he said. "And that's exactly what Derrik did, and exactly what Sir Eldon was hoping Derrik would do. You see, just before reaching the hill, he split off what few knights he had and..."

The door to the room opened, and with a rattle of hinges, in stepped Melody Gemcroft.

"Am I interrupting?" she asked. She wore a long crimson dress, and despite the Gemcroft family crest sewn into its sleeves with golden thread, it only seemed to make Melody all the more a stranger in Nathaniel's mind, highlighting just how unknown she was to him.

"Not at all," John said, and Nathaniel wished he had the courage to disagree. As frustrating as his studies with John could be, he still preferred them to the lectures Melody gave him when alone. Lectures about law, order, and the gods in particular. The way Melody talked about the gods unnerved him, made him wish he could pretend neither existed. That and the dreams...

"I fail to see why Nathaniel must learn such uncivilized matters," Melody said, crossing the room on bare feet and standing beside the table. Nathaniel felt squished between the two, an adult on either side of his chair. "Will Nathaniel one day lead men to war on the battlefield?"

"A strategic mind excels in all battlefields," John said, "not just those in brute warfare. And though he may not believe it himself, Nathaniel here has a good mind for it, should he ever focus on the little details and stop wildly guessing when he doesn't immediately know the answer."

Nathaniel felt his ears turning red. He hated when adults talked about him when he was in the room. It always embarrassed him, no matter if they were praising his virtues, condemning his failures, or pitying him for his missing arm. The pity was the worst, though, always the worst.

"I should go back to my room," Nathaniel said, and he pushed back his chair in hopes one of the two would move out of the way so he might leave. "I haven't practiced my numbers for today."

"Very well, we can resume this tomorrow," said John. Nathaniel hopped down, and he hid his smile at the sudden freedom.

"Mind if an old lady walks with you?" Melody asked, and that freedom died.

"Of course," Nathaniel said, knowing it'd be akin to suicide to deny the request, particularly in front of John. Doing so would have earned him a reaction little different from if he spit at Melody's feet.

His grandmother offered him a hand, and he took it. Despite the veins along her hands, her fingers were still surprisingly soft and warm. Just thinking that made Nathaniel feel awkward, and he wished he were anywhere but with her. Still, he had no choice, and he walked with his head slumped and eyes cast to the floor. From his experience, acting like the carpet was the most fascinating thing ever was the best way to slide through conversations with his grandmother.

"You would do well to listen to John," Melody said as they walked down the hall, passing by soldier after soldier keeping guard. "Even if it seems rather…unnecessary. The future is always chaotic, and the skills you end up needing may surprise you."

"You think I will ever lead soldiers in a fight?" Nathaniel asked. It sounded stupid to his ears. Surely Melody didn't think differently?

"Wars have caused stranger things," Melody said. "And a war is coming; have no doubt on that. You've seen the visions. You know what approaches."

Even harder now did he stare at the floor. Of course, she mentioned his visions. Why did she always have to mention the visions? Could she not see they terrified him? Could she not just let him be instead of dragging him into stupid conversations and asking stupid questions?

"I guess so," he mumbled.

They were almost to his room now. Desperate, he silently begged that she would leave him be when he got there, but he knew she wouldn't. She'd come to him for a reason, and just what, he'd soon discover.

"We'll need to make preparations soon," Melody said, making it sound no different from if they were preparing for a picnic. "Perhaps bring in some more mercenaries from the south. John's men will help, but they won't be enough. I fear nothing will be enough. If only we knew more of his arrival..."

They were at his room now, and he tried to let go of Melody's hand so he could open the door, but she refused. Instead, she opened it for him, then stepped inside after.

Waiting for him on his bed were the bowl, silver chains, and various gems of the chrysarium. The very sight of it made Nathaniel's stomach clench.

"Grandmother?" he asked.

"We need to know," she said, walking over to the curtains and pulling them shut to darken the room. "Too many questions, too many threats to Luther's plan. We *have* to know anything and everything that we can." She turned to him. "You've been blessed with the sight by our beloved Karak, and such a blessing cannot go unused. It is a sin to take the gifts we've been given and bury them deep in the earth to remain hidden forever."

"I don't want to," he said, first quietly, then louder. "I don't want to!"

"You must!"

She reached for his shoulder, and he yanked away.

"I'll tell Mother!" he shouted at her, and this finally seemed to make her pause. His grandmother's eyes narrowed, and suddenly he felt very young and very alone.

"You won't," she said.

"Why not? I don't want to *do* this anymore."

"Because deep down, you know I'm right." She took a single step toward him, her body shrouded in shadows due to the heavy curtains. "Because you've seen his face, haven't you? Never the same, except for the eyes, those burning eyes. Even thinking about him makes you scared, doesn't it? Well, he makes me scared, too. He's old, as old as mankind itself, and we must prepare for his arrival. We must be *ready*. This city must be made righteous. It must be made faithful."

She pointed to the chrysarium.

"Karak's voice waits for you in the darkness. Do not deny the power of our god. The coming days are the prelude to the fated hour. This is your chance, Nathaniel. Your chance to be something special. Your chance to change the fate of the entire world."

Every word she said put a weight on his shoulders, and he felt it settling, felt it pushing down at his resistance. Was he really so important? These visions, if Karak had chosen them for him... did it mean he was special? As special as his grandmother claimed?

"I don't understand them," he said.

"Just try," she said. "And even if you do not, I and those I serve still may."

Slowly, Nathaniel approached the chrysarium as if it were a snake that might bite him. It'd been several weeks since he last succumbed to one of the visions, at least while awake. His dreams, on the other hand, he never remembered come morning, but every time he awoke, his heart was racing, his hands shaking, his body covered with sweat. The very idea of seeing whatever it was, of whatever his mind somehow blanked out, terrified him to his very core.

His fingers touched the bowl, and he was surprised by its warmth. Swallowing down a dry lump in his throat, he leaned closer, staring into the very center of the slender bowl. Beside him, Melody began to pray, her words spidery things that made no sense to his ears. The gems rattled, glowing from their centers as if an infinitesimal fire had begun to burn within them. Melody's words quickened, the darkness in the center of the chrysarium deepened, and then the gems lifted one by one into the air, stretching the length of their thin silver chains. Nathaniel felt himself being pulled into it, felt his mind giving in to whatever power resided within the gems and the words his grandmother spoke.

The shift was harsh, a jerk that made his very mind ache. He saw not the bowl, nor the darkness, but instead a great chasm. It seemed to go on for miles on either side of him, and the fall down was so great that the few trees growing at the far bottom looked no bigger than tiny green dots. Water flowed down there as well, a meager river that seemed almost mocked by the grand size of the chasm.

Even in death, the faithless may be made to serve, said a voice, and it rumbled across the very sky like thunder. Nathaniel found himself unable to look away despite the great distance of the chasm and the fear it put into his gut that he might fall. Down there, he saw movement, just the faintest hint of it, like observing ants, only even smaller. What it might be, he didn't know, but the movement continued, becoming vague shapes crawling up both sides of the chasm. Time passed, and while he was aware of its passing, it still seemed like the minutes were but seconds vanishing with each breath he took. The vague shapes gained clarity, and he saw they numbered in the thousands.

They were rotten, broken, bone and flesh, and they were dead.

Higher and higher they climbed, and Nathaniel realized they would soon reach his side of the chasm, their skeletal fingers reaching up toward the top, and he let out a scream of terror. Compared to the voice that had spoken before, he felt miniscule and worthless, but it seemed the very sky recoiled at the noise he made. Clouds swirled, the sky turned red, and suddenly he stared into the face of a man on the other side of the chasm, only the man's face never remained the same, the nose shrinking, the lips widening, forehead deepening, only to reverse as his cry continued to echo throughout the dreamscape.

Even in death... said the man, and Nathaniel wanted to hear no more. He begged for safety, for escape, for anyone to stop the being on the other side of the chasm, and then he felt himself flying. The world passed beneath him as if he were a bird, and for a brief moment, he thought he caught sight of the glow of the chrysarium's crystals at the edges of his sight. Then his movement stopped, and below him was a great building, shaped as a black spire rising out of the cracked earth. He fell through its ceilings until he was in a small, cramped room full of books, desks, and a lone bed.

All sound ceased but for the turning of a page. Then another. There was a man at a desk, and he wore black robes. His head was bowed, his long hair gray. Hovering above him, Nathaniel stared down, confused as to who he saw and why.

"We save this world by healing it," said the man, and he sounded tired, very tired. "Not with fire, not with destruction."

Nathaniel felt an impulse, and he obeyed, reaching down to touch the shoulder of the man. Just before he could, the chair turned, and in the chair was a dying man, his throat cut. Despite it, still he talked, even letting out a laugh.

"Fire and destruction," he said, his eyes clouded gray, his voice losing strength. "Forgive me, Jerico, but I saw no other way."

Nathaniel could take no more. He slammed his eyes shut, and he begged to be home, to be in the arms of his mother. A roaring filled his ears, his entire body shook, and suddenly he was back in his room, his grandmother lurking over him.

"You were not out long," she said, taking the chrysarium from him. Nathaniel looked at her, then away. He didn't want to talk, didn't want to be with her. His heart pounded in his chest, and he felt the vision chasing after him, the man with the ever-changing face lurking just behind his neck.

"What did you see?" she asked, the question he knew she

would ask. He thought to tell her of the man at the chasm, but the very idea of it made his throat constrict. Instead, he thought of the second man, the dying one, and he hoped that by his speaking of him instead, she might leave him alone.

"I...I saw a man in a tower," he said. "An older man with gray hair."

Nathaniel hadn't expected her to know him, nor react, but instead, she froze as if he'd flung a rope around her neck and pulled it tight.

"An older man?" she asked. "His robes, were they black, like a priest's?"

He nodded, and he watched her swallow.

"Did he say anything to you?"

Nathaniel felt a shiver crawl up his spine as he thought of the man's cut throat, and of the way his eyes had turned a cloudy gray.

"He was dying," Nathaniel said. "His throat was cut. He said he only knew fire and destruction. That's when I woke up."

He'd thought the second vision would be easier, less frightening, but the way Melody grabbed his shoulders terrified him. She fell to her knees, staring at him as tears filled her eyes.

"No," she said. "He can't be dying. He *can't*. I need him, I need...We need..."

She started crying, and she pulled him against her, holding him with his face pressed against her neck. Her entire thin body seemed overwhelmed by her sobs. Nathaniel waited it out, awkward and confused.

"I'm sorry," she told him when she regained control. "It's only that...sometimes when you love someone, love them so much, you'll forfeit everything to be with them. And if this world were just, that sacrifice would mean something, but it never does. This world is cruel and horrible, and it's only going to get worse without Karak here to guide us."

She leaned back, eyes red, her hair sticking to her face, which was wet from her tears.

"I'm sorry," Nathaniel said. He wasn't sure for what, but it felt like the appropriate thing to say at the time.

"Shh," she said, touching his face with her shaking fingers. "It's not your fault; you see only what you were meant to see. But if Luther falls, we'll need you all the more. So much will rest on your tiny little shoulders..."

When she stood, he went to the windows and pulled back the curtains, letting in the light. Immediately, he felt better, the images fading in Nathaniel's mind, becoming like dreams, hazy and distant.

"Not yet," Melody said, and she walked back to the curtains, shutting them, spoiling his relief. "I must use it myself."

"May I go?" he asked, and he could not describe the relief when she said yes. He bowed his head in respect, then rushed to the door. As he stepped out into the hallway, he turned to shut the door, and as he did, he saw Melody on her knees before his bed, the chrysarium settled atop the blankets.

"Luther?" he heard his grandmother ask. "Luther, are you there? Please, my love, answer me..."

He shut the door and hurried away.

CHAPTER 9

Let me tell you, Brug," said Tarlak as he slumped back in his chair, "this whole city's gone insane."

The squat man stood behind him in his room, a small apple in each hand. He alternated bites, each one spilling juice down his beard.

"Give me some credit," Brug said, mouth half full. "I've been telling *you* that for years."

"Well, you weren't right before, but you're sure as the Abyss right now."

He pushed back his chair and stood, then gestured to the scattered pieces of paper on his stained oak desk. Every single one was a letter written to him from those who had, until recently, been on his payroll to leak him information about the various thief guilds of Veldaren.

"Six resignations," he said. "From carefully worded apologies to ones merely telling me to do fairly difficult things to myself using *other* parts of myself. Not a damn one of them is willing to cross the Sun Guild. Either they're scared witless, or they're making more money than I'm offering."

"These guys were greedy, cowardly turncoats," Brug said, "and now you're surprised they're acting out of either greed or cowardice? You might want to rethink who's the insane one."

Brug took another large bite of the apple, then tossed the core to the stone floor. Tarlak frowned at it, then waved his hand, vanishing the apple with a puff of smoke.

"Lazy bastard," Tarlak muttered.

The other man shrugged.

"Fine, I'll toss the next one out the window, Your Highness, just like you could have done if you walked five feet and picked it up yourself."

"What, now *I'm* the lazy one?"

Brug shrugged.

"If the pointy yellow hat fits..."

Tarlak froze, then let out a groan.

"Come on," he said. "Let's head out to the city. Bad enough without Haern patrolling and keeping us informed, but now everything's changing at a whirlwind's pace. Let's see just how much the Sun Guild's really taken over."

The two headed down the stairs, then exited the stone tower into the early-morning light. They left the King's Forest behind, following a path across the grass toward the main trade route leading to the west gate entrance of Veldaren. As they walked, Brug kept glancing over his shoulder, and come the third time, Tarlak couldn't keep his curiosity at bay.

"What's the matter with you?" he asked.

"We're being followed," Brug said, trying to keep his voice low.

"Followed? By who, and how? We're in the middle of a damn road."

To accentuate the point, he spun in a full circle, hands out, to show there wasn't anyone either ahead or behind them on the road for at least half a mile. Brug's neck turned red, but he refused to back down.

"I'm telling you, I keep seeing something out of the corner of my eye, but whenever I look back, they drop to the grass where I can't see. You think, given all we've done, we might not have a few enemies?"

"Plenty of enemies, sure, but competent enemies? That I'm more skeptical of."

Tarlak gave another scan, not caring if their pursuer actually saw that they were aware of his or her presence. The grass on either side of the road was tall, up to Tarlak's waist, so someone could easily be following them. Bigger question was why... and whether or not their intentions were lethal. Given their various fights with the Bloodcrafts only weeks prior, Tarlak did not feel all that hopeful.

"Stand still," Tarlak said, putting a hand on Brug's shoulder. He closed his eyes and spoke a few words of simple magic. Before his friend could ask what was going on, a heavy wind blew in from the east, strong enough they had to raise their voices to hear each other.

"What's the point of this?" Brug asked.

"Just a precaution," said Tarlak. "Let's see him fire an arrow or crossbow through this. Now come on; the wind won't last but a few minutes."

They continued on toward the city entrance, directly into the unrelenting windstorm. Tarlak glanced over his shoulder occasionally, but the whipping of the wind made it all but impossible to catch a sign of movement.

At the gate, Brug flashed one of the soldiers a pendant hanging around his neck, that of a triangle with the left corner unconnected and the bottom line used to mark the center of a capitalized E. They passed through without further question.

"Where to now?" Brug asked.

"We wanted to know how much Muzien controls," Tarlak said. "So, let's go to the one place he'd be insane to take over. Copper Road should belong to the Ash Guild. If we find the mark of the Sun there, then we know things have definitely gotten out of hand."

As they walked, Tarlak kept his eyes open for the telltale four-pointed star signifying the Sun Guild's presence…and it didn't take much effort to spot it. It seemed at every corner he found one of their tiles dug into the center of the street or placed at the entrance of a small shop or bakery. After a bit, he began to count, and once he reached thirty he gave up.

"If Thren were still around, I think he'd be jealous," Brug muttered as they passed by yet another tile, this one buried in front of what had once been a tannery.

"If Thren were still around, I doubt there'd be so many."

"I wouldn't be so sure, not anymore."

Honestly, Tarlak felt it hard to argue. With Haern's help, he'd slowly learned how to identify those of the underworld, from the lower-positioned members with their simple colored bands around their arms, many of them also farmers, workers, smiths, and bakers, to the higher-ups with their patches, their earrings, and eventually the highest ranked with their colored cloaks. As Brug and Tarlak passed through the major intersection at the center of town, he took a quick count of all he saw. Over two dozen yellow armbands, fifteen with the marked earrings, and another seven with the four-pointed star sewn onto their chest.

Of the other guilds, he saw not a cloak, not an armband. Nothing. Tarlak continued to turn, then stopped, frowned down at Brug.

"Well," he said, "shit."

"Truly, you are a wizard with a silver tongue."

"Try not to feel too jealous."

They continued east, leaving more of the hustle and crowd behind the farther they went. Tarlak took his hat off ten minutes later, glanced inside it, and then put it back on his head.

"We're still being followed," he said.

"How do you know?"

"My hat said so."

Brug's bewildered look gave Tarlak pause.

"Your...hat?"

"There's a mirror inside it. Did you think my hat actually..." He let out a sigh. "Ashhur save me from the company of my friends."

They were approaching the wealthiest parts of Veldaren, and Tarlak knew the Connington mansion wouldn't be far off. He glanced around to either side, looking for a suitable place.

"There," he said, nodding at a two-story house, its outside painted a faint gray, the roof sharply slanted with wooden tiles painted black.

"Anything special about that one?" Brug asked.

"No fence, no guards. Come on."

Tarlak left the road, following the short walkway across the poorly tended lawn to the home's front door. A quick check and he found it locked, but that he could deal with. Putting his hands together, he whispered one of his simpler arcane spells. The tumblers inside the door clicked and shifted, and moments later, he pushed the door open and stepped inside. Brug followed, then Tarlak flung it shut and redid the bolt.

"What all did you see in your hat?" Brug asked as the two remained in the cramped entranceway.

"A handsome red-bearded devil."

"I meant our shadow."

"Standard fare," Tarlak said. "Lots of gray, lots of cloak. Imagine being stalked by Haern, only bigger."

"Fun thought."

They turned about, and Tarlak winced at the sight. The outside of the home looked like any other, but it hid an inside that was thoroughly vacant. The floors were bare, the walls stripped of paintings and mirrors, leaving bright squares to mark where they'd been. As they walked farther inside, they found more bare rooms, plus rows of cabinets that had been ransacked some time before.

"Cheery place," Brug said.

"Owners must have fled Veldaren not long ago," Tarlak said. "Let's hope they won't mind our using it for a moment."

Brug was without his armor, but he had his punch daggers with him at all times, and he readied them as he stood at the bottom of the stairs, looking up. Tarlak kept his attention bouncing between the front door, which he'd locked, and the many windows along the sides of the house.

"Do you think whoever it is will make a move here and now, when we're ready?" Brug asked.

"Not sure," Tarlak said. "They'd have to be absurdly—"

The window past Brug on the far side of the house shattered, and Tarlak spun that way, a bolt of lightning already flying off the palm of his hand toward the noise. His friend dropped to his knees and ducked his head, smart enough to know such a reaction was appropriate whenever Tarlak cast his magic. The bolt blasted past Brug, through the doorway, and into the other room, the sound of it deafening in the enclosed space. The intruder was already rolling on the ground, the blast passing just above him.

Out from the roll he came, swords drawn. Tarlak saw his attire, his weapons, thought nothing of it. What did sear into him, awakening horrible memories, was the man's face, an oval of white paint thickly smeared across dark skin. Before Tarlak could react, Ghost lifted a sword and pointed it at him, an eyebrow raised in surprise.

"Didn't I kill you?" he asked.

"Didn't Haern kill you?"

Ghost shrugged.

"Fair enough."

Fire flung from Tarlak's hands, three balls that exploded the moment they crossed through the doorway. Brug dove to one side, letting out an angry cry that Tarlak couldn't quite decipher. Ghost avoided them as well, vanishing out of sight behind the doorway.

"Get over here, Brug," Tarlak said, slowly backing away toward the front door.

"I'm not scared of that bastard," Brug said, stumbling to his feet and then clanging his daggers together. "That's him, isn't it, the one who killed Senke?"

Tarlak let out a deep breath at the mention of the name.

"It is," he said. "Now get over here before he kills someone else."

Brug took a step toward him, a second, and then Ghost lunged through the doorway, swords lashing out. The first hit only air, misjudging the distance, and for the second one, Brug crossed his daggers and blocked it just in time. His positioning was bad, and Ghost kicked him once in the stomach, then the face. The impact of it sent him sprawling backward, his body rolling to a stop at Tarlak's feet. Before Ghost could finish him off, Tarlak extended his hands, screaming out the words of a spell. A wall of solid force shimmered into view for but a second, then flung outward, slamming into Ghost and sending him rolling away.

"You couldn't just stay dead?" Tarlak shouted as he dropped to one knee, checking to make sure Brug was all right. The man's nose was bleeding, but he didn't seem too badly hurt.

"How do you know I'm not?" Ghost asked, still positioned out of sight behind the doorway in the other room.

"I don't think you'd be too scared of me if you were."

He sent another bolt of lightning through just because he could, then pulled on Brug's arm.

"Get off your ass," he said as the man staggered back to his feet.

"I'm going to kill him," Brug said, wiping his face and smearing blood across his sleeve. "I swear, Tar, I'm going to kill him."

"More than welcome to," Tarlak muttered, staring at the door and waiting. Ghost was patient, maddeningly so. If he'd only show himself so Tarlak could properly burn him to ashes like he deserved...

Still nothing. Tarlak dared a glance at Brug, who was inching forward, daggers raised.

"Ghost?" Brug asked after another moment.

The door behind them shattered and Tarlak spun, hands whirling through the air on instinct. Ghost came crashing through at a full sprint, the mansion's front door but a nuisance for him to slam aside. In a panic, Tarlak extended his left hand, and from its center appeared a single long, slender shard of ice, wickedly sharp at its point. It flew through the air, straight at the charging Ghost.

The man crossed his arms and dove, slamming into the wall of the hallway while turning his body to the side. The shard flew harmlessly past, and then Ghost continued on, his pace hardly even slowed. As the giant man leaped through the air, Tarlak knew he was a dead wizard, but he kept casting anyway, twisting his fingers into the necessary shapes, human mimicries of the arcane runes necessary to put form to the powerful magic that dwelled within him.

As Ghost's swords came slicing in, Brug leaped into the way, letting out a battle-mad howl. His daggers smacked aside both thrusts, and then he ducked his head and went charging in, both arms punching. Within the cramped space, Ghost could only leap backward in an attempt to gain space as well as recover his positioning. The first two of Brug's punches missed, the third and fourth he parried aside, opening up room for an attack.

But despite all his screaming and wild attack, Brug had no desire to continue the assault, and the moment Ghost parried, Brug turned and dove to the ground toward Tarlak, and the wizard felt the briefest moment of appreciation for the man's ability to improvise in a hectic situation.

In that exact moment, Tarlak activated his spell. A red line spread across the floor of the hallway, and then it erupted, a burst of fire that crawled up the hallway and rolled across the ceiling, forming an impenetrable wall of flame between Brug and Ghost. Tarlak had hoped the man would be caught trying to pass through, but Ghost did not. Instead, when the fire dissipated seconds later, leaving the walls charred black and smoke billowing across the ceiling, Ghost was nowhere to be found.

"Damn it, too many exits and entrances," Tarlak said.

"Up the stairs, then," Brug said, scrambling back to his feet. "If we're going to fight, let's make it harder for him to come to us."

Sounded like as good a plan as any to Tarlak. He followed Brug up the circular staircase, climbing into a second story that appeared even more dilapidated than the lower. There were only two rooms, each barren with large glass windows. Tarlak smelled the distinct smells of alcohol and urine, and he wondered if others had been making use of the building since its owner's departure. Tarlak remained at the top of the stairs, while Brug turned back and forth, keeping an eye on the windows of both rooms.

"What'd we ever do to that bastard to make him come back for us?" Brug asked, still keeping his head swiveling.

"He beat us bloody, tied us up, killed Senke, and nearly killed me as well," said Tarlak. "If anyone should be hunting, it's us..."

"You're right, of course," said Ghost, leaning around the edge to appear at the foot of the staircase. Tarlak flung a small ball of fire his way, but the man easily sidestepped out of sight, the fire harmlessly splashing across the dirty floor and vanishing without catching.

"About what?" Tarlak asked, another ball of fire hovering above his palm. "Us needing to hunt you?"

"Indeed, but you misunderstand my being here."

"Are you here to kill us?"

"I am."

Tarlak laughed.

"Then I think we understand you just fine."

Ghost dashed in front of the staircase entrance, going from the left side to the right. Tarlak felt baited, and he kept his spell at ready. When Ghost vanished from sight, he shouted back up the staircase.

"I do not come for you out of malice," Ghost insisted. "And I bear you no grudge for what you've done."

"Bear *us* a grudge?" Brug asked, standing beside Tarlak looking bewildered. "*You* killed Senke, you stinking son of a bitch. Haern said you were dead, and that's exactly what you should be."

"Keep your eyes open," Tarlak whispered, grabbing his friend by the arm. "He won't charge the stairs, so he'll have to come through a window."

Brug's face was red with fury, but he nodded and continued to scan both the rooms. Tarlak cracked his neck, then continued focusing on keeping the fire burning on his hands. Just in case Ghost tried to make a desperate climb...or finally came crashing through one of the many upper-floor windows.

"Your friend never killed me," Ghost shouted after a moment. His voice sounded distant, and Tarlak guessed him slowly shifting toward one of the windows to the outside. "I wish he had. Then I'd have been spared the past four years. I'd have been spared their touch, their needles..."

The voice trailed off to nothing. Climbing on the outside, surely, but where? Which side? Still above the staircase, Tarlak glanced left, right, turned his attention back to the stairs. Behind him, he heard Brug shifting on his feet, trying to remain loose. The waiting was driving Tarlak mad, and he hated how Ghost was controlling the entirety of the fight. If only he could find him out in the open!

To his left, he heard the shattering of glass. He spun that way, and Brug rushed toward it without the slightest hesitance. The window was beyond where Tarlak could see from his position, and as the glass fell upon the upper floor, he felt a warning in his gut he dared not ignore. Despite the danger, despite how horrible a position Brug would be in if left to fight Ghost on his own, Tarlak turned and slammed his hands together. Seeing nothing, hearing nothing, he still cast his spell, pointing his hands down the stairs and unleashing a massive barrage of fire, as if his palms were the mouth of a furious dragon.

Just as the fire began to roll, Ghost appeared from around the left corner, legs pumping, swords drawn, his large body traveling at a bewildering speed so great that he was halfway up the stairs before he could even register the fire bathing him. Tarlak heard him scream, and it sent chills racing up his spine. Ghost dropped to his stomach, hands crossing to protect his face. The moment he hit the stairs, he rolled, and Tarlak doubted if he cared about the blows he took as he rolled down. Anything would be better than the fire.

"You killed my best friend," Tarlak said, looping his hands

around once, ice shards growing in the air before him. "Whatever torture you suffered, you deserved a hundred times worse."

He flung the shards, aiming to spear Ghost through the chest. The man was tougher than Tarlak guessed, though, and even as he lay at the bottom of the stairs, his arms and face horribly burned, he was still not beaten. Even as Ghost screamed, he rolled along the floor and out of the way. Out of sight, Tarlak swore and rushed down the steps, wishing he were half as fast as the giant man. At the bottom of the steps, he saw what he knew he'd find: no one.

"You get him?" Brug asked, rushing down the stairs after him.

"He's badly burned, but he might live," Tarlak said, looking left to right as he briefly thought of chasing. But he couldn't even guess whether the man had fled out the window or the front door. Haern was the tracker in their group, not him.

Furious, he punched a wall, then again, tempted to tear the whole building down with his magic in an attempt to accommodate the overwhelming anger he felt.

"I don't get it," Brug said, sheathing his daggers and then gingerly touching his bruised nose with his fingers. "He was dead, wasn't he? Where was he all this time if not?"

"I don't know," Tarlak said. "And honestly, I don't care. All I care about is that the next time I see him, he dies, and this time, I'll burn his damn body to make sure if he does come back it'll have to be as an actual ghost."

"Be careful what you wish for," Brug said.

Tarlak chuckled.

"Come on," he said. "Let's get back to the tower and out of this awful city."

CHAPTER
10

There was nothing special about the town of Trass, at least to Haern's eyes. They were traveling south, following the Rigon River's western bank, and had passed through many such towns. All around were well-tilled fields, and many towns had shops set up to sell plows and repair nets, and barter away the day's latest catch or harvest. But apparently, Trass had what they wanted, for when Thren led them down the street toward the ramshackle inn, he beamed.

"Truth be told, I didn't think it would take this long," Thren said to them as he headed toward the inn's door.

"I'd be inclined to believe you if I knew what we were looking for in the first place," said Haern. He felt uncomfortable as he always did when walking the open street in daylight. His attire, with his long cloak and his low hood obscuring his face, would earn him strange looks in Veldaren. Out in a land of farmers and fishers? He and Thren were oddities, and ones people knew to rightly fear. Men and women veered away from them when they passed. If not for Delysia accompanying them, dressed in her priestess robes and with the symbol of the Golden Mountain clearly showing on her chest, they might have openly demanded their departure.

"Information," Thren said as he opened the door to the inn and stepped inside.

The inn was small, and down the corridor past the innkeeper, Haern saw what he guessed were only two rooms. An older man with sores on his face sat on a wooden chair beside the corridor, arms crossed over his chest as he slept. Thren walked up to him and kicked the chair.

"Wake up," he said.

The innkeeper startled, and seeing Thren, he glared.

"Five copper a head," he said. "Though I should make it six for waking an old man so rudely."

Thren chuckled.

"The sun marks the sky," he said. "And I wish to talk to someone unafraid of its light."

The innkeeper narrowed his eyes.

"So, you're one of them?" he asked. Thren nodded. "All right, then. Go to the commons and ask for Maneth. If you're looking to talk, he's the one best at it."

Thren dipped his head in thanks, then turned and strode past Haern and Delysia and out the door.

"I take it we're meeting an informant?" Haern asked, hurrying after.

"Something like that," Thren said, looking left and right in search of the commons. "The Sun Guild's been steadily moving east over the years, and even the smaller towns have someone to collect modest dues in return for guarantees no one else will try to muscle in on their trade. Such protection is easily worth it, for it also deters any bandits from trying to rob the place. No one of intelligence willingly makes an enemy of the Sun."

"Except us," Delysia said.

Thren cast her a smile.

"Yes, except us," he said. "Now let's go find this Maneth."

It took only a few minutes of wandering for them to stumble upon the commons, a large expanse with only a single ancient oak growing in its center. In its shade were several groups of people talking, women holding babes as their children played, along with many tanned men drinking, most of them naked from the waist up. As Haern approached, he felt all eyes turning their way.

"Well met this fine day," Thren said to a group of three men drinking. "I'm looking for a man named Maneth. Might one of you be him?"

"I'm Maneth," said a man leaning against the oak. He was also bare chested, his shirt wrapped around his waist. Unlike the others, his tan was lighter, his arms less toned. "Care to tell me why three strangers odd as yourselves have come traipsing through our town?"

"I have four reasons," Thren said. "Each one a point, and each one made of gold."

Maneth grunted.

"Get out of here," he told the others.

"But we were..."

"Out!"

The men muttered but wandered away, and the women quickly beckoned their children to their sides before they could carry them off. Haern watched them leave, and there was no denying the fear in their eyes. It wasn't much, just a hint. Maneth didn't command power himself, but they feared what he represented.

"Well, then," Maneth said once they were alone. "Care to tell me your names and why you've come all this way to seek out the Sun Guild? Any idiot can tell you three aren't from around here."

Thren grinned.

"My name is the only one that matters. I am Thren Felhorn, of Veldaren."

Maneth didn't even try to hide his surprise.

"Thren?" he asked. "You're not lying to me, are ya?"

"Not many men are brave enough to pretend to be me."

Maneth let out a dismissive snort.

"If you say so. Still, you match the stories I've heard, most of them, anyway. Must say, you traveling with a priestess of Ashhur doesn't quite fit. Care to tell me why you're with this barbarian, sweetheart?"

He likely thought Delysia would blush or appear flustered by the sudden question, but she only flashed him a smile.

"Someone must keep the barbarian in line."

Maneth laughed, loud and boisterous.

"Indeed, indeed. Well, Thren, let me formally introduce myself. I'm Maneth Trout. I grew up here, believe it or not, then trundled all the way north to Mordeina thinking to make myself a fortune. Joined the Sun Guild only to find myself sent back home to keep an eye on things. If you're looking for information in these parts, I'm sure I know a little something about everything the heir of Muzien might need to know."

Heir of Muzien?

Haern looked to his father, curious as to what that meant, and it seemed Thren wasn't too keen on the title, either. Haern caught his brief flash of disgust before he smoothly smiled it away.

"Let's find out," Thren said. "What do you know of the Stronghold?"

It was the second time for Maneth to laugh in surprise.

"The Stronghold? I know you don't mess with it, Thren. That's the dark paladins' home. Unless you want to walk in bowing your head and carrying a bagful of gold in offering, I'd stay far away."

"We have no plans to do either," Haern said. "There's a man inside we need to kill."

Maneth glared at him.

"Thren, tell your lackey to stay out of our business," he said.

Haern's hands were moving for his swords when Thren reached out and grabbed his shoulder.

"Now's not the time for a temper," he said.

Haern let go of the hilts, did his best to ignore Maneth's ugly grin. As he stood there seething, he felt Delysia's hands slip into his, and she leaned up to his ear so she could whisper.

"That's right; behave, lackey, or no dessert for you."

He heard her choke down a laugh, and Haern found himself unable to remain angry, not with her so close.

"Listen," Maneth said, turning his attention back to Thren. "We don't mess with servants of Karak, and they don't mess with us. It's a nice agreement we've reached in Mordeina, and thankfully, it's made its way down here to little old Trass. If you're thinking of infiltrating their home, you've come to the wrong guy."

"You know I'm not buying that," Thren said. "Muzien has a plan for anything and everything, and taking out the dark paladins in their home will certainly be one he's prepared for."

Maneth shrugged.

"If he has, he sure as shit hasn't told me. You're on your own with this."

Haern could see his father's displeasure, but at the same time, neither did he look surprised. Apparently, contacting a member of the Sun Guild had been at best a reach.

"Thank you for your help, however little it was," Thren said. He turned to Haern and Delysia. "Let's go."

"Hey," Maneth said, taking a step after them. "Just because I don't know how you'd get into that damn place doesn't mean I'm empty of ideas."

Thren looked back over his shoulder.

"I'm listening," he said.

"About ten miles south of here along the river is a town called Leen. There's a paladin of Karak who preaches to the people. I've met him a few times; his name's Jorakai. If you were hoping to find out any weaknesses or vulnerabilities of the Stronghold, well..." He shrugged. "Perhaps you can have a nice, long, painful chat with Jorakai."

Thren nodded but said nothing. As the three left the commons, Haern moved in step beside Thren.

"What next?" he asked.

"Next, we refill our supplies," Thren said. "And after that, we head south."

They'd traveled only a few miles before night fell and they were forced to make camp. Haern and Delysia prepared a fire, cooked some of the fresh meat they'd purchased prior to leaving Trass, then ate in silence. Thren, as had been his custom over the past week, let them be, always saying he preferred solitude whenever asked. Haern was never sure if he lingered about, watching, or if he truly did want to be away from them.

Delysia tossed aside the bones from the leg of a chicken, the remnants of her meal. That done, she slid closer to both Haern and the fire, both of which were in the center of the matted grass that served as the seldom-traveled road.

"This plan is reckless," she said, stirring him from his thoughts. "You do know that, don't you?"

Haern took another bite, tossed a bone into the fire.

"Of course it is," he said. "The whole idea is reckless, but what else could possibly work? One nice thing about insanity is that no one can predict it."

"You're going to torture a man for information, a man who'll be trained to withstand it. This won't be quick and it won't be easy. Is that something you can do? Something you *want* to do?"

"What do you want from me, Delysia?" Haern asked. He kept his irritation out of his voice, but she no doubt sensed it anyway. "No, I don't want to, but this is a paladin of Karak we're talking about here. They aren't good men. They aren't noble. They're killers of a mad god, and if Luther's using them as his own personal bodyguards, then we need to find out what they know. We have to discover any secrets, any weaknesses, and yes, that means we'll have to shed blood."

She pulled her knees up to her chest and curled her arms around them.

"Hours," she said. "It's going to take hours."

"I'm better than that, Delysia. He'll talk, no matter his training. I learned from the best, remember?"

Her face darkened.

"And that is something to be proud of?" she asked him.

To that he had no answer. Was he proud of it? It was a skill, one he'd rarely used but learned nonetheless. Part of him wanted to be proud, to brag of how no punishment could break him, yet all would break to him if given the time. He was the son of Thren Felhorn, and he'd learned many things from his father and his cavalcade of tutors.

"And when you're done," she asked, "after you've tortured and beaten this man, what then will you do?"

Haern lifted his hands in surrender.

"We cannot have him warn the Stronghold of our approach," he said. "Which means I'll do what needs to be done."

Delysia stood, went to her blanket, and wrapped herself tight atop her bedroll.

"Good night, Haern," she said. Her back was to him, and he knew it was intentional. Haern watched her, let out a sigh, then tossed the rest of his own meal.

"Maybe you should have stayed home," he whispered.

Haern stood and wandered north, following the road. He wanted a moment to himself, to think without anyone's presence. He'd been a loner all his life, needing times of solitude even when a child. Patrolling the rooftops of Veldaren used to give him all he could possibly want of quiet and isolation, but traveling with Thren, and now Delysia, had worn on him over the weeks. So, upon the path he walked, short grass crunching beneath his feet, as he gazed up at the stars.

"I do this for hundreds of thousands," he said to the sky, imagining Ashhur up there among them, gazing down. It made his presence feel more real, made it seem as if his questions were heard, even if he expected no answer. "Hundreds of thousands, and all I have to do is kill a few evil men, men who worship your brother. Will you judge me for this?"

"Ashhur might," said Thren from behind him. Haern felt his neck flush, and he turned to see his father approaching from farther down the road. Embarrassed at having such a private moment overheard, he didn't know what to say, only kept walking as his father quickened his pace to catch up.

"You have no reason to feel guilty for what we are to do,"

Thren said. "Especially not because of what you think some god in the stars might say."

"You know nothing of my beliefs," Haern said. "And I will not listen to you mock them."

Thren looked his way, his face lit by the moonlight. As he often did, he looked disappointed.

"I do not mock, but neither am I ignorant of what you believe, not if you confess Ashhur as your god. Though you must forgive me for my surprise. Much of what you do seems contrary to his teachings, so it seems odd to me that you might question him now."

Talking of gods with his father stirred dozens of buried memories, each one making him grow angrier. He thought of Robert Haern, executed for teaching little Aaron Felhorn of Ashhur. He thought of Delius Eschaton, stabbed in the chest for daring to speak out against the thief guilds and demand a better way. Worst, though, was of that single arrow piercing Delysia's chest in a moment of prayer.

"You would never understand," Haern told him. "You're everything Ashhur hates."

At this, Thren laughed.

"Perhaps, but you insult me by pretending I know so little. I know plenty, Watcher. I know of his forced forgiveness, of his belief that even the lowliest man or woman is equal to the greatest of kings. Delusions, lies, fairy tales, call them what you want, but they don't fit the real world. The scum you kill, the scum that serve me, would you put them as your equal?"

"No, but that's not what Ashhur…"

"That's *exactly* what Ashhur means," Thren said, refusing to let him finish. "The soul of a man who murders children and fucks their corpses is just as precious as the little children who that man kills. Equal, Ashhur says, equal in need of forgiveness, equal in value in the eyes of a weak, blind god. But this world has monsters, Haern. It has people like me, and if you think I'll be defeated by a righteous man who bends his knee instead of striking back, then you're just as delusional as Ashhur."

Haern felt his hands curling into fists, and great as his anger was, he still felt helpless.

"You don't see it," Haern said. "The absolute beauty in witnessing something this whole world views as wretched and worthless be lifted up, loved, and made valuable again."

"What you see as beauty, I see as travesty," said Thren. "Let a man reap what he sows from his actions, not be spared it by a moment of weakness and a few words on his tongue. The gods are a blight on our world, all three of them, and the sooner we excise their presence, the better."

They ceased their walking, the campfire dwindled far behind them. Haern felt his emotions all stirred, his tongue unable to articulate what he felt or his heart know for certain what that might even be. Over and over, he saw the arrow piercing Delysia's chest, and it was the only argument he had, the greatest denial he could offer, but to speak of that moment would reveal his identity to his father, and right then, the very idea terrified him.

"You're wrong," he said, the only argument he could summon. "You'd have us abandon everything and descend into anarchy."

"The strong take from the weak," Thren said. "I need no other universal truth than that."

Haern started to argue, then froze. The path they walked upon, while grass, was still short and bent from the occasional carts and feet that traversed it. Beyond it was far taller grass stretching out across the plains, and in that grass he saw movement. It wasn't much, just a swish of blades against the soft wind, or a deepened shadow where there should be none.

"Thren," he said, lowering his voice. "We're being watched."

Thren's hands drifted to the hilts of his swords as he curled around, standing in front of Haern.

"I see them," he said. "There's...shit."

From the tall grass they emerged, twelve men, six wielding crossbows, six wielding swords and daggers. Their clothes were dark grays and browns, all but for the small yellow star sewn upon their chests. Across their mouths, they'd tied thick cloths hiding much of their faces. They formed a circle surrounding Haern and Thren, and leading the band was a smugly amused Maneth, the only one with his face exposed.

"Well, now," he said, grinning as he tossed his dagger from hand to hand. "You two seem rather unhappy. Did I interrupt a lovers' quarrel?"

"What business do you have with us, Maneth?" Thren asked, still poised to draw his blades. Haern shifted so that his own back was to Thren, doing what he could to prevent them from being surprised by any side.

"Come, now," Maneth said. "Don't treat me like an idiot. You should never think you have the jump on Muzien. You think we haven't heard of your rebellious actions when Grayson moved into Veldaren? You should have helped him. You should have gladly welcomed the Sun Guild's arrival, but it seems you did not."

"Did you hear what happened to Grayson?" Thren asked, body tensing. "Did you hear how I slit him open and had him bleed out before me?"

Maneth's smile faltered the tiniest bit.

"Muzien feared as much," Maneth said. "There'll be no allies for you in the west, Thren. We've all been told to keep an eye out for your passing. The Spider Guild is no friend of the Sun, not anymore. Now lift up your hands and surrender. Our orders aren't to kill you, just bring you back to the Darkhand. That is, so long as you don't resist…"

Haern scanned their ambushers, taking stock of where they were, what threat they presented. The men with melee weapons frightened him little. With his and Thren's skill, they'd need far more than six to take them down. The crossbows were a different matter. All it'd take was one good shot…

"I'm impressed by your confidence," Thren said, "but if you think a few local members of the Sun Guild you rounded up on short notice present *me* any threat, you're out of your damn mind. Get out of my way, Maneth, before I send your head to Muzien in a bag."

"We might not be as skilled as you," Maneth said, "but our master is wealthy beyond measure, and that lets us afford such wonderful toys…"

He flung his dagger, and it twirled end over end toward Thren's chest. Haern braced, expecting the attack to begin, but it did not. Thren drew his own swords with blinding speed, and with one blade, he batted the dagger out of the air. Instead of it flying away, it shattered, exploding into shards that pierced Thren's chest. Accompanying its breaking was a tremendous burst of smoke, and the moment Haern breathed it in, he felt as if his lungs were on fire. He readied his swords, holding his breath even as his eyes watered. The smoke continued to spread, and his eyes itched as if someone had tossed pepper into them.

Behind him, Thren fell to his knees, screaming out in pain as blood dripped down his chest.

"Take Thren," Maneth said to his men. "Kill the lackey."

Despite the smoke in his eyes, despite the burning in his lungs, Haern grinned.

Lackey? Oh, how wrong he was about to show that bastard to be.

As much as the smoke burned, he knew it would aid in disguising his movements. He spun in place once before dropping to the ground, his cloak whipping above him. He heard the twang of crossbow strings, felt tugs on his cloak as the bolts pierced through, and then he was on the move, his swords drawn and hungry in his hands. He leaped opposite of Maneth, crashing into two men with daggers. Neither looked prepared for his sudden onslaught, and he gave them no chance to recover. The first failed to parry his thrust in time, and as the saber drove into his belly, Haern batted aside the other's dagger and then cut across his face. The man stumbled away, and when Haern yanked his blade free, he leaped at the man, burying both swords in his chest to finish him off.

Shouts of warning called from all sides, but the exchange had lasted only seconds, and so long as he kept moving, he knew he had a chance. To his right he rushed, to where a man was frantically trying to reload his crossbow. A single cut and down he went. Two more beside him readied their weapons, and they rushed headlong into his charge. Haern's eyes were filled with water as he stood before them, batting their swords about as if they were playthings. A buzzing grew in his head, a strange feeling that filled him with worry. His throat felt raw, his breath shallow. The smoke was still affecting him, and he pressed his attack before the two could try to take advantage of it. A well-placed kick to the groin sent the man on his left to the ground, and he rammed both his blades into the throat of the other. A step, a shift, and he pushed the tip of a saber through the eye of the man he kicked.

"Just fucking die already," Maneth shouted, hurling two more daggers. Haern spun, twisting to move his body out of the way. Instinct told him both were like the ones that had taken down his father. When they hit the ground behind him, they shattered, and shards shot high into the air. Haern dropped just before, curling down to avoid the upward spray of metal. With them came the smoke, now overwhelming. Haern pressed his cloak against his mouth, and breathing through it did help, but there was little he could do for his eyes.

Sight useless, he closed his eyes and remained hunkered down in the smoke, trying to decide his next move. He'd killed less than half of the ambushers. Not good enough. Disabled as he was, there'd be no winning against such overwhelming numbers...which meant doing something to change the situation. Despite his light-headedness, he rolled out of the smoke toward the tall grass and then broke into a run. He heard another twang, saw a bolt zip by mere inches from his head. Another twang, and this time he was not so lucky. Pain shot through him as a heavy force smacked into his right side, just left of his shoulder. Letting out a gasp, he pushed himself on even as warm blood ran down his back. More cries, but Haern trusted his speed, and he ran until he felt his lungs ready to burst. Feeling he'd gained enough distance, he dropped to the ground, sliding on one leg and then flipping about to crouch on his knees. The grass around him was plenty high enough to hide in, and finally in fresh air, he rubbed at his eyes, wiping away the water and forcing himself to see through the sting.

It looked like three of them had originally given chase, but he heard Maneth screaming at them to come back. Together they circled around Thren, who remained prone. His father made no sound, but best he could tell, the man was still alive. Haern wondered if the shards had driven in deep enough to fatally wound his father, or if there were some sort of toxin on them, but he'd have no chance to find out until the Sun Guild killers were dealt with.

"Looks like Thren brought the best with him!" Maneth

shouted out in Haern's direction. "You're good, no question there. But are you loyal?"

Maneth knelt down beside Thren, lifted his head up by the hair, and pressed a dagger against his throat.

"We were ordered to take him alive," Maneth continued. "But damn it, sometimes accidents happen. So, what'll it be? You willing to watch your boss die, or will you come on out like a good little lapdog?"

Perhaps a member of the Sun Guild would give their life for Muzien in a heartbeat, but Haern knew they were wrong if they thought the Spider Guild still had that sort of loyalty. Thren looked pale, his chest a vague blob of red from where Haern lurked. The knife slowly scraped up and down against Thren's neck, mocking Haern.

Deep down, part of him wanted to remain, to let him bleed out. All his confusion, all his worries, it'd all end right there, and by the hands of another. After what his father had told him, after his disregard for anything Haern believed…was there really anything human left to save? But without Thren, any hope of succeeding in finding Luther in the Stronghold dwindled down to nothing. Which was greater, his desire to help the people of Veldaren or his desire to finally be free of his past?

"Come on, now," Maneth shouted. "I don't have all night to wait. Not care for your master? Fine. How's about this, then? Your cute little priestess who was with you…where do you think she is? If we go looking for you, we also go looking for her, and I swear she won't be too happy when we find her."

That ended Haern's argument. Still crouched, he slowly made his way forward, the grass scraping against his face and hands as he pushed through. He kept his breathing steady, which seemed to help with the lingering effects of the smoke. His right arm was already starting to go numb from the pain, and the slightest movement sent jolts of agony throughout his body. Seeing the remaining men with masks across their faces, he wished he could have been equally prepared. If he could only breathe normally, he might have a chance. But weak lunged and wounded by a crossbow bolt still lodged in his shoulder? It was a madman's hope.

Still Maneth lurked over Thren, and clearly his patience was nearing its end.

"You have to die, you know that," Maneth continued. "Can't have anyone chasing after us. But that pretty redhead, she won't know we took Thren, nor where we're taking him. She can escape this. If you care for her at all, then give yourself up."

Haern's jaw clenched tight as he neared. He cared for her, there was no doubt to that, but Maneth was delusional if he thought Haern would willingly give himself up to save her. No, he'd go down fighting, taking as many with him as he could. Two had reloaded their crossbows, and they scanned the grass, searching for movement. Haern slowed, only halfway there. He wiped at his eyes again, clearing away the building tears. They felt like a swathe of cotton was pressed against them, constantly rubbing up and down every time he blinked.

"I said, come on out!" Maneth shouted, temper lost. Haern thought to call out in return, to mock him, but someone else answered in return.

"Leave us," said Delysia, walking toward them from back down the road, her white robes seeming to glow in the moonlight. She walked with her head held high, her hands at an angle from her sides. Haern panicked at seeing her in the open, and he wondered what madness possessed her to go walking straight into their midst. His legs tensed, and he prepared for a charge.

"Well, hello, beautiful," Maneth said, turning toward her. "We were just about to go look—"

Light circled around her hands, like whips made from the sun, and then she clapped them together. The following sunburst was blinding in the darkness, and even Haern had to look away from its shine. He heard screams, the twang of crossbow strings, but when he managed to clear his eyes and look, Delysia remained unharmed. She continued her approach, lips in a constant murmur of prayers. When she neared the first of them, a man still clutching at his face and a crossbow limp in his free hand, she lashed at him with her left hand. The light struck him like a sword, cutting into his body and dropping him to the ground. Her other arm extended the opposite direction, and twin circles of golden light twirled out, cutting into the chest of another. The power of it lifted him off his feet, breaking bones in his arms and chest. When he landed in the tall grass, he showed no sign of moving.

"Kill her!" Maneth screamed, but when the last of his men moved to attack her she simply showed them her open palms. Pure white light shone upon the men as it radiated from the center of her hands, releasing a sound like the constant ringing of a bell. Her red hair billowed behind her, twirling in a sudden storm of wind. The ringing grew louder and louder, until it was like a thunderclap, each boom a force that blasted the men backward as if struck by the fist of Ashhur himself. Against such power, they had no chance to endure.

Her face still calm as ever, Delysia walked up to Maneth, who had fallen to his knees, now alone but for the bleeding body of Thren at his side. She reached down to take him by the chin, lifting his head up so he might look upon her. As he did, he drew a dagger from his belt and moved to stab her chest. Haern felt panic shoot through him, but it was all for naught. Delysia's eyes flared brilliant white, and Maneth screamed, the dagger falling from his hands. When the priestess released him, he staggered to his feet and stumbled away. As Haern watched, he took a few wild steps, a hand out before him. Blinded, Haern realized. She'd left him blind.

Haern rose to his feet, having watched the entire display take place over what seemed like mere seconds. There was no reason to hide now, the men broken, blinded, or unconscious. Maneth continued staggering until one of his men managed to take him by the arm, and together they made their way north. Those that were wounded joined them, limping and clutching their wounds. They said nothing as they left, offered no threats, no promises of retribution. Haern could hardly believe it.

"Delysia..." he said as he made his way through the grass, his right arm limp against his stomach.

She ignored him, instead kneeling beside his father. She put a hand to his chest, an ear to his lips.

"He's alive," she said. "But he won't be for long."

No hesitation, no debate. She put her other hand atop the first, clean, pale skin mixing with blood, and then bowed her head. He heard her whisper the name of Ashhur, saw a soft glow spread across the bleeding skin. It was nothing like before; instead of hurting his eyes, it was soothing, a reassuring sight in the darkness. For several minutes Delysia prayed, stopping only to remove a hand and toss yet another shard of metal that somehow appeared in her palm.

At last, she wiped her hands clean on the leg of Thren's pants, then stood, pulling hair from her face that had stuck to the sweat running down from her brow.

"Your turn," she said, coming over to glance at the bolt in his back.

"You should rest first."

"I have all night to rest."

He winced as he felt her touch the skin around the entrance to the wound.

"It hit bone," she said. "I can't push it through, which means I have to pull."

Haern slowly lowered to his knees, took in several deep breaths, then braced himself.

"I'm ready," he said.

"This will hurt."

"I know. Do it."

She was right. It hurt. As he clenched his teeth together, forcing away the pain, he heard the soft murmurs of her prayers, the gentle ringing accompanied by the light around her hands. Slowly the pain faded, becoming a tingling ache.

"Thank you," he said, slowly rising back to his feet.

"Go back to our camp and get our supplies," Delysia told him, settling back down beside Thren. "He needs a blanket."

Haern stood there, unwilling to leave. He stared at the face of his father, his skin ashen as he slept.

"You should have let him die," he whispered.

Delysia looked up, and there was no hiding her glare. Rising, she took a step closer and then slapped him across the face.

"I save people," she said. "I don't leave them to die. Not when I have a choice. Now go get your father a blanket. Tonight will be cold, and he'll need it."

Haern opened his mouth, closed it, and then left to do as she asked.

CHAPTER
11

The night was deep as, from the nearby rooftop, Cynric watched the Sun Guild surround his guildhouse with their torches held high.

"I used to think Veldáren was the most dangerous city in all of Dezrel," said the master of the Wolf Guild. "But now I see differently. We have grown weak, soft. We should have crushed the Sun Guild the moment they stepped foot into our city, but instead we listened, we bartered and hid. Only the Ash resisted. Why did we not? Why did we act so timid?"

Beside him on the rooftop were seven of his best men, the most trusted and loyal. All of them had filed their teeth down to fangs, in mimicries of their guild leader.

"We sensed the change in the wind," said one of them. "The Sun Guild could have been an ally against the Trifect."

"And now they are our executioners," Cynric said. "The Trifect is more ally than foe in this battle. What a twisted world we live in."

They fell silent as below them Muzien called out to the guildhouse for the Wolf Guild's surrender. Cynric smirked when he heard it.

"Corner any animal, and it will bite," he said. "And we are no timid animal. We are wolves."

He turned to the seven.

"I may never see any of you again, but know you are my best, my bravest, and I take pride in having your allegiance. Go, and show the Sun Guild that we will make them bleed before we break."

They each dipped their heads in respect, then scattered in all directions along the rooftops, where the remaining fifty of Cynric's guild waited in ambush. Now alone, Cynric leaned back on his haunches and looked up to the moon, and slowly he breathed in and then let it out.

"Shame you're not with us anymore, Thren," he whispered.

The other guilds had always mistrusted the cold-blooded man, but Cynric had known Thren's heart. He'd sensed the ambition within it, the craving for an empire. Such desires fitted Cynric just fine, and together they'd orchestrated the Bloody Kensgold, killed Maynard Gemcroft, and burned Leon Connington's mansion to the ground. That same power, that commanding presence, would have served them well tonight.

Cynric drew a long dagger from his belt.

Victor had suddenly grown timid, the Trifect silent. Thren was gone, as was the Watcher. Veldaren's salvation would have to rest in his hands.

Again, Muzien cried out for surrender. He was a wraith-like figure, looking thin in his long coat. The circle of torches around the building lifted higher, and the whole of it carried the feel of a religious ceremony. Cynric smirked. At least Muzien had a sense of showmanship about him. The Darkhand shook his head, and he turned his back to the building. The rest of the Sun Guild, at least thirty by Cynric's count, advanced upon the building. Within were only three men, those willing to die for the cause, and Cynric waited for them to act.

The Wolf Guild's headquarters was a two-story building, full of curtained windows, and from three different windows they appeared, all facing Muzien. The three held crossbows, and they fired wildly, unable to aim for a single moment due to the sudden barrage of bolts unleashed at them by Muzien's men. Still, the damage was done, Muzien untouched but two men on either side of him dead with crossbow bolts deep in their bodies. A good start.

Cynric turned and ran from the guildhouse, knowing time would be short. Already the building burned behind him, the Sun guildmembers throwing torches through windows and pressing them up against the base. A glance at either side showed the rest of his guild following suit, racing fast as they could along the rooftops.

The plan was simple. Muzien would never leave himself vulnerable, Cynric knew that, and those thirty men were but a scrap of the Darkhand's total power. He'd have had more men ready, waiting to attack the moment the Wolf Guild dared attempt an ambush. So, they wouldn't ambush Muzien at all.

They'd ambush the ambushers.

Cynric's men had located them prior to the attack, two different sections of thieves gathered on opposite sides of the Wolf Guild's headquarters. Heading toward the south, escorted by twenty more Wolves, Cynric approached the two alleyways where the Sun guildmembers gathered. They waited patiently, over forty of them, with two at the end of the alley, keeping watch for Muzien's signal. Cynric didn't wait, didn't slow down or even fire a crossbow bolt or two to soften their ranks. Blind, overwhelming fury was what he needed to take down his foes. Upon their prey they descended, and he howled to announce his arrival.

He landed atop one man, his heel colliding hard with the man's neck so that it snapped upon slamming to the stone ground. A slash, and the woman beside him gasped as blood gushed out the length of her throat. All around him, he heard his enemies crying out in surprise, heard them drawing weapons and shouting conflicting orders. Amid the chaos, Cynric felt right at home. As his men continued to fall upon them from the rooftops, Cynric charged three to his left that had put their backs to a wall. The first rushed at him, thinking to catch him off guard, but Cynric easily shoved the dagger aside, drew a blade with his free hand, and slashed across the man's face. Unable to stop to ensure its fatality, he continued on, wielding both blades now. The remaining two threw up swords in defense, and he nearly laughed at the attempt.

They wanted to swordfight, to thrust and parry in the dance people like Thren and the Watcher excelled at. But that wasn't Cynric's game. He was never much of a dancer.

Cynric crashed right into him, twisting his body out of sheer reflex to avoid his prey's weak thrust. His knee drove into the man's stomach, his daggers stabbed chest and shoulder. Even Cynric's forehead slammed the man in the nose, splattering blood across both their faces. Spinning his body in a half circle, he yanked his daggers out of the first man's chest only to whirl around and bury them in the face of the other, one piercing the eye, the other an open mouth. His death scream was gargled nonsense as the blood poured down the blade.

Cynric kicked him in the stomach for good measure as he drew the weapons free. He took no time to assess the battle, for the sounds of combat told him it was not yet over, and by sheer ferocity, he would find new opponents to face. Running full speed along the wall, he leaped up so he could kick off it, and then elongated so that he soared through the air, slamming dagger-first into another of the Sun Guild, who fell backward out of panic at the sight of Cynric flying at him, blood dripping down his face and past his maniacal grin. The two collided, rolled along the ground, and all the while, Cynric kicked and slashed and bit. Coming out of the roll, his foe was dead, and already he searched for another. He found one in a woman battling another of his Wolf Guild, her back to him. On his knees still, he slashed her heel, and as she crumpled backward, he lifted his other dagger so he could stab her throat on the way down.

Rising to his feet, he let out a deep breath, his combat rush settling. The fight was over, only a handful of the Sun Guild left, and they quickly died to the now-overwhelming numbers of the Wolves. Cynric took a quick count of the dead, and for the forty they killed, they'd lost only seven in return.

"Jaff, lead three Wolves down into the slums," Cynric said. "Milly, take four and patrol east of here. Engage any of the Sun Guild you see, no matter their number. They *must* remain scattered as long as possible." He turned, pointed at those in the group who were most coated with blood from the previous fight. "You three, come with me."

With that they scattered, Cynric leading his group back north. If they'd succeeded at the northern ambush site as well, then Muzien should have been left isolated with his men back at the Wolf Guild's headquarters. Soon, Wolves would come from all corners, firing crossbows, surrounding them, spurring them into a retreat. As for Cynric, well, he knew where that retreat would lead to. It'd taken patience, but at last he'd found the simple home Muzien retired to when he needed to sleep or plot out his next phase of Veldaren's takeover. It was a gamble, but Cynric had to believe that Muzien, upon realizing his own ambush had failed, would try to return to where he was safest until he could regroup and reassess the situation.

The night was full of cries of the dying when Cynric found him. Muzien hurried down the center of the street, dark coat flapping behind him, two members of the Sun Guild in escort. Cynric led his own men to block the path, and he bared his sharpened teeth in greeting.

"Did you have fun burning down my home?" he asked as on either side of him, his Wolves unleashed bolts from crossbows. The two escorts died, but the one aimed for Muzien somehow missed despite the short distance, the bolt veering off just past the elf's head. Muzien never even flinched.

"Burning down an abandoned building?" Muzien asked, walking toward them as if unbothered in the slightest by their arrival. "No, I found no enjoyment in that."

Cynric drew his daggers, and the other three dropped the crossbows and readied their own blades.

"Killing *you*, though," Muzien said, pulling his swords from their sheaths, "in that I will take great pleasure."

"As a pack," Cynric said in a low voice to his crew. "Don't hesitate. Don't even think. Surround him, then take him down."

The four moved forward, keeping a wide berth as they moved to put a man on all sides. Muzien stayed where he was, swords pointed to the ground as he watched them. The smile on his face never faltered.

"You'll die last, Cynric," said Muzien. "Consider it my gift to you, one final chance to pledge loyalty before death."

"And consider this my gift to you," Cynric said. "My blade in your gut!"

He leaped forward, and the other three joined, rushing in from all sides. Cynric knew no opponent, no matter how skilled, should have been able to withstand them. His men were ferocious, unrelenting, and when they came crashing in, they should have overwhelmed their foe with a flurry of steel. The night would be theirs, followed by all of Veldaren.

The moment of the attack, Muzien sprang to his right, assaulting Cynric's fellow Wolf with a double slash that moved so fast, Cynric could barely see it. Steel flashed in the moonlight, followed by blood. Cynric shifted the angle of his run, and he swung his swords from left to right, hoping to bury them in Muzien's side. The other two reacted similarly, either thrusting with their daggers or chopping in with both weapons in an attempt to overwhelm the elf.

Muzien's movements never halted, his feet never still. On one foot he spun, his swords lashing out, and the night rang with the sound of steel hitting steel as he batted away all three of their attacks. Cynric swung back in as Muzien continued to spin before him, but he hit only cloak. The elf had danced away, down the street directly opposite Cynric, but before he could follow, Muzien had already turned about. Having escaped their cage, he sprang back onto the offensive, tearing into the remaining two that had accompanied Cynric. The Wolves stood side by side, lifting their weapons to defend, but watching Muzien move was like watching a ghost of the fighter Thren had been during his rise to power. Before Cynric could rush to their aid, both were falling back, Muzien's twin blades slashing in tandem, constantly shifting their angle, and the elf's body twisted and slid, fluid as a river.

The man on the left died, a sword piercing his neck so fast, it seemed his throat opened by itself, spilling scarlet blood down the front of his shirt. Cynric took his spot as he fell, trying to aid the last member of his guild, perhaps the last in all of Veldaren. As the Wolf took another step back, slashing with the dagger in his right hand while attempting to parry Muzien's thrust with the left, Cynric swung both his swords, all his strength behind the chop. If he could only hit the damn elf, get him bleeding…

The sword in Muzien's left hand, which had been thrusting in to pierce a vital lung, instead curled right, smacking aside the Wolf's own thrusts. With his other blade, he lifted it up in defense, planting his foot to steady himself as Cynric's swords connected. Despite all Cynric's strength, despite how wiry the elf seemed, he resisted it with ease. It was as if Cynric had smashed his swords against the side of the king's castle, so badly did it hurt his hands.

Press harder! Cynric screamed to himself as he pulled back and slashed again and again, beating his swords at the elf as if he were a tree to be felled. Muzien took step after step backward, alternating which of his swords blocked the blows, always matching Cynric swing for swing. There was no moving him out of position, no tiring him, no fooling with a feint. At last, Cynric tried desperate surprise, flinging himself forward out of sheer madness, with no care for what Muzien might do in retaliation or counter. Instead of skewering the elf or being skewered in return, Muzien twirled around him, coat flapping in the air, and assaulted the other Wolf who had fallen back to give his guildmaster space to fight.

Two hits knocked his swords away, the third took his life.

"What the fuck are you?" Cynric asked as he stood there trying to catch his breath. "We had you trapped. You should be dead."

Muzien shook some of the blood off his swords, chuckling as he did.

"Did you?" he asked. "Look around, Cynric. Tell me, do you think it is *your* trap we are in?"

Cynric glanced to the rooftops, and he felt his stomach tighten. All along them he saw men and women watching, the four-pointed star sewn on their chests. The way they lurked there, silent and still as statues, infuriated him more. This wasn't some damn ritual for them to observe, and for Muzien to be so confident in his abilities, so unafraid of Cynric's blades…

"You're down here, and they're up there," Cynric said. "If it's a trap, it's a poor one."

"They're only eyes in the night, to bear witness to your death," Muzien said. "Forget them, Cynric. We are alone here, just the two of us. Again, I offer you a chance to live. Men will serve you, just as they do now. You will have a position of power and respect. Would it be so terrible for you to cast aside your cloak and bear the star?"

Cynric stood tall before them all, and he puffed out his chest.

"I won't be made into your pet, nor beaten and bludgeoned until I obey. Kill me if you can, Muzien. I may die, but I'll die fighting. What other end could I have hoped for?"

The elf shook his head.

"If you see defeat as your only future, then your mind lacks imagination, your spirit void of true ambition. Die well, Cynric, and know the Wolf Guild dies with you."

Muzien charged straight ahead, building up a frightening speed before vaulting into the air. Cynric estimated the distance, saw he'd come up short, and used the heartbeat's time he had to brace himself for the eventual assault.

Except a ring on Muzien's blackened hand flashed when he landed, and suddenly there were two of the Sun Guild's master. One dashed to the left, the other to the right, and Cynric was baffled as to what to do. Once they had him flanked, they rushed in simultaneously, the coordinated attack leaving him helpless. With no choice, he moved to block the strikes from his right. His blades passed right through Muzien's, scattering the image like smoke.

Something sharp pierced his back. A hand reached around his neck, holding him still as he bled.

"Your pride cost you your life," Muzien whispered into his ear. "Do you feel it piercing your flesh? Bleeding you dry? Pride, in a meager creature of failed gods? Fools, all of you, your whole damn race..."

Swords fell from Cynric's limp hands. He opened his mouth to retort, some last insult against the elf's victory, but then a sharp pain spread across his throat, and when he breathed in, his lungs filled with blood. When he fell, he was still gagging, failing to gargle out a final curse against Muzien and his blasted Sun Guild.

Muzien looked down at the dead body of the former Wolf Guild's master and shook his head.

"If only you had served," he said. "In time, you could have earned a place of honor at my side."

Not that it surprised him, though. It was a cruel self-fulfilling prophecy. Those he wanted at his side were the strongest, the bravest, the ones with a sense of pride and destiny to their lives. Yet those same people would always be the ones who would resist him, who would deny the perceived insult at having anyone else lord over them as master. Muzien needed to find such people when they were young, before they'd tasted power, such as he had with Thren Felhorn.

Muzien glanced up and down the street. He heard distant sounds of combat, but it had mostly died down from what it'd been only moments before. The Wolf Guild would be defeated soon, their numbers too thin to cause much permanent harm. If anything, Cynric's ambush had made things interesting compared to some of the others. At least the Wolves had had the wisdom and strength to fight, unlike the Hawks, who had only burned. As the days of his takeover faded into history, Muzien would let his men talk of this night with wonder and pride, reminiscing on the ferocity of their foes, the cleverness and brutality of their final death throes.

The Hawks, though, would never have their name whispered again.

"Scour the city for any who remain in hiding," Muzien called up to those on the rooftops. "Search until dawn, then consider the matter finished. The few you miss will not dare bear the cloak of their fallen master."

The rogues saluted, then dashed away. Alone, Muzien continued his way back toward his home in the eastern quarter of Veldaren, not far from the city's entrance. Normally, he'd have stayed back to enjoy the last of the hunt, but Daverik was waiting for him, and Muzien knew the priest was an annoying sod whenever their meetings did not begin on time. So he walked, refusing to give Daverik any more haste than that. He took in the sight of the city as he did, amused by what he saw. The night life had slowly died off since his arrival, a fear growing in the populace at what the omnipresent symbol of the Sun meant to them. Doors to the various taverns were shut instead of left open in an attempt to entice more clientele by the sound of merriment within. Many of the street women had taken to lurking deeper in the dark spaces of the alleys, and it wouldn't surprise Muzien if many others had gone to the brothels, seeking their protection.

Change was frightening, and all of them could sense the change blowing the wind. But they'd yet to see his true revealing to the populace. No, Muzien had something special planned for that defining moment, when the entire city would witness their new lord and then bow in obedience.

Muzien's home was plain, a one-story building with a front door and a single window without glass or covering beside a thick brown curtain. The wood was old but sturdy, the roof flat with wooden slats to keep out the rain. Muzien knew such a bland outer appearance would prevent anyone from thinking it would be his home, but that was a common shortcoming of humans. They assumed a man of wealth and power could not bear to live without it, even for a moment. Muzien flexed his dark hand, whose ache had never left him over the decades.

Yes, he'd sacrificed far worse than a comfortable bed and vaulted ceilings to accomplish his goals. Let the humans remain blind fools. Was that not the reason he'd come to live among them in the first place?

"I hope your wait was not long," Muzien said as he stepped through the door.

"Longer than I would prefer," said Daverik, the priest waiting with his back against the wall. He'd positioned himself facing the window, and Muzien had little doubt the man would have leaped through if he had felt himself in danger.

"I had business to attend to first," Muzien said, walking past Daverik to the far wall. Lifting up a board from the floor, he reached down into a deep pit dug into the earth, then pulled out a cool glass bottle. He removed the cork and drank it straight, without glass or cup.

"Were you successful?" Daverik asked.

"I always am."

Daverik smirked.

"Come now, even for one as skilled as you, I find it hard to swallow that you yourself believe that. What of Grayson's first attempt to move into the city?"

"Grayson's attempt," Muzien said, setting down the bottle. "Not mine."

"And your other apprentice, Thren Felhorn, would you consider him a success as well?"

Muzien narrowed his eyes.

"You had a reason to meet with me, priest, and I suggest you get to it before my mood sours."

Daverik reached into his pocket, pulled out a bag tied with a red string, and tossed it to him. Muzien caught it in one hand and, with a twist of his fingers, removed the knot to glance inside. Rattling within the small pouch were over two dozen gold coins.

"This is a pittance of what I was promised," Muzien said.

"It's all I can procure for now," Daverik said. "Everything else has gone to the guards to ensure they continue looking the other way when your wagons pass through our gates."

"The guards are greedy, then. Many still hold out their hands, demanding coin so we may smuggle in your tiles."

"*My* tiles?" asked Daverik. "They bear your symbol, not mine."

Muzien took another drink, then pushed the cork back into the bottle.

"My symbol," Muzien said, staring into Daverik's green eyes, "but your coin, your request. I am content to scrawl the symbol of the Sun with chalk, to carve it with a knife, or even paint it with blood so all may know. But you insist on stone and even tell my men where to place them. If you think me daft, Daverik, you should reconsider while you still have the chance. I'm fond of games, and it's clear you are playing one... but no one has ever turned against me and lived. I pray you remember that."

Daverik pushed aside the curtain so he might look outside, then let it drop.

"All I do, I do for my god," he said. "I do not play games."

Muzien couldn't help but laugh.

"You are mistaken. The only thing the gods know are games, just games, and we are their pieces."

"What do you know of gods?"

Muzien took a step closer to the priest, and he held out his blackened, aching hand so the man might see its charred flesh.

"I was marked by the goddess Celestia herself," Muzien said, his good mood from crushing the Wolf Guild leaving him. "I know more of the gods and their foolishness than you can possibly imagine. I do not care what Karak intends for this city. All I care is that the true city, the real world underneath, remains in my hands. I would have an empire that stretches from coast to coast, and not even a god will prevent that."

"I seek to save the lives of hundreds of thousands," Daverik said. "No matter how important you think you are, you are still nothing compared to the importance of what we do. Keep out of our affairs, and we will let you rule like the king you've always pretended to be."

"Enjoy your battle for souls," Muzien said as the priest headed for the door. "I will remain here, lording over all that truly matters."

Daverik opened the door, shook his head.

"The things of men and kings turn to ash, held only by hands of bone," he said.

Muzien lifted his blackened hand, and he smiled despite the burning anger in his chest.

"Even a hand of ash and bone may still wear a ring of gold," he said. "Even a darkened hand may force a man to kneel. We are the dust, priest, swirling against the stones of time and the will of gods. To either, we mean nothing, but to each other... to each other, we rise and fall, shine and dim, build great kingdoms and burn others to the ground. Nothing we do matters but what echoes on in the night, and I swear to you, I care not for my soul, but I do care for the echo."

Muzien turned away, heading once more for his bottle.

"The next time you say the name of a god in my presence, I will kill you," he said. "Pleasant dreams."

He drank, and Daverik left him, and as the alcohol burned down his throat, he offered his own goodbye to the Wolf Guild.

"Echo on into the night," he whispered. "Remembered, and lost only to the echoes of others just as proud, just as meaningless."

CHAPTER

 12

Haern's shoulder had nearly recovered by the time the three of them walked into the town of Leen. It was a far more populous settlement than Trass, largely due to the modest docks built on the Rigon River. Many people walked about, their clothes simple and homespun, their faces tanned from working the fields, long days fishing in the boats, and sailing both up- and downstream to sell their goods. Already feeling like he stuck out as an oddity due to his clothing, the blood on his shoulder and all over Thren's shirt did little to help.

"You should be able to find suitable clothes here," Delysia said as they approached a large inn. She gestured to the river, where a couple ramshackle booths were selling food to the men, others replacement gear and clothing.

"I'll smell like fish for weeks," Thren said.

"Better than smelling like blood."

Haern and Delysia stepped into the tavern as Thren headed

off to the meager market. Inside, a weathered man, much of the top of his head both bald and tanned, greeted them warmly.

"Two rooms," Haern said, dropping coins atop the man's desk. "The other is for a friend," he added at the man's raised eyebrow.

"Of course," he said.

As Delysia put away their things in their room, Haern returned to the man up front, who was clearly wary. Given his hood and clothing, Haern couldn't blame him.

"I'm looking for a paladin of Karak named Jorakai," he said. "We heard he was here?"

"Jorakai will be here tomorrow," the innkeeper said. "He comes every sixth day to give another lecture. You wanting to take a listen?"

"Something like that."

"He comes early, so don't go sleeping in."

Haern bought a bit of bread left over from the morning, brought it back to their room, and shared it with Delysia. Thren returned not much later, wearing a white shirt with long sleeves. He tossed his old bloody and torn shirt onto the floor beside their bed.

"It'll suffice," he said. "You discover anything about Jorakai?"

"Tomorrow," Haern said.

Thren shrugged.

"Good," he said. "I need a long sleep in a comfortable bed, anyway."

Come the next morning, the three of them joined the rest of the gathered crowd at the docks. It looked like much of the river work was put on hold, and Haern was surprised to see over sixty people there to listen to the dark paladin preach. They sat on blankets, many sharing food with their families. Staying near the back so they could quietly observe, Haern waited with his arms crossed.

"Why must we listen?" asked Haern. "I've heard enough of Karak to last a lifetime." He winced at a half-forgotten memory, that of him lost in a strange room of Karak's temple, the great Lion demanding his obedience.

"Before we make a move on him, I want to take measure of the man," Thren said. "We'll learn plenty by how well he controls the crowd."

A few more people came in late, taking seats around the outer ring, and not much later, Jorakai arrived, having been waiting in a nearby home. He was a tall man, his skin even more tanned than the people of the village. Much of his hair was shaved but for a single stretch forming a long ponytail he tied behind his head. He wore the armor of his order, heavy plate mail stained black with a silver lion painted across his chest. Its mouth was open in a roar, its teeth bared, its claws raised to strike. Attached to his back in a loose sheath was an enormous two-handed blade.

"Karak's peace be with you," he said, and his voice carried with ease.

"And peace be to you," responded the crowd in kind.

"Peace," Thren said, letting out a snort. "If you can call slavery 'peace,' I guess..."

A few of the people on the outer ring heard him and glared his way, but he only smiled in return.

"We live in exciting times," Jorakai continued, and he slowly paced before them, turning his head so he might address all parts of the crowd. "With the fall of the Citadel, our world of Dezrel may finally see a glimmer of hope, see her people return to the true god, to the times of obedience, times of peace. Order. At last we have a chance for there to be order, in all our lives!"

A few clapped, and others said "amen" to punctuate the paladin's sentences.

"Such exciting times," Thren said, looking disgusted. "He

tells this to fishermen and farmers. The most excitement they'll see in their lifetimes is a sick child or a bandit raid. No wonder they'll cling to such a false story. To think I believed it'd be through weakness or desperation he converted the people, but instead, it is merely boredom."

"Perhaps it is all three," Haern said.

"Keep your voices down," Delysia whispered to the two. "We stand out enough as it is."

Haern glanced at her, saw the way her skin had paled.

"Are you all right?" he asked her.

She nodded, continuing to watch as Jorakai preached.

"I know the weaknesses in your hearts," the dark paladin shouted, his voice bleeding with sincerity and anger. "I know those of you who lust after women, with hands you fail to control. I know you who let your tongues rule your minds, who will murder a man with your words far worse than my blade ever could. Worst of all, I know many of you doubt. Where is the Lion, you ask? Where are his people, his faith, his power? But the sick branches must be burned so the healthy may live. The rotting hand must be cut to spare the arm. If you have doubt, now is the time to silence it! If you sin with your tongue, now is the time to remove it from your heads. Karak seeks grand gestures, not simple, cowardly steps to be undone mere days later."

Jorakai was shouting now, his deep voice thundering over the crowd.

"Who are you to give in to your own desires? What worth are we as pathetic, dying humans to demand our will over the will of the one who created us? When your eyes wander to the chest of a woman not your wife, *kneel* to the Lion and beg for forgiveness. When you spread lies about a man or woman, *kneel* to the Lion and beg that he rip out your tongue. We are the creators of chaos, and if our world is to find order, if it is to have meaningful change, then that change must start with us, the faithful. It won't come from the unbelievers. It won't come from Ashhur and his doctrine of turning blind eyes to sin and opening his arms to all the failures and hypocrites of the land. Us, my friends, it comes from us! Sacrifice your will to the Lion. Sacrifice your desires, your pride, and know that Karak is Lord!"

Haern felt Delysia clutch his arm as she leaned against him, and he was surprised by the intense look in her eyes.

"Karak would make them slaves," she said, and she shivered as a song of worship began. "I'm sorry, I can't listen to this."

"Go," Haern said. "There's no reason for you to be here, not for this."

She took his hand, squeezed it, then left for their room. Haern watched her go for a moment, then brought his attention back to the crowd. The song they sang was a somber one, yet the people seemed willing enough to cry it out at the top of their lungs. Jorakai maintained the chorus, his deep voice leading the others.

"Pray to Karak," he said as the song dwindled down. "Pray to the Lion, and sacrifice daily your weaknesses upon his blood altar. Deny yourselves, and be made strong. Give up your own childish rebellion, and be made whole. So is the word, so is the truth, and so is the way."

The crowd murmured a conjoined "amen," and then the sermon was over.

"Before I forget," Jorakai shouted over them, apparently not finished. "I will not be here the next sixth, but the day after. My travels will take me to Yarsville, then to Arlet, and it will add an extra day on my return ride."

That was it, then. Several came up to him, confessing private worries, others packing up their blankets and their children so they might begin their work on the river and in the fields.

"What do you think?" Haern asked as the crowd began to disperse.

"I think he's a man like any other," Thren said. "And like any other, we'll make him bleed, and we'll make him talk."

"He said he's traveling to Yarsville soon. Do you know where that is?"

"Doesn't matter," Thren said. "He said he'll ride back from it, which means horses, which means he won't be on a boat. Go find Delysia; tell her to get ready. When Jorakai rides out, we'll be waiting for him on the road."

Yarsville was to the west of Leen, following a well-worn road through the fertile farmlands near the river. Trees were sparse, but the grass was tall, and Haern saw little point in trying to find a particularly clever ambush place.

"He's one man," Haern had said. "Take out the horse, and he'll be ours. Don't need to leap from trees to pull that off."

So, they waited near the bottom of a hill, the tall grass keeping them hidden while elevation let them have clear sight of the road for over half a mile. Haern and Thren lurked on opposite sides of the road, while Delysia sat next to Haern.

"You don't need to be here," Haern told her as the day passed into night.

"Yes, I do," she said.

"Why? I know you don't want us doing this."

Delysia kept her eyes on the road, refusing to look at him.

"Turning my back to it doesn't change what it is you'll do. If my choices are hiding like a coward or staying to ensure your safety, then I'll stay."

As it had been for the past week, the night was bright, with sparse clouds and a glittering field of stars accompanying the moon. They should have had no problem seeing Jorakai on his ride nor hearing him, but it seemed he and his horse traveled in shadows, for he crested their slender hill without their having heard or spotted his approach. Haern startled at the sudden proximity, and he had no time to whistle out his signal to Thren. They'd meant to leap out simultaneously, cutting at the legs of the horse to bring it down, but with such speed, he wasn't sure he could manage. Sprinting through the grass, giving no thought to remaining hidden, he lunged . . . and missed.

Rolling along the ground, he watched as Thren leaped out farther ahead, and his strike was far better aimed. His short swords cut into the back tendons of the horse's rear right leg, and it let out a wail that was dreadful to hear. The horse continued ahead a few more steps out of sheer momentum, its right leg crumpling each time it tried to apply weight. Haern rose to his feet as Jorakai dismounted, gently tapping the beast on the neck as it whinnied in pain.

"Nesme has long served me faithfully," the dark paladin said, drawing his sword over his back and holding it before him. "Whatever gold you thought to take from me, it will not be worth the suffering you'll endure at my hands for such insolence."

Fire enveloped the enormous blade, black flames flickering with violet at its tips.

"We're not here for gold," Thren said as he and Haern stepped away from each other, giving themselves space to fight, while Delysia remained in hiding. Slowly, they approached the paladin, spreading out even farther to ensure an attack on one meant he'd leave himself vulnerable to the other. Jorakai eyed the two of them, feet firmly planted where he was. The fire on his blade grew stronger with each passing moment, and it seemed the very light of the stars dimmed, their illumination drawn into the blade and snuffed out forever. Yet despite the darkening of the world around him, Jorakai seemed to shine brighter, every curve and dent on his black plate mail vibrant, most of all the lion on his chest, which shimmered blue-violet.

"If not gold, then what?" asked Jorakai. Despite the ambush, he didn't sound worried, just annoyed by their presence. "Revenge, perhaps? Have I killed someone you loved? Or are you some of Ashhur's more fanatical faithful? If you're seeking a martyr's death, I'll gladly give it to you if you think it will earn you a better seat for eternity."

"Information," said Haern, taking several more careful steps so that he and his father were on opposite sides of the paladin. "Drop your blade and tell us what we need to know, and your death will be quick and painless."

Jorakai grinned a wolfish grin, exposing his teeth.

"I'm not the one dying here tonight."

He lunged at Haern, the movement stunningly quick for one bedecked in plate mail. The great sword swung in a wide arc, aiming to cleave him in half at the waist. Haern twisted, bracing both his legs as he put his sabers in the way. He expected the blow to be strong—he'd fought people like Ghost whose arms were like tree trunks—but when Jorakai's blade hit his own, he feared his life was at an end. His arms jarred toward his chest, the ground giving way beneath his feet as he skidded backward half a foot. A scream escaped his lips as he pushed against it, fighting the fire and steel that pressed for his waist. He felt no heat despite the proximity, instead a biting cold that stole his breath.

At last he shoved the blade away, and when the paladin moved to swing again, Haern was already rolling, desperate to avoid another until he could recover. The block had lasted no longer than a second, yet it felt like an eternity. Sliding to a halt, he spun to watch as Thren assaulted Jorakai, his blades whirling. Jorakai took step after methodical step backward, holding his great sword by the hilt as well as with a gauntleted hand midway up the sword. As if it were a staff, he shifted and turned his sword, batting away Thren's attempts to stab and cut. A few slipped past, but Haern had a feeling Jorakai was letting them, for they were weak and struck his plate mail, unable to find a crease and lacking the strength of a mace or ax to punch through the armor.

Armor wasn't Jorakai's only advantage. With his great reach, and even greater strength, he appeared able to halt Thren's assault at any time. As Haern ran to join in, the paladin swung his sword in another wide arc. Thren dared not block, not after witnessing Haern's struggle, and instead, he dropped to his knees underneath, then rolled away as the great sword curled back around and stabbed deep into the earth where he'd been. Haern came crashing in while the sword was still embedded in the dirt, both feet slamming into the man's chest in an attempt to knock him away from his blade and leave him vulnerable.

It felt like ramming feetfirst into a giant. Haern somersaulted off, his feet barely touching ground before he leaped in again, this time slashing toward Jorakai's exposed face with one blade while thrusting for the gap at the armpit with the other. The paladin tore his blade free, chunks of dirt flying as he whipped it around, blocking both strikes, then continuing its turn to deter Thren's attempted charge from the other side, again beating him back. Still, they were together now, and Haern swung and stabbed, forcing Jorakai to turn his attention in his direction lest he be cut down.

Jorakai continued to swing in long, wide arcs, his burning blade crackling as it cut through the air. Haern felt himself finally settling into a rhythm, knowing when the paladin would turn his way, and therefore retreating, and when to come rushing back in while his father attacked from the opposite direction. They'd scored no hits yet, but Jorakai was clearly getting frustrated, constantly turning back and forth, sometimes blocking the attacks with his swords, sometimes using the armor on his elbow and arms.

At last, Haern saw an opening. With Jorakai in mid-spin, his back was to him, and in that instant, Haern dropped to one knee, and as the burning blade cut above his head, he stabbed deep into the paladin's calf. Before he could suffer any retaliation, he danced away, ripping out the saber as he did. Blood flew, and by the scream Jorakai let out, Haern knew the fight was theirs. Rather than press the fight he stayed back, lurking along with his father as they watched Jorakai lean most of his weight on his good leg.

"What do you want from me?" he asked, taking a hobbling step forward. "What wisdom do you think I have that you can take by the sword?"

Thren joined Haern's side, and shoulder to shoulder, they prepared a charge.

"Don't worry," Thren said. "You'll tell us soon enough."

Together they rushed him, and as he was unable to properly brace himself, his sword carried only a shadow of its former strength. Haern put both his swords in the way, and as he blocked it, his left foot kicked out, ramming into the dark paladin's throat. Thren was left unblocked, and he took advantage of it, jamming one of his short swords into the knee of the man's good leg while slipping the other through a crease at his side. Jorakai crumpled to the ground from the combination of their attacks, and when he hit, the sword fell from his hand. The fire surrounding it faded away, and it seemed the stars shone brighter for it.

Thren was on top of him in a heartbeat, knees pressing on Jorakai's shoulders to pin his arms, his swords crossed beneath his chin, gently touching the skin of his neck. The paladin's breaths came ragged and uneven as he tried to recover from the blow. Haern paced before the two, pausing only to kick the great sword out of reach.

"If you'd only surrendered, you'd have spared yourself the pain," Thren said, bent down so he could stare into Jorakai's eyes.

Haern had hoped for surrender, maybe exhaustion or hopelessness in Jorakai's response. Instead, he heard laughter, and he knew they would need to earn their answers that night.

Fingers touched his shoulder, and he turned to see Delysia there, withdrawing her hand to wrap both around her waist as she watched, her upper body hunched as if she were cold.

"Give me one moment," she said, her red hair taking on a bluish tone in the moonlight. "I will not stop you, but I may at least reduce the torment he must suffer."

Haern stepped out of her way and gestured for her to continue. Thren eyed her warily, but he said nothing as she knelt down above Jorakai, her hands lying flat on either side of his face. The paladin glared up at her, his smile momentarily fading.

"What is this?" he asked, his voice hoarse. "A priestess of Ashhur come to join the fun?"

She ignored him and instead dipped her head and closed her eyes. Words of a prayer slipped from her lips, soft and indiscernible. Light glowed around her fingertips, then rolled over her hands and onto his face as if it were made of liquid. It settled on his lips, waiting, and then when he breathed in, the light slipped between his lips and vanished down his throat.

"I cannot make him speak," she said, rising to her feet. "But when he does, he may only speak the truth."

She walked past them, and Haern reached out to take her hand. She let him, smiling faintly, then pulled away so she could return to the road. Haern watched her go, then brought his attention back to his father, who was gesturing for him to come nearer.

"Your swords," he said.

Haern hesitated, an irrational fear of a trap soaring through him, but he fought it down and then handed over one of his blades. Thren took it, flipped it around, and then jammed it through Jorakai's right palm. As the man screamed, Thren gestured again.

"The other."

He almost didn't give it to him. Almost.

Now with both of Jorakai's hands pinned to the ground, Thren rose to his feet, his own short swords twirling in his hands.

"I want to make this perfectly clear," Thren told him. "You will suffer greatly tonight, though for how long is up to you. If you cooperate, it will only be minutes. If you don't, it will be hours." He smiled at Jorakai. "And if you piss me off, I will make it days. I know ways to hurt a man without killing him, dozens, really. If I must, I will try every single one, break every bone, tear every muscle, stab your eyes, your lips, tear your genitals from your body with my bare hands...I'll do it all, do you understand?"

Jorakai was laughing through it all, just laughing.

"You damn fools," he said. "Nothing but damn fools."

Thren smiled right back.

"We'll see."

He began his work, starting with dislocating fingers. Haern watched, a rock building in his stomach. He told himself this was a man who deserved no better, a servant of a dark god, but it mattered little as the man's screams grew louder. Those screams only paused when Thren would ram his elbow into the man's throat, constantly keeping his breathing ragged and uneven.

"We need to get inside the Stronghold," Thren told him when he paused for a moment to put away one of his swords. "The building must have a weakness, a secret entrance or a lapse in the patrols. I want to know when and where."

Still laughing. Jorakai was still laughing.

"You don't understand," he said, even as he struggled to breathe. "You won't break me. You'll never break me."

Thren glanced over his shoulder, and his worried look was enough. Delysia's spell was supposed to keep him from lying. Did that mean Jorakai spoke the truth, or merely that he *believed* it to be true?

"Most men claim they can't be broken," Thren said, taking his other sword and pressing it against Jorakai's left eye. "Most men are wrong."

"I am the servant of the Lion, the sharpened claw to rake the world," Jorakai said. "What you'll do to me... do you think I have not undergone worse? In the pits of the Stronghold, we are made pure. There we are broken and remade strong. There is nothing you can do, *nothing,* that will match the black fires that have seared my skin and the teeth that shredded me down to the bone."

Laughing, still laughing.

"You will never breach the Stronghold," he said. "It is built for war and guarded as if it were the greatest of treasures. Whatever you want in there, you won't get it, you hear me, you bastards? You. Won't. Get it."

Thren ripped out his eye anyway, then tossed the orb over his shoulder so that it landed at Haern's feet.

"I think," he said, "we have made a mistake."

When Jorakai's screams stopped, he resumed his mocking.

"The windows are barred," he said. "The doors always guarded. There are no gates, no tunnels, nothing but that front entrance. Who is it you seek there, you fools? One of us? Or do you think you'll take our gold and jewels?"

Out went the other eye.

"Nothing for you," Jorakai screamed. "Nothing but a death far worse than mine. Go there, I beg of you. Go willingly into the hands of my brethren and their pits. What I suffered for weeks, you will suffer for *decades*."

Thren abandoned his short sword, instead drawing a thin knife from his belt and beginning to work. After finishing with the face, he moved downward. He cut and thrust, opening up the man's belly so he could reach his hands inside. Jorakai could no longer laugh, only scream as Thren shouted.

"You think *I* will suffer?" he asked. "You think I fear your pits and lions? Your home is a home like any other, and I will break into it. I will find the man within who has toyed with my life and manipulated me like a pawn in his fucking game!"

Haern put his hand on his father's shoulder.

"Enough," he said. "Let him die."

Jorakai's face had turned pale, and Haern knew he'd pass out soon enough from the pain. His empty eye sockets looked up to the stars, and the sight of them reminded Haern of the Widow's victims from months before. To find him party to one doing the same filled him with unease.

"He deserves worse," Thren said, refusing to look back at him.

"It doesn't matter if he does. We'll gain nothing from him. Let him die."

Thren stood, his hands slick with blood, so red they seemed to glow in the night.

"If you want him dead, then you kill him," he said. "Otherwise,

I want this bastard to suffer. However slim the connection, he is part of what is happening in Veldaren, and we need to send a message."

"What message?" Haern asked. "Who will know of his death? Who will see it? This is for your own enjoyment, nothing else, so don't lie to me, nor to yourself."

Thren froze, his eyes meeting Haern's, and they were filled with fire. Haern felt a tingle travel down his spine, and more than anything, he wished to have his swords in his hands.

"You of all people are the last allowed to say that to me," he said, his voice dropping, his words shaking with intensity. "Not you, not a man who is a living lie. Deep down, past the cloak and the hood and all your protective shadows, I know the monster you truly are. Never again, you understand? Never dare tell me that again. No matter what this man says, we'll go to the Stronghold, we'll break inside, and we'll find our prey. No building is impenetrable, not to us. Now clean up your mess."

With that, he walked away, leaving Haern alone with the dying man. Jorakai was breathing slowly now, each one accompanied by a wheeze due to the damage of his throat. Haern put his foot on a wrist, then withdrew the blade stabbed through the palm. He stared down into those two bloodied caves that were now the paladin's eyes.

"Why did your god try to manipulate us?" Haern asked him. "Why would he work with the Sun Guild to help move them into Veldaren?"

Jorakai's lips peeled back into a gruesome smile. Several teeth were missing from where Thren had pried them out with a knife.

"I cannot decide if you're deluded or merely stupid," he said, coughing and spitting blood to the side. "I don't know who you are. I don't know where you're from. Whatever you think happened, Karak had nothing to do with it. No priest or paladin worthy of their title would aid the Sun Guild."

Haern was again perplexed. How could that not be a lie? Luther had worked with Grayson in organizing the Sun Guild's initial arrival to Veldaren. So, unless they'd been lied to before...

"The priest named Luther," Haern said. "Tell me where he is, and I'll give you mercy."

The paladin let out a chuckle.

"Mercy? Why should I want your mercy?"

Haern knelt down, and he felt a shadow cross over his soul.

"You may have my mercy," he said, "and if not, I will have Thren return so he may resume his work. Your choice."

Jorakai let out a sigh, and his entire body seemed to relax.

"So be it," he said. "Luther is a disgrace, an insult to our order. We are holding him in the highest room of the Stronghold as our prisoner."

The words left him stunned.

"Prisoner?" Haern asked.

"Prisoner," Jorakai said. "Are you satisfied?"

Disgraced? Prisoner? Suddenly, his earlier confusion clarified. What if the priests and paladins of Karak were in the dark when it came to Luther's actions? Given Jorakai's reaction to the idea, it had a sort of logic to it. Did Luther hide his involvement for fear of retribution from his brethren? Or were his actions the reason for his imprisonment? Above all, what would cause a priest of Karak to risk so much that he'd hide his plan from his own order?

Even more unsettled, Haern placed the tip of his sword against Jorakai's throat.

"Thank you," said the paladin. "Send me to my god. Let me find succor in his embrace."

"I've seen the Lion," Haern told him. "You'll find no succor, not with him. Only fire."

He thrust, twisted the sword, then pulled it free. The paladin bucked for a moment as he failed to draw breath, and Haern watched until the body fell still. He felt no pleasure, but no shame either, no guilt. Just exhaustion.

Yanking free his other blade, he held both out wide and looked up to the stars, to where he pictured Ashhur looking down upon him.

"What we do, is it madness?" he asked. "Is it wrong?"

There was no answer, as he knew there wouldn't be. But deep down, the answer was obvious.

It'd taken both of them to handle a single paladin of Karak, and now they headed for their home, to where they were raised, trained, and sent out into the world to spread their order. What they did, it wasn't hopeless. It wasn't madness.

It was suicide.

"I do this for others, not myself," he insisted. "I do this to save those I love. I have to. Even my father...somewhere in there, he knows I am his son, and he's ready to die for me. It has to mean something. All of this. Luther, Thren, Delysia..."

There was no confirmation given to him, nothing but the blowing of a cold night wind across the blood on his blades.

CHAPTER

13

Ghost didn't know where he was going or even where he wanted to go, but he knew he had to keep moving. The pain was unbearable, his skin feeling as if it were constantly aflame. Not that he could see it, his eyes always watering from the pain. He tried brushing at his arms once, but that had only made the pain worse, so much worse. With each step he took, he cursed the damned wizard in yellow and the fire he'd bathed him in.

He was walking down a street; that was the one thing Ghost knew for sure. His eyes were locked on the ground, watching himself as he took step after step. With each one, it felt harder to move, his feet growing in weight. His stomach was tight, and even the slightest movement of his legs sent waves of pain bouncing throughout his body, overwhelming him, preventing him from even knowing the source exactly. Was it his arms, his legs, his face? Did it even matter?

At last, he could go no farther. He dropped to the ground,

and at the impact, he screamed. It must have been loud, for the scream made him feel better, if only momentarily. He rolled onto his back, and that helped a little. Lying there, he stared up at the night sky and wondered what the point of escaping the gentle touchers had been. They'd never hurt him, not like this. Perhaps because they couldn't. Perhaps because this much pain, this much fire, meant he would soon die.

Ghost closed his eyes. At that moment, death sounded like a fine alternative.

"Mister, are you…oh gods, mister, who did this to you?"

Despite the pain, Ghost cracked a smile and laughed.

"That bastard in yellow," he said, not bothering to open his eyes. He was dying, he was certain of it now. Better to fade away, to pass in his sleep, the waves of pain carrying him off to an ocean of fire or pearl or whatever it was eternity had waiting for him.

"Yellow?" asked another voice.

"I don't know, he looks…"

And then the voices faded, and he knew darkness, but not for long. Movement, something lifting him, multiple hands on his arms and legs. He opened his eyes once, and he realized he was screaming again. It was odd, for he could not hear it, but he knew he was. He had to be. His lungs burned, his throat tense, his mouth open, and in the distance, he heard a sound that just maybe might be him…

When he awoke, he lay on a bed and was dressed in a simple robe that felt like little more than a white sheet sewn together with three holes left at the top. His tongue felt swollen, his throat parched. Something was missing, he knew, and he felt afraid to move as he looked around, as if movement might awaken whatever was missing. And then he realized what it was. The pain was gone. Somehow, it was gone.

"Gods damn it all," Ghost said, and he sat up, taking in more of his surroundings. He was in a small room lacking any decorations, and the only furnishing beyond his bed was a chamber pot in the opposite corner. The walls appeared to be made of a pale stone, and above him was a small window with light streaming in. The place felt familiar, but it was still taking him time to figure out where. There were cobwebs in his mind, and a distorted feeling, like a reminder that a great amount of time had passed since he fell in the road. The daylight in the window alone helped confirm that.

There were no signs of his clothes, and Ghost felt panic when he saw his weapons were missing as well. The panic ebbed when he realized how foolish it was to think whoever had kept him alive would suddenly wish to do him harm. Ebbed but never vanished. So many times, the gentle touchers had come with their bandages, sewing kits, and alcohol, fixing him up, allowing him to heal, all so they could start anew in a week's time, eager to try something different on his chained body. The window was tall and thin, and for all he knew, the door was barred from the outside.

Ghost lay back onto the bed, and he took a deep breath. He'd delayed long enough, but now he had to look. He had to know. Pulling back the blankets, he looked to his exposed arms, and he winced at the river of scars, pale white veins that swirled into one another to mark the fire's damage. Casting aside the rest of the sheet, he saw his legs were no better. Forcing his dry mouth to swallow, he closed his eyes and touched his face with his fingers, feeling along the skin of his cheeks and forehead. Even there, he felt the subtle change, the mark of deep scars.

"All over," he whispered, and he tried to decide how he felt.

Truth be told, he didn't even know. His physical appearance was not something he cared much for beyond what he could convey to others, to manipulate or frighten with the size of his muscles or the contrast of the white paint across his face. But for the burns to have healed already, the pain gone and replaced by scars, gave him a clue as to where he might be. Who else could possibly have such skill?

Gingerly, he swung his feet off the bed, stood, and then made his way to the door. Deep in his chest, he felt shame and embarrassment. Gods help him, how many times had he come there in desperate need of aid?

"Calan," he said, banging on the door. "Calan, I'm awake."

Twice more he had to knock before he heard movement from the other side. The door swung open, and a young priest stood in a hallway before him. Despite his best attempts to hide it, the boy was clearly disturbed by the sight of him.

"I will fetch the High Priest shortly," said the boy. "I was told to tell you to stay here when you awoke, while I go get him."

"Then go fetch him."

Ghost flung the door shut, then sat back down on his bed. He ran his hands along his arms, feeling the scars. More and more, it felt like his body was awakening, and with it his scars were beginning to itch. He desperately hoped it would stay that way, just an itch, and not the searing pain he dimly remembered.

Several minutes later, the door opened, and Calan stepped inside.

"I must say, this is hardly how I wished to meet you again," said the priest.

"I agree," Ghost said. He'd stood upon the old man's entrance, and now he felt unsure of what to do. By the Abyss, he didn't even have real clothes, just the thin sheet. So he sat back down, looked to his hands.

"How did I get here?" he asked.

"Two nights ago, some men found you in the middle of the road on their way home from a night of drinking," Calan said, sitting on his knees in front of Ghost and reaching out to take his left arm and examine it. Slowly, the priest ran his fingers along the scars, and a faint glow shimmered across the fingertips. With their passing, the growing itch faded away.

"They carried you here," he continued, switching to the right arm. "Well, carried might be generous. You're a large man, after all, so they more dragged than carried. They dumped you at the doors to our temple, waited until someone came for you, and then left."

"I suppose I should be grateful."

"Given the condition you were in, you should be glad they didn't leave you for dead," Calan said. "It wouldn't have taken much longer, I assure you."

Ghost let out a sigh.

"Forgive me . . . and did you say two nights ago?"

Calan nodded.

"You've been in my care all the while. Ashhur's blessing has allowed me to keep you asleep through the pain and recovery." He turned Ghost's arm over, and he ran a finger over one of the deeper scars. "I'm sorry, Ghost; I did my best, but the burns were so terrible and covered so much of you. I could do nothing about the scars."

"A mirror," Ghost said. "Do you have a mirror?"

Calan met his gaze.

"I'd suggest you wait a bit longer before that," he said.

The answer did little to ease Ghost's mind.

"If you insist," he said.

"I do," Calan said, now moving to the legs. More blue-white

light swelled on his fingers, barely perceptible. "Do you know who did this to you?"

"Whoever they are," Ghost said, "it is of no business of yours."

Calan stopped what he was doing, and he stood.

"If you do not trust me, then so be it," he said. "You are healthy enough to leave this place. Go and do so with my blessing, but I have others who need my attention, and should go to them instead."

"Wait," Ghost said, before he could go. "Please, forgive me. Just, having you help me makes me feel...ashamed. I will better control my tongue, I promise."

Calan hesitated, then returned, standing before Ghost, and he put both his hands on Ghost's face.

"I can do little to help the scars," he said. "But I will do what I can, at least for your face. This will hurt, but I trust you can handle a bit of pain."

Ghost closed his eyes and waited for it to begin. Calan began whispering words of a prayer, and then he felt it, a sharp tingling as if spiders were crawling across his face, each one with little hooks at the ends of their feet. The sensation increased, and he heard a ringing in his ears so loud, it overwhelmed Calan's prayers. Sudden as it began, it ceased. Ghost opened his eyes, and the priest took a step back to observe his handiwork.

"Better," he said. "I'm sorry, Ghost; this is the best that I can do."

He reached into his pocket and produced a small circular looking glass. Ghost accepted it and, refusing to show any reluctance, held it up before his eyes.

The scars ran over every inch of his face, starting from the top of his head down to the base of his neck. The work of

Calan's magic was evident, for the skin, while raised, was not discolored like the rest of his body. It still gave his entire face a sickly, distorted look, and he put away the glass, unwilling to look at it more.

"My things," he said. "Where are my things?"

"Just outside your door," Calan said. "Your clothes were burned beyond repair, but we purchased you replacements that should fit well enough. As for your swords, though, you will have to wait until you are ready to leave."

"I'm ready now."

"Are you sure you would not prefer something to eat first?"

The rock in Ghost's stomach shifted, reminding him of just how long it'd been since he ate or drank. But staying inside the temple was something Ghost just could not handle right now.

"I'll swing by the market," he said. "Thank you for what you've done."

"Of course," Calan said, though he did not step aside, instead leaning his weight against the door so that he blocked the way. He stayed there, arms crossed, examining Ghost.

"The man who burned you," he said. "Were you trying to kill him?"

This was it, of course, what the priest wanted. Ghost swallowed down an exasperated sigh.

"Yes," he said. "I was."

"Did you want to?"

The question was so odd, and not what he expected. He opened his mouth to answer, then paused so he might think it over and answer truthfully. The priests had clearly done much for him. Was it really so much to ask in return to tell him the truth?

"No," he said.

"Then why? For money?"

Ghost shook his head.

"I do this because I must, priest. I owe someone my life, my life and beyond. She saved me from the darkness, pulled me out. Killing is what I'm good at. It's what I'm *best* at, and if I must kill a few more times before I am free, then I will do so to repay my debt."

Calan continued staring at him with his soft blue eyes, and then abruptly stepped aside.

"If you feel you must, then so be it," he said. "Though if I were you, I'd ask myself if this woman has truly saved you from darkness, or merely pulled you from one and thrown you into another."

"Stop it," Ghost said. "Stop judging me; stop staring at me like you can see everything I am. You'd condemn me for kill-ing…then why save me, Calan? Why, if you knew the reason for my injuries? No one held a sword to your neck. No one forced you to heal these wounds."

The songs Melody had sung when she was down there, her cries of faith, he remembered the few which spoke of Ashhur, of the anger and abandonment. Calan seemed nothing like the cowardly god Melody had decried, yet at the same time, he acted hypocritical, condemning him for his deeds yet still healing him to do them once again. It left Ghost baffled and furious.

"Listen well," Calan said. "If you wish to see the measure of a man, do not judge him by how he reacts to your successes. Judge him by how he reacts to your failures. Ashhur teaches us that if we see a man fall, we reach down our hand so they may take it and stand again."

He gestured to the door.

"Your clothes and swords await you," he said. "Go, return to the lady who saved you. See the truth of whom you've sworn your life to, and how great your debt truly is."

Calan left him, and he offered nothing else at his departure. Ghost stepped out the door, took his clothes and dressed. They were simple enough, brown pants and a white shirt that was surprisingly too large. His boots had survived, though, and as he strapped them on last, he let out a deep breath.

Ghost had always considered himself wise, never stubborn, never one to close his eyes to the brutal truth of the world. The priest's words left him disturbed, and there would be only one way to solve it. Out the door he went, into the hallway. He found the same boy from earlier keeping watch, and when he asked, the boy pointed him toward the entrance. Ghost walked across the red carpet, his weight causing his boots to sink into it, leaving deep imprints after his passing. When he stepped into the main worship hall, he hooked to his left, and at the grand doors surrounded by pillars, a young priest waited, two swords in his arms.

"Take them, though I pray you have no need of them," said the priest.

"You'll be praying for a long time, then," Ghost said, and he strode out of the temple, down the steps, and then hurried north, to the Gemcroft family mansion.

With his clothes new, and his face lacking any paint, he strode unworried up to the mansion's front gates and demanded the guards there deliver a message for him.

"Don't see much reason why we should," said one of the guards, sniffing.

"The choice is yours," said Ghost, "but I will come again, and again, until Melody knows. When she discovers a message she has waited for was delayed because of your laziness, tell me, how do you think she will react?"

The two guards glanced at one another, and the one on the right shrugged.

"Fine," he said. "What's your message?"

"Tell her a ghost waits for her in the market."

The left guard lifted an eyebrow.

"That's it?"

"That's it. She'll understand."

With that, he walked away, toward the nearby market to wait. He searched his pockets, and sure enough, the coin Bill Trett had given him was still there. Pulling out the bag to scan within, he saw that they'd not even taken a single piece to cover the cost of the healing, or to replace his clothes. Shaking his head, he drew out a handful of coins, bought a meat pie from a portly man at a stall, and then found himself a vacant spot against a wall to eat. He wolfed the food down, each bite seemingly making him hungrier. His appetite was like a dormant beast, suddenly awakened. When finished, he returned to the stall, bought another, and finished it as fast as the first.

Finally sated, he crossed his arms, leaned his head back against the wall, and watched the men and women as they passed. Envy built in his chest as the time dragged on, childish as it was. A woman browsed a nearby stand, bickering over the cost of apples while her son tugged on her hand, crying against some surely horrible slight. Two skinny men passed by in front of him, each with the four-pointed star on their sleeves. They were laughing, one of them telling a story to the other. Young and old, those browsing, those hoping to steal, all able to live within the day. All in their own world, focused on primal needs like food and a warm place to sleep. Who of them could understand what it meant to be in darkness for years, stuck with needles and knives, bleeding, always bleeding...

And then he saw the one woman who could understand. Melody Gemcroft casually drifted through the market, browsing with a slender bag on her left arm and a wide violet hat atop her head. She looked like any other well-to-do woman, and she smiled just as easily. For a moment, Ghost looked once more to the market, to those he had dismissed so quickly, and wondered how many others hid their pain and past as well as Melody hid hers.

"It's a fine day to take in the sights, isn't it?" Ghost asked her as she walked past. She glanced his way, and he could tell she had something pleasant yet dismissive to say to him. The comment died when her eyes met his and she realized who he was.

"No paint," he said. "I'm sure that made it more difficult."

"Nor the hair on your face when I last saw you," she said, crossing her hands before her and smiling as if she'd just met a long lost friend. "What you did was dangerous. Zusa suspects me already, and if she can use you to...my god, Ghost, what happened to your arms?"

Ghost grinned at her, hardly surprised it took her so long to notice.

"You sent me after a wizard who likes to play with fire," he said. "Did you not think I might get burned?"

He'd thought she'd be gruff, uncaring of his wounds. So many men and women he'd done jobs for had been like that, viewing him as an expendable tool, a walking killing machine they fed with coins and forgot about when the job was done. Melody, however, grimaced with pain and took his hands in his.

"Your face, too," she said, looking up at him. "Forgive me, Ghost, I thought you could kill them with ease. Your reputation spoke so highly of you."

"Consider me still working to remove the rust."

He swallowed, and strangely enough, he realized he was nervous. This was something he had little experience about. As a mercenary, he'd never before failed to kill a target once they'd been found. In truth, the Watcher had been the first. Now that he was to tell Melody, he felt anxious, but why?

Judge him by how he reacts to your failures.

"Melody," he said, glancing about to make sure no one was close enough to overhear. "I'm sorry, but I cannot do this. The wizard is too powerful, and by all rights, I should be dead. Even with surprise, he defeated me, and now he will be prepared. I will help you with the others, but in this, I have failed you."

Ghost did not know how she might react. Having others around in the market made it even harder to predict. But out of all his guesses, pity was the farthest from his mind, yet she took a step closer and put a hand on his scarred face.

"You poor thing," she said. "Your time in the pit has left your soul broken, hasn't it? But I can look in your eyes and see buried in you a man who would never admit defeat. We must free him once again."

Ghost frowned, confused.

"I don't understand," he said.

"You will. Follow me."

She took his hand, and it surprised him further. She was a pale thing of white next to him, her hand dwarfed in the black of his own, and the looks they received were far from flattering. Melody leading the way, they left the market and traveled east, heading deep into the wealthiest parts of Veldaren. The traffic thinned out more and more until they were alone on the road, approaching a secluded area built close to the eastern section of the stone wall surrounding the city. Before what appeared to be nothing more than a dark mansion encircled by tall iron gates, Melody stopped, and she looked to either side to ensure no one watched.

"I see through your illusions," she whispered, putting her hands on the gate. She beckoned he do the same, and still confused, Ghost obeyed.

"I see through your illusions," he repeated.

Immediately, the house before him changed, and he let out a gasp. It was a towering building, just as large as the temple to Ashhur, yet it was built with black marble, and leading toward it across the grass was a walkway of obsidian. Rows of pillars lined the exterior. Carved lions roared from either side of the entrance, mouths open, teeth bared. The light of the day seemed denied to it, a shadow cast across the entirety of the building with no discernible source.

"Welcome home," Melody said as the gate opened, and she stepped inside.

Ghost had never considered himself afraid of anything, and only that stubborn pride allowed him to follow without hesitation. Even through his boots, it felt as if the obsidian beneath his feet were warm, uncomfortably so. At the temple, the doors opened before their arrival, and an elderly man with gray hair and deep black robes stepped out, nodding his head in respect.

"Lady Melody, you are most welcome as always," said the man. "May we know the name of your guest before we permit him entrance?"

"I have none," Ghost said, before Melody could answer for him. "Mine was lost long ago."

The priest looked him over carefully, then nodded.

"Even the nameless may find comfort within our walls, if their hearts are true," he said. "Come. Do you wish to speak with Pelarak?"

"With Daverik, actually," Melody said as they stepped through the doors. "Tell him I must meet with him in the room of purity."

Ghost followed, and they passed through a cramped entranceway and into a grand worship hall. So much of it felt like a mirrored image of the temple to Ashhur, yet when he entered the hall, he felt his breath catch in his throat. Towering over everyone was a statue lit by violet flames that put off no smoke. It was of Karak, he had no doubt, for who else could it be? The god was carved of stone, the likeness frightening in its lifelike pose, in the raw power conveyed by that raised fist defying the heavens. What looked like fresh blood stained the statue's greaves, and more dripped from the serrated sword Karak held. He looked beautiful yet dangerous, powerful and unrelenting. The very thought of standing in Karak's presence in the ancient times, when he supposedly walked the land, filled him with both wonder and terror.

Melody slowly approached the statue, and the guide allowed it. On either side were many pews, and several younger men sat in them, lost in prayer. The sound was like nails scraping against his spine. How he wished they might sing a song like Melody sang instead. Bringing his attention back to her, he saw her kneeling before the statue, head bowed, a single hand lifted above her, timid as a child as she touched the very foot of the statue. It lingered there but a moment before she stood, and when she turned back to him tears were in her eyes.

"I am ready," she said.

Several corridors led out from the grand hall, and through one of them they exited, the path slowly slanting downward. Ghost felt as if he were descending into the pit of the world, with their only light that of the purple torches that burned on either side, letting off no heat, no smoke, just a glow whose very presence filled him with unease. Deeper and deeper they went, until they reached an abrupt stop at a door. Their guide opened it, revealing within a simple square room, its brick walls barren, its floor empty. Inside was an even deeper darkness, lit by two torches that burned at the center of the ceiling.

Ghost nearly turned away and left. Entering that room was a bad idea, he knew it, but Melody was so peaceful and seemed so earnest to help him. Calan's challenge remained in his mind, and deep down, he wanted to know how this woman who had sung him to sleep for hundreds of nights would react to his failure.

Melody stepped into the room as if oblivious to his hesitation, walking to the center before sitting on the bare floor.

"Daverik will join you soon enough," said their guide. With that, he left. Berating himself for his cowardice, Ghost stepped into the room, sitting opposite Melody. The floor was cold, and he kept his arms crossed over his chest to keep warm.

"Where are we?" he asked her.

"The room of purity," she said. "It is a special place within the temple. It's said Karak himself meditated here for days as he prepared for his holy war against his brother, and his tears have blessed the very stone with his power. Be careful what you say and do here, Ghost. We've left the realm of man. Veldaren's king has no power here, only the true King."

The door opened, and in stepped a bald man, his features sharp, his large lips pulling back into a smile as he offered Melody his hand so she might kiss it. Following him into the room was a startling sight, a woman dressed similar to Zusa, only her face was fully covered but for an open slit across her eyes, and even that had a thin strip of white cloth to hide her features. She was taller than Zusa, too, and moved with an easy grace, her hands always close by the hilts of her daggers belted to her waist. Ghost figured the man to be Daverik, though he could only guess as to the strangely dressed woman.

"Welcome to this sacred place," Daverik said, turning to Ghost. "Melody has told me of your purpose. You are Luther's executioner."

"I suppose," said Ghost, hiding his confusion. Luther? Who

was this Luther? And Zusa, the Eschaton, the Watcher...were these people Luther wanted dead, and not Melody?

"But he has failed," Melody said, rising to her feet. "He tells me the wizard's power is greater than his own."

"Is this true?" Daverik asked.

Ghost almost denied it. He could try again, find new ways to surprise Tarlak Eschaton and his oafish friend. But Calan's wisdom kept echoing in his mind, and despite his fear, despite the chill of the floor beneath him and the cold wind that somehow blew softly from the corners of the sealed room, he vowed to continue to the bitter end.

"It is true," he said.

"I suppose I should not be surprised," Daverik said. "And the Watcher defeated you years ago as well, did he not?"

"He did," Ghost said, and the words were ash on his tongue.

Daverik paced before him, hands behind his back. He looked lost in thought, puzzling over something.

"What will you do, now that you have abandoned your task?" he asked him.

"If I am of no more use, I would travel west," Ghost said. "Find a life for myself somewhere, in a place where I no longer must wear paint on my face."

Daverik ceased his pacing.

"Your life was sworn to Karak," he said. "And such vows can never be escaped."

He opened his hand, and suddenly it felt like every bone in Ghost's body weighed a thousand stone. Trying to draw his swords was like lifting a boulder with a lone finger. He collapsed onto his back, gasping for air. The very act of lifting his chest was a burden. The muscles in his neck and arms bulged as he tried to stand, to fight against whatever foul magic was upon him, but he could not pull his body from the stone.

Above him, Daverik resumed his pacing.

"There are too many like you in this world," he said. "Willing to abandon everything at the first struggle. Willing to sacrifice vows, beliefs, anything and everything sacred and blessed to avoid risks, to shed no blood, to give up nothing of meaning. But you are too powerful to be so weak, Ghost. There is a brilliant soul within you, aching for meaning, for purpose. And I will free it for you."

Daverik leaned down so they might stare eye to eye. Ghost struggled, wanting to do nothing more than strike the man across the face, but he was helpless.

"I will make you serve," the priest whispered. "I will grant you power untold and a responsibility to use it that matches such power. And when you taste victory, when you hear the Lion whisper to you, 'Well done, my son,' then you will thank me for what I am about to do."

He stepped away, and Ghost stared up at the ceiling. Above him were the two torches, and he realized now that there was more to the ceiling. Faint white lines were drawn across it, forming a powerful feline shape. The torches were the eyes of the Lion, and they burned down at him, and it was at them he stared until Daverik's hand settled upon his face. Even through the fingers, he still saw the eyes burning.

"Karak, my god, hear me," said the priest. "Here in your presence, I present to you my offering."

The fire grew, and in the far distance, Ghost heard the roar of a lion. The sound sent a chill throughout his body, and more than ever, he wished he could move, wished he could scream. Beside him, he heard Melody praying, her beautiful voice no longer a comfort, her song just as terrifying as the low growl that came from behind his head. All sense of time left him, and it seemed Melody's prayers became an unending chorus, punctuated only by Daverik's demands for order, for retribution. Brighter and brighter the fire burned, the lion above him closer, angrier. Many times he heard it roar, and within its mouth he saw the reaches of eternity.

Say your name.

He didn't know who asked him, didn't know from where the sound came. The voice was deep and cold. Its rumblings pulled him from his dream-sleep, reawakening an awareness of the floor beneath him, the torches above, the touch of Daverik's hand against his face, and how hoarse Melody's voice had grown from her singing.

"I don't know it," he answered, his own voice a whisper.

Then what are you?

What was he? What else could he be? After years in the dungeons, after a lifetime knowing only murder and payment?

"Ghost."

As you are called, then so shall you be.

The darkness swallowed him. The roar of the Lion overwhelmed him. Only the twin torches remained, furious eyes burning violet. From Daverik's touch at his forehead he felt electricity piercing him, traveling down his spine, and into his arms and legs. He flailed, unable to fight the motions. Everything burned with pain, and when he opened his mouth to scream, he swore he saw smoke exhaling from his lungs. If his cry made a sound, it was pitiful and insignificant, the Lion's roar easily drowning it out so it went unheard, at least by him. He wanted to pass out, begged for unconsciousness to take him, yet it felt as if the pain would find him even there, overwhelming his dreams, piercing the unconscious veil.

"Your life is Karak's," he heard Daverik say. "And no matter the cost, you *will* repay your debt."

The hand vanished, and with it went the pain. Ghost let out

a gasp, the sudden calm just as startling. His body felt his own now, and he stood with ease. Gradually, his sight returned to him, and he saw Daverik beside him in the center of the room, with Melody and the faceless woman safely by the door. All three appeared exhausted, Daverik in particular.

"What did you do to me?" Ghost asked the priest.

"I gave you the strength to complete your task," he said, and he sounded out of breath. "As well as motivation to ensure you do not try to abandon your obligations."

"Obligations?" said Ghost. "I suffered through that, and you think I'll keep up my *obligations?*"

He drew one of his swords and took a step forward, but Daverik lifted his hand. It was a simple motion, like one might use to dismiss a child, yet to Ghost, it was the hand of a god blasting him backward. He flew, his sword falling from his grip. As he fell back, he braced for hitting the wall...but then he was through the wall, and all he saw was darkness. Panic struck him in his chest, and he struggled to move, crawling forward as if he were in freezing water. With a gasp, he emerged back into the room, stepping out with clothes perfectly clean and free of the dirt and stone he knew he'd just been struggling through. He fell to his knees, relieved to be where his vision made sense, where his senses of touch and smell weren't overwhelmed with strange sensations.

"I don't believe it," he said, staring at the floor.

As you are called, then so shall you be.

Ghost. It was no longer a name. No longer a disguise.

Melody walked over, and slowly she knelt beside him and put a hand on his shoulder. The touch was strangely loving, and he looked to her, torn between asking for forgiveness and trying to rip out her throat before Daverik could react. She said nothing, only reached into his pocket and pulled out the container of paint she'd given him before. With a pop she opened it, then held it out for him to take.

"Put it on," she said. "This is what you are, what you were always meant to be."

He took it from her, dipped a hand into the white. As he smeared it across his face, he swore it burned far worse than it ever had before. That done, he stood, retrieved his sword, and glared at Daverik.

"You tread dangerous ground," he told him.

"In this age, we all walk in danger," Daverik said. "You no less than others." He turned to Melody. "Alyssa's stubbornness will be our undoing. We have no more time to wait, Melody. Ghost, Deborah, the two of you will go and kill her protector. Once Zusa is dead, overthrowing Alyssa will be a sure thing."

"I don't need his help," Deborah said, glaring at Ghost.

"She defeated all of you together," Daverik said. "Keep your pride to yourself. You'll need Ghost's help with this."

Ghost looked to his hands, covered with paint. His feeling in them was already fading. It was like a limb falling asleep, only across his entire body. Panic pounded in his heart, but he did his best to hide it.

"No," he said.

Daverik crossed his arms, and despite Ghost's defiance, he seemed only amused.

"No?" he asked.

"No," Ghost repeated. "I won't do this. I am not your slave."

"I don't think you understand," Daverik said, taking a step closer. "But this will help. Speak it again. Tell me you refuse to kill those Melody instructed you to kill."

"I will not kill Zusa, nor the Watcher, nor the Eschaton," he said.

The moment the words were gone from his lips, he felt a pain stabbing him in the forehead. It was incredible, like a metal spike jamming through his skull and into his mind. Emotions flooded forth, panic, terror, anger, and helplessness. Again, he dropped to his knees, and he let out a scream that this time echoed on and on in the cramped space.

"There is now a curse upon your body, Ghost," said the priest. "Should you fail at your task, it will take your life. You have no choice in this. If I were you, I'd control my thoughts. Even the temptation to disobey will prove...uncomfortable."

That was it, then. His choice was made for him, all because he followed Melody down into the pit. He glared at her, wishing her could make her suffer for betraying his trust, but she only smiled back at him.

"Soon, you'll know," she said. "Offer up yourself as sacrifice. There is such beauty in the surrender."

Ghost rose back to his feet, swearing a vow that made his head ache just by the thinking of it.

I will never surrender. Not to you. Not to anyone.

"Go," Daverik said. "Both of you. Kill Zusa so we may prepare the way."

Deborah cast him a foul look, then turned to leave. Ghost thought of making his way back through the tunnel, past the great statue of Karak, and decided anything would be better than that. Taking a deep breath, he leaped, his hands reaching for the sky. As he thought, the stone ceiling was nothing to him, and he rose and rose, dirt and rock passing across his eyes, and somehow he could see it, though he knew there was no light for him to see. At last, he tore up through the very street, not far from the iron gates. It was dark now, and he wondered just how long he had lain on the cold stone floor. Upon reaching the night air, he felt his ascension cease, and he hit the ground with a satisfying thud. Glancing east, he saw the telltale signs of the rising sun. *All night?* he wondered. What had felt like mere moments of agony, of having the spells branded upon him, had taken all day and night.

Slowly he stood, staring at the temple, which was once more just a plain, well-crafted mansion. A plan forming in his mind, he waited until Deborah emerged from the mansion's door. She quickly saw him, and still frowning, she went to his side.

"I'll have no need of you," she said, "but Daverik insists. Are you ready to kill for our god?"

She didn't even wait for his answer, just turned and ran down the street. Ghost smiled, feeling the paint cracking on his face.

"Yes," he lied, following her into the morning light.

CHAPTER
14

King Edwin Vaelor had just blown out the last candle in his bedroom when he heard a man clear his throat. He froze, sudden fear paralyzing him where he stood. The little orange dot that was the candlewick slowly faded out, completing the darkness.

"Who's there?" Edwin asked. His room was large, without windows. Too easy for someone to climb in. All day and night, guards watched the doors to his room. No one should have been inside, yet when a soft chuckle greeted his words, there was no doubt that someone was.

"I've been curious to meet you," said the invader, ignoring the question. The voice came from his large four-poster bed, and when Edwin took a step back, the man shimmered into view. His ears were maimed, and he wore a long dark coat, his shirt and pants a pale gray. Both hands were resting easily on his lap as he sat on his bed. Edwin could not puzzle out where the light was coming from, for it just seemed that amid the darkness, there was the elf, as if his very skin and coat glowed the softest of colors.

"Scream and you'll die," said the elf, tapping his fingers on the hilts of his swords.

Edwin almost did anyway, nearly shrieked for his guards to come and rescue him, but the elf's tone was so commanding, so certain of itself, that he kept his mouth shut.

"Excellent. You're capable of behaving. That's a good sign, Edwin. If you continue this, then you might live through the coming months."

"Who are you?" Edwin asked as the elf rose to his feet, still atop the bed. He seemed so thin, but what muscle was there looked corded and tight, a feline predator eager to pounce on its prey.

"You should know if your advisors are worth anything, or if you would bother to listen to them if they are. I am Muzien the Darkhand, come from Mordeina, and you and I must have a few words. Between us, I would like there to be an understanding."

Edwin felt a tremble work its way up and down his neck.

"I do know," he said. "You came here from the west. Gerand assured me you would be no more a bother than any other of the guilds."

Muzien flashed him a smile.

"He was wrong."

Off the bed he jumped, landing silently mere feet away from the king at the foot of the bed. He did not draw his swords, yet Edwin tensed anyway, expecting to die, or at least to suffer some sort of horrible injury. Despite it, he did not cry out for guards, and he felt ashamed at his own cowardice.

"What...what do you want from me?" Edwin asked, trying to muster up some kernel of bravery.

Muzien took another step, his smile fading away. It felt like he was being analyzed, dissected with his innards revealed, and the elf did not appear impressed with what he found.

"You will continue to rule because I allow it," he said. "Not because of your soldiers, and not through your birthright. The Sun comes to Veldaren, and you will not interfere with its rise. At any time, I can kill you; do you understand? If you fear death, then stay clear of my path. Tell your soldiers to look the other way when they see the four-pointed star. They are not to investigate killings done with my mark left upon them. They will charge us no tariffs to enter the city, they will investigate none of my merchandise, and your tax collectors will never see a single coin come from my pocket. Am I clear, or must I carve it into your chest so you will remember?"

Edwin swallowed down what felt like a jagged stone in the back of his throat.

"I'll make sure my soldiers know," he said.

Muzien smiled.

"Not so hard, is it? Obedience will come naturally, I assure you, just as it does for all humans. You were never meant to lead, only serve."

He turned, leaped back onto the bed, and then continued to walk. Whatever light kept him visible faded away, and come the room's descent into total darkness, Edwin turned, ran toward the door, and beat his fists upon it as he screamed.

"*Guards!*"

The following morning, Guard Captain Antonil Copernus stood before the western wall of the castle, arms crossed over his chest as he glared at what he saw. Every few feet, forming a line that covered the entire wall's length, were stone tiles of the Sun

Guild, each one bearing their four-pointed star. They'd been placed sometime during the night, dug into the hard earth and then left for his guards to find come their morning patrols.

"What do you want us to do with them when we're done?" asked one of his soldiers as he knelt before a tile, trying and failing to get a grip around it with his fingers.

"Grab a shovel," Antonil said as five more guards showed up to help with the removal. "And hurl them outside the city from the wall. May not mean much, but a symbolic victory is still a victory."

"In this case, I'm afraid it is neither," said Gerand Crold, coming around the corner. He looked exhausted, the smile on his face clearly forced. Time had not been kind to Gerand, his hair now fully gray, deep wrinkles under his eyes made worse by the scar that ran from his left eye to his ear. When he talked, he sounded painfully tired.

"How so?" Antonil asked the king's advisor.

"Leave them," Gerand said, ignoring him and instead addressing the soldiers. "Put your shovels down and leave them where they lie."

Antonil grabbed Gerand's arm and pulled him away from his men.

"Care to tell me what's going on?" he asked.

"Unhand me and I will."

Antonil let go, and he took a step back, mad at himself for losing his temper.

"Forgive me," he said. "Now please, tell me what reason justifies leaving such blatant disrespect for our liege in plain view of the castle."

"If you think this is my doing, you're wrong," Gerand said. "I bring orders from King Edwin himself. The Sun Guild's to be untouched."

Antonil felt as if he'd been slapped by a metal gauntlet.

"Untouched? What does that mean, untouched?"

"It means exactly what it sounds like it means," Gerand said. "All markings of the Sun Guild remain where they are. No apprehending their members, no questioning their merchants, nothing."

"We're to let them have free rein of the city?" Antonil asked, stepping closer and lowering his voice. "Has the king gone mad?"

"Truthfully? Yes, he has." Gerand rubbed his eyes, which were painfully red. "I've been talking to him all night, Antonil, so whatever anger you have, you can stop directing it at me. I've never seen him this scared. Even Thren Felhorn didn't frighten him so badly as this Muzien bastard has."

"But you're asking me to tell my men not to do their jobs," Antonil insisted. "You're asking me to have them ignore their duties, and allow petty crimes to . . ."

"You still don't get it," Gerand said, shaking his head. "Petty crimes? A member of the Sun can stab one of your guards to death, and you're not to do a thing about it, Antonil. Have I made myself clear yet?"

Antonil fell silent. Gerand waited for him to respond, and when it was clear he wouldn't, he let out a sigh.

"Don't think of ignoring this edict, either," he said. "My orders are very clear. Anyone who antagonizes the Sun Guild in any way and therefore puts the life of His Majesty at risk will be permanently banished from the city. Not that I expect those who are banished to get very far. Muzien doesn't seem like the sort of fellow to let interlopers off lightly . . ."

"Gerand, you can't let him do this," Antonil said. He stared him in the eye, hoping that somewhere in him was an honorable man who knew such conditions could not be allowed to pass. "For the gods' sake, you're his advisor; he'll listen to you."

"And you're his protector, yet Muzien slipped past your guards and patrols right into the king's very bedroom," Gerand said. "If you'd done *your* job, I'd be able to do mine. But now the king is a frightened child doing anything and everything he can to stay alive. My words mean nothing, as does your indignation. The Sun Guild owns Veldaren now, Antonil, and if you hope to remain part of its population, then start swallowing that fact down through any means necessary."

With that, Gerand stormed away, mumbling to himself as he headed around the corner and back to the castle entrance. Antonil watched him go, ideas in his head slowly forming.

"Sir?" asked one of the soldiers beside the castle, and Antonil turned to see that all of them had stopped their work, waiting for his orders. He saw their loyalty, knew their opinions of the king. If he asked them to disobey, and march right through the gates of the Abyss, they'd follow with a song on their lips. But he would not ask that of them.

Yet.

"Leave the tiles be," he said. "Resume your morning duties."

They saluted, and he saluted back. That done, he knew he should gather together his captains and inform them of the king's unofficial edict, but there was something he had to do first. Unescorted, he walked down the street, leaving the castle far behind him. He saluted the soldiers he passed, did his best to hide the miserable feeling in his chest. All around him, he saw his citizens—men, women, and children who relied on him to keep them safe. Except safe was last thing they'd be unless they bent knee to a foreign elf instead of their own king.

Damn you, Muzien, Antonil thought. *Just you wait until the Watcher returns.*

Haern had come to him just before his departure from the city, letting him know things might grow a little more restless than usual while he was off doing whatever it was he planned on doing. Antonil knew not to ask where he went, only trusted the mysterious protector of Veldaren to be doing what needed to be done. Still, "restless" did not describe the upheaval taking place during the weeks of his absence. It wasn't chaos; it wasn't like the early days of the thief war with mercenaries storming the streets, fighting the guilds in open warfare. It wasn't even like Lord Victor's initial attempts at cleaning up the city. Everything about it felt too insidious, too inevitable. Street by street he walked, seeing stone tiles proclaiming the territory of the Sun Guild, and he knew there was painfully little he could do about it.

But he had to try, and that's why he arrived at Victor Kane's repurposed tavern and dipped his head in respect to the guards at the door.

"I wish to speak with your master," he said.

They did not have to ask who he was, his polished armor and royal tunic on his chest clearly labeling him as a servant of the king. One of the guards banged on the door, and when it opened, he spoke to the man within.

"Sir Antonil wishes to speak with Victor," said the guard.

The door shut, and moments later, it opened completely, and a soldier gestured for Antonil to enter. He did, stepping into the dimly lit tavern, only now it served just Victor and his men. Many of the tables had been pushed aside, leaving a wide-open space before the bar. As Antonil walked in, he noticed bloodstains on the floor, and in nearly shocking amounts. He knew there'd been a battle inside it before, when Thren made a move to kill Victor, but that was months ago. Surely it should have been cleared up by now.

"Welcome to my home," Victor said, sitting at one of the few remaining tables. He had two tall drinks before him, the glasses overflowing with foam, and he gestured for Antonil to take a seat. Antonil did so, and after hesitating, decided that despite the early hour, he really could go for a drink.

"So, what brings you here?" Victor asked, his own drink going untouched.

"Insanity," Antonil said, thudding his glass back down onto the wooden table. "Insanity brings me here. Insanity in my king, insanity in his advisors, insanity in the streets, the guilds, everywhere. The whole damn world's gone insane."

"Since entering Veldaren, I've often wondered if I'm the only sane person left," Victor said, grinning.

"That, or the only one insane enough to fight against the way the world is moving," Antonil said. "But in the end, it doesn't matter." He glanced over his shoulder, to the man guarding the door. "What I speak, no one but us must hear. Are we safe?"

Victor nodded.

"My men are loyal. Whatever you need to say, say it."

Antonil took in a deep breath, drank a bit more from his glass, and then let it out.

"I'm here to commit treason, Victor."

To his credit, Victor handled the news well enough.

"Go on," he said.

"Muzien and his Sun Guild have gotten to the king, and he's given them complete immunity in all things. My guards aren't to touch them, aren't even to give them strange looks no matter what crimes they commit. I swear, this whole city's rotting beneath me, and no matter how hard I try, the wood keeps peeling, the stones keep cracking. I won't let this happen. I won't sit back and watch my beloved city break. Not without a fight."

Victor pushed aside his alcohol and leaned forward on his elbows.

"What are you telling me?" he asked. There was no denying the eagerness in his voice, in the way his eyes shone.

"I can't fight Muzien, not openly," he said. "But I have men who are loyal, and access to the king's armory. If you'll stand against him, I will ensure you have soldiers and weapons for them to wield. Our nation has not fought a war in over a decade, but I feel this is the closest we will be in my lifetime. I have no intention of losing."

Antonil stood.

"You marched into this city proclaiming to cast out the men hiding in the shadows. By Karak, you even swore to remove the shadows themselves. Well, the city's only darkened, Victor, and I need all the help I can get. Will you accept? Will you put your neck on the line where I cannot?"

Victor pushed aside his own chair as he stood.

"You are a rope thrown to a drowning man," he said. "Give me soldiers, and I will save our city. I swear it upon my life and the honor of my family."

Antonil could hardly believe the words he was saying, but it felt good. Terrifying, but good.

"When do you need my men?" he asked.

Victor scratched at his chin as he thought, his eyes staring into nowhere.

"Not yet," he said. "I'll come to you when I am ready. There is one more ally we need, and with your promise, I feel I can at last win them to my side. We must be strong, and when we strike, it must be overwhelming. Right now, Muzien views us as ants, insignificant to his plans, and we must keep him thinking as much. By the time he realizes his error, I pray we'll be hoisting his head on a pike over the walls of the castle."

He offered his hand, and Antonil clasped it and shook.

"Good men like us," Antonil said, "we are the only hope this city knows."

"This city doesn't want good men," said Victor. "I've watched it chew up and spit out dozens of men who thought themselves good, who thought they might bring about change. We commit treason and plot death in the shadows. We're no longer good, but we're what this city needs."

Harsh words, but Antonil could not deny them.

"May it be enough," he said, and with a salute, he exited the tavern and made his way back to the castle, to inform the soldiers of the city that until further notice, the Sun Guild ruled the streets.

CHAPTER
15

The hour was early when Zusa heard word of Victor's arrival at their gates.

"I can send him away," she told Alyssa, who was lounging in a warm bath beside her.

"He will only come with the same promises as before," Alyssa said, eyelids closed and head tilted back so her long red hair was fully submerged. "Gods, I am tired of listening to it. I'm not sure there is a more stubborn man alive on the face of Dezrel."

Zusa sat at the edge of the tub, dressed in her elaborate dark wrappings, and she drummed her fingers atop the hilt of one of her two daggers.

"I can make him stay away forever," she said.

"He's stubborn, not dangerous," Alyssa said, and she laughed.

"I merely meant to frighten him."

Alyssa turned her head to the side, and Zusa easily recognized it as the equivalent of a glare ever since her mistress lost her eyes.

"Is that so?" Alyssa asked.

Zusa scratched at her neck.

"Maybe?" she said. "He *is* rather annoying…"

Alyssa laughed again, and it warmed Zusa's heart to see her do so. They were in an extravagant washroom, full of mirrors, white walls, and gold-tinted frames, and the air was heavy with the scent of lilac. Alyssa was nearly hidden by the steam, they'd heated the bath so hot, but it was one of the few things that could truly relax the lady in charge of the Gemcroft fortune.

The door cracked open, and a female servant stepped in and bowed with her hands behind her back.

"Milady," she said, "Lord Victor refuses to leave the gates and insists I relay another message."

"What is it?" Alyssa asked, her good humor replaced by annoyance.

"He says he must speak with you, and it is most urgent."

"He always insists that is the case," Zusa said.

The servant woman blushed.

"Yes," she said, "but—but this time he said to tell you that he has spoken with Antonil Copernus, and that he has learned of matters most urgent to the well-being of this city…and of a potential ally."

It was the clear the woman knew she was relaying information that was both private and dangerous, and she grew more nervous with every word. Alyssa let out a sigh, and at her nod, Zusa rose from her seat at the tub and gestured for the woman to go.

"Bring him, and put him somewhere he can wait," Zusa said. "Alyssa must first dress appropriately for the meeting of a man of such…high regard."

The servant curtsied again, then hurried out of the room. At the shutting of the door, Alyssa rose from the tub.

"My towel," she said, holding her left arm out and waiting.

Zusa retrieved one from a cabinet, then sat patiently as Alyssa dried herself. She pondered over what Victor had come for this time, how it might change things.

"If Antonil has sworn to help Victor against the Sun Guild, it may only make matters worse," she told Alyssa.

Alyssa pulled the towel from her body and wrapped it about her head. That done, she reached out and waited for Zusa to take her hand and guide her from the tub. From there, Zusa led her from the room into the adjacent bedroom, where atop the bed, the maidservants had already laid out her clothes for the day, a simple enough dress the color of grass. A younger girl waited patiently in the room to help, but Zusa dismissed her with a wave and began dressing Alyssa herself.

"Muzien's left us alone," Alyssa said, and she sounded troubled. "Compared to the other guilds, he's almost…civilized."

"You fool yourself if you think it will last," Zusa said, lacing up the back of the dress. "We will be next, I assure you."

"We don't have to fight him," Alyssa said, and Zusa's deft fingers stopped their weaving.

"I fear I misheard you," she said.

"No, you didn't. We don't need the Watcher's truce. There was a time we merely endured the thief guilds, accepting their take as a part of doing business. Why not return to that? Muzien may seek the same. It was Thren who sought to unite them, to lift up the underworld as if it were a conquering army."

Zusa turned Alyssa around so she might look upon her face. With Alyssa's eyes unfeeling glass, there was nothing she could read in them, but there was no hiding the defeat she heard in the woman's voice, the tension in her neck, the exhaustion tugging at her lips.

"Now is not the time to surrender," she told her mistress. "You have been strong your whole life, and—"

"And I am tired of being strong," Alyssa said. Water built around her eyes, dripping down in slender tracks. "Look what being strong has cost me. I've lost my father, I've lost friends, my sight...it'll cost me you one day, I know it, and it will cost me my son. I cannot do this anymore. If Victor wants to fight a war, I won't help him do it. I won't give him my hand just so he can lead me into more fire and bloodshed."

Slowly, carefully, Zusa wrapped her arms around Alyssa's neck and pulled her close. She said nothing, only held her as her mistress silently cried.

"What about Nathaniel's future?" Zusa asked after the moment passed, and she sensed Alyssa's composure returning.

Alyssa stepped away, and she turned so Zusa might finish putting on the dress.

"It's the only thing I have left," she said.

"And is that not something worth *fighting* for?"

Alyssa crossed her arms, and Zusa wondered where the laughter had gone she'd seen only moments before. Where was the joy? Was the mantle of leadership truly so heavy?

"What is it you want from me?" Alyssa asked her. "Truly, what? Do you want to see me married? Do you want us to run from Veldaren, dragging Nathaniel with us so we might escape and leave the scum to pick apart our remains? Or do you want me to die fighting a war we cannot win, spilling blood as I have spilled it so many times before?"

Zusa took Alyssa's hand into hers, and she squeezed her fingers tight.

"I'd have you know joy," she said. "I'd have you feel safe. I'd see you smile again and give not a damn for what all others would think or do."

Alyssa smiled at her, and it was so sad, it broke her heart.

"My hope for that is gone," she said. "It left me the moment Stephen ripped the eyes from my face."

She gestured to her dress.

"Am I presentable?"

Zusa swallowed down a knot in her throat.

"Beautiful as always," she said.

"Good. We have left Victor waiting long enough."

She offered her hand, and Zusa took it and led her down the hall. After asking a servant for Victor's whereabouts, she found him waiting in the garden behind the mansion, nestled between the long east and west wings of the building. He sat on a cracked marble bench, chin resting on his fist as his eyes stared far into nowhere. As usual, he looked prepared for war instead of a casual conversation. When he noticed their arrival, he bolted to his feet, then bowed low.

"Lady Alyssa, Zusa," he said, addressing each in turn. "Thank you for agreeing to visit with me on this fine morning."

"Better sense would have had me send you away," said Alyssa as she sat next to him on the bench. Zusa remained standing, lurking behind the bench with her fingers tapping the sides of her daggers. With each passing day, her trust of Victor had shrunk. It was more than just his stubborn display the last time he'd spoken with Alyssa, at how he'd laid his hands upon her. There was a hunger in his eyes, a desperation that belied his handsome smile. The morning sun might have lit up his blond hair like spun gold, but to her eyes, he was the rotting corpse of a beggar with outstretched hands.

"Better sense," said Victor, leaning back and feigning being relaxed. "Now, when have either of us been known to be well in supply of that?"

"I'm not here for idle banter," Alyssa said, not bothering to hide her annoyance. "You're lucky to be in my presence after your last visit, so make this quick. You said you brought word from the Guard Captain... What is it, and how could it possibly change any answer I've given you before?"

Zusa slowly paced behind them, only half listening to Victor as he began making promises of Antonil's aid. It was intriguing, of course, but she doubted it would influence Alyssa's decision. Victor wanted her hand in marriage, and it'd take more than some extra soldiers and illicit coin to win that. Her eyes were on the garden, the soft violet columbines and pink roses buzzing with the occasional insect. She couldn't shake the feeling that something was amiss. It was like a familiar presence in the back of her mind, no stronger than the buzz of the honeybees flitting from flower to flower.

Again she scanned the garden, searching for the source. It was as if the more primitive part of her mind had spotted and recognized something she did not. Somewhere lurking in the rosemary bushes, hiding behind one of the slender birch trees, perhaps? Or...

She looked to the rooftop of the mansion overlooking the garden, and there she saw it, the crouched specter of a faceless woman, the only one Zusa knew to still be alive.

"Deborah," she whispered, and she felt ice chill in her veins.

Deborah leaped from the rooftop, and Zusa could tell she knew she'd been spotted. Drawing her daggers, she took a step, meaning to fling herself between Alyssa and the faceless, only to realize as the woman's trajectory neared that her mistress was not the target.

She was.

Zusa backflipped away as Deborah slammed into the dirt, the impact seeming to have no effect on her body. Her pale cloak settled about her shoulders as she crouched there, daggers in hand.

"You've insulted us long enough," Deborah said as the tall woman rose to her full height. "Today, you will go to Karak, and you will find no mercy in his fire."

"What is the meaning of this?" Victor asked, leaping from the bench and drawing his sword.

"Stay back," Zusa said, the muscles in her legs tensing. "You have no place in this fight."

"Zusa?" Alyssa asked, and she clutched Victor's wrist in alarm. "Zusa, what's going on?"

She had no time to answer, for Deborah launched herself into an attack, her body turning in midair to add strength to her downward slashes. Zusa blocked one of the strokes as she fell back, the other coming up short so that it knifed the air before her chest. Instead of taking the opening before her, Zusa continued to retreat, wanting to gain space between them and Alyssa. Besides, she sensed if the fight remained near, that idiot Victor would try to get himself involved. Legs pumping, she leaped once, and then again, soaring through the garden so that her toes brushed the tops of the birches.

The air whipping the cloak about her body, she turned to see Deborah following, the pull of the world meaningless to her as well. As she fell toward another tree, she braced her legs, and upon slamming into its trunk halfway up its length, she kicked off, flying back into the air. Her body extended, her daggers reaching out, and with Deborah still falling, she should have been easy prey.

"*Karak!*" Deborah shrieked, and the word was like a thunderbolt. Zusa's upward momentum halted, and she screamed as she felt her bones rattle from the sudden shift. And then it was Deborah who slammed into her feetfirst, blasting her abdomen. Together, they fell to the earth, the other woman's weight atop her, and she knew upon landing she'd be crushed. Letting go of the dagger in her left hand, she reached out to grab Deborah by the elbow and then pulled with all her might. The motion tilted her just enough so that when they hit the soft grass, it was side by side. Zusa's head struck dirt, and her vision blacked out as her stomach heaved its contents up and out her throat.

Panic overwhelmed her as she crawled on her knees, still struggling to see. If Deborah had managed the landing better than she had...

Something hard struck the side of her face, and out of instinct, she flung her other dagger in the way. The metal rang against metal, and as the scattershot stars in her vision gave way to sunlight, she caught sight of Deborah preparing another stab. Wishing she still had her other blade, she continued to retreat, twisting her body out of the way to avoid the thrust and then parrying aside a second and third from Deborah's other hand.

"Did you think I would come unprepared?" Deborah asked as they stepped onto a cobbled walkway running through the center of the garden, the faded violet stones cool beneath Zusa's feet. "The deciding hour approaches, and Karak has rewarded our faithfulness above all others."

"That's wonderful," said Zusa, spitting out a bit of bile that had collected in the back of her throat. "A shame you'll die anyway."

Deborah stepped closer and closer, head tilted to one side, staring out through the thin white cloth covering the opened slit across her eyes.

"Still in denial," she said. "Still a fool."

Again she rushed in, and Zusa twisted and danced side to

side, parrying whatever she could not avoid. Back onto the grass they went, the march of their combat taking them toward a shallow pond near the heart of the garden. Surrounding it were five rowan trees, tall and thick with creamy white flowers. Zusa tried to retake control of the engagement to fight her way past Deborah, but the woman battled as if possessed, denying her any escape, her daggers always there. Closer and closer to the pond they went, and Zusa knew if she were forced into it, it'd hamper her ability to dodge, leaving her trapped.

"You humiliated me when you escaped our dungeon," Deborah said, slashing out for Zusa's face. She knew it'd be blocked, but she wanted Zusa kept on the defensive, wanted her to feel overwhelmed. Again and again, slashes to the face and chest, Zusa forced to shift her weight side to side to brace accordingly. They were between two of the trees now, the pond so very near.

"You humiliate yourself every day you wrap your face in that mask," Zusa said, her pride stirring in her chest. She was far more experienced than the whelp she faced, and even lacking a weapon, she should have been able to find victory. "You humiliate yourself every day you let Karak rule over you like a slave."

Deborah's controlled demeanor broke for just a moment, and she stretched forward for a killing lunge. The overextension was all Zusa needed. Sidestepping the thrust, she trapped Deborah's wrist between her elbow and her side, and she kicked as hard as she could into the woman's armpit. She heard a pop from Deborah's shoulder, followed by a scream. Zusa let her go to block a desperate swipe, then flung herself into the offensive. Deborah was wounded now, her right arm pressed against her waist as she battled solely with her left. For Zusa, who needed no advantage, it was more than enough.

"Every day," she shouted at Deborah, her own anger letting

loose, her dagger a winding cobra always on the strike. "Every single day, you humiliate yourself! Slave! Fool!"

Deborah had her back to the tree, unable to dodge, and letting out a wordless cry, Zusa thrust for Deborah's heart. But the shadows were deep beneath the yellow leaves, and instead of piercing flesh, her dagger thudded into the ashen bark, the faceless woman falling into the dark as if it were an open doorway. Zusa spun, knowing Deborah would reappear from another section of shadow nearby, one of the trees or . . .

From beneath the pond, Deborah emerged, water splashing out in all directions as she lifted into the air, rising as if she were a forgotten beast of the ocean deep. One arm she held against herself, the other stretched out to the side, both her legs dangling. Her wet hair rose as if she were amid a torrent of wind, her eyes shining a bright white from behind the cloth. Her mouth opened, and all her rage and fury came shrieking out in a single word.

"*KARAK!*"

The noise pierced like the cry of an eagle, the very air shimmering from its force. Drops of water caught in its path turned to mist. Zusa crossed her arms and dug in her heels, but it meant nothing. The cry tore into her, ripping gashes into her wrappings, blood pouring down like rain. Her feet left the ground, but it was not for long. Her back slammed into a tree, stealing away her breath. After such a noise, she wondered why no guards had come to save her yet, to protect their lady of the house. Not that it would matter. No one would come in time to save her, not from the demon that landed just beyond the water's edge, a hungry dagger in her left hand.

"If only you had remained loyal," Deborah said as she stalked closer. "If only you could have accepted the gifts Karak had to offer. Your place in our order will never be forgotten, Zusa, but it will forever be tainted by your heresy."

"Give it time, girl," Zusa said, laughing even as she slumped to the ground, convinced several of her ribs were broken, due to how painful it was to breathe. She let out a sigh as she looked up at the faceless woman lurking above her. "Give it time. No animal ever truly loves its cage."

Deborah grabbed Zusa by the hair, pulling her head back to fully expose her throat. The other readied a dagger.

"May the fire take you," she said, and Zusa could do nothing to stop the fatal thrust, only laugh.

Ghost remained atop the mansion as Deborah leaped off, hoping to overtake Zusa before the woman could realize the ambush was upon her. Together, they'd climbed to the top after finding a gap in the patrols, though Ghost had more floated upward than climbed. He couldn't do it in open space, but while clutching something solid, he found he could will himself to rise or fall. As he watched Zusa and Deborah crash into each other, he laughed at the order the faceless woman had given him.

Stay out of my way, even if it looks like I may lose. I'd rather die than accept your help.

"Only fair," Ghost muttered as he watched the fight. "I think I'd rather die than help you in the first place."

Even saying the words made his head ache with a steady throb. Closing his eyes, he focused on Zusa lying before him, her body bleeding from multiple wounds, and that seemed to make it go away. As he did, he heard sounds of alarm to his right. Opening his eyes, he ran along the rooftop to the corner, not a single step making a noise, and then peered down over the edge. Several soldiers were drawing their weapons and moving to join the fight. Ghost felt his face twitch at the sight of them. Letting them interfere would be dangerous, and given how even the fight between Zusa and Deborah appeared, the slightest aid could be enough.

"I'm sorry," he said, leaping off the side.

Swords drawn, he crashed down atop the rearmost soldier. Ghost felt no fear for his body, no danger at the great height from which he fell. His blades smashed through the man's armor and into the soft flesh beneath, slicing off one arm and shattering the collarbone of the other. Upon hitting ground, he did not stop, only continued on. As his head slipped beneath the dirt, he felt his vision shift, gaining a greater awareness of his surroundings. It was as if he could feel the vibrations of the soldiers above him, could see the great expanse of dirt and rock in all directions. When he pulled his swords to him, he saw their steel was immaculate, whatever blood that had stained them unable to pass through the ground.

He moved without needing to run, merely by thinking of the direction and willing himself to be there. It wasn't far, and when there, he jumped. The physical action may not have been necessary, but it felt natural, and he emerged from the ground before the remaining soldiers, head bowed, swords out, and a smile on his face.

Their fear at the sight of him was overwhelming, and to his otherworldly senses, it smelled like a fine perfume.

"Fall back!" the foremost man shouted before Ghost took off his head. The other two impressed him with their bravery, ignoring the command and instead slashing out at Ghost with their swords. Ghost blocked them both, pushing aside their strokes as if they were children. Another step, closing the distance, and they were his, their weapons positioned awkwardly, given his new proximity. One stab through the throat killed the first; a looping slash cut the other across the belly just beneath his breastplate. As he fell, innards tumbling, Ghost showed him mercy and opened his throat as well.

More would be coming, he knew, which meant Deborah needed to end her fight soon. Running back to the garden, he watched the women battle in midair, smashing into one another. As they fell, Ghost felt himself cheering for Zusa. Had he not promised to kill her last? But no, his opinion was now irrelevant. He felt the curse pulsing in the veins of his face and neck, boring deep into his muscles, or whatever it was his body now had. When Zusa slammed hard to the ground, seeing it filled him with a sensation almost sexual in its pleasure.

Yet deep down in his chest, Ghost felt only rage and sickness.

Swords still drawn, he flew across the grass of the garden, doing his best not to think. Not to breathe. He embraced that rage, clung to it like a shelter in a thunderstorm. It pushed aside his doubt, denied the curse pounding angrily in his veins. Focus only on the act, on the betrayal they'd committed.

I am not yours, thought Ghost as he came barreling in toward Deborah, who knelt triumphantly over Zusa. *Not your puppet. Not your slave.*

He leaped, legs extended, and slammed straight into her chest with his feet. The woman let out a startled cry, rolling along the ground several times before she could skid to a halt. The faceless woman glared at him from behind the white cloth of her face, her legs crooked beneath her like a spider, much of her weight supported on one hand still clutching the grass from halting her roll.

"I should have known as much," Deborah said, and she coughed. Dark blood spread across the wrappings of her face around her mouth.

"Indeed, you should have," Ghost said, fighting to concentrate. Zusa lay beside him, and it felt like every part of his mind was screaming at him to finish her, to drive a blade through her eye and out the back of her skull. Instead, he grinned at Deborah and remembered the hours he'd lain on a cold floor while above him roared the phantom image of the Lion.

The woman's eyes narrowed, and when she attacked, Ghost was ready. Instead of meeting her head on, he leaped backward, arms crossed over his chest. His body passed through the tree Zusa leaned against, and he felt a chill spike up his right leg as it brushed Zusa's body. Pushing it out of mind, he jumped as high as his legs would let him...which was much, much higher than it had ever been prior to becoming whatever Daverik had made him. He soared through the branches, felt the moisture of the leaves as they slid through his face, and then was falling. Deborah had hesitated upon his disappearance, and when she looked up, he realized she had deciphered his maneuver.

"*Karak!*" she shrieked, waves of power rolling across him, knifing into his exposed skin. For a moment, he hovered there in the air, his fall countered by the shriek, and then he landed, his blood splashing all across the grass. Deborah was on him in a heartbeat, slicing and stabbing with her daggers. Ghost blocked the first two, the third sneaking through as he struggled to regain his sense of balance and vision. As he felt pain from her blade cutting into his forearm and saw the blood spill, he confirmed that blades could still hurt him, at least when he was in the open instead of shifting through walls or the rocky ground.

Good to know, he thought, though that knowledge would benefit him for only moments more. Deborah pressed the attack, and it took all his skill to keep her at bay. At least the ache from the curse had subsided. Battle was a wonderful medicine, and he much preferred the pain from the cuts of blades over the insidious pulse deep in the center of his being.

Into the dirt Ghost dropped, and when he reemerged behind

Deborah, she had already turned, blocking his slashes. She lunged toward him, her daggers a flurry of steel, and he blocked them with growing confidence. Her skill was great, but damn it, prior to fighting the Watcher, he'd never even considered someone could be greater than he, and it was time he remembered that.

Parrying aside one thrust, he stole the offensive, his feet a blur beneath him as he shifted closer and closer, giving her no break. Her defenses grew desperate, they both could tell, and then she inhaled deep.

"*Karak!*" came the cry, only this time Ghost denied it with every piece of his soul.

"No!" he screamed, swords crossed before him as the power rolled forth. "Not...this...time!"

His swords opened, and he pushed aside the attack as if it were just another blade. He saw the fear in Deborah's eyes, that flash of doubt, and he knew the end had come. Into her chest his swords sank deep, and as the blood flowed, she looked up at him with a mixture of fury and confusion.

"No one..." she said as he pinned her to the dirt. "No one can...can resist..."

Ghost knelt down close, and he ripped off the wrappings that hid her face.

"I just did," he said, kissing her forehead. "And I will again. My life is my own, precious. A shame you never felt the same about yours."

To that she could say nothing, for her eyes had rolled back into her head, her movements merely the final twitchings of a dying body. Ghost pulled free his swords and looked about. All around him was a scene so bizarre he could only laugh. Dozens of soldiers had come in from outside the mansion, and they'd formed a circle around him and Deborah. How long had they been there, he wondered, watching their fight? He could only guess. It'd taken a knife-edged focus to defeat Deborah as well as keep all thoughts of Zusa from his mind.

"I mean no harm," Ghost said to the soldiers about him. "I killed the invader, or have you not noticed?"

To the front pushed a man in fine silver armor, a yellow circle with wings upon the front of his tunic.

"What is the meaning of this?" he asked, his own sword drawn.

"This has nothing to do with you," Ghost said. He saw where Zusa lay against the tree, Alyssa huddled over her, and then he pointed.

"Only her," he said.

A shadow crossed over the man's face.

"Get out," he said.

"With pleasure."

Ghost dropped into the dirt, the last sound he heard before the earth swallowed him that of the guards' gasps. Like some strange worm, Ghost swam through the ground, focusing on exiting the compound. As he did, he felt a sensation building in his stomach, and with each passing second, it grew stronger. His speed slowed, and his otherworldly vision dimmed. For a panicked moment, he thought he'd be lost underground, forever entombed as the powers Karak had given him diminished.

And then the pain hit.

It was like a lightning bolt through his mind, a crystal-tipped spear ramming into his gut. He felt like he needed to breathe, yet couldn't. Over and over, he saw Zusa in his mind, lying there, her life ready to be taken by the faceless woman, yet he'd stopped it. He'd *saved* her, and now he heard a deep voice chanting as if from some great distance.

Betrayed.

"No!" Ghost screamed, but it was only the whisper of a man long buried in a grave.

Betrayed.

"I was never your servant," he said, clawing in an attempt to climb back to the surface. The pain heightened, and a multitude of colors swam across his vision. It was like razors cutting across his skin. His movements ceased, for he was unable to focus on anything, to move, to climb. A swirling vertigo overcame him, and he felt as if he were falling amid a great fire.

Fight it, Ghost knew he had to fight it, but how? Only one thing had worked before, and so he tried it out of desperation. He thought of Tarlak, and of how he would sneak into the wizard's home. He filled his mind with images of the man's death, by poison, razor wire, and blade. As the pounding in his skull faded, the thoughts grew soothing, his promises calming. Yes, he could kill the wizard, he told himself. The man was a nuisance, and his magic had left him horribly burned. Killing him was good. Killing him, he could do. Over and over he swore, and desperately, he tried to believe it.

At last, the voices were gone, his sight returned, and with a gasp, he emerged from the ground in the open street just outside the Gemcroft mansion. Blood poured down from his body like rain, marking the place of his emergence. Ignoring the surprised cries of those around him, he ran, wanting to get as far away from a certain woman, whose name he'd not dare think, as fast as he possibly could.

CHAPTER
16

Marion smiled at Thren from the other side of the bed, her face glowing in the early-morning light that streamed through the stained glass of their room. Their blankets were bunched around her waist, revealing her full breasts and even fuller belly. Thren put a hand atop her belly, feeling the movement of the little life within.

"I say we name her Mary, after you," Thren said, his fingertips circling Marion's navel.

"Seems a bit prideful," Marion said. "You're the one wanting a legacy, not me."

Thren laughed.

"Well, then, what name would you prefer?"

She shrugged.

"Mary is fine. And if it's a boy?"

He kissed her lips.

"Aaron," he said. "After my father."

"I didn't think you knew your father."

Thren pressed his forehead to hers.

"He's but a distant haze in my mind, but it doesn't matter. He was my father, and it is only right to respect him."

Marion winced once, then rubbed her belly, a sign Thren had long deciphered as their child turning in the womb fast enough to make her uncomfortable.

"Aaron it is," she said, staring down at her stomach as if she could see through the layers of skin and right into the face of the life yet to be born. "Tiny little Aaron..."

Thren reached for her face, wishing to kiss her again, to feel her warmth against his body, but she was not there. He paused, confused, for he was in an empty bed. The room was dark. Whatever light had shone through the window moments ago was gone. Frowning, he slid naked off his bed and began to dress. When his breeches were tied, he strapped on his sword belt, then strode shirtless toward the door. Something, or someone, was outside his room. He knew it, deep down he knew it, though the knowledge disturbed him. Where had Marion gone? Why had the day vanished so quickly? Had he fallen asleep again?

He touched the doorknob, found it ice-cold. His frown deepened. With how hot the summer had been, even nightfall shouldn't have cooled his house so well. Sensing a trap, he put one hand on the hilt of a short sword, then pushed open the door with the other. He rushed on through, meaning to attack whoever laid an ambush, but the scene was too bewildering for him to react beyond gaping.

"Hello, Thren," said an older man, his hair gray, his skin starting to wrinkle. Around his neck was a silver chain decorated with the emblem of a lion, and it hung before his dark black robes. Instead of being inside his house's hallway, they stood in a plain field with but a single tree in the distance. The sky was filled with stars, and slowly they moved across the horizon, as if locked in a dance that baffled his reeling mind.

"Who..." Thren asked, trying to make sense of things. The grass was cold and wet beneath his feet, and when he looked behind him, there was no sign of the doorway he'd just entered, only more fields stretching on for hundreds of miles, ending at a deep white fog.

"Come, now," said the stranger. "You aren't as slow as this. Where you are, *when* you are, should be easy enough to decipher."

When? What did he mean by...

And then the past years came slamming into him. Marion's murder, Grayson's arrival in Veldaren, Randith's death at the hands of Aaron...all of it, he remembered all of it, and in doing so, he knew where he must be.

"I'm dreaming," he said. "But no normal dream. Who are you who would dare enter a man's most private sanctuary?"

"A desperate man," he said. "A man I believe you've come looking for. My name is Luther, and I am a priest of Karak."

At the word *Karak*, it seemed the sky rumbled, and along the horizon, he watched a red line pierce the hills, signifying the rising of a blood-colored sun.

"Luther," said Thren, and the name felt heavy on his tongue. "So, you've come where you think me vulnerable, is that true? Would you kill me in my sleep, where I have but thoughts and dreams to defend myself?"

Luther smiled, and it was strange, for he seemed so non-threatening, just an aging man in the crossroads between his middle years and the elderly stage beyond. He still had all his hair, but his smile looked tired, his eyes heavy with many, many years of struggle.

"I'm not here to harm you," he said. "Hard as it may be to believe, I'm here to help you."

"Help me?" Thren swallowed, and he wished that the stars above him would vanish. He felt too exposed, a vulnerable speck atop a thousand miles of grass. Deeper grew the red horizon, and with it, he heard the sound of screams.

"Do you hear that?" asked Luther, and he joined him in watching the sunrise. "That sound is the wailing of those yet to die. But they will die. Their souls cry out in the void, for they know what comes for them. What I've tried to stop."

The leaves atop the lone tree turned yellow, then black, and as they began to fall, Thren heard the softest of snaps from each and every one.

"Why are you here?" Thren asked.

"As I said, to help you. You seek to find me in the Stronghold, and I would have words with you. You won't reach me, not through force, nor through stealth. The way is too well-guarded, the paladins too skilled in battle for you to overcome them all." He took a step closer, and with each step, the world silently shook. "But there is a way. The Stronghold was built atop Ashhur's fallen Sanctuary, its very construction meant to blaspheme and insult. Because of that, there are many secret ways, gaps between the walls, and places where the new could not fully destroy the old."

"You mean to trick me," said Thren. "You'd have me walk into a trap."

The stars twinkled out one by one, the red growing across the skyline, streaks of yellow starting to poke beyond the hills. The fog that had hidden the horizon began to fade, revealing rows of snow-crested mountains, and with the light shining upon them, they seemed to shimmer as if their tips were made of gold.

"I only seek to spare your life," said Luther. "I have need of you, if you would only trust me. On the northern wall of the Stronghold, twenty paces in from the eastern corner, you will find a patch where the grass does not grow as deep. Dig to reveal the door. From there, you must climb, always climb, never once descend. You will not like what you find otherwise. Come the top, you will find a false wall, and beyond that, you must follow the stairs to the highest floor of the Stronghold. My room is there, and I wait for you within."

It seemed too easy, too good to be true. Thren pondered drawing his swords and stabbing the priest through the neck, to see if dying in a dream meant dying in the waking world, but when he moved to do so, his swords were gone. Glancing back up, he saw Luther smiling at him and shaking his head as if Thren were a disobedient child.

"You have no choice in this," said the priest. "Come speak with me, Thren. Hear what I have to say."

"You continue to treat me as if I am your puppet," Thren said. "I will kill you for this, for everything you've done."

"Perhaps you will," said Luther. "But I forfeited my life long ago..."

The wind picked up, the stabbing spears of light reaching from horizon to horizon. The lone tree in the distance died, its branches collapsing as the earth swallowed it whole. Amid the rising sun, Luther smiled, his body fading away as a terrible rumble overwhelmed it all.

"Oh, and Thren," shouted the priest to be heard over the noise. "Come alone."

And then, the dreamworld was gone, the light breaking everything, and it was only when he gasped in a waking breath that Thren realized it was from the steady opening of his eyes.

"I don't understand the need for secrecy," Haern said as the three of them traversed the thick wheat fields that grew around the

Stronghold. Thren led the way, with Delysia staying at Haern's side. "Who was the contact that gave you the way inside?"

Thren kept his back to them, a barely visible specter in the deep night.

"It was a contact," Thren said. "That's all you need to know."

Delysia grabbed Haern's arm, slowing him down so she could brush his ear with her lips.

"He's lying," she whispered.

"Are you sure?"

He glanced at her, saw her nod. Taking in a deep breath, Haern let it out with a sigh and decided to press the issue later. The wheat in the fields was tall, but following Thren was easy enough. Several days before, he'd informed them of how he'd learned of a way inside, yet gave no more information beyond that. For all Haern knew, it'd be through another contact, a secret entrance, or a magical bird that would fly down and offer to carry them to the tallest tower in exchange for their souls.

"There it is," Thren said, and he pointed. Casting aside his thoughts, Haern followed his father's outstretched hand, and then he saw it: the Stronghold. Even at such a distance, over a mile away, it was an imposing building. In the moonlight, it was a thick, rectangular spire, its walls seeming to be of a black even purer than the darkness. From where they were, he could see faint dots of red and yellow, torches burning around the lower rings. If forced to guess how many floors the building had, Haern would venture at least fifteen. The entire structure had a proud feeling to it, a defiant fortress rising into the dark night sky. The only parts that looked simple and rustic were the stables attached to the side, wood pens covered by a thatched roof.

"I hope your contact was trustworthy," Haern said as they quickened their pace. "I doubt the people inside will be too forgiving of trespassers."

"Trustworthy as any other man in this world."

Haern chuckled.

"And by that, you mean not at all."

Thren glanced over his shoulder, then grinned.

"Perhaps it's not a miracle you've survived as long as you have."

They said nothing as they crossed the distance, pushing through what seemed like a never-ending field of wheat. Closer and closer loomed the Stronghold, and as they neared, Haern better saw the slender windows outlined by the torches hanging just above, saw the crenelated top, the sharply curved supports along the bottom, making it seem almost as if the building itself were a long-buried weapon wielded by men the size of mountains.

No wonder everyone thought we were mad to sneak inside, thought Haern. The structure itself was frighteningly imposing, and then there was the matter of the dangerous and skilled residents within. And apparently, their secret method for scaling those walls had come from a source Thren was either too embarrassed or mistrustful to reveal to him and Delysia. *Not exactly something to inspire confidence in the heart,* thought Haern.

At last, the field came to an end, leaving a hundred-yard stretch of smooth, short grass between them and the building. After pausing momentarily to ensure no patrols walked the area, Thren stepped out and gestured for them to follow.

"Close enough," said Haern. "I'm not leaving this field until I know what I'm getting into."

Thren turned about, a frown on his face and impatience in his blue eyes.

"There's a hidden entrance," he said. "A tunnel dug beneath the grass we can use to climb near to the top. After that, we'll find Luther in the highest room of the Stronghold. Will that suffice?"

"How did you find out?" Haern asked.

"A contact of Muzien's. Now let's go."

"You're lying," Delysia said, stepping out from the wheat. "And you should know better than to do so in my presence. What are you hiding, Thren?"

Thren crossed his arms and his frown deepened.

"A dream," he said at last.

Haern blinked.

"A dream."

"Yes, a dream," Thren said. "Luther used a spell of some sort to come to me while we slept. He knew of our approach, and he claimed he wished for a meeting."

Haern rubbed his eyes, tried to think.

"A meeting?" he said. "Did he say why? And why not come to us?"

Thren shrugged.

"He's being held prisoner," he said. "At least, that is what he told me. Now, is that enough, or must I go alone?"

"This is insane," Delysia said, turning to Haern to plead her case. "It's a trap of some sort; it has to be. Don't go in there, either of you. No good will come of it."

"I'm going," Thren said, and it was clear there'd be no debate, not with him. "Question is, is either of you willing to follow?"

With that, he turned and sprinted toward the towering spire and the shadowed recesses that swelled around its base. Haern watched him, pulled from his thoughts only by Delysia taking his hand in hers.

"You don't have to do this," she said.

"Then why else have we come all this way?" he asked her.

"I don't know," she said. "Because you thought it was the right thing to do, or that maybe you could salvage something good in your father. But I'm telling you, whatever you find in there will not be worth the risk. Please, stay with me. For once, just this once, will you trust me?"

Haern ran a hand through her fiery red hair, felt the strands slipping smoothly through his fingers.

"I won't make him go alone," he said. "I won't abandon him now."

"He's abandoned you your whole life," Delysia said, her voice a whisper, the words a serrated blade. "He's done nothing but leave you alone. Don't follow him, Haern. You won't find any answers in that horrible place."

He kissed her forehead, and she let out a sigh. Reaching down his shirt, she pulled out the pendant of the golden mountain that had belonged to Senke. Closing her eyes, she whispered a prayer over it. The metal shone briefly, a reassuring glow in the darkness, and then faded.

"Should something go wrong," she said, "should you find yourself at your lowest, clutch it and say Ashhur's name, and the magic will release. It's the best I can do."

"I won't need it," he said, slipping the pendant beneath his shirt. "I promise. Just wait here until I come back, and you'll see, I'll be just fine."

She squeezed his hand, he squeezed back, and then he was running. With each step, he wanted to look back, to see her, to find comfort in her presence in the fields, yet he refused. The Stronghold was ahead, and on his knees his father dug, hands into the green earth. By the time Haern reached his side, he'd already uncovered a small set of wooden planks, which he pulled up one by one.

"And to think I always believed dreams were worthless," said Thren, grinning up at Haern as he gestured to the circular tunnel leading deep underground. "We should be able to crawl through it just fine."

"Sounds pleasant," said Haern, fighting another stolen glance to see if Delysia watched. Looking back to the tunnel, he shuddered. Years before, his father had taken him into the temple of Karak, seeking to cure him of his fledgling belief in Ashhur. Now here he was, following the same man into the fortress of Karak's paladins. He prayed he might escape as unscathed as he had from the temple.

"Lead the way," Haern said, gesturing to the pit entrance.

"Stay close," said Thren, falling to his stomach and beginning to crawl. "The way will be dark, and I would hate to lose you."

With that, he vanished within, sliding and squirming over the dirt and into the harder stone. Taking in a deep breath, Haern looked to Delysia, who remained at the edge of the field of wheat.

I'll be fine, he whispered, blew her a kiss, and then dropped to his belly. Headfirst, he followed Thren into the darkness.

The way was tight at first, but after twenty feet or so of crawling, it expanded so that his shoulders needn't be scrunched so tightly. The stone was wet and cold beneath his hands, the angle sharply downward for much of the way. The sound of his crawling seemed thunderous in the confined space, equally so the noise of Thren scraping along ahead of him. Haern felt his heartbeat beginning to increase, felt the early tickle of panic poking around the edges of his mind. He could see nothing, hear nothing but the sound of his breath, the rustling of his clothes, and the scrape of his sheaths against the stone. How long did the tunnel go? What if Thren had been lied to, and they'd soon be trapped down there forever? Every sliding step he took, he felt loose stones, and he told himself not to imagine what it'd be like if the tunnel caved in, trapping but not killing him.

"Wait," said Thren, and his voice sounded like a roar in the silence.

"What?" Haern whispered. He knew it was foolish whispering, given how deep beneath the earth they were, but he did so anyway. In that darkness, he felt painfully vulnerable, and it was a feeling he'd be glad to be rid of. Facing off against dozens of dark paladins felt preferable to another twenty minutes in that deep passageway.

"I've found a gap just ahead," said Thren. "I can feel it with my hands. The tunnel's shifted vertically, and just over the gap I can feel a sort of ladder. Climb carefully. I don't know how far down that tunnel goes…"

"Will do," said Haern. He waited until he heard movement, then continued on ahead. Thren grunted, there was the sound of rocks clacking and falling against one another, and then silence. Haern made sure to check every movement carefully, sliding his hands along the stone before advancing. Sure enough, within another ten feet, he felt his hand move right off the stone, feeling only open air. Pulling back, he felt for the exact edge, then slowly advanced toward it. Now closer, he reached out again, and the inability to see what he was reaching for, yet knowing he leaned out over an unknown pit, made his stomach twist and dance. When he touched a wall, followed by a steel rung just beneath it, he let out a sigh.

"I'm just above," he heard Thren say. "Tell me when you're safely across."

"I will."

Haern grabbed the rung, braced himself, then extended his other hand. The weight pulled him over the chasm, and he felt himself hanging, feet on the edge, hands on the rung. By his guess, the pit beneath him was only a few feet wide, but being unable to see, he felt like it was a thousand. Another breath, and then he took a blind step. He dropped, pivoting along the rung so that he swung toward the wall of stone. He expected to find more rungs, but instead, his feet hit smooth stone, and he dangled there, clutching the steel with both hands. He was on the bottom rung of a ladder, he realized, and if he planned on getting anywhere, he needed to stop panicking. It was just darkness, he told himself. Darkness was his friend. Something about the confined spaces messed with his mind, and again he wished he could see, if only the tiniest of light, so he could find his bearings.

Planting a foot against the wall, he pushed off it as best he could and reached up for a second rung. He found it, and telling himself to not even think of letting his grip slip, he pulled himself up higher. A grunt, another kick, and he ascended again. The fourth time, he was able to put a knee on the rung, and he breathed a sigh of relief.

"Are you across?" he heard Thren ask from up above.

"Yes," Haern said, pressing his forehead against one of the rungs, immensely comforted by its smooth, cold feel. "Yes, I'm on the ladder."

"Good."

He heard a rustle of movement, and Haern shifted so instead of his knee, his foot was on the bottom rung, and he was eager to begin his climb up through whatever unknown shaft they'd found themselves in. He reached up to grab another rung, then felt his heart leap into his throat as a hand clasped his wrist.

"I'm sorry," said Thren.

His father flung out Haern's wrist, and at the same time, he felt a heavy weight crash against his right arm. Before he could even brace himself, another kick hit him in the face, then his left hand. Balance lost, he fell, still reaching for a rung. Twisting, reaching for the other side of the tunnel they'd come from, he scraped his fingernails against smooth stone, and then he was falling, falling. So stung by the betrayal, so frightened of the unbreakable darkness, Haern never screamed as he plummeted into the unknown.

CHAPTER

17

Luther sat in an uncomfortable wood chair, a book open before him and his back to the door, when he heard the faint metal click of the lock opening. He paused in the middle of turning a page, and as he held the coarse paper between his fingers, he let out a soft breath.

"At last," he whispered.

A dagger jammed through his left hand resting atop the desk, spearing through his palm and pinning it to the wood. Into his mouth pressed a heavy cloth, gagging him as its wielder shoved his head backward, allowing a longer blade to push against his exposed throat. Luther let out a moan at the pain, from both the stab wound and the awkward angle his neck was forced into. Above him he saw no one, just his drab ceiling. The cloth tasted of dirt and blood, and it built up a cough he had to struggle to suppress.

"I know the power a man like you can wield," said his

intruder. "The moment I hear anything that sounds remotely like a prayer or spell, I will cut open your throat and leave you to bleed all over your book. Am I understood? Say nothing, just blink twice."

He did so, feeling remarkably calm despite what he knew was to happen. Carefully, he raised his free hand, allowing his intruder to take it, wrench it behind his back, and bind it to the chair. When that was done, the blade returned to his throat.

"Remember, not a single sound that makes me nervous."

Out of his mouth came the cloth, and Luther gave a soft sigh.

"Thren Felhorn," he said. "You've finally arrived."

To Luther's right was his bed, and sliding into view was an older man clothed in plain colors and wearing a pale gray cloak. His hair was short and blond, his face marked by scars and age, yet his blue eyes still seemed to shine with life. He sat on the bed, sword still in hand.

"It seems I have," he said. "You've been playing dangerous games, priest."

Luther smiled despite the pain spreading up his hand from the dagger. With the blade still in him, the bleeding wasn't as bad as it could be, but even the slightest twitch of his fingers dramatically increased its agony.

"As have you," he said. "There are few with the skill, and the audacity, to come to the Stronghold in search of prey." He did his best to look over his shoulder at the door. "I take it the guard posted there is dead?"

Thren twirled the sword in his hand.

"He is."

"A shame. Mihir was a good man."

"He died a quick death, if that makes you feel better."

Luther chuckled.

"Little can make me feel better, Thren. I fear my capacity for joy has been permanently ruined."

Thren ignored him, instead continuing to twirl the sword, slowly, his fingers in masterful control of the leather and steel. He stared at Luther, analyzing him, judging him.

"Why?" he asked.

Luther shifted, trying to find a measure of comfort, given one hand was stabbed and bleeding and the other roughly tied behind his back.

"Such a large, vague question," he answered. "One my order has devoted a great many of its years to solving. Could you be more specific?"

"I'm in no mood for jokes or sarcasm, priest. You know who I am, which means you know why I'm here. You sent the Sun Guild into Veldaren with aims to kill me. I want to know why."

"Untie my hand, and I will tell you," Luther said.

Thren tensed, the twirling of his sword halting.

"I am no fool," he said.

"And neither am I. You are here, which means I am a dead man. But even if I could, I would make no move against you. I've been waiting for you, Thren. Waiting for you to do the impossible, and to come to me, because truth be told, I need you alive. Why else would I have come to you in a dream to show you the way?"

Thren looked undecided, and it was clearly an emotion he was unaccustomed to. Debating wordlessly with himself, at last he sat up from his bed, cut through the ropes holding Luther to the chair, and then sat back down on the bed. The dagger he left embedded.

"There," he said. "Now talk. Why did you want to destroy my Spider Guild?"

"I had no animosity toward your guild in particular," Luther said. "I needed all of the guilds weakened so the Sun Guild might come in as I requested. You were the strongest of them, the one most likely to withstand their arrival. I expect you to be familiar with such a role by now, Thren. The tallest must first duck the swing of a reaper's scythe."

"And the Widow?"

Luther thought of what he'd known of Stephen Connington, and he shook his head sadly.

"A poor child with a horrific past," he said. "His mind was damaged beyond repair. I did my best to contain his more vile habits, to direct them to better uses, but over such distance, my control was limited."

Thren stabbed his sword into the wood floor, put both his hands upon the hilt, and rested his lips against his knuckles. The man stared at him, his concentration frighteningly intense.

"For what reason?" he asked at last. "What is your hope, the goal of your little game? Have Karak's followers decided to make a move on my city?"

"In a way, you are right," Luther said, "but not how you believe. The paladins and priesthood have nothing to do with my plans, Thren. I am very much alone but for a trusted few."

"You can't expect me to believe that," Thren said. "You're a powerful priest of Karak, hidden in the top of the Stronghold..."

"Held *prisoner* atop the Stronghold," Luther interrupted. "Or did you not notice the guard and locked door?"

"Something else I fail to understand. Why are you a prisoner here?"

Luther thought over the past months, of his vague letters to Daverik and his shadowed conversations using the chrysarium.

"I presented ideas some might consider... heretical," he said at last.

Thren stood, and he pointed his sword at Luther, the tip hovering less than an inch from his neck.

"You're lying," he said. "I may not bow to Karak, but I know enough about those who do. A heretic of Karak within the faithful? You'd have been sacrificed within hours, yet here you are. I don't believe it."

Luther laughed.

"Then your mind is more closed than I thought. My faith has never wavered for my god, Thren, not once. They performed every test, subjected me to fire and spell, and always the outcome was the same. There is no denying my beliefs, and given my years serving the Lion, there are many who would defend my zeal. So, here I am, locked in a room, a thorn in the priesthood's side that they cannot decide how to deal with. Perhaps in a few years, they'll poison my food or send in a younger paladin with a blade. Perhaps they'll merely leave me here to wither away and die. In the end, it doesn't matter. The next few months are the ones that will decide the fate of our world, and I doubt I will live to see them."

The conversation was clearly not going where Thren had expected it, and after a moment of doubt, he sat back down on the bed, sword across his lap.

"Enough cryptic talk," he said. "The fate of our world? I'll not hear such tales. Whatever you're doing, you thought it was the best for your god. You want Karak's presence strengthened in Veldaren somehow, just admit it."

"I have *betrayed* my god, you damn fool," Luther said, his voice rising loud enough to spur Thren back to his feet. Knuckles smacked across his mouth, cutting open a lip, and as the blood dripped down, Luther laughed at how ridiculous it felt that the sting in his mouth momentarily hurt worse than the dagger still embedded in his hand.

"At least, betrayed who he is now," Luther continued despite Thren's glare. "My heresy was in suggesting that the god we know, the god we think we serve, is not the same god we first worshipped when he walked the lands centuries ago. My only wonder is if our god himself changed...or only our understanding of him, an understanding largely shaped by a single man. The First Man, once known as the Eveningstar, the only human crafted by the hands of both brother gods prior to the war that tore them apart. He is a wretched being who denies death's authority over him, a man who sows chaos while preaching order. Life is nothing to him. *Humanity* means nothing to him."

"His name?" asked Thren. "What is his name?"

Luther felt a weight settle on his chest.

"He is known as the prophet, the beast of a thousand faces, the voice of the Lion. His name is Velixar, and for the past year, I have done all I can to protect our world from his coming wrath. Even if it meant disobeying my order. Even if it meant plotting in secret and bringing chaos and disorder to your city of Veldaren."

It was too much for Thren to take in, Luther could tell. The man stared at him, meeting his eyes as if to force the truth from him through sheer conviction. Luther met that stare unafraid. He felt no shame for what he'd done, and every word he spoke was the truth, for the first time confessed by his lips to anyone other than himself. Even in his prayers to Karak, he had denied himself full honesty, for what did it mean to pray to a god while working against his own prophet? What kind of man would worship a god yet still deny what he might have become?

Only a madman, Luther knew, and it fit him perfectly. A madman plotting against his own order, a madman spurring chaos into an already-broken city.

"The Sun Guild?" Thren asked. "What is their part?"

"I needed someone who could stand against you all," Luther said. "Someone with no connection to the priesthood in Veldaren. Muzien has eyed your city since you and Grayson went there to conquer it, and when I came to him offering bribes and the aid of Karak, his ears were listening. All I requested was that he transport the stone tiles bearing the symbol of his guild that I made for him into the city. Those tiles... I've personally cast spells upon every single one prior to my imprisonment. Those tiles are the key, Thren, the key to saving Veldaren from the prophet's return. Muzien's rise, his takeover of the streets... all of it is merely my means to an end."

"That end being saving the city from this prophet, Velixar," Thren said. "Why do you fear him so? Does he command an army? Will he lay siege to its walls? What threat can he possibly present to our world that would leave you so terrified?"

Luther swallowed, and he almost lied. This was a truth known to a rare few, and telling a man like Thren Felhorn was a leap of faith so great, it was a stretch even for him. But in the end, he knew he had to trust his instincts. Thren could be one to bear the necessary burden, but only if he knew the truth in its entirety.

"Karak and Ashhur are not from this world," Luther said. "They came from another, one they fled from out of failure. Humanity's birth here, overseen by the elven Goddess, was an attempt at redemption that went predictably awry. The world they came from, one of thousands, is a dangerous place now... and it is behind Veldaren's throne that the brother gods first stepped into our world. That place is a crack in a sheet of armor, a torn thread in a great tapestry, a doorway between worlds that the prophet must not be allowed access to at all costs."

Thren's blue eyes bored into him, filled with doubt. Luther

knew he had to convince him, and he prayed the words would come to his tongue at the proper time.

"So, this prophet," Thren said slowly, as if everything he'd heard was tumbling and clicking in his mind, a puzzle stubbornly coming together. "This…Velixar…seeks access to the throne. That is what you're telling me?"

"It is," Luther insisted. "He's tried before, and he will soon try again. He cannot succeed. If he does, devastation will envelop the land, of a scope we have not seen since the Gods' War ages ago. There are more gods than Karak and Ashhur, and Velixar would have them come into our world in an attempt to free Karak from his prison. Mankind will be decimated, and whatever freedom you think you know will vanish. The prophet would have all living men and women kneel before the Lion. Those who refuse will receive death. Do you understand, Thren? Why I've done all I've done? Why I have sacrificed everything to prevent the complete ruination of our civilization and the end of all free will?"

"You're a madman," Thren said.

"I've long thought the same of you…though I tend to use it as a term of respect."

Luther reached into his robe, and from around his neck, he pulled out a slender amulet crafted of gold and with a roaring lion etched into its circular center. Thren tensed at the sight of it, sensing a trap, but then Luther tossed it onto the desk before him.

"It was a last resort," he said. "I've tried convincing my order to turn against the prophet's ideals, to realize they were a sickening distortion of the god we all loved. In return, I received accusations of heresy. A god cannot change, they tell me, even though our own doctrines have changed again and again. You must believe me, I've tried everything, all I know, but this world is stubborn, full of bleak hearts and wounded children.

The tiles are all across Veldaren by now, but they're nothing without this amulet. It's the key, Thren, and I want you to have it. The fate of our world, I want it in your hands."

Whatever anger and confusion Thren had shown was lost, now replaced with a look Luther recognized, oh, so well: exhaustion.

"Why me?" he asked. "I don't know you, have never even heard of you. I've not once bent the knee to Karak. My connection to the priests in Veldaren is sparse and only when absolutely necessary. I want no part of the gods, no part of their war, their dogma and traditions."

"Exactly," said Luther. "You have always cherished your humanity above gods and kings, and not once have you hesitated at the thought of blood on your hands. Right now, I need someone like you. Someone who will have the courage to do what I cannot to protect our world."

"This amulet," Thren asked him, lifting it off the desk. "What does it do?"

"With a word, it activates the magic I've placed within the tiles," Luther said.

Thren's frown deepened.

"And what exactly will that magic do?"

This was it, the last piece of the puzzle. If Thren refused, there would be no other to take up the mantle. Taking in a deep breath, he pushed away his fear, his nervousness, and told him everything. As he spoke, he watched an awakening horror spread across the master thief's face. When Luther finished, Thren had fallen perfectly still, and it seemed even his breathing had stopped.

"Do you understand now?" Luther asked him. "Why I trust you? Why I feel you are one of the few with the strength to bear such a burden?" He chuckled. "The gods help me, I know

I could not. I am weak, and so I have remained here, hiding like a coward. It was only when I heard of Grayson Lightborn's death that I knew you would come for me. You've brought me hope, Thren. Seize it. Declare to the world we will be the pawns of gods no longer."

The pain in his hand was increasing, and he could see parts where it was darkening, congealing against the shining edge of the blade. He stared at the red and black, unable to meet Thren's gaze.

"You've played me, my guild, my entire city as if you were a god," Thren told him, and the sharpness of a blade pressed against his back. "You know I cannot let you live after that."

Luther slowly nodded, and he took in a deep breath. This was it, a moment he'd long known was coming. Eternity approached, yet which god would want him? Ashhur, who he had preached against all his life? Or Karak, whom he now actively betrayed?

"Will you do it?" he asked. "If the gates fall, if the prophet's army marches upon the castle, will you do it?"

Thren ripped out the dagger from his palm, and Luther choked down his pained cry. As warm blood spilled across his desk, seeping into the pages of the book before him, he felt water building in his eyes.

"I don't know," said Thren, but he put the amulet around his neck, and for Luther, that was sign enough.

"Do not fail me," he said, and he heard his voice crack. "You need to be strong, or the whole world suffers. There's good in what I've done, but unless you're strong, it'll all have been in vain."

"Strong?" Thren said softly. "It is all I know. When my childhood died, Muzien left me with little else."

The sword at his back pulled away, and he knew it prepared

for a thrust. The cruelty of Luther's plan, its sheer hopelessness, rushed through his mind. It burned him with guilt, and
he loathed it, yet amid such thoughts came the words of a lost
friend, and he spoke them aloud as if they came from the grave.

"We save this world by healing it," Luther whispered. "Not
with fire. Not with destruction." He felt tears running down
his face. "Forgive me, Jerico, but I saw no other way."

Forward came the blade, pain bursting into him, and as the
blood poured across his chest, he closed his eyes and gave up
his breath.

CHAPTER

18

Haern didn't fall very far, or for very long, before he landed on stone. It was sharply curved and perfectly smooth. He grabbed at it, searching for handholds, but there were none to be found. Down into the darkness he slid, unable to slow his descent. Haern tried kicking to one side, hoping to wedge himself in whatever chute he was sliding down, but he only succeeded in turning himself a different direction, and headfirst he flew.

The stone vanished, he was falling, and then he landed upon uneven ground. He heard the rattle of bones, felt pieces of something sharp digging into him. Letting out a groan from the pain, he rolled over and felt at what he'd landed on, for he had no hope of seeing it in the pitch black.

They were the bones of a man or woman, long since deceased. It did little to improve Haern's opinion of his situation.

"Left to starve," he muttered. "Gods damn it, is this how it all ends, starving in the darkness?"

"Not quite," said a voice, and the surprise nearly stopped his heart. He rolled to his knees and turned to face the direction the voice had come from. At first, he thought his mind played tricks on him, but he saw the faintest hint of blue light twinkling in the distance. As he watched, it grew stronger, larger, until he could see clearly the blue flame of a torch, only it burned on nothing, merely floated in the air like a bizarre sun. With its light, he could better see the reaches of his room, though it was less of a room and more of a cave. There appeared no doors or further passages, just a circular dome with a ceiling covered with stalactites, maybe a hundred feet from one side to the other. Covering the floor were bones, and sitting beneath the magical torchlight, his face an ashen gray and his rustic armor covered with dust, was a man with a long scar on his cheek.

"Welcome to my home," said the man. "It has been a very, very long time since I had company."

Haern stood, both hands falling to the swords at his belt.

"Who are you?" he asked. "Where am I?"

"Beneath the Stronghold," said the man. "In a place forgotten by most, though I would guess you knew that. As for who I am, well..."

He rose to his feet, dust billowing off of him. His armor groaned with each movement, and the way he moved, the way his joints cracked, made it seem as if he were a statue come to life. When at his full height, he stood at attention and saluted.

"Boris Marchant, at your service," he said, his deep voice scratchy and frightening in the enclosed space.

"Well, Boris," said Haern, trying not to panic, "care to tell me how to get out of here?"

Boris laughed.

"Look at me," he said. "If there were a way out, do you think I would still be down here?"

It was hardly what Haern wanted to hear, not that he could deny the logic.

"Perhaps you want to be down here," Haern said, hoping to keep the man talking. Something about him unnerved Haern immensely. He hardly carried the look of a paladin of Karak. In fact, he bore no markings at all of the god. His clothes were ratty and torn, and his armor was of a most peculiar make. He'd not seen banded mail of that style before, nor did he recognize the crudely drawn golden hawk on his chest. Much of it was crumbling along the edges, the metal tinted with green. At his side was an ancient sword, still sheathed.

At Haern's words, Boris erupted into laughter that went on for far too long.

"Want to be down here?" he asked when finished composing himself. He wiped at his face as if to remove a tear, yet there was not a hint of moisture on his skin. "Oh, no, good sir, I do not want to be down here. I have not wanted to be down here for decades, yet still I am."

"Decades?" Haern asked. "Then the paladins must bring you food and drink."

Boris shook his head.

"I do not require food to live, nor drink. Not here, not in this prison the prophet made for me."

Haern felt all the more certain something was amiss. The man looked to be in his thirties, a far cry from a man who had spent decades in isolation. And what man alive could survive without food and drink? He looked at the pale skin, the body covered with dust.

Unless he wasn't alive . . .

"My name is Haern," he said, deciding to introduce himself. Until he knew what was going on down there in that blue cavern, he'd try to play along. "And forgive me, but I still do not understand. You say you've lived here for decades without food and drink...I do not see how that is possible."

Boris sat back down on the smooth floor, and it was as if he were settling into a throne of bones, judging from how many were piled on either side of him.

"Sit," Boris said. "There is nowhere to go, and we have all the time in the world."

Haern did so, but only after ensuring he sat on no bones.

"When I say there is no escape, you must believe me," said Boris. He pointed to the blue light above him. "It lights only when the night is deep and the moon shining. I have used it to count the days as they pass, and those days have passed into years, and years into decades. For over five hundred years I have dwelt underneath the Stronghold, for that is my curse."

"They will not let you die?" Haern asked.

"Oh, I am already dead, but they will not let me pass on. I am bound here, forever bound until the curse is broken."

Haern shuddered at the thought of such torture. To be alive yet alone, locked in solitude with no hope of escape as the years rolled on and on, with no promise of relief?

He glanced at the bones around him. Well, not quite alone...

"What did you do to deserve such punishment?" he asked.

"I stole from him," Boris said. "Jacob Eveningstar, Karak's special little chosen servant. I never thought he'd find me, that he'd know I took it...but he did, oh, yes, he did, Haern. He found me, and he dragged me here, back when the Stronghold was first built. They flung me into the depths of this cave, sealed me in, but not before he used his magic. The prophet is powerful, so very powerful. 'You will not die,' he told me. 'Not until Karak once more walks the land.'"

Boris gestured about his prison.

"And so I wait." He grinned. "Tell me, Haern, does Karak walk the land?"

"No," Haern said, the very thought of it unnerving. "No, he does not."

"Of course not. I doubt he ever will. And so it goes. I'd ask you what transpires above ground, but after the first two centuries, I learned nothing changes. The names of rulers shift and dance, a few wars move the boundaries of lords like pieces in a game, but nothing ever truly changes."

"Used to ask...the bones, they throw prisoners down here to starve with you?"

"Only the most disloyal," Boris said. "Only the ones the paladins feel are truly deserving of such punishment. I am sent the heretics, the doubters, the men who turn from Karak and seek another way. When they are found, they are cast into the pit, where I wait like a monster from stories they tell their children."

Boris settled in, throwing more of his weight against the wall. It sent up a cloud of dust, and it shimmered a pale blue in the ethereal torchlight.

"What does change," he said, his voice quieting, "is the *reason* I find men and women thrown down to join me in this pit. So, tell me, Haern, what crime have you committed against the Stronghold? You hardly look like one of their paladins. Did you steal from them, perhaps, or get caught blaspheming a bit too loudly in a tavern?"

Haern normally would have been amused at how wrong his guess was, but there was no room for humor in that dark void. Returning to a stand, he walked toward the wall opposite Boris, his eyes scanning the ceiling. He knew he'd fallen down from somewhere, a chute or hole, and it had to have remained. Yet despite how well the phantom torch lit the walls and the floor, it seemed powerless to light the ceiling. Was it because of how high it stretched up, Haern wondered, or were tricks in play, games messing with the heads of their prisoners?

"What is it you're looking for?" Boris asked. "I told you, there's no way out."

"I wasn't thrown in here by the paladins," Haern said, ignoring him. It seemed best that way. "My...friend and I were breaking into the Stronghold, and we used a secret path to climb to the top. I slipped, fell, and landed in here."

On the other side, Boris broke out into creaking laughter, his voice as pleasant as rust.

"Breaking *into* the Stronghold? You must have balls the size of cantaloupes, boy. Did someone fill your head with wild stories of Karak's treasure stored in its depths? I've had my fair share of fools and blasphemers, but I think you might be the first treasure seeker to stumble down the pit without them knowing it."

Haern grinned despite himself.

"Always happy to be a first," he said, grabbing a bone and flinging it at the dark of the ceiling. Instead of continuing on, he heard an immediate clack.

Ten feet up, maybe eight, he thought, feeling a glimmer of hope. The shadows were there to hide the size. Perhaps if Boris could boost him, or he could use his cloak and swords to form some sort of grappling hook...

"But treasure is not why I'm here," Haern said, grabbing a few more bones, small pieces that looked like parts to a finger, and methodically walking in a circle from where he thought he'd landed, throwing them straight up to hear the *clack* of the bone hitting hard stone above, followed by another as it landed.

"Then why are you here?" Boris asked. He watched Haern work, clearly curious but saying nothing about it.

"I sought an audience with a priest," Haern said, scooping

up more bones. "A man named Luther who was supposedly imprisoned here."

"Luther?" asked Boris, and the recognition was enough to bring Haern's attention back his way. The gray-skinned man worked his jaw as if chewing something in his mouth, and the slopping noise he made was stomach-turning.

"You know him?" Haern asked.

"I do," Boris said. "He's the first of Karak's order to come down to speak with me in over a century. An intelligent man, perhaps too intelligent for his own good. It's going to cost him his life."

Well, thought Haern, at least there was a silver lining to his fun little drop. Perhaps he could learn a bit more about Luther and what he was hoping to accomplish in Veldaren. Tossing a few more bones into the air, all three hitting stone, he returned once more to the light of Boris's ethereal torch.

"What did he want from you?" Haern asked.

"I knew the prophet," Boris said. "Not well, but I was there when he was alive. Before he changed his name and became the thing with many faces he is now. Luther wanted to know what he was like, what he wanted, what he'd be willing to sacrifice..." Boris laughed. "And so I told him. A man who would imprison me for centuries, all for stealing a stupid book? He'd sacrifice everything, do anything, to achieve what he wanted. And no matter how loyal you think those pieces of shit upstairs are, Velixar makes them look like fair-weather faithful."

Haern saw Boris had begun to breathe heavily, and both his hands were trembling.

"Is something the matter?" Haern asked, taking a step backward. With another round of creaks and groans, Boris rose to his feet. His sword remained sheathed at his side, but Haern did not wait to draw his own blades and settle into a comfortable combat stance.

"I'm sorry, Haern," said Boris. "I've waited as long as I can."

"The bones," Haern said. "All the victims. You're their executioner, aren't you? Why, if you hate Karak so much?"

"There's no way for you to understand," said Boris, and he sounded sad. "You see, Velixar was a cruel one, and he was clever. Very clever. He knew what it'd be like to be down here alone, to crave company. I'd give so much for you to remain with me, Haern. I'd love to hear you speak of the outer world, of nations, your family, your friends. I yearn for stories like a drowning man craves land, but it never matters. Velixar did not just leave me imprisoned here. He filled me with a need."

Boris took a step closer.

"A need to feed," he said. "To taste blood upon my tongue. To tear flesh apart with my bare hands. I've fought it, Haern, but you are one of many, and I have long learned how useless it is to try."

Another step.

"The paladins send me company," he said. "Send me men and women who hate Karak as much as I do, who could ease my burden even if only for a few days, yet all I can do...what I *must* do...is kill any hope I have of escaping my solitude."

"Stay back," Haern warned, "unless you wish to test your claim at being unable to find death."

Boris smiled so wide, it stretched ear to rotten ear.

"I will feed," he said, and he licked his lips, his tongue like a dry sponge, and it left no moisture upon his cracked skin. "Many have tried, Haern. They always die, and as I feed, I cry their names so they may be remembered among the bones."

His mouth dropped open, thin lips pulling back to reveal chipped teeth stained by the blood of the dead. From his throat came a screech, animalistic in its sound and intelligence, and Haern felt his skin crawl. Weapons ready, he braced himself as Boris charged, sword still sheathed. Against a normal foe, Haern would have thought it an easy victory, but the bones all around him provided ample warning. The man raced toward him like a bull eager to ram its target, the popping of his bones and clanking of his feet on the stone only heightening the horror of his mindless shriek.

Just before reaching him, Boris spread his arms as if to embrace him in a hug, and Haern leaped to one side, twisting his body in the air so he could lash out with his left hand. The sword sliced along the side of Boris's neck, severing what should have been his jugular vein. But when Haern landed and he looked, he saw no blood, just a dry tear in the side of gray flesh. Boris turned, and the only visible life in him was the amused twinkle in his eyes.

"I don't bleed," Boris screamed, flinging himself at Haern again. Haern jumped back, slashing Boris's throat and face. More cuts, doing nothing.

"I don't sleep."

Haern found himself running out of room, the gray man faster than he had any right to be. There was no hesitation to his moves, nor the slightest fear of harm coming to himself. Nearly trapped against the wall, he waited for another lunge from Boris, then dropped to a roll, slicing out in hopes of taking out the tendons in Boris's legs. Instead of leaving him hampered, though, Haern's swords caught on the thick banded plates protecting him, unable to penetrate further.

In mid-roll, Haern could only try to kick out fast enough to avoid Boris as he dropped atop him.

"I don't breathe."

Haern felt Boris's hand catch his ankle, putting an end to his roll. He slammed onto his stomach, one of his swords slipping from his grip as his face struck the stone floor. Meanwhile,

Boris tugged and tugged, his mouth open, his tongue hanging down like a dead gray worm as he pulled Haern's leg closer.

"All I know to do," he said, "is eat."

With nothing else to do, nothing else to try, Haern took his sword, twisting to a sitting position, and plunged it straight into that gaping maw. It punched through the back of his throat and out the other side, lodging in tight. Haern released it when it was sunk all the way in, leaving Boris snapping his teeth down on the metal of the hilt. As the ancient man hacked and coughed, his head shaking violently as he tried to expel the blade, Haern repeatedly kicked the hand holding him. Fingers snapped one by one, and the moment he was loose, he rolled away before Boris could attempt to grab again.

Now free, he reached for his other sword and stalked back toward Boris.

"I'm sorry, Boris," he said. "But I have a priest to find."

He slammed the blade with all his strength against the man's throat until it hit bone. The power of it knocked him to his back, and Haern struck again and again, as if he were a lumberjack trying to fell a tree. At last he heard a crack, and at that, he reached down, pinned Boris with his knees, and then twisted the head until there was a second, far louder crack.

"Gods damn it," Haern said as he stood, holding Boris's head in his hands. "Let go of my sword already."

Sheathing one blade, he pulled the other from the head's mouth, the blade sliding out through the hole it'd punched in the back of the head. Inspecting the weapon in the blue light, he saw no gore, no blood or goop or anything. Just dust. Shaking his head, he rolled the head toward the other side of the room, where it came to a thumping halt.

"Enjoy your rest," he said, eyes scanning the darkness above him. "But it's time for me to get out of here."

Boris had said no one ever escaped, but with him there to attack and kill presumably unarmed and perhaps even bound men and women, he doubted anyone had been given sufficient time to try. Scooping up another handful of bones, he returned toward the middle and began tossing. On the fifth try, he heard a different sound, one that gave him pause.

Metal?

He threw a few more, some ringing of metal, yet a few falling silently back down.

A grate, he realized. He didn't remember one upon falling down into the chamber. Perhaps it had been already open, or loose enough he hadn't noticed during his fall? For all he knew, it shut by magic. What did matter, though, was that he had found his exit. Clearing a spot beneath so he could easily relocate it if need be, he stood there, arms crossed, mind racing. He needed some way to reach it, preferably a rope. It was only a few feet above his head, and he didn't need much to try to grab ahold and test its resilience.

Glancing over at Boris's body, he had a thought, one so absurd he laughed aloud.

"Surely you won't mind," he said as he knelt down beside the headless body. He lifted the man's left arm, analyzing it. The fingers had curled in upon death, and testing them, he found them rigid. Flipping it over, he found the buckles to the banded armor and quickly removed them. The shirt beneath had long ago faded into nothing, and Boris's skin beneath was sickeningly pale and cold to the touch. Tugging on the arm, he found the joints even stiffer than they should have been so recently after death.

No blood, he told himself. The body was far from normal, so just maybe...

He removed the chest piece as well as the shoulder pads,

wanting a clear view of the dead man's shoulder. With that done, he began hacking into it with a sword. Each cut made a sickening cracking noise, and after several swings, he grabbed the arm and began to wrench it violently side to side until at last he heard a pop. A few more swings and he cut the thing loose, not surprised to find that the connection between the arm and shoulder was much stronger than a normal corpse.

"I'm counting on you," Haern said, carrying the arm back to the grate. "Just . . . hold together, all right?"

There was no swivel at the elbow, no movement whatsoever. Wielding it as he would a club, he held it by the far end of the arm, a bizarre extension with curled fingers reaching up into the black void unlit by the blue torchlight. Praying for a miracle, he swung the club, ramming the fingers into the grate. He heard a scraping sound coupled with a crack he could only assume was one of the bones in the fingers breaking. Trying not to get his hopes up, he closed his eyes and pulled.

The fingers held, and the grate swung down with ease. The torchlight just barely shone upon it, and Haern could tell it was thoroughly rusted over.

"No escape?" muttered Haern. "I think you're about to help me prove you wrong, Boris."

Using the arm as a rope, he pulled himself up off the ground, not bothering to test the weight. The last thing he wanted to do was add any extra strain, even if for a moment. Up the arm he went, and when he reached the grate, he stretched to his limits, fingers searching for a hold. When he found one, a jut of stone the grate's hinge was connected to, he wanted to cry. Now with something firm to hold onto, he pulled himself up and into the tunnel. The sides were cramped, the rock uneven, so when he pushed against one side with his feet, he was able to successfully wedge himself into the entrance.

Before he could ascend higher, he heard a rattling, a rolling, and then the most sickening popping sound.

"*Haern . . .*"

Just his imagination, he told himself. Haern reached down, grabbing Boris's arm and wrenching it free. He might need it again on his climb, he decided. Still, he didn't like the way it flopped over his back, suddenly not so rigid.

"*Haern, don't leave me.*"

Not his imagination, then. He heard the scattering of bones, the groaning of leather straps and the rattle of armor.

"*Don't leave me down here!*"

The arm vibrated across his back. Haern pulled it off him, and then it suddenly tugged hard down toward the chamber. He just barely released it in time before it could pull him back inside. The arm hit the ground, then rolled out of sight. Another sickening pop followed.

"Just climb," Haern whispered, pushing away all thoughts of Boris reassembling himself, condemned to remain inside the blue-fire chamber, fed the scraps of Karak's unfaithful. "Nothing else, just climb."

Keeping his legs braced, his back pressed against the stone, he pushed himself upward with his arms, nice and slow. Once high enough, he took a step, one foot above the other. It was tedious work and put tremendous strain on his legs and back, but it was something he knew he could endure for hours if need be. He just had to be careful. One slip, one slacking of the pressure, and he'd be tumbling back down the tunnel.

He doubted Boris would be so polite and talkative the second time around.

"*Haern . . .*"

Boris's voice followed him, a ragged, fading whisper. It took many steps, and at least ten minutes by his guess, but eventually, he was high enough in the darkness to be free of the man's haunting cry. He prayed he never heard the cursed man's voice ever again.

Inch by tedious inch he climbed. Occasionally, he found handholds in the stone, and he used them to rest his back. He tried not to think about how long he was down there, nor his escape. All he thought of was his father telling him "sorry" before sending him tumbling down into the pit. Whenever Haern felt his legs starting to wobble, or his back locking up from the strain, he thought of that "sorry" and used it to push on higher. The tunnel gradually shifted, the slight variations required to prevent someone from plummeting straight down to their death. Sometimes, they were just soft enough that he could sit for a moment and catch his breath before continuing. Sometimes, they forced him to twist and shift the way he climbed, lest he slide right back down.

At one point, he felt his foot slip into the air, and at first, he thought he'd missed, but then he realized it was a secondary tunnel connected to the first. It was somewhat perpendicular to the one he climbed, and he grabbed ahold of its sides with his fingers and pulled himself into it. Letting out a gasp, he lay on his back and willed his muscles to relax.

"Almost there," he told himself, though he had no idea if it were true or not. "Almost there."

The question now was where to go: up, or follow the other chute? In the end, he decided to continue his climb. His gut said the other direction led to wherever the dark paladins tended to dump their victims. The higher tunnel with the ladder? That one he had a feeling they knew nothing about. Well, no one but Luther, if the priest, or his father, were to be trusted.

As much as he hated the thought of doing so, he returned to a crouch, then extended so that he was leaning against the far side. Spinning about so his back was against it, he stepped one step to the left, a firm foot pushing against stone, and began his climb. More time. More inches by painful inches. When the pain in his back didn't seem able to get any worse, he felt it strike something sharp. Despite the pain, despite the darkness, a laugh escaped his lips that took almost a minute to cease.

It was one of the rungs pounded into the stone that formed the ladder.

Once he had a firm grip and his weight was fully supported by the ladder, Haern hung there, once again debating. He could leave, he knew. The exit was just opposite him. He could crawl through the dark until reaching Delysia, and together they could flee the Stronghold, leaving as if they'd never been. But above him was where Luther should be, and where his father had gone. Leaving now, giving in . . . he couldn't do it. He had to know. So, up the rungs he went, and after the tedious process earlier, the ladder felt like a gift from the heavens.

Multiple times he felt the soft blowing of cool air upon his neck, alerting him to side passages, but he never took them. Luther was supposed to be at the top, so to the top he would climb. As he did, he listened to the noises that came to him through the stone. They were distorted, of course, but he still found himself occasionally surprised by the proximity or clarity he heard. Much of it was soft discussion, deep voices talking about things he could only guess at. Once he swore he heard a man in prayer, and on another floor, two men arguing. Whenever he heard such sounds, he slowed his ascent, always fearful that somehow they might also hear him scurrying up the walls like a rat.

At last, he reached the end of the rungs. He reached out behind him, but the wall was solid. Steadying himself, he paused a moment, felt the softest flow of air from his left. Taking his foot off the rung, he tested, and sure enough, he found a tall tunnel. Slowly, he shifted his weight off the rungs and into the short tunnel, at the very end of which he saw the tiniest slivers of light, like cracks in a wooden door. To his eyes, though, they were blinding, and he blinked and kept his gaze to the side until he might recover.

It turned out his comparison wasn't far off. It did seem to be a wooden door before him, slender and rectangular. He could only guess as to what it appeared to be from the other side, as well as how he might open it. Slowly, he ran his hands along it until he found a single bit of metal for him to grab. Gently, he pushed inward, then pulled toward him, and he found the door had far more give into the room than out.

Putting his ear to the side, he listened for signs of life, heard none. Double-checking his swords at his waist, he pulled his hood low over his face and took in a deep breath. This was it. Time to discover just where he was. He pushed against the metal knob, heard a crack, and then the rectangular slab of wood swung out. The light inside was blinding, even though it was only two separate lanterns on each side of the room with tall slender candles burning within them. Squinting against it, he dipped his head so his hood would block much of the light, and with what vision he had, he checked his surroundings.

Haern found himself inside what appeared to be a library, with four free-standing shelves of books before him. Turning about out of curiosity, he looked to see what it was he'd emerged from. Shutting the entrance, he saw that it was an enormous wooden carving that had been mounted upon the wall. Etched into the wood with amazing detail was a lion devouring a stag, with the carver having used heat to blacken wherever there was supposed to have been blood. Testing a corner, he found that pulling against it made the wall itself open up to grant him entrance back into the darkness.

Should be easy enough to remember, Haern thought to himself as he reshut the door. If he were to somehow get lost, all he needed to do was find a library and the giant wood lion carving within it. Getting to it without being killed or spotted, however, he had a feeling would be the real trick. Hurrying past the rows of bookshelves, all of which were blessedly empty of any odd midnight readers, he reached the door and put an ear to it. Again, he heard nothing. Opening it, he found himself facing a large set of stairs curling around the outer walls of the Stronghold. To his right, they descended, curving out of sight, and so he hurried left, moving ever higher. A red carpet ran along the center of the stairs, its edges laced with gold-colored thread. The stone shaping the walls and stairs was a deep gray, with spiderwebs of black racing all across the surface. Candles hung above him, high enough he felt glad he wasn't the poor soul who had to change them somehow when they burned low. A glance out one of the thin windows showed him just how high up he was, and he fought down a shiver. He'd never been inside a building as tall as the Stronghold. Not even the highest towers of the king's castle in Veldaren could compare. Haern had never considered himself afraid of heights, but peering out that window made him think all men could be made afraid of them if the ground were far enough away.

The stairs curled up into the next floor, the grand wooden door to it closed. Haern heard muffled prayers from within despite the lack of any light shining through the cracks. Deciding to check higher first, he continued on, resolving to return only if he could not find Luther in any of the floors above. A few more steps up, and he knew that his search was over. Lying before an open door, throat opened and armor bloody, was a young man. Haern stepped over him, peering into the final room at the uppermost reaches of the Stronghold. Inside he saw a small bed with violet sheets, a slender, half-empty bookshelf, a glassed window facing the east, and a desk. Slumped over the desk was an older man in black robes.

Haern stepped into the room and drew his swords, even though he knew what he would find. There was too much blood on the chair, too much blood on the floor. Coming up to the man, he pulled on his shoulder, and his body slumped back, head lolling.

"Damn it," Haern whispered.

His father had beaten him to the top, learned or taken whatever he needed, and then fled. He was too late.

"What did you want from us?" Haern asked the body. The man looked like any other, skin starting to wrinkle, hair all gray. There was dried blood on his left hand, and a fatal wound to the back. Haern had a feeling the wound to the hand had been first, a way to prevent the priest from casting any potential spells. Had Thren interrogated him afterward? A cursory glance showed no additional stab wounds, no obvious broken bones. Whatever information Luther gave, it must have come easily.

His eyes fell on the book that lay open before him. It was stained with blood, but the lone paragraph on its pages was still legible. Based on the pen and inkwell on the desk, Haern assumed the writing to be Luther's. The script was tight, carefully controlled, and reading it did little to illuminate matters.

Tonight he comes, I know it. I would pray, but what god would answer? I condemn a city to save a nation. Perhaps Karak would be proud after all.

No answers, just as Delysia had promised. Only death and betrayal. His only hope now was to find Thren, assuming the man even stuck around to be questioned. He felt a momentary rush of panic, thinking of Delysia lying dead by the exit to the building, and he pushed it down. For her to die while he was crawling up from the pit, to die while waiting for him to return from a place she'd begged him not to go...

"Luther?"

He turned around to see a boy no older than twelve carrying a lit candle in one hand, five more unlit in the other. The boy stood just before the body of the dead guard, his jaw hanging open. Haern swore, leaping toward the door in hopes of stopping him before he could escape and sound the guard. But the boy had no desire to run. The candles dropped from his hands, and before Haern could reach him, he'd already drawn a slender dirk from his belt and begun shouting at the top of his lungs.

"Intruder! Intruder! Intr—"

Haern batted aside the meager weapon, and momentum unchanged, he slammed into the boy with a sword leading the way. The boy's cry halted as he doubled over, a sword buried to the hilt in his gut. Haern stared right into his eyes, horrified by the sight. There was no doubt, no sorrow, no confusion... just rage.

No different than I was at his age, thought Haern, and he felt a chill as if a ghost had crossed over his grave.

Cries from below quickly echoed the boy's warning, and Haern swore again. He had to get out of there now, before they could overwhelm him. He flew down the stairs, trying to push the memory of the boy's dying face out of his mind. At the floor beneath, he found the door open and a man standing before it. He was stout and not very tall, but he held an enormous sword in one hand, its blade wreathed with black flame. Contrasted against the plain white bedrobe he wore, the sight would have been comical if not for how the paladin nearly skewered Haern as he ran down the steps.

"Who sent you?" the man asked, pulling back for another thrust as Haern dodged the first.

"Luther did," said Haern, hoping to confuse him. Based on the glare he received, Haern decided he'd hit a nerve, and the burning blade slashed down with all the man's might. There wasn't much room in the stairway, but Haern was more than agile enough to slide to the side, the fire and steel cutting the air before him. The sword smacked into the stone steps, immediately charring the red carpet and cracking the step in two. Haern gave him no chance to recover, his right arm swinging out so his sword opened the man's throat. A follow-up kick sent the body tumbling, the sword clattering along with him. Haern winced at the cacophony it created. If there was anyone in the Stronghold who hadn't realized he was inside, they knew now.

No time, no time, no time.

Haern ran, wanting nothing more than to see those beautiful oak shelves full of books. Instead, he found two more men armed with swords rushing up the stairs, the blades of both paladins wreathed with flame.

"Sorry, can't stay long," Haern said as he lunged with both weapons. He knew they would successfully block the attacks, and when they did he felt a tingle in his hands, as if the sting of the flames had traveled through the steel of his swords, through the hilt, and into his flesh. It kept them back, though, just enough that he had room to leap headfirst into the library. He rolled along the carpet, then skidded to a stop so he could turn and fight. He had room now, and every intention to use it.

"You will suffer for this insult!" one of the paladins cried, and Haern grinned at him. *Suffer? No, not today.* He attacked the man just as he tried to rush through the doorway, sabers a blur. The paladin tried to block, and there was no moving that dark blade, no forcing its position like he might against a normal opponent. But Haern had speed, and due to the surprise nature of the combat, neither paladin had their armor to rely upon. When the paladin tried to counter as a way of buying himself some space, Haern blocked it with ease, then stabbed him through the belly. As he doubled over, the other paladin shoved the body forward, using it to keep Haern from attacking while he was limited by the doorway.

"Karak guide my hand," said the paladin as he grabbed the hilt of his sword with both hands. The dark fire around its steel grew stronger, and the very sight of it made Haern's head ache. He moved to attack, but the fire flared, and without knowing what it meant, Haern fell back. So badly did he want to flee to the wood carving, but if any caught sight of where he was going, there was too much of a chance they could decipher where he might exit. Better they thought he vanished like a ghost than into a cramped tunnel in their very walls.

"Karak be my strength."

The paladin swung, and it was as if he wielded an inferno with his hands. Haern retreated until his back was to a bookshelf, bumped it, scattered books to the floor.

"Karak be my victory!"

A massive downward chop, but Haern was already moving. The sword hit the stone, the books erupted in flame, and then came the smoke. Haern slid to one side, then pushed off into the air. Twirling, all cloaks and swords, the paladin could only guess where to position his blade in defense. He guessed wrong.

The man's body crumpled to the ground as Haern landed. He was given no chance to celebrate nor retreat, for more men were running into the library, all wielding swords or axes. Knowing his time had long since run out, Haern did not engage them, instead racing toward the fire and knocking more books into it. As the smoke billowed, Haern grabbed one that was already aflame, the violet fire consuming it eerie to witness and powerful in its heat, and then hurled the book into another shelf. It caught as if doused with lantern oil.

Deeper toward the back of the library he ran, dodging desperate swings as the men rushed into it. They were trying to be methodical, sealing off the exit and lining the far wall so that there'd be no aisle he could hide in, but that only gave him more time. He knocked over another shelf, then assaulted a paladin that had been chasing him. Their weapons clashed, and though all feeling was gone from his hands, Haern still managed to slice out his heel, then finish him with a stab to the neck in passing. From the other side, he heard men shouting, asking where he was, and debating what to do about the flames that were leaping from bookshelf to bookshelf as if containing a life of their own.

Keep on arguing, thought Haern as he raced for the enormous wood carving and his escape.

Just before he reached, it a burning blade swung into his vision. On instinct, Haern dropped to his knees, the sword searing the air above him. The heat was incredible, terrifyingly so. Whirling about to face his opponent, he found an older man with gray hair, his black armor decorated with the silver skull of a lion. His strength was incredible as he pulled the enormous sword back around for a second swing, faster than most men could wield a dagger. Haern knew blocking was impossible, and trying to time the swing right, he dove underneath, hoping to come out of his roll beside the man and stab him in the neck while he was vulnerable.

Except as he dove into the roll, the sword dipped, swung with only one hand. Coming up for the stab, Haern found a mailed fist already waiting. It struck him square in the face, blood blasting from his nose.

"*Karak!*" cried the man, and suddenly, that fist felt like the hammer of a god. The blow rocked through his body, straining his bones, filling his throat with a scream that sounded far too horrific to be his own. Legs suddenly resisting him, he dropped to one side, limbs curiously asleep. Trying not to panic, he glared up at the older paladin, who knelt down before him.

"You're either a brilliant man or a fool," said the paladin as arms grabbed Haern from all sides. "In our dungeon, we'll see which of the two you truly are."

Something hard hit him from behind, and then the darkness took him.

CHAPTER

19

The last thing Alyssa did that night, as she did every night, was remove her eyes. Despite the insistence of the craftsmen who'd formed them, despite her own fingers that could confirm their smoothness, she still felt as if they were covered with a thousand jagged slivers that sliced into her vacant eye sockets. Only once had she tried sleeping with them still in, and she'd awoken halfway through the night to find her fingers digging into her sockets, which were wet with tears.

There were no servants with her in her room, Alyssa at last left in solitude. They'd check on her occasionally, she knew. At the foot of her bed, resting atop a table, was a brass bell she could ring if she ever needed anything, not that she ever did. She was blind, not an invalid, and whenever she needed something, she left her bed, walked across the cold floor, and opened the door to ask the servant waiting outside. She remembered when Melody first suggested the bell, except the bell was to have been hooked to a rope hanging beside her head. She'd threatened to set the entire bed on fire if she ever discovered such a set up.

What I'd give to have seen their faces, Alyssa thought as she set the eyes into a glass with a thin layer of alcohol at the bottom. *They must have thought me out of my mind.*

It wasn't that much of a stretch, really. She'd long felt the eyes of her enemies circling her. Now without her own, she knew it was only a matter of time before they closed in, snatching at whatever they could get. Her only hope rested in people like Zusa and John Gandrem protecting her interests, and even then, they faced an impossible task.

Alyssa removed her robe and slid naked underneath the silken sheets. They were cold, and she shivered, arms crossed and knees drawn to her chest, as she waited for them to warm. Her breathing steadily slowed, and head sunk into a giant feathered pillow, she tried to relax. Yet she couldn't. Something bothered her, even as the rest of her body warmed. A window, she realized. The quiet of her room was not complete, the soft rustle of air she felt on her cheek not supposed to be there. Sitting up with the blankets pulled to her chest, she addressed the darkness.

"Who is there?" she asked. "Say your name now. If I hear any other noise, I will scream for my guards."

"Your senses are to be commended," said a deep voice at the foot of her bed. "Given what I know of your personality, you might have been a fine member of my guild in a different life."

"Who are you?" she asked, though in the pit of her stomach she felt certain she already knew.

"Come, now, surely you can guess?"

Spoken with such confidence, such condescension. *You are a child to me,* that voice said, *just a silly, stupid child,* and it annoyed Alyssa to no end.

"There are plenty in this city with the skill to sneak past my guards," she said, hoping to deflate him the tiniest bit. "Is there a reason you think you are special?"

The intruder laughed. Controlled. Amused. A predator's laugh.

"I need not think it," he said. "I *know* it, and you do too, don't you, Alyssa? The moment I spoke to reveal my presence, a chill ran down your spine, and with an absolute certainty came to you a name. Please, say it, and don't lie. It proves nothing if you lie."

Alyssa swallowed.

"Muzien," she said. "Muzien the Darkhand."

The elf clapped, and she wondered if the servant outside her door would hear it. Pulling the blankets tighter about her, she slid her free hand underneath her pillow, to the dagger hidden there.

"See, was that so hard? Now spare me your sarcasm and petty attempts to insult me while hiding your fear. We have things to discuss, you and I."

"I will have no business with you," Alyssa said. "And if you've come to kill me, just do it now. I will not beg for your amusement."

"Amusement?" Again Muzien laughed. It was from a different direction than before, and when he spoke again, the location had changed once more. He was moving about her, constantly forcing her to readjust his mental position in her head. Anything to make her uncomfortable, she realized, as if being naked and helpless were not enough to accomplish that.

"My dear, if I wanted amusement, I would have gone elsewhere. Tonight is business, whether you wish it or not."

Her fingers closed about the dagger's hilt. With her blankets raised, her actions should have been hidden. There was no chance she could strike him when ready, but if he were to make a move on her, thinking her helpless...

"Get on with it, then," she said, raising her voice the slightest amount. If only the servant outside would hear her voice, realize she spoke with someone when she was supposed to be alone.

"Gladly."

So close to her right ear she felt the heat of his breath on her skin. Her entire body tensed, and in that half second, she felt a tug on her blankets and movement beneath her pillow. Before she could react, Muzien ripped the dagger from her hand. A soft thud told her it landed on the carpet below, far out of reach. She thought to dive for it anyway, but a hand closed around her throat and slammed her back down atop her pillow.

"Now is a time to listen," the elf whispered into her ear, "not make foolish plans to attack me, nor vain attempts to alert the servant outside your door. I killed her, Alyssa. She's bleeding out in your closet as we speak, so before someone notices her absence, you and I must come to an understanding. Have I made myself clear?"

His grip tightened, and though she opened her mouth to answer, she could not make a sound. Her hands clutched at his wrist, fingernails scratching hard enough to draw blood, yet it relented not the slightest amount.

"I asked, Have I made myself clear?"

It loosened the tiniest bit, and she gasped in air.

"Yes," she said, voice hoarse and painful to her own ears.

"Excellent."

Gone was the hand, her bed shifting as his weight upon it was removed. Alyssa lay there, still covered by the blankets, and did her best to regain her composure.

"I saved you for last," Muzien said, and by the way his voice traveled, she imagined him pacing before her at the foot of the bed. "Every other man and woman of power in this city, I have crossed paths with. No one may claim I came to Veldaren like a thief in the night. No one may feign ignorance or surprise by what happens tomorrow. For everyone, from the highest king to the lowliest serf, there are only two options: compliance or rebellion."

"Compliance with what?" she dared ask, and it hurt her throat to speak.

"My demands," Muzien said. "You see, Alyssa, the night is mine now. I own it and keep it in my pocket like I would a coin or key. No one will take it from me, nor challenge me for it. The Sun Guild has claimed every street, every corner, every shop, every stall. Even the king has agreed to look the other way, granting us immunity from his soldiers and guards. So, as you sit here, I want you to realize how alone you are. You've proven troublesome in your past, fiery and stubborn, but now is a time for wisdom, not passion. Can you do that for me, Alyssa?"

She wanted to tell him to go fuck himself, but that would only make her night worse. Instead, she nodded and kept her mouth shut.

"Excellent. Quiet, obedient. You're learning, so here is the next lesson. The deal you've struck between the Trifect and the thief guilds, this Watcher's truce, it ends tonight."

"You'd plunge this city back into chaos?" she asked.

"On the contrary, Alyssa, I would give it a proper peace. What you've created is a mockery of order, and it was doomed to fail whether I came here or not. But here I am, and I will not allow it to stand. The guilds are mine, all of them. The men who signed those signatures are either dead or bow their knees to me. We will do whatever we wish to do, take from whomever we wish to take. Only one thing will stop us: gold."

"That's it? You just want protection money? How is that any different from what we had before?"

She felt the bed sink the tiniest bit from the elf sitting on one of the corners.

"It comes down to power, Alyssa. There will be no enforcer beyond myself. The terms will be decided by me and me alone. You will hand over coin, and through my good grace, you will be spared any wrath. The same will go for every other shop and tavern and brothel that operates within Veldaren's walls. No one will sell the smallest scrap of bread without my approval and my cut. Consider it a tax paid to the rightful king of our fair city."

Alyssa was stunned by what she heard. The elf believed it, every word. He truly thought the entirety of Veldaren was his. The frightening part was how close to the truth it might actually be.

"You reach too far," she said. "The king will call his armies from across Neldar. Lord Stern Blackwater in Angelport will hear of this, and he'll prepare his own mercenaries. Even the temple to Ashhur will not stand for your enslavement."

"King Vaelor could summon soldiers," Muzien said, and he was close again, lurking, a cat playing with a mouse. "The priests might stumble out of their temple, hopeless to discover what is happening underneath their noses. Yes, even Stern might head north to protect his fellow members of the Trifect. But do you know what all those require, Alyssa?"

She felt his hand grab her face and turn it hard to the left. The skin was scaly and hot to the touch. It felt like the hand of a monster, and she whimpered at the pain it caused in her neck.

"What?" she asked as the silence lingered.

"Bravery, and I sense none of it in this forsaken place."

He let her go, and she heard footsteps as he moved away, toward the door, she guessed.

"Tomorrow, I announce my presence to the city," Muzien

said. "My time of meetings and games will be over. This is your only chance, Alyssa; now give me your answer. Will you pay for protection against my might, or must I bury you like all others who have dared oppose me?"

She should do it, she knew. When Thren Felhorn had united the thief guilds, they'd been near impossible to destroy, and this elf seemed superior to Thren in every way... even in arrogance. It'd be so easy, too. All she had to do was whisper those simple words "I will" and she'd be in his pocket, no different from anyone else in the Trifect. No different from the other thief guilds or even their cowardly, infantile king.

No different...

"I never bowed to Thren," she said. "I never bowed to the guilds nor the pressures of my title. I won't bow to you, Muzien. Threaten me all you wish, but I'm tired of hiding in my home, trembling like a child."

She thought he might react in anger, or even kill her, but instead, he laughed.

"Curious," he said. "Daverik assured me the Gemcroft family would readily accept, yet that seemed counter to everything I knew about you, my dear Alyssa. It is good to know that my opinion of you was more accurate than that of a lowly priest."

Priest? thought Alyssa. *Daverik? What nonsense is this?*

"You have your answer," she said, doing her best to sit up straight and control the quiver in her voice. "Now leave me be."

Muzien *tsk*ed at her from across the room.

"You're making a mistake, Alyssa. No one must die needlessly, but then again, needless death has always been the mark of your house. As you humans like to say, 'It is your funeral.'"

Something heavy landed in her lap atop the blankets, and she felt it with her fingers. The bronze bell the servants kept at the foot of her bed.

"You may summon your guards now," Muzien said, and she could imagine him standing before her, so smug, so certain of himself. "It will be the last time they ever have warning."

She heard footsteps, the sound of her door opening, followed by the shattering of a window in a distant room. Despite her hatred of it, she shook the bell with both hands, shook until she heard her door opening, heard the heavy boots of her guards rushing in. But one person, one whose footsteps were silent, arrived before any guard could.

"What happened?" asked Zusa, voice hovering just beside her.

"Muzien was here," she said. "He wanted my allegiance."

"What did you tell him?"

Soldiers were coming into the room now, and she felt their presence like a suffocating blanket. Still naked, she clutched her blankets tightly to her to preserve some modicum of modesty.

"Get those men out of here," she said. "I need to dress."

The grumblings of the guards were obviously unhappy, but they reluctantly obeyed. Once they were gone, she heard a closet opening, followed by a sharp inhalation of air.

The body, thought Alyssa.

"Muzien told me he killed Sally," she said.

"He did," was all Zusa said. The closet door shut, and a moment later, a simple, lengthy shift dropped into her hands.

"Dress," Zusa said. "But talk while doing it. What was your answer to the Darkhand?"

Alyssa lifted her arms, let Zusa begin to slide the shift over her head.

"I told him no," she said.

"You did?" Zusa said, and she sounded surprised. "But I thought you were willing to let this all go? When we spoke earlier..."

"I know what I said," snapped Alyssa, far harsher than she

meant. "But damn it, Zusa, is this what I've become? Cowering in my room, wallowing in self-pity because a sick little boy took away my eyes? All I want is for Nathaniel to become something great. Something amazing. It won't happen this way, though. My anger and sorrow once made this entire city tremble with fear. I thought to learn from that, to humble myself... but the world will only see it as weakness, not strength. So then, let's be the strength they understand."

The shift on, Alyssa reached out a hand until she felt Zusa's face press against it.

"Are your blades still mine to command?" she asked.

"Now and forever," Zusa said.

"Then find this Daverik. Muzien spoke his name, and said he was a priest. Somehow, it seems he is involved with the Sun Guild's arrival."

It took little skill to sense Zusa's sudden unease.

"I know who he is," she said. "Forgive me, Alyssa. I should have killed him months ago. The faceless woman who attacked you was loyal to him as well."

"Can you find him?"

"If he is in the temple, he is beyond me. I have already failed once to take his life in his sacred home. But if he is nearby, perhaps aware of Muzien's plan..."

The door opened, and Alyssa heard her mother gasp.

"My dear, are you all right?" she asked.

Alyssa took Zusa's hand, squeezed it tight.

"Go do what needs to be done," she said. "I'll be fine."

Being left alone with Melody was hardly a pleasant thought, but she needed Zusa out and about, ensuring the safety of her home. No doubt the woman was already itching to do so, at least to discover how Muzien made it past their guards.

Zusa's lips pressed against her hand, and then she was gone.

Alyssa remained in the center of her bed, and she felt it give as Melody sat at the foot.

"You poor thing," her mother said. "You must have been so frightened."

Alyssa laughed at the absurdity as she put back in her eyes.

"I was," she said. "But for once, I think I feel like myself again. We have much to do tomorrow, and I hope you will help me as you've always promised."

"Of course," Melody said. "Whatever you need of me, I will do. I take it this has to do with that ... *elf's* visit?"

"In a way," Alyssa said, scratching at her neck. Something about the fabric of her shift made her skin itch. Yet it seemed the blankets bothered her as well, and with the way her heart was racing in her chest, she wondered if she were about to suffer a panic attack. It was odd how calm she felt, as if her body were simply betraying her, or perhaps better understanding how to properly react than even she did. This would change everything, she knew. Stepping back out of the shadows and into the light with a target painted across her forehead ... it'd been so long since she had the courage. Could she do so again?

"Did he tell you what he wanted?" Melody asked. Something about the way she asked put Alyssa on edge. It was as if she were asking a question to which she already knew the answer. Or perhaps it was only the flurry of panic she was fighting down.

"Bribes," she said. "For protection. Our deal between the Trifect and the guilds is over, and Muzien aims to replace it."

"How much did he request?"

Alyssa shook her head.

"I didn't ask. It doesn't matter. Giving that elf more power than he already has is suicide."

"Have you thought that *refusing* him is suicide, not the other way around?"

Alyssa sighed. Not that she was surprised by the question, just exhausted by it. Of course, her mother would doubt her. Of course, she'd act as if her decision were the wrong one.

"We've endured worse," Alyssa said. "It's time to rid ourselves of these miserable whoresons like I should have done years ago."

Melody cleared her throat. It was the act of someone preparing to broach a subject they were clearly nervous about.

"I know you think you're doing what is best for the family," she began, "but perhaps it would be appropriate for you to let someone else handle matters while you recover?"

Whatever exhaustion Alyssa had felt quickly vanished.

"Recover?" she asked. "Recover from what?"

"Your...troubles," Melody said. "Ever since you lost your eyes you've been sullen, quick to anger, and no longer caring for the future of the Gemcroft family line. Right now, we need a leader who may show patience and forethought, not someone who can only think of herself and her son."

Alyssa's dagger was still on the floor by the bed, and it was a good thing for Melody.

"A leader like you?" she asked. "That's what you mean, isn't it?"

There was a pause, and Alyssa had a feeling it was from her mother stupidly shaking her head as if she might see it.

"It's not," Melody insisted. "I will accept the burden if I must, but it doesn't have to be that way. There's still hope for you, my sweet little girl, but only if you remove the hardness about your heart."

Zusa, thought Alyssa. *Damn it, why didn't I keep you with me?* No doubt she was scouring the grounds, but inside was where she needed her. Inside was where the true threat lied.

"Don't dance around this," Alyssa said, her patience wearing thin and annoyed that it only seemed to affirm part of what Melody had accused her of. "Whatever it is you want, come out and say it."

"Karak…"

"No," she interrupted, anger burning in her breast the moment she heard the god's name spoken. "No, anything but that. I will not hear it, Melody. Not a word about your damned god's promises, his wisdom, or any help you think his followers can give us. I will not bend the knee to a corpse to avoid bending it to a thief."

"No, little girl, you *will* listen," said Melody, and a change had come about her. Her voice was authoritative, the very presence of her in the room far stronger. "Even if it takes years, you will listen. I won't lose you, not like I've lost everyone else."

The bed shifted as Melody stood from it and went to the door. When Alyssa heard it open, she reached down, searching for the dagger Muzien had thrown to the floor. Her fingers brushed wrapped leather, she grabbed the hilt, and then she sat back upon the bed, hiding the blade beneath her left thigh.

"Summon John Gandrem. I would have words with him," she heard the muffled voice of her mother say to someone outside the door. A female voice gave an affirmative on the other side, and then followed soft footsteps on the carpet as Melody returned to the bed.

"John won't help you," Alyssa said, trying to believe it herself. "He's always been loyal to our family line, and he won't dare try overthrowing me for an imposter."

"I'm no imposter," Melody said. "I endured all those years married to your father, and then many more locked in Leon

Connington's cell, a plaything for him and his gentle touchers. Your trials are but a joke compared to mine, yet I have emerged stronger, while you wallow in bitterness. John sees it just as well as I. Given the choice, you or me, you know who he'll choose."

"Father disowned you," Alyssa argued.

"No, he didn't," Melody said. "He never had to. I was dead, remember?"

It was true, of course. Alyssa knew her claim was stronger than her mother's, especially since she was the one with a male heir...but if someone wanted to believe otherwise, if someone like John wanted to put the strength of his soldiers behind Maynard Gemcroft's wife instead of his daughter...

"I'll kill you," she said. "You won't take all I've built from me."

"Only for safekeeping," Melody said, and by the sound of her voice, she was coming around the bed, closer and closer. "For you and for Nathaniel. Someone needs to be strong. Someone needs to have conviction and make the decisions necessary to save our world from the coming storm. Don't you understand? I care for your son's legacy just as much as you, but unlike you, I won't be blinded by fear. I won't be lost to..."

Alyssa lunged with her dagger drawn, thrusting in the direction of Melody's voice. The blade found resistance, followed by a scream, and it put a smile on Alyssa's face.

"Alyssa, stop this!"

It was John's firm voice. Alyssa ignored it, instead trying to thrust again. This time, she caught only air, and she slid off the bed, thrusting once more toward the sound of movement and crying. A hand caught her wrist, and another struck her across the face. The pressure tightened, and before she could fight it, the blade was yanked away.

"Enough," John said. A thud at her feet told her he'd dropped the weapon, and now two strong hands held her wrists, keeping her trapped. She fought down the indignity of struggling and instead tilted her head so she could better listen to her mother's tears.

"Is it fatal?" she asked, and by the way John sucked in a breath of air and tensed, she could tell he was stunned by the coldness of her voice.

"No," Melody answered for her, and Alyssa's heart sank. "Just a cut across my arm."

"Damn," she whispered.

"Alyssa, your wild behavior has gone on far enough," John said. "I understand you have endured many trials, but I will not sit idly by while you let your depression and guilt bury the legacy of your father and endanger the future of your son."

"Of course you won't," Alyssa said, and she laughed. "You'll do exactly as Melody says, won't you? Did she fuck you for it, John, or only offer promises?"

She couldn't see him, but she hoped the older man's face flushed a bright red.

"This will only be temporary," John said, "until it's clear to us you are in a right state of mind. Either that or Nathaniel is old enough, and mature enough, to handle the estate's matters."

"Send out a rider to look for Muzien, or a member of his guild," Melody told John. "Tell them we'll accept any reasonable terms he offers us. Do it quickly! As for Zusa..."

"My men are ready," John said. "I do not trust her to take this well."

Alyssa laughed, loud enough to ensure they turned her way.

"That is putting it lightly," she said. "She'll kill you both for this betrayal. There'll be no stopping her."

"We'll see about that," said John. "But until she acknowledges Melody's right to rule, that woman is a danger to every single person in this home. Keeping her from you will be a challenge, but as much as it will pain me, I know of a place to keep you secure..."

The way he said it told her immediately where they would take her. She didn't know if it made her want to scream or cry.

The wall of noise about her, of men grunting, armor creaking, convinced her at least ten men escorted her down the hall. Perhaps it was twenty, but their fear of Zusa was obvious. They took a turn, then another, and as she counted her steps, her fears were confirmed. They were taking her to the cells, the cold, drafty cells her father had thrown her into in an age past. Zusa had helped rescue her from them before... but could she do so again?

A heavy door opened, John barked an order, and then she was physically lifted into the air and carried down the stairs. It was pointless to resist, but she did so anyway.

They more tossed her into the cell than anything else, and she rolled along the cold, hard ground before coming to a stop at the far wall. A blanket followed, landing atop her leg. It was a painfully familiar act of kindness.

"I want ten men down here at all times," John said. "And that door is never to be left unlocked or unwatched..."

His voice trailed off as he gave his orders. As the cell slammed shut, she heard her mother calling to her.

"I do this for you, Alyssa," Melody said from the cell door. "To save you, to save us all. You'll understand one day, my daughter, but I think we all need our moments of darkness first, to humble us and break us down. It's been a long time since you were humbled. Consider this a needed first step toward the truth."

Alyssa stood, fighting off a wave of pain from several new bruises. Slowly, and with eyelids wide to ensure her mother saw the torchlight reflecting off her artfully crafted glass eyes, she walked to the bars of her new prison.

"The darkness means nothing to me now," she said, and she shoved the offered blanket back through the bars. "And it will take more than a cold draft to break me."

"I endured nine years in a far worse dungeon," Melody said. "I know what it takes to break a man or woman, and I assure you, I have the patience to wait that long if it will save your immortal soul."

Alyssa pressed her face to the bars, entire body trembling with rage.

"Zusa will kill you," she whispered.

Melody's whisper back was full of venom, a hatred Alyssa had never heard before in her voice.

"Let her try."

CHAPTER 20

The first thing Haern did when he awoke was turn to the side and vomit, his stomach unloading everything it had. Eyes closed, he endured the sensation of vertigo, knowing he might not have very long to react, and his life could still be on the line. The last thing he remembered...what was the last thing he...

"Welcome back to the land of the living," said a deep voice. Haern snapped his eyes open. He was in a small cubical cell, with every wall but one made of solid stone. The open one was before him, and blocking the way was the older man with the silver lion upon his chest. His eyes were a cold gray, his voice deep and demanding obedience.

Haern tried to move from where he lay and found himself shackled. His wrists were bound together with manacles, as were his ankles. A chain connected the two, short enough so that he could not extend to his full height. His swords were gone, as were his cloak, his hood, his various daggers and blades he kept for emergencies hidden across his body, and his belt of tools to pick locks and disarm traps. Haern thought to attempt an escape anyway, but the room was small and dark, and the paladin still had his enormous sword. Dizzy and bound as he was, he had little hope for escape against a man with such skill and presence.

"I hope I wasn't much of a bother," Haern said. "Those books I burned, were they valuable?"

"Priceless beyond compare," the paladin said, reaching down and grabbing him by the front of his shirt. With ease, he lifted Haern up and then flung him against the wall. Haern let out a gasp as his head hit, adding yet another wave of nausea to his already-unhappy stomach.

"Well, then," Haern laughed, "good to know I'll have left a mark."

The dark paladin stood and crossed his arms. He didn't seem angry, nor amused. Instead, he appeared...curious.

"My name is Carden," he said. "High Enforcer of our mighty god's paladins. Who might you be?"

Haern shrugged as best he could, given the chains and manacles. What did it matter if he gave a name?

"Haern," he said. "At your service."

Carden's eyes narrowed for the briefest moment.

"Well, then, Haern, would you care to tell me why you killed a priest that was under our care?"

They don't know about Thren, Haern realized, and he made sure not to let his smile show. Of course they wouldn't. No doubt they assumed all the deaths had been at his hand alone, for what evidence did they have to the contrary?

"Is this an interrogation?" Haern asked, and he lifted his bound hands before him, rattling the chains. "Forgive me, but I assumed you'd at least rough me up a little before trying to get something out of me. I'm almost insulted you thought an unbarred cell and some manacles would break me. Or was your charming personality to do that instead?"

If Carden was annoyed, he didn't show it. Instead, it seemed his amusement grew.

"Listen well, Haern," he said. "In killing Luther, you did me a favor. He was a heretic and a deceiver, and in time, he would have hung by his thumbs from our doorway once we proved his blasphemy. But you also slew students of mine, faithful sons of the Lion. This fortress of ours is sacred, and by all accounts impregnable. Yet somehow, they are dead, and here you are. I'd have your reason, and I'd have your method for entry. That's all. Once you tell me both, I'll grant you release."

Haern grinned at him.

"That's it? Those two things, and I walk out of here?"

Carden reached down, grabbing him by the neck, and lifted him off the ground before slamming him against the wall.

"You won't walk," the man said, deep voice rumbling. "You'll die, Haern. That's your release. You are in the dungeons of the Stronghold. No one escapes from here. No one. Your stay can be for hours, or it can be for decades. The choice will be yours and yours alone, but know that in the end you will tell me. My home has a weakness, and I will not relent until it is found."

The hand closed tighter around his throat, making it hard to breathe. Despite it, Haern smiled at him, choking out his reply.

"Prepare for me a bed," he said. "I'm not going anywhere."

Carden punched him in the stomach with his other hand. It seemed like he put no strength into it, no real effort, but the blow was like a sledge blasting into his body. He let out a strangled scream, and as crackling black energy leaped from the fist into him, he felt his muscles spasm uncontrollably. Every nerve inside him flared with pain, and it was like being stabbed in the gut, only so, so much worse. Seconds dragged on, and then Carden let him drop with a great rattle of chains. Haern gasped in air, sinking into himself, pulling up the training techniques his father had taught him as a child. Pain was his servant, not his master. Put it away. Shove it into a corner.

The dark paladin paced before him, just two steps before he had to turn around and go the other way. The open exit past him was dark, and dimly Haern wondered how they planned to seal him in once Carden left.

"Tell me, Haern," the paladin said. "Do you believe in something?"

"I believe you'll roast in the Abyss," Haern said, rolling over onto his side and letting out another gasp as the last of his pain receded away.

"I was hoping for something more interesting than that," Carden said, halting his pacing. "But I have a feeling you and I will have many hours to spend in each other's company. You aren't one to break easily; that much is obvious. I've had grown soldiers weep and beg for forgiveness after a single touch of my fist, yet you endured it well, remarkably so. Still, this world is one of challenges, and I should expect no less from one insane enough to break into our home. So, tell me…what is it you truly believe in? Is it Ashhur? Karak? Do you worship coin, revenge, or perhaps does the lust of a woman's flesh guide your actions?"

Haern felt a numbness spreading from his stomach, tickling his other limbs as Carden knelt down and gripped him by the neck one more time.

"Do you know who I worship?" the paladin asked as he pulled Haern closer so he could whisper into his ear. "*Karak*."

At the name of his god, power flared through his hand, this time with the pain focused solely on Haern's neck. Every muscle in his throat constricted, robbing him of breath, straining his neck, whipping his head back with terrible force. Haern did everything he knew to push it away, to put himself into a different place where the torture was a distant, foreign thing, but there was no way, not against that pain. Unconsciousness was his only hope, and he tried to let himself go, to fall back into the empty embrace, but Carden was far too skilled for that.

The pain relented, Haern sucked in air like a drowning man, and then to the ground he dropped. On his back, he groaned, staring up at the flat stone ceiling above him. What was it Tarlak had told him before he left? *Damn it, Haern, I've heard horror stories about their dungeons...*

"It's interesting, the way you break a man," Carden continued, deep voice calm as ever. "Some you can break through fear. Fear of promised pain, fear of death, fear of a return of the pain they've already experienced. That's the easy kind, though you have to be careful. Some men try to trick you, pretending to break easily, thinking their lies will both protect and spare them. Time and patience root out those deceivers."

Carden tapped a mailed finger at his lips as Haern's heart finally returned to a normal pace.

"Some, though, are too strong to give in to fear," he said. "Some find a way to endure the pain. Hope, you see. They cling to a hope, no matter what it is, and hold on tight against every punishment imaginable. Sometimes, it's hope for escape. Sometimes, it's hope for a better life. Sometimes, it's gods or a belief in their ceasing existence come death. Which means pain becomes pointless in breaking this type of man. Instead, I must break their hope."

The paladin's cold, hard boot pressed down on his chest.

"So, I ask again... what is it you believe in, Haern?"

Don't tell him, thought Haern. *Tell him nothing. Deny him everything.*

Smoothly, as if terribly pleased with himself, Carden bent down, reached into Haern's shirt, and pulled out Senke's emblem of the golden mountain. He casually twirled it in his hands, the slender chain still around Haern's neck. A gleam seemed to shine in Carden's eye.

"And there it is," he said. "Did you think we missed it when we searched you? Come, now; think better of us than that. Ashhur's symbol of endlessness, his reminder of humanity's inability to reach his own holy heights. You surprise me, Haern. Is this merely a good luck charm? Your cloaks, your sabers... you have the look of a man from the thief guilds of Veldaren. They tend to view themselves as gods, with no patience for others. Chance is their friend, guilt a thing to be mocked and ignored. They live in sin, and they love every minute of their squalor. Is that you, Haern? Does this emblem mean anything in your shadowed life?"

Haern wanted to deny him even the slightest information, but to lie meant to deny the god he worshipped. He couldn't decide if it would be right to do so, so instead, he kept his mouth shut. At least with silence, he told no lie.

"Well, then," Carden said, shrugging. "I take it you won't mind if I destroy this."

His fist tightened, dark fire sparking from his fingers. Seeing the emblem starting to bend, Haern could not help himself. Before him was the last remnant of his friend Senke, the last reminder of the risks the man had taken to help him and of how integral he'd been in pulling him out of the streets and into his new family, the Eschaton. Through everything, he'd kept it with him, always around his neck, always reminding him of all the things his father would have him reject.

"Stop!" he cried. "Just...leave it be."

Carden tilted his head to the side.

"So, you do believe," he said, his fist easing its pressure. "Not some trinket, then. Good. This will make the breaking that much more pleasurable."

The paladin drew his sword, and across its enormous blade, fire immediately burst to life. It was dark as night, if not darker, with the very center a deep violet that made Haern's stomach twist just looking upon it. Releasing the emblem, Carden lowered the blade so the fire burned mere inches from Haern's neck.

"Your god is one of weakness," he said. "An imprisoned child whose dreams cannot live in this world, and whose hope is a pathetic excuse for reason and sanity. Eternity will roll forever and ever on, and one day, the brother gods will war again. Those children, those souls who think themselves safe in his embrace, will kneel before the Lion and face true judgment for their sins. And you...what sins do you hide? I'll find them all, Haern. I'll listen to every last one. You're in the heart of the Stronghold, a place of tremendous power sworn to the true deity of this land."

The fire began to sear into his skin. Strangely, it did not char the flesh, only ignite horrible pain. He fought, but the magic of it held him still, tightening every single muscle in his body so that he could not run, could not turn away. Even screaming was denied to him.

"Every day you will feel the pain of Karak's anger," Carden said, voice like a demon, words the condemnation of a furious god. "Every night, you will weep and cry for salvation. Keep your pendant around your neck. Stare at it. Hold it. Caress it while you weep. Feel it against your flesh as the pain rips through you. Day after day. Night after night. Tell yourself that is your hope. Tell yourself it must mean something. But I know what will happen, know it like I know the sun will rise, come the morrow. I've seen it a hundred times before, and in your eyes, I will see it again: the realization that no matter how greatly you suffer, how loudly you pray to your god, *he will do nothing*."

The fire was leaping off the blade like water now, curling around him, seeping into his skin like rain into a parched landscape.

"He'll love you from afar," Carden said. "Love you as you suffer, love you as you die. That is the sickness you worship. That is the impotence you've given your life to serve, you poor damn fool."

The paladin leaned down so his lips brushed against his ear.

"You may scream now," he whispered.

Haern did, howling at the top of his lungs, releasing every bit of his pain and rage. The sound echoed within his cell, and to his ears, it belonged to a wild animal. Certainly not to anything human. At last, his lungs gave way, and the pain became something he could bear as Carden stood and sheathed his blade on his back.

"Watch carefully," he said, and it seemed as if the previous tortures were but a dream, and he was a kind host describing an offered room. Touching the wall, Carden closed his eyes, whispered something in prayer, and then suddenly, a wall of flame rose from the floor, sealing Haern inside his stone cube. It burned, shimmering, black and violet, swirling like water running upward to the ceiling. Just looking at it made Haern sick, no different from the fire that burned around Carden's blade. The paladin examined the wall of fire, and he nodded, pleased.

"Only the faithful can pass through unharmed," he said.

"Even our younger members find it difficult to endure. The other walls are solid stone, so your only exit is through the flames...but there is no hope beyond, Haern. Here in this dungeon, there is but one door, and it can only be opened from the outside. There is no escape, I promise you. In case you thought to take your chance with the fire, I thought it best you know the pointlessness of such an action."

The man stepped through the flames, and as the violet fire passed across his skin and armor, it did not burn, nor did he show signs of pain.

"Oh," the paladin said from the other side. "So you know... these flames are designed to burn, and hurt, but very rarely will they kill. Though if you stay within them long enough, if you can endure the pain, you just might find death. Consider that a gift we offer the strong...but only a very few have managed it. But who knows...perhaps you'll be one of them?"

With that, he was gone, leaving Haern alone in his prison, sick before the glow of the fire, in pain from the torture, and his chest aching from where the pendant of the golden mountain rested against his skin. Tears running down his face, he clutched it with a shaking hand, felt the cold metal dig into his skin.

"Ashhur," he prayed, turning his back to the flame. "Please, Ashhur, I know you hear me..."

One day. Just one day, and he felt a quivering in his chest, a breaking of something so vital to everything he knew.

Just one day.

"Delysia,' he whispered, and his tears fell harder.

CHAPTER

21

Just after dawn, when all his men were in place, Muzien strode into the marketplace, pockmarked Ridley at his side. He kept his hood off, wanting others to see his face, his scarred ears, and know exactly who he was. The four-pointed star was sewn large on his tunic, and it amused him to see the way the commoners' eyes widened upon his entrance. How long had he been in Veldaren, a few months at most? Already they feared him. But not enough. Not yet.

They would, though, after today.

Waiting for him were several crates stacked together in the heart of the market, and he leaped atop them and looked about. In all directions, he saw members of his guild watching at the various entrances and exits, and each one saluted with their left hand to show they were ready.

"People of Veldaren!" Muzien screamed, and his voice carried over the rest, for he knew how to project his authority, how to command the attention of any in his presence. "Come forth, and witness the rise of the Sun!"

Frightened murmurs rapidly spread, and with his face like stone, he watched their reactions. Many turned to flee, recognizing him, but there was nowhere to go. From all corners came members of his guild, bearing torches in one hand and brandishing swords in the other. Following his strict orders, they said nothing, only blocked the people's way with fire and steel. Muzien's reason had been simple. The people were sheep and needed to learn to behave without word or order but by the mere sight of the four-pointed star.

A circular gap spread about Muzien, no one wanting to be near him where he stood. Muzien waited, knowing there was no reason to hurry. The king was in his pocket, the remaining guilds all but crushed. Who else could stand against him?

"Come closer," he yelled to them, estimating nearly two hundred trapped there in that center stretch of the marketplace. "To me, now, for I would have you watch!"

More members of the Sun Guild came through the alleys, pushing people in, threatening with club and blade when necessary. The two hundred bunched in, unable to flee, unable to hide. Muzien nodded, pleased with the efficiency of his guild. Many members were newly recruited, either from other guilds or the streets, but they were learning swiftly. Again, he felt a pang of frustration. Why had Thren Felhorn struggled for so long, when he lived with such fertile recruiting ground?

Muzien stayed there, merely watching, wanting the people to grow accustomed to his presence above them. Sealing in the circle of people were two dozen Sun Guild members holding torches aloft. It conveyed the feeling of a ritual, and Muzien knew how powerful rituals could be. It gave the humans a sense of awe, of belief that their ephemeral lives might somehow continue on while connected to things greater and more permanent than they. Even the most mundane of events could carry the weight of mysticism and power by adding a few ancient words and predetermined motions.

From the north, pushing through the crowd, came two city guards, prodded on by more members of the Sun. Neither had drawn their weapons, and they looked equally terrified by the sudden events. Muzien crossed his arms at their approach, still saying nothing. At last, he hopped down from the crate and walked toward them. He saw fear in their eyes, and it made him sick.

"Give me your sword," he said, extending his hand.

The one on the left was an older man, his face scarred from an ancient cut running from the left side of his chin to his right eye. At Muzien's demand, he shook his head and looked away. The man on the right, far younger, glanced around at the people, the torches, and blades, and then drew his sword and slowly flipped it around so he might extend the hilt in offering.

Muzien took it as all eyes of the marketplace watched. Symbols, thought Muzien. Symbols and rituals, all carrying power. Let the city see who the guard truly feared, and obeyed.

"Bring me the merchant," Muzien said to Ridley, who put his fingers to his lips and blew. From the other side, the crowd parted and into the empty circle came a scrawny merchant with a waist-length beard. He looked middle-aged and, given his pallid skin and recessed eyes, of poor health. Muzien didn't remember his name, but he knew what he was there for.

"This man," Muzien cried, "denied us our right. Veldaren is mine now, and if you would seek protection in my city, then your coin must go to my hands and no others. This fool, this oaf, dared to reject my outstretched hand. He dared to believe he would not suffer the consequences."

Muzien took a step closer.

"He was wrong."

He kicked the merchant in the face, knocking him onto his back, and then struck with the guard's offered sword. Over and over, he hacked into the merchant's neck, purposefully ensuring no blow snapped the spine. He wanted carnage; he wanted brutality. Let them watch as the blood flowed, the flesh separated, and the stupid man flailed and screamed as the blood poured down his opened windpipe. Blood splashed everywhere, and with one final hack, Muzien ensured a spray went across his own face and clothes. Another turn, and he flung the sword to the feet of the soldier who offered it to him. The crowd gasped at the sight of him, fine elegance covered with crude gore.

"You obeyed, and so you live," Muzien said to the younger guard. He turned to the older. "You hesitated, and you refused."

Two steps and a thrust. That was all it took. No one saw him draw the dagger from the belt at his waist, no one dared to move as Muzien jammed the blade into the older guard's neck, twisted it once, and then jerked it free. The body collapsed, and with that done, Muzien tossed aside the dagger as well. With his darkened hand, he beckoned the other city guard to leave him be.

The market was deathly silent now but for a few children crying in their parents' arms. It put a smile to Muzien's face. What he stood in now, that combination of awe and terror, was something his elven brethren would never understand. With their skills, they could instill a fear no human could match. They didn't need to hide in forests. They didn't need to stalk roads with arrows to win a war against mankind.

They only needed the ability to sacrifice, to kill, to live among the wretches. Everything else came in time.

"Hear me, people of Veldaren!" Muzien cried, hopping back up top of the crate. "Here at the dawn, you will witness the rise of the Sun!"

"*The rise of the Sun!*" cried the members of his guild in perfect echo.

Muzien turned, let his eyes fall upon them all.

"The city is mine," he said. "I own its streets. I own its castle. From the lowliest whorehouse to the greatest of the bazaars, it is mine. No guard will stand against me. No thief will steal from me. To no king, no lord, no priest will I bow. I bring you fire that will cast light upon you, but that same fire will also burn."

He lifted his forever-burned hand above him so all might see it.

"I am the Darkhand," he said. "In the west, I am the lord of shadows, the king of riots, the bringer of ghosts, and now I come to you. Upon every street you have seen my symbol, and even those of you who are blind will have felt it with your fingertips. Yet still you hesitate to serve. Men deny me protection money. Women sell their bodies, then hide my portion in cupboards and jars. Others yearn for former guilds or whisper the name of the Watcher as if he might save you."

Muzien let his words echo, let the moment linger. This was it, the grand proclamation that would spread throughout Veldaren, the nation of Neldar, and all the way to the southern oceans of Omn. He wanted every word right, every syllable filled with ice and conviction.

"There is room for no other in your hearts," he said. "Let go of your false hope. Deny your past, forsake your gods, abandon your king. *I* am your king. *I* hold the essence of your existence within the palm of my hands. Your coin, your lives, the very blood in your veins, it is mine, and I am a jealous master. Today, at this beautiful dawn, you will finally learn the truth, and like the children you are, I will teach it to you in the simplest of ways. I am your god, and I will have my tithe."

He nodded to Ridley, and immediately, the man barked out

commands, sending the men with torches back to the various exits so that there'd be three blocking each one. Soft murmurs grew among the people, confusion as to the lesson and what was expected of them. But he would not tell them. Like dogs, he would show them.

"Kill one of every ten," he ordered Ridley.

The man hurried off, bouncing from exit to exit, relaying the orders. The two hundred in the market waited, eager, wanting to leave but fearful to disobey after the death of the guard and the merchant. When the first of the exits opened up, people surged forward, and Muzien watched as his men let one through at a time, counting. At the tenth, one of the three stepped forward, stabbed with his dagger, and then shoved the corpse out of the way.

More exits opened, and despite the screams, despite the bleeding, the people continued to surge toward them, eyes low, heads downcast, murmuring prayers and clenching fists as they hoped they might not be the tenth.

"Glorious," Muzien said when Ridley returned. "Is it not glorious?"

"Only you would find beauty in this," Ridley said.

"The weak die before us, and with each corpse, they learn no one will save them," Muzien said. "After today, we will hold the very heart of this city in our hands, and it will never be tempted by another."

He headed toward the southern entrance of the market, left alone so that it would be ready for only him. Reaching into his pocket, he pulled out a cloth and began wiping the merchant's blood off his face.

"Come share a drink with me," he told Ridley. Behind him, a woman let out a wail as her child was knifed through the throat.

"I feel a celebration is in order."

*   *   *

Tarlak sat in his chair before the fireplace, glass of wine in hand. *Today will be a good day,* he told himself. *No matter if I have to drink until it comes true.* He was bringing the last of the glass to his lips when Brug's voice sounded in his ear, ruining whatever hope he had of accomplishing his modest goal.

Get to the market, damn it, and hurry!

The wizard winced, annoyed by the volume of his friend's voice. Every member of his mercenaries had a ring they could speak into a single time, sending a message across the wind for him to hear, and he'd always stressed for them to whisper. Brug, however, seemed to have forgotten that instruction; either that or he wanted to make sure his words pounded throughout Tarlak's brain like a thunderstorm trapped in a teakettle.

"I'm coming, I'm coming," Tarlak said, cracking his knuckles and rising from his chair. The market was several miles away in the city, and he had no intention of walking. If Brug wanted him to hurry to the market, then by the gods, he'd hurry. Teleportation was always a tricky business, and one of the key requirements was to have a strong mental image of where he was going. Going to a busy, ever-changing market would be a nightmare, so instead, Tarlak focused on a spot nearby, then opened his eyes as he spoke the necessary words of magic. A blue portal ripped open the fabric of space before him, and before it could close, he stepped on through.

He emerged on top of a large stone building, one of many shops that formed a border around the large open market. Wondering what was so important, he leaned over, spying down at the very center of the market, and that was when he saw the crowd attempting to disperse.

"What in blazes..." he wondered aloud, for it seemed like

the crowd was fleeing through several entrances and alleys, and at each one, they passed three members of the Sun Guild. At first, he thought they were fleecing the crowd, demanding coins or reaching into the pockets of those that passed, but instead, he saw nothing. They were only letting them by, watching, as if they were searching for someone they…

One of the exits was directly to Tarlak's left, and as he watched, one of the Sun guildmembers jammed a dagger through a woman's throat and kicked her to the side. Her body toppled to the ground, and as she landed, Tarlak realized others lay around here, all perfectly still, like corpses.

Eyes widening, he looked to the other exits, saw similar piles, and on the far side of the street, he watched a child no older than ten get lifted off his feet, stabbed in the stomach, and then carelessly tossed among the bodies.

Fire burst around Tarlak's hands as he stepped to the edge of the building.

"Oh, fuck you, Muzien," he said as he leaped off.

He landed between the three blocking the exit beside him, a great burst of air billowing from his feet right before he touched ground. As he halted in midair, he stretched out either hand and let his anger flow in the form of fire. The flames exploded on either side of him, burning their flesh, incinerating their bodies and that damned four-pointed star sewn onto their shirts. The third rushed at him, drawing a dagger, but Tarlak turned and aimed a palm his way. More fire, this time in a concentrated bolt that struck him in the face. The man screamed as his skin peeled.

"Get back!" Tarlak screamed, not to the thief but to the others trying to pass through. Not waiting to see if they obeyed, he clapped his hands together and then flung them downward. From the clear sky sounded thunder, and then a bolt of lightning struck the burning man, the power of it lifting him from his feet before dropping him onto his back, smoke rising from his skin as the fire on his face slowly spread to consume the rest of him.

Now unblocked, the people poured out the exit. Tarlak pushed through, far from satisfied. Once free of the people, he caught sight of a battle raging on the opposite side of the marketplace. It was Brug, hollering and banging his plate mail as he fought against three of the rogues. In his heavy armor, he was fairly well defended, and his flailing with his punch daggers was unpredictable to say the least, but Tarlak knew they'd get a knife in eventually. Brug wasn't good enough to handle more than one opponent at a time, at least not for long.

Breaking out into a sprint, he ran a list of spells through his head, trying to decide on the best one for the situation. There were too many people everywhere, too many innocents he might hit. Still, he wouldn't let these bastards live, not after what they'd done.

"Brug!" he screamed as he neared. "Get your head down now!"

His friend heard and promptly obeyed. His three opponents, however, did not understand, and when they turned to face him, he skidded to a halt, flung his hands outward, and unleashed a massive blast of air. It lifted them off their feet and sent them sprawling, nothing fatal, but Brug recovered far faster than they. He'd already stabbed one before the other two were up, and by then, the people had scattered, and Tarlak finally had room to play.

"You like killing?" he asked, hurling a jagged lance of ice the size of his arm. It pierced the chest of one and burst out his back, the clear blue shard stained red. "You like suffering?" Another shard of ice, this through the leg of the only survivor. He dropped to one knee, screaming at the pain. "Then have a nice taste of it for yourself!"

The man tried to stab Tarlak, but Brug was there, grabbing his arm and breaking it. The dagger fell, and Tarlak leaned out and clenched the man's throat in his fingers.

"Tell Karak hello for me," he said, and then he let his power roll forth, an invisible force that shattered the man's spine. Letting out a curse, he flung the body down, looked about the marketplace. It was empty of all but the corpses, the rest having escaped the exits. None lingered of the Sun Guild.

"Damn it!" Tarlak screamed, kicking the body.

"I'm sorry, Tar," Brug said, sheathing his daggers. "I wanted something fresh to eat and decided to swing by. If I'd only gotten here sooner, we might have stopped this. I waited until you got here too, waited like a damn coward."

"Stop it," Tarlak said, taking in deep breaths to calm himself down. He put a hand on Brug's shoulder, tapped the plate mail. "You did what you could. Better question is, what in Karak's name happened here?"

"I heard the Darkhand just before he left," Brug said, gesturing toward a pile of dead behind him. "He called this his tithe."

Tarlak shook his head. He knew the Sun Guild's arrival meant bad tidings, but this? This made Thren Felhorn look sane.

"I don't understand," he said, walking toward the center. "Where are the guards? The city watch? Why did no one..."

He froze, for at one of the exits stood Lord Victor Kane, arms crossed over his chest as he looked upon the carnage.

"You!" Tarlak screamed, pointing a finger as he hurried over. "Did you watch all this? Did you know this was happening?"

Victor nodded.

"I watched like the others," he said.

"Then why didn't you do something?" Tarlak asked. "Where's your soldiers? Why didn't you stop this?"

"At least two hundred watched him butcher a merchant,"

Victor said, his face hardening. "Two hundred men and women who did nothing as a guard of the city died for refusing to be a pawn of the Darkhand's game. And then as their own people shed blood, nine living for every one that died, do you know what they did, wizard? *Nothing.* They kept their eyes shut, their heads down, and prayed that they wouldn't be the unlucky tenth. Tell me, Tarlak, why should I fight for a city that won't fight to save itself?"

"But that's *why* you fight," Tarlak said. "Because you're the one who's strong enough. You're the one willing to risk everything; you're the one that knows something has to be done. Isn't that what you wanted to do, to inspire the city, to give them hope?"

"Hope?" Victor laughed. "Look around you, Tarlak. This is the hope our fair city now dwells in, and I say they've earned it."

"Is that it?" Brug asked as Victor turned about and walked down the alley toward the street beyond. "You're giving up?"

Victor glanced over his shoulder.

"Not giving up," he said. "Just changing how I play the game. From top to bottom, this city is wretched. I've stopped trying to polish the skin of a rotten apple. We need true change, starting at the crown itself. I just pray I didn't take too long to realize it."

Brug moved to follow, but Tarlak grabbed his arm and pulled him back.

"Let him go," he said. "We have bigger problems to worry about than that jackass."

The shorter man nodded, and he looked back to the market, the disgust and sorrow as plain as the beard on his face.

"You're right," he said. "But what do we do about it?"

As the city guard finally arrived from the north, wordlessly gathering the bodies onto a wagon, Tarlak had no answer.

CHAPTER 22

The first sign to Nathaniel that something was amiss was when he woke to find it wasn't one of his mother's servants opening the door to his bedroom but instead Lord John Gandrem.

"John?" Nathaniel asked as he sat up, using his lone hand to rub the sleep from his eyes.

"Forgive me for waking you so early," John said, though he hardly sounded apologetic. He was dressed in his finest, his tunic clean and his armor shining. Something about it put Nathaniel even more on edge. John looked as if he were going to march to war, and he'd not worn his armor since the first day he arrived at their mansion.

"It's all right," Nathaniel said. He didn't move to leave his bed, though, instead sitting there, waiting, not even asking a question. John clearly wanted him to ask, to broach whatever subject needed discussed, but Nathaniel wouldn't give it to him. There were so few reasons for John to be waking him, and with how cautious he was acting, how careful, it meant it was more than simple training or an interesting piece of gossip. His thoughts leaped to his mother, and he did his best to keep his lip from quivering as he anticipated hearing something dreadful.

"Nathan..." John paused again, crossed his arms. "Your mother has proven herself unfit for leadership, at least as of recently. I don't mean to disparage her character, but I fear losing her eyesight has sunk her into a pit she needs to find a way to climb out of."

"What did you do?" Nathaniel asked, unable to help himself. John looked offended at the unspoken accusation, and he sat up straighter and gave him a stern glare that made Nathan dip his head in respect.

"I did what needed to be done," he said. "For the safekeeping of your family and your own future. No harm has come to your mother, I assure you, but for now, all important decisions involving your family's wealth and that of the Trifect will be made by Lady Melody."

At his grandmother's name, Nathaniel pulled his blankets higher up on his chest. The idea of her in charge left him with chills. Her secretive talks of Karak...how secretive would they remain if the house was now under her control? Would he be able to avoid them any longer?

"You betrayed her," Nathaniel said. This time, he did not wilt, despite the glare he received as John's face gradually turned red. "Overthrew her for my grandmother."

"This isn't some sort of coup," John said. "It's only until she realizes this is what's best. Your mother's life is in no danger, Nathaniel, nor is her eventual rule. But Melody has just as much right as your mother, and right now, she's the more capable head of the household."

It sounded like shit to Nathaniel, just lies and shit, but

he kept his mouth shut, not wanting to deal with the reprimand John would give him for using such language. Instead, he finally pushed aside his blankets and stepped onto the cold floor. A glance out his window showed the morning sun just barely rising above the walls of the city. He went to his dresser as John remained standing at the door.

"When can I see her?" Nathaniel asked as he pulled open a drawer and reached for a new shirt.

"You should talk to Melody first," John said. "Listen to her and pay your respects. Once you do, I feel you'll be in a more proper frame of mind when visiting your mother."

"Do you have her locked up?"

John stood up a bit straighter.

"She's being kept in a safe place, yes."

Not a coup, thought Nathaniel. Of course not. Only his mother was imprisoned, someone new was in charge of his family's affairs, and the whole thing was being reinforced by John Gandrem's soldiers.

But not a coup.

"Can I eat first?" Nathaniel asked.

"Of course," John said, and he opened the door to leave. The hard image he conveyed softened a bit, and some of the warmth that had made Nathaniel trust the man came forth. "Nathaniel . . . I understand this is difficult; I really do. But we live in a very harsh world, and those at the top are always in danger of being toppled by those beneath. I fear your mother's decisions of late put everything your family has built in danger, and it would not be the first time, either. Now is not a time for rash decisions but for calm, careful planning and acceptance of the world as it currently is. Please remember this, and do not treat your grandmother harshly. All we do, in some way or another, is for you."

He left, shutting the door behind him. Nathaniel wanted to scream and throw his chamber pot at the man, but he kept the reaction choked down. It wouldn't do anything. It wouldn't help anything. To them, he was but a child, and his worth was only in his last name and in the man he might grow up to be. Right now... right now he was a scared little boy who they hoped would not cause too much of a scene as Melody seized control. Perhaps John was right. Perhaps he should just do his best to get along, to make sense of things, to see it from their point of view.

Despite the light streaming through his slender window, much of his room was still dark. Nathaniel pulled off his old shirt and slid on the new one, and as he pushed his head through the collar, he nearly screamed at the sight of Zusa crouching right in front of him, her body bathed in shadow.

"Shhhh," Zusa said, shoving her hand over his mouth and holding him close. Her eyes darted to the door, and she tensed to see if somehow any had sensed her arrival despite Nathaniel having not made a sound. When it was clear no one was at all aware, she pulled back her hand and then kissed him atop the forehead.

"I am so glad you are safe," she whispered. "I feared the worst when John's men began spreading the news of Melody's control."

"I don't think they'll hurt me," Nathaniel said.

"I don't think they will, either," Zusa said. "It's your mother I fear for. If she's to have any hope, we must act now."

Her haste, her desperation made sense to Nathaniel. John had often drilled into him the importance of time, of how each day a man sat on a throne strengthened people's belief that it was his, no matter his birthright or claim.

"What will you do?" Nathaniel asked. "Kill them all?"

He'd meant it as a bitter joke, a way to convey to Zusa his inability to see what she might accomplish on her own. The

way her face darkened and the sheer stubborn ferocity he saw
in her eyes made him think twice.

"They have her held in the mansion's old cells," she said. "At
least a dozen soldiers bar the way, more than I fear I can handle
on my own. But your mother has allies outside the household,
Lord Victor in particular. I would ask for his help first before I
try assaulting John's fighting force alone."

"Then why haven't you gone to him already?" he asked.
"Leave me. I'm safe here."

Zusa shook her head.

"Time is of the essence, little one. Each passing day strength-
ens Melody's claim. I need Lord Victor to act without alerting
John or Melody to his possible interference. That means I need
someone he'll trust more than myself, without question, without hesitation. That's you, Nathaniel. Your testimony will push
him to action; now, are you ready? Doing so puts your life in
danger, more so than if you remained behind."

In the end, it was no decision, only a matter of finding the
necessary bravery. Deep in his heart, he knew his mother had
earned far better loyalty and respect than to have her household stolen away from her in the deep of night. He would not
sit idly by in a comfortable prison while his mother's only true
friend risked her life to free them.

"All right," he said. "Tell me what to do."

She took his hand in hers and crouched down so her beautiful brown eyes could stare into his.

"Hold on," she said, "and trust me."

Zusa grabbed his blanket with her other hand, pulling it off
the bed. Together, they moved into the corner of the room, and
she held the blanket above them, blotting out what morning
light could reach them. He felt her hand tighten, sensed the
woman tense.

"This will be...uncomfortable," Zusa said. "Once we're outside, there's no turning back. No matter what, run where I tell you to run, and do not once stop. No one will hurt you, but they'll hurt me, and I have no intention of leaving you behind."

"I understand," he said.

"I pray you do, Nathan. Close your eyes. It helps lessen the discomfort."

He did, and he felt her strong arms close about him, pulling him to her breast. It made his skin tingle, and he was glad for his fear, for it kept him from focusing on the strange feelings that filled him with being so close to the woman. Her grip tightened, and suddenly, it felt like he was falling. Everything darkened, the blanket vanished, and then the shadows were replaced with the bright morning light outside. Together, they rolled, Zusa coming up on her knees and Nathaniel doubled over, clutching his stomach as he retched uncontrollably.

"Vomit later," Zusa said, one hand on his wrist, the other grabbing a coiled rope that seemed to have been waiting for them beside the wall. They were in the garden, with a few trees separating them from the large fence protecting the mansion grounds. John Gandrem's men patrolled the area, and a squad of three nearby noticed their sudden appearance and let out a cry of alarm. With a fierce tug, Zusa pulled him to his feet, and he flailed his legs to keep pace as she made for the nearby wall. The squad of three moved to intercept, and with Nathaniel slowing her down, she knew they would not make it in time.

"Keep running," Zusa said, thrusting the coiled rope before him. He let go of her wrist to take it, and he held it to his chest as if his life depended on it. The rope was heavy, and with his having but one arm, it forced him to double over a bit to use his stomach to help hold on. Walking in such a way was awkward, his movements slow, but he pressed on anyway. Ahead of him, he watched Zusa draw both of her daggers and approach the squad of three that blocked her way.

"Move aside," Zusa told them.

"We've been ordered not to harm you," said one of the guards. "Not unless you give us no choice."

"Move out of our way, or stand your ground and die," Zusa said, daggers twirling in her hands. "That's the only choice I leave you with."

They were three, well armed and armored, while she was a lone woman with slender daggers. Nathaniel knew they would not listen, not with several more men running from further up and down the mansion grounds. So he kept going, following Zusa, trusting her. The woman crouched down, and she looked like a snake coiling for a strike. One of the three moved to attack, and that was enough to send her into motion. Zusa spun, a rotating blur, her dagger smacking aside the guard's thrust with ease. She continued forward, arm lashing out, deflecting a stab from a second guard, then assaulting the first with brutal efficiency. Nathaniel's eyes widened at the blood that flew from the man's neck and face as her daggers raked across him.

The other two tried to cut her down while she had her back to them, but before they could even complete their swings, she had already turned, dropping to her knees and arching her back so their weapons passed harmlessly above her. And then she was snapping forward, legs kicking, daggers thrusting. At such close range, they could not hope to withstand such skilled brutality. One tried to flee, but he died with a dagger to the neck. The other tried to wrestle her to the ground, but she stayed just beyond his grip, her blades finding the gaps in his armor at the neck and beneath the arm. Within moments, he was bleeding, and as Nathaniel ran through the bodies, he saw the man fall, screaming out in pain from yet another deep cut.

"Hurry!" Zusa shouted, pulling the rope from his hand and racing to the wall. Looping one end into a knot quickly enough that it seemed like magic, she flung it so that it looped over one of the spikes at the top, pulled it tight, then offered it to him. Nathaniel felt his neck flush, and he lifted his only arm.

"I can't climb," he said.

Zusa hesitated the slightest moment, and he realized she'd not even thought of such a problem when planning his escape.

"Damn it," she said, pushing the rope against his chest. "Hold on!"

More soldiers were coming, and Nathaniel stood there, feeling helpless and a burden as Zusa leaped screaming into the first two to near. He saw the fear on their faces at her attack, knew from countless lessons with Lord John that the fight was already won before it even began. Steel flashed, blood flew, and then Zusa came rushing back to him, having earned them another brief moment of reprieve before more arrived.

"You may not climb, but you can run," Zusa said. "When I pull, you run, understand?"

He didn't, but he nodded anyway. With only two steps to build speed, Zusa vaulted into the air, soaring as if she weighed nothing. As she passed over the gate, her dagger lashed out, cutting the rope and grabbing it with her other hand. As she disappeared over the other side, Nathaniel realized her weight would pull him, and attempting to help, he put a foot on the wall and tried to lift into the air. With shocking strength the rope yanked him upward, and he moved his feet one after the other in an attempt to keep up. Faster and faster he climbed until he was reaching the spikes at the top.

Momentum carrying him forward, he did the only thing he knew to do: at the very top, he jumped. Soaring over the spikes of the fence, he saw Zusa waiting for him, and she did not betray his trust. Into her arms he landed, firm but gentle.

"Well done," she said, taking his hand and setting him down. "Now come. Victor's place is not far. If you tire, let me know so I may carry you."

They hurried, Zusa glancing behind her several times to see if any chased. Twice, she looked worried, and she tugged him along at a speed his feet could barely maintain. Down streets and alleys they twisted, and he doubted they took anywhere close to a direct path, all to fool any potential followers. At last, when it felt as if his legs could take no more, and he was finding a way to swallow his pride and ask to be carried, they arrived.

"What reason brings you here?" asked one of the soldiers guarding the door to what might have been an inn prior to being boarded up.

"I need to speak with Victor," Zusa said.

"And who might you be?"

"Who I am doesn't matter," she said. "But with me is Nathaniel Gemcroft."

That was enough to get them moving. Into the building they went, and it was dark and stuffy. They stood in the center, ignoring the tables, until from down the stairs came the regal Lord Victor. The man smiled widely, and he dipped his head in respect to his guests.

"Welcome," he said. "Unexpected company you may be, but please, consider yourselves at home. Sit and let my servants get you something to eat or drink if you'd like."

Once Nathaniel was comfortably seated, as well as having turned down the offered meal despite the hunger in his stomach, Victor sat opposite him. The lord did his best to look relaxed, but Nathaniel could sense the serious atmosphere filling the room, and he felt ready to shrivel beneath the man's fierce stare.

"So," Victor said, "I suspect something significant is occurring for you two to be here, so would you care to explain just what that may be?"

Zusa spoke up first, and Nathaniel was glad for it.

"Melody Gemcroft has enlisted Lord John Gandrem's aid in overthrowing Alyssa for control of the Gemcroft fortune," Zusa said. "We have little time before she consolidates her power."

Victor's face darkened.

"You have proof?" he asked.

At that, Zusa gestured toward Nathaniel, and he felt his skin shrivel.

"Tell me everything," said Victor, leaning forward, smothering him with that hungry, intelligent stare.

"John came into my bedroom this morning to wake me," Nathaniel said. "He said . . . he said my mother is not fit to rule, and that Melody's claim is just as strong. She's in charge now; that's what he said."

"For how long?" Victor asked.

Nathaniel shrugged.

"Until he thinks my mother ready."

Victor looked to Zusa, and he rose from his chair.

"I take it time is of the essence?" he asked.

"Too many of our business associates, even those of the Trifect, will gladly accept Melody's takeover," Zusa said. "Especially if they think Melody easier to manipulate or bully than Alyssa."

Victor went to the door, opened it, and spoke to one of his guards stationed outside.

"Send for Guard Captain Antonil," he said. "Tell him it is of the utmost urgency, and tell him I come calling for the aid he once promised."

That done, the man strode back into the room, hand on the hilt of his sword.

"After Muzien's display in the marketplace this morning, Antonil will do everything he can to aid me and, by extension, anyone who will stand against the elf," Victor said.

"Muzien?" asked Zusa. "I don't understand; what does he have to do with—"

"It doesn't matter. When I say Alyssa will stand against him, her past deeds should convince Antonil. His men will join mine in an attack on the mansion. Once Alyssa is freed and Melody our prisoner, any and all chance of a coup dies."

Victor moved closer to her, leaning down and whispering even though Nathaniel could still hear.

"I mean this," he said. "Both Melody and John must not suffer harm. I want to question them, to know how much of this was planned and for how long. Keep your daggers under control when we assault the mansion. Is that clear?"

"I will lead the attack," Zusa said. "Beyond that, I am Alyssa's servant, not yours."

Victor ignored her, instead kneeling down in front of Nathaniel so they might look eye to eye.

"I'll save your mother," he said, putting a hand on his shoulder and squeezing it. "Have no fear of that. And even if something should go wrong, remember you'll always be safe in my care."

Nathaniel tried to smile, to thank the man, but Victor was already moving on, calling out for his men, organizing, preparing.

"Zusa?" he said as the woman lurked by the door, watching.

"Don't worry," she said, glancing his direction. "I will be there, leading the way."

"You won't let them hurt her, will you?" Nathaniel asked, unable to shake the dread building in his heart.

Zusa shook her head, blood on her clothes and drying in her hair.

"Alyssa is not the woman who must fear this morning," she said, and there was death in her smile.

CHAPTER
23

An eighteen-year-old Melody Gemcroft knelt in prayer, a book open before her on a slender bench. Towering over her, illuminated in violet light burning from torches that never flickered or dwindled, was the statue of Karak, carved when he first walked the land, waging war against his cowardly brother. It was the third night in a row she'd come to Karak's temple, yet her fervent prayers seemed to do little to diminish the fire burning in her breast.

"You seem troubled," said a priest, joining her at her side. Melody opened her eyes and smiled at Luther, the man leaning down over her, always quiet, always willing to listen.

"Forgive me," she said, "but I cannot speak of why. It shames me just thinking about it."

Luther sat down on the bench she knelt before, and he glanced at the book she'd been reading. It was a series of stories, supposedly told to Karak's people in the earliest days of mankind.

"If a burglar has broken into your home, do you know how you flush him out? Not by hiding him but instead opening all your doors and windows and letting the world in to see. If sin has taken residence within your heart, bare it now. We're alone here, you and I, alone before our god. The only shame you should feel is letting your pride stand in the way of the purification of your soul."

Melody trembled. Of course, it was Luther who would know what to say. Of course, it would be to him she must confess.

"Lust," she whispered. "I suffer lust, and for a man not my husband."

Luther leaned over further, hands clasped together, and he stared at her with those intense eyes of his.

"Do I know who the man is?" he asked.

Melody looked away, nodded.

"You do," she said. "You know him well."

Her heart raced in her chest, and she felt her neck flushing red. Of course, Luther would figure it out. She was never good at keeping secrets. But Maynard was always so cold to her, and though he knew the servants told her of his midnight trysts with the quality whores a man of the Trifect could buy, he never seemed to care. Sometimes, she tried talking to him, to broach the subject of him coming with her to the temple. Perhaps if they could share in their faith, if he could see how it wounded her when he cavorted with sinful women...

But then there was Luther at her side, listening, understanding, his words firm yet kind, knowledgeable yet humble.

"The role of a wife is not an easy one," Luther said after a lengthy pause. "There is a reason Karak calls us his bride. It carries expectations, faithfulness, and sacrifice. But Melody... there is...You've sworn your life to the temple, have you not?

You are Karak's bride, and let no man of this earth defile you nor burden you with shame."

She nodded even as she struggled to understand. What was it he was telling her? What was he asking of her?

Luther offered her his hand.

"I am the temple," he said. "And I would never defile your body."

She took it, and together they stood.

"Where are we going?" she asked.

"To my chambers," he answered. "So together we may worship and offer our blessings to the Lion in a way your husband would never understand."

She knew what it meant, yet was scared to think it. Was it a test? Or perhaps her sinful mind perverted something meant to be simple and pure? The walk down the hallways of the temple to Luther's private study was a nightmare. But the moment inside his room, when he slowly removed her clothes, his lips caressing the length of her neck before traveling down to her naked breasts? A blessed dream.

Years passed.

They lay together in her bed, her clothes cast off one side, his priestly robes the other. Luther had come to the Gemcroft mansion for months now, always in the guise of private lessons. In a way, Melody considered them just that. They still bowed their heads in prayer. He still imparted wisdom to her, but it wasn't always in the ways of Karak's strength and order. Sometimes, it was in more carnal things, and as a teacher, he was better than Maynard could ever hope to be. Usually they were more careful, more discreet, but Maynard had left earlier that day for a meeting with James Keenan to the south in Angelport.

Weeks, she thought. *We shall have weeks together, just he and I. Praise Karak, I have so badly needed this.*

"Are you ready for more?" she asked him, her head on his chest.

"I am always ready if you are in need, Melody."

Her hand traveled down his body, and she cupped his manhood, which was still soft and wet.

"You don't seem it," she said. "Are you sure you don't need more time?"

Luther smiled at her, a smile that showed there was wisdom he had she did not, yet instead of belittling her, it only made him eager to share it.

"I have a hand and a mouth," he said, "and neither will tire before you do, I promise."

Before he could show her, the door to her room opened. An angry rebuke was on her tongue for the servant foolish enough to enter before knocking, but it died without a single word spoken. Melody clutched her blanket in both hands, and she felt as if she shriveled several feet before the deadly, cold glare of her husband. Beside him stood a man in the black robes of Karak, and he seemed no more pleased than Maynard.

"Get dressed," Maynard said. "Both of you."

That was it. Nothing else before he shut the door. Melody sat there, naked, mouth open, and skin covered with goose bumps. It seemed all the world was crashing down, and she wanted to vomit.

"Get dressed, Melody," Luther said, and he seemed strangely resigned. "We both knew it was only a matter of time."

But she didn't know. She thought it could be kept a secret, or that Maynard would not care if he learned. How many whores had he slept with? How many times had he spit in her face with his behavior? Why must she be treated differently?

The unfairness lent her a spark of anger, and she used that to push her numb body from the bed so she might put her clothes back on.

When both were finished, Luther went to her, and he kissed her forehead.

"I don't know what fate awaits us," he said. "But know I will always come back for you."

"Thank you," she said, and she felt tears running down her face. "They won't hurt you, will they?"

Luther smiled at her that same, wise smile.

"Do not worry for me," he said. "You're the one who must be strong."

His arm around her waist, he opened the door for her, and they stepped out into the hallway. Maynard was there, along with several more priests, and together, they walked across the hall, down the stairs, and to the grand foyer, where over a dozen more in black were gathered.

"I want him punished for this," Maynard said. Melody tried staying at Luther's side, but he gently pushed her away and went to his brethren. Despite their glares, he kept his head high, and there was no shame in his walk.

"His punishment is ours to decide," said their head priest, a man Melody had long admired named Pelarak. "Not yours. Leave us to punish our own, just as we will let you decide the fate of your wife's infidelity."

They put hands on Luther's shoulders, guiding him toward the door.

"Luther!" Melody cried. "I'll be strong, I promise. I'll be strong!"

Maynard struck her with his fist to silence her. The blow knocked her to the floor, and as she looked up at him, blood trickling down her chin, she swore not to cry. No matter what he did to her, she would not cry. All her tears would be reserved for Luther, and Luther alone.

"Apologize," Maynard said when the priests were gone, and they were alone.

"No," she said, holding a hand to her mouth. She felt the beginnings of panic crawling up and down her chest, but she fought it down.

"You've humiliated me," her husband said, and he reached down to grab her by the hair and yank back so she might meet his eye. "Now beg for forgiveness, and maybe I will have mercy."

She laughed at him.

"There is only one to whom I would beg for forgiveness," she said, "and it is not you."

He raised a hand to strike her, but it did not come. Instead, he let her go, and he shook his head. To her shock, there were tears running down his face as well.

"You make me do this, then," he said. "Remember that. Everything that happens, it's your fault, and that damn god of yours."

He called for soldiers, and they took her to a carriage. She didn't even get a chance to say goodbye to her daughter. Maynard joined not much later, and in the deep of night, they rode through the streets of Veldaren. Melody sat quietly, watching out the window with a mercenary at either side of her. At first, she did not know where they went, but as they neared their destination, a creeping certainty came over her.

When the carriage rolled to a stop before Leon Connington's mansion, she knew it to be true.

They took her in, and Leon was waiting for her at the door.

"Make it quick," Maynard said. She watched as her husband pulled out four coins, two gold and two silver, and dropped them into the fat man's eager hand.

"It'll be masterfully done," Leon said. "I promise."

They took her deep into the mansion, down the stone steps and into the black dungeons. Maynard never said a word to her, neither in anger nor love. The moment those coins changed hands, she was gone, and she knew it. Into a cell they took her, casting her onto the hard floor and leaving her in total darkness. There she remained, and for how long until Leon came to her, she could only guess.

"Are you in here, my little doll?" he asked, light of torches flickering across his face. On either side of him, holding the torches, were men in strange clothes. The gentle touchers, Melody realized, and she felt her creeping horror growing in strength.

"You promised it'd be quick," Melody said as the men with the torches lifted her from the ground, each holding a wrist with a frighteningly strong grip.

"I promised it'd be masterful," Leon said. "Not that it'd ever be quick."

They chained her to the wall, her struggles not even an inconvenience. She cried as the fat man loomed closer, his breathing heavy.

"I always thought you were beautiful," he said. "So much better than that uptight prick Maynard deserved."

He leaned in, she screamed, and then his lips were on her body. Thrashing, kicking, it all was hopeless. Chained to a wall, chained and helpless as his trousers dropped to the floor, and in the torchlight, Leon smiled the sickest of smiles.

"But now you're mine," he said. "All mine."

And there was nothing she could scream or do to deny it.

Years passed.

The darkness had closed in on her, and she much preferred it to the alternative. People meant the rare gentle toucher, come to experiment with a few of his needles and knives should Leon take too much time between his visits for the torturer's liking. Or worse, it meant Leon himself. His touch was everything Luther's was not: sick, greedy, hateful. Not once had they moved her to a different cell, and as she lay on the cold stone, she could trace her fingers along the dried spots of her own blood.

In the distance, she heard a door opening, and she tensed. That was the door from upstairs, the groan of its hinges much deeper and louder than those of the one leading to the rooms the gentle touchers slept and ate in. Upstairs meant either new prisoners...or Leon. As much as she felt guilty for it, she prayed it was someone new coming down to suffer as she did. Anything was better than Leon's touch. Anything.

A man came to the entrance of her cell, but it was not Leon as she feared. Instead, it was one of the gentle touchers, but the way he stood there was off. He had no desire to perform his art upon her, she could tell. Then, what?

"I have a gift," said the elderly man. "One we've been paid a handsome sum to bring to you, so I pray you appreciate it."

The cell door opened, he stepped inside, and then he placed an object on the floor, one which left her bewildered. It was a slender bowl, and in its center, held by thin silver string, were gems of a rainbow of colors. She took it onto her lap, cradling it as if it were a child.

"What am I to do with this?" she asked.

"Pray," said the gentle toucher. "That's all we were told."

With that, he left her holding the strange object.

Pray? she wondered. *Pray what? And why?*

It'd taken weeks before she discovered it. Many times she'd closed her eyes and prayed, clutching the strange shallow bowl in her hands, yet nothing ever happened. It was only after one of Leon's visits, as she lay on her side staring into its center, that she decided to try again. This time she would watch it, she decided, determined to see if her prayers did anything to the device. Never before or after did she notice a change, but just perhaps during...

And then as she prayed with her eyes open, focused on the bowl, she saw the colors begin to swirl within the gems. Hope blossomed in her breast, the emotion strange and foreign after her time in the cells. Her prayers faltered for a moment, the colors dimmed, and with frantic strength, she begged Karak for mercy and guidance. Back came the colors, and they were the greatest gift she could have ever imagined. The gems lifted into the air, straining the lengths of their silver chains.

And yet it was not done. As she stared into its center, yearning for freedom, she found herself sinking into a vision. She saw mountains, forests, the waters of the Rigon flowing beneath her as she soared with the wings of a falcon. Her prayers spilled from her lips as if they were those of another, or perhaps from some more primal part of her mind. She saw flowing fields of grain, the walls of the city of Veldaren, and then the barren wastelands of the Vile Wedge. It seemed nothing could contain her, her mind able to go wherever she desired.

And what she desired most was her former lover, Luther.

She tried to imagine his face, where he might be, and then suddenly, she saw him huddled before a desk, his back to her.

"Luther?" she asked aloud, her voice sounding distant.

Melody? Melody, is that you?

Nothing then could stop her crying. She felt tears running down her face, the first tears she'd cried in over a year. The image shifted, and suddenly, she was looking up at him and he looking down. He was so beautiful, so kind, and it ripped her heart to pieces that she could not reach out and stroke his face.

"I'm here," she said.

Praise Karak. I feared the men would only keep the chrysarium for themselves despite all I paid.

"The chrysarium?" she asked.

The device you hold.

He held one as well, she realized, and she was peering up from it. A magical thing, a blessed gift.

"Can you free me from here?" she asked him.

Not yet, said the priest. *They have banished me west and forbidden me to travel anywhere east of the Rigon. I'm sorry; it will take time, but I promise I will return. Can you survive until then?*

She smiled, and despite its darkness, the world was suddenly the brightest it had been in what felt like a dozen lifetimes.

"Yes," she said. "So long as I can see your face, I can endure."

The colors faded, her earlier fervent prayers no longer able to sustain the contact. As the gems slowly fell one by one into the center of the shallow bowl, she felt her faith in Karak renewed. She was not forgotten. Not abandoned.

Heart filled, she began to sing her praises to her god, and her voice echoed throughout the dungeon, in stark defiance of its somber hopelessness.

Years passed.

Something was different; there was no denying that. It'd been months since Leon came down to touch her or witness the torture of others brought in for the gentle touchers' care. Even the gentle touchers themselves seemed off. Old men who used to exude calm control now seemed nervous when they gave her her daily bowl of broth or cup of water. Their glances were furtive, their tongues harsh. What could it be, she wondered, but she had no answers, at least none she dared hope for. Because only one made sense, especially with how often they came to talk with the imprisoned boy beside her. Stephen, Leon's boy.

When they came for him, it was at night, and she slept. She awoke to see only a passing glimpse of him, a ghostly image lit by four carried torches. It was a procession, she realized, but to a coronation, or a funeral? But deep in her heart, she knew it had to be true. Leon Connington, somehow, someway, had found his way into the grave.

I hope they had to chop you up so you'd fit in a coffin, she thought. Karak's fire could not be hot enough for a man like him. Only in the deepest, darkest pit would he find appropriate torture. But what of Stephen? Had they found a replacement? Was he considered a threat to the ascension? She prayed Karak keep him from harm. He was such a sweet thing, full of anguish and hurt, but only because he craved love so desperately, love he never got from his heartless father. The hour passed, and she heard nothing. Sleep finally came for her, and she relented. She dreamed of open fields, and of Luther waiting for her there. For some reason, she could not go to him, only cry out from a faraway place. Sometimes he heard her, sometimes not, but he always looked so sad.

"Melody?"

A voice from the gate. She opened her eyes, her heart leaping into her throat. There before her was thin, frail Stephen, his pale skin seeming to glow amid the light of the torches held at either side of him. She'd seen him before, only rarely, during the times Leon allowed him to leave the cells and venture into the reaches of his mansion. He'd always looked tired then, defeated, but not this time. Now he was all smiles, his shoulders pulled back, his head held high.

"I'm lord now," he told her as one of the gentle touchers opened the barred door to her cell. "They've acknowledged my right. You're free, Melody. We both are."

Slowly, she rose to her feet, and she gripped the chrysarium tightly in one hand. She stepped toward the door, and she felt lost in a dream. It couldn't be. She couldn't be so blessed. But she was, and she fell into Stephen's arms, clutching him with all her might as her tears ran forth.

They gave her a finely decorated room upstairs. It was night, and she was glad, for even the light of the many candles hurt her eyes. Servants had bathed her, washing away the gunk from her hair and the layers of dirt and shit from her skin. Fine silks wrapped about her body afterward, her neck splashed with perfume. When she stepped into her new bedroom, she felt she stepped back in time, to when she was the wife of Maynard Gemcroft and a powerful lady of the Trifect. And she would have that power again.

But first...

"Luther?" she said as she took the chrysarium into her hands. "Luther, I have such wonderful things to tell you!"

She saw his face, and when he asked, she blurted out everything, of Leon's death, Stephen's ascension, and her freedom from the cell. She thought he'd be happy, and he was, but the joy was tempered.

This was meant to be, Luther said into her mind when she was done. *Dark times come for Veldaren, Melody, but you can help us fight them. Stay hidden and do not reveal yourself to the Gemcroft family just yet. Stephen needs you to be with him, to teach him how to act, to speak, to rule as a true lord. All these things he won't have learned in the dungeon.*

"Yes, of course," Melody said. "I owe him all this and more."

Not just that, Melody. I have seen Veldaren's future, and it is full of flames and death. We can stop it, though, with your help.

"What must I do?" she asked. "Tell me, and I'll do it."

I will, said Luther. *But not yet. I cannot come to you, but a friend of mine can. His name is Daverik, a priest loyal to the*

Karak that was. When he comes to you, listen well, and obey without question. Can you do that, Melody?

"I can," she said. "Anything and everything, I'll do it. Karak has given me freedom. Whatever life I have left is his."

My beloved Melody, I pray you never understand the sacrifice you've sworn to make. The most frightening thing a god may do when offered a life is say yes.

Years passed.

Melody sat in her room in the Gemcroft mansion. The door was locked, though she knew it would not hold long when the soldiers came for her. Tears ran down her face, and her trembling hands held the sides of the chrysarium. She was hunched over on her bed, and she felt more trapped than she had during her final years in Leon's horrible prison. Down there, she always had the hope of escape. Now, though? Now there was no escape. She *had* escaped, yet no peace had awaited her, no happiness. Just a cruel, cold world in desperate need of cleansing.

"Luther?" she whispered, trying her best not to cry. "Luther, please, are you there? I've done all you've asked, and it's not enough. It'll never be enough."

She'd watched from her room as Victor Kane's forces rushed the gate, with men of the city guard accompanying them. They'd had no warning, no chance to prepare. Melody berated herself for not having expected it, but John insisted to her they would hold. Their claim was strong, and if given a chance to argue the law before the king, he felt strongly they would be proven correct. It was all nonsense, though. Men with swords came for their heads. No claim or law would protect them, not when the city guard itself was out for blood.

From the window, she'd watched, and prayed, and felt her tears building as John's men fell one by one. The wretched betrayer, the former faceless woman Zusa, was the worst. She'd leaped over the gates protecting the compound as if the distance were nothing, and with some sort of blasphemous magic, she shattered the lock so the rest of the men could come charging in. *If only Ghost had killed her as he'd promised,* she thought. With Zusa at the front, John's men could do nothing. They tried at first, but as the blood flowed, she watched them throw down their weapons. They would not bleed for her, die for her. From the cries she heard repeating throughout the mansion, it seemed like John might have even ordered a surrender.

So stupid, she'd thought. *The law does not protect the faithful, not in this godless city.*

After that, she'd shut the curtain, granting her the necessary darkness, and then found the chrysarium. Only one person could help her, and begging for Karak's strength, she prayed for there to be no weakness within her come the end. Into the chrysarium's empty center she stared. She'd done her hurried best to block the windows, but she didn't need the darkness like she had before. Her focus was greater, her faith even stronger. Within the gems appeared the light, and dipping her mind into it, she vaulted across the many miles, granted sight of distant places and people. Right then, the one person she needed more than anything was her poor, beloved Luther. She needed to hear him tell her it would all be made right, that her sacrifices had made a difference.

The vision came, first cloudy, then stronger. It was Luther, and he was in the same room he'd been in for the past year. He sat at a wooden desk, book open before him, head down. Normally, the sight of him would have made her heart feel light, but this time, she knew something was wrong. He was too still, positioned too awkwardly to be asleep. And then she saw the blood staining the back of his robe.

"Luther!" she screamed. "Luther!"

The image shifted, and she saw him from the side. His face was still, his eyes locked open. No breath. No life.

From a faraway place, she heard soldiers shouting, and she pulled up from the vision as if rising from the grave. Her tears fell upon the chrysarium, whose gems had fallen dark. *Dead*, she told herself. Luther was dead. He wouldn't be there to calm her, to whisper words of Karak's wisdom. Just a corpse.

Pounding on the door. She looked over to it, a growing horror in her chest. This was it, then. No more future. Another pounding, and then the door burst open. Melody wasn't surprised to see it was Zusa who came rushing in, a dagger drawn, her face revealed in purposeful blasphemy against her beloved god's command. If only she could have removed her from Alyssa's side. If only Zusa had not forever tainted her daughter's opinion of the Lion. Then she wouldn't be sitting there helpless on a bed as Alyssa's well-trained attack dog came barking in.

"It's over," Zusa said, smacking the chrysarium from her hands and then grabbing her neck with her free hand. Zusa's fingers tightened, choking the breath from her as she lifted her to a stand.

"Then finish it," Melody said as she felt the dagger's edge press against her throat. Their eyes met, and she tried to show the woman the strength of her will, the lack of fear for her death. Zusa hesitated, and when Alyssa arrived at the door, accompanied by soldiers as well as Lord Victor Kane, her indecision only deepened.

"Do it," Melody insisted, grabbing Zusa's hand and pushing the tip hard enough to draw blood. "Do it, or I will."

"Zusa, stop!" Victor ordered, panic in his voice.

"You nearly destroyed everything," Zusa said, soft enough so that only she could hear. "But you failed, Melody. Know that as you burn in Karak's embrace."

Knifing pain, all across her throat. She tried to breathe, but blood interfered, her severed windpipe unable to draw air. As the blood flowed and her vision darkened, she heard her daughter scream her name, not that Melody cared. Alyssa was dead to her, they were all dead, and they'd suffer at the prophet's hands. Collapsing onto the bed, she reached out, bloody fingers clasping sheets, reaching for the chrysarium. Light-headed, she felt its polished surface, and with the last of her strength, she pulled it to her. Her blood spilled across the shallow bowl, covering the priceless gems. She stared into it, imagining Luther's face, wondering what his own final words and thoughts had been, and if they were of her.

Luther...she mouthed, unable to force out the air to make a sound. The darkness enclosed around her, her body now a foreign thing. As she fell through the world, she felt the heat of flames, heard the roar of the Lion.

CHAPTER
24

Haern was given no indication of time beyond his own innate tracking. Carden came back twice, his only words delivered with his fists and the sadistic gleam in his eye. After the second time, Haern assumed it nightfall, for no one came to deliver him pain. At no point was he given food or water, and as he lay on the cold hard floor, he could feel his body starting to rebel. All he had were the enclosed walls of stone and the final wall of flame, a fire that gave no heat, no light, only discomfort.

Though the fire was strong, he could still see through it to whoever might stand on the other side. For a long period of time, perhaps half an hour at his estimate, he saw no one. It didn't mean he was unguarded, but it helped convince him that night had returned. He waited longer, just to be sure, and that was when his guard finally arrived.

"What are you doing awake?" asked the man, though he seemed more of a boy than a man. Seventeen at Haern's estimation, maybe eighteen. He wore light mail, and at his waist was a sharpened sword. The fire made it difficult to know for sure, obscuring the color of his hair and eyes, eyes that glared at him with surprising hatred. It was that hatred that put a smile on Haern's face, and he positioned himself to a stand best he could given the manacles, and since he could not walk he rolled along the wall until he was as close to the fire as he dared be.

"I take it you drew the shortest straw of your friends," Haern said, and he was annoyed at the weakness of his voice. Coughing to clear his throat, he made sure his mocking laughter was much stronger.

"It is an honor to ensure the captivity of Karak's most hated," the guard said.

"Oh, of course," Haern said, leaning his head back and closing his eyes. He couldn't quite stand erect, not with how short the chain connecting his wrists and ankles was, but if he bent his knees, he could straighten his back enough so it didn't hurt. "I'm sure lots of things you're told to do are an honor to Karak. Heathen fools like me might not see the honor in it, but I'm sure that's my own failing, not you being lied to. Staying up late in a dark cell while the rest of your friends sleep? Truly an honorable role."

The man glared, and it was enough to confirm to Haern the Stronghold was indeed asleep. Taking in a deep breath, he willed his strength to return. The sessions with Carden had taken a lot out of him, and being deprived of food and water made matters all the worse. Still, if there were to be any hope of escape, it'd be now. Pulling at his shirt, he felt Senke's pendant to Ashhur, the cold metal tingling to the touch.

You promised to help me when I needed it most, thought Haern. *Well, I don't think the need gets much worse than now.*

Still, he had to make sure everything was ready. The wall

of fire was a few feet to his right, and the guard several feet beyond that. He needed him closer. He needed to be sure.

"You really do seem to hate me," Haern said. "Not sure what I might have done to earn it. Did I kill a family member?"

"You butchered two of my friends last night," the guard said, and he took a step closer.

Haern grunted, almost feeling foolish. Hard to remember at times the paladins were just people, fellow classmates who'd worked together to take down a brutal invader to their home. People with twisted values and an eager desire to see him suffering, but still people.

"Did I, now?" Haern said, feeling only the tiniest bit of guilt as he prodded the man further. "Care to give me a hint as to who they were? I mean, it's all a blur, and I don't think anyone stood out as having any skill..."

The man turned away, clearly trying to keep his temper in check. Haern gauged the distance. Still not close enough...

"That's fine; don't talk to me," Haern said, eyes closing as if he were tired. "I'm capable of talking enough for the both of us when I feel like it. You know, your kind isn't much for talking, I've noticed. Dying, that you're good at. Living a lie, serving a mad, imprisoned god, now that you're *really* good at."

The man stepped closer to the wall of fire, putting a hand on the stone beyond its reach and leaning closer as he glared.

"You'll be down here for years," the young man said. "Decades from now, I will come down here to watch you suffering still. We'll all take turns breaking you, humiliating you. Do you think your petty little words mean anything compared to that?"

He was inches away from the fire, which cast a purple hue across his skin. If he hoped to make himself look intimidating, it worked, but he also put himself within striking distance.

"My words?" Haern said, pulling the medallion out from

his shirt and holding it with both hands. "Not really. But this might mean something. *Ashhur!*"

At his words, a bright light flared from the medallion, rolling in all directions like a wave. Without waiting to see what it did, nor daring to give his guard a chance to react, Haern leaped with all the strength his coiled legs could muster, dropping his hands to ensure they could reach full extension. Under the strength of the light, the wall of fire faded away, and as Haern came leaping through, he twisted and lifted his arms as he slammed right into the guard. Together, they toppled to the ground. The landing jarred his shoulder, but he'd positioned his arms perfectly, wrapping the chain around the young man's neck. Sword trapped beneath them both, there was nothing he could do as Haern lifted his arms and kicked his legs, tightening the chain, strangling the breath out of the man. Twice he kicked, crushing his windpipe, for when he glanced about, he saw he was in the center of a long hallway...and at the far end of the hallway was another man in armor leaping to his feet.

"Joffrey!" the other man cried. Haern curled back in, bound hands reaching down to the dead man's belt...and the lone key attached to it. He freed it easily enough, but with the lock facing him, between both his wrists, he had no choice but to put the key into his mouth, then curl up even more so he could insert it. Keenly aware of the charging man, Haern jammed the key, gripped it tightly with his teeth, and then twisted his head one way while turning his wrists the other.

With a pop, they came off, and just in time. Haern rolled to his left, over the body of the dead man, as an enormous sword stabbed into the hard stone floor. His ankles were still shackled together, but with his arms free to move, he reached out and grabbed the handle of the dead man's blade. Pulling it from the sheath, he flung the weapon into the way as a second strike came crashing in. The blades smacked together, and Haern grimaced at the jolt to his arms. Above him, the guard leaned more of his weight into his sword, trying to crush him. The man's eyes were wide, lips pulled back to reveal his clenched teeth.

"Try harder," Haern told him, unable to help himself.

The man pulled back to swing again, but Haern was faster. Kicking his feet to give his upper body an upward motion, he thrust his sword with his arm extended to the limit. The tip of his sword slipped into the man's belly, and the sudden pain froze the man in mid-swing. Turning the sword to open the wound further, Haern dropped back to the ground as the man staggered backward. Calmly, Haern let go of the sword, found the key he'd dropped, and removed the shackles from his ankles. Meanwhile, the wounded man rushed to the door of the dungeon at the far end of the hall, both hands clutching his bleeding wound to staunch the flow.

Picking up the sword, Haern broke out into a run, closing the distance between them. Around the man's neck whipped his blade, and then a single cut dropped him to the ground. Hovering over the body, Haern took in a deep breath and checked his surroundings. The hall appeared to have a total of ten cells, each with an open face at the end, presumably for the same black fire to seal in any prisoners as they had with Haern. Other than Haern's cell, which still burned with the black-violet flame, the others appeared empty. Down one way, he saw the hall come to an abrupt end at a stone wall, while in the other direction, it ended at a larger opening, plus a wooden door heavily reinforced and barred with iron.

Glancing down at the pendant to Ashhur still dangling from the chain around his neck, Haern lifted it to his lips and kissed it.

"Thanks, Del," he whispered, tucking it back underneath his shirt.

Jogging down the hallway, he reached the door. In the opening around it were two tables, and on one he saw a pitcher, which he grabbed and greedily drank the water within. That done, he set it aside, scanning around him. On the other table, in a haphazard pile, were his belongings. Taking his cloak, he wrapped it about his shoulders, then grabbed his belt. Checking his swords, he saw they were recently sharpened, and he shuddered. He had a feeling that in a few days' time, if not that following morning, those blades would have been used on him. Last, he put on his hood, felt its comforting shadow envelop his features.

Much better, he thought. Now came the one last tricky part: getting through the supposedly locked and barred door of the dungeon. Already fingering his lockpicks, he approached the door, searching for any sort of keyhole. There was none. Wincing, Haern began to feel across it, wondering if there might be a hidden lever somewhere, maybe a weakened spot of wood he could pry into. Laughter from the other side bolted Haern back to a stand. He peered into the small circular window near the top, which had three bars preventing anything larger than a finger from slipping through. Shaking his head at him from the other side was his father.

"I'm starting to think my rescuing you was unnecessary," he said.

"Just open the damn door."

Still chuckling, Thren vanished from the window. Haern heard something heavy scraping against the other side, followed by a thud. After a rattle of keys, the door swung open, revealing Thren with his swords and the bodies of two young paladins on either side of the dungeon entrance. Behind him was a set of stairs leading higher into the Stronghold.

"Follow me," Thren said. "We don't have much time before people start noticing the bodies."

There was only one way to go, which was straight up the stairs before them. They curved sharply around, and after only a dozen steps or so, Thren stopped and motioned for Haern to be quiet.

"The entrance is just ahead," he said. "I've killed the guards there, fools still convinced they had to be afraid of what's outside instead of what's in. The door's been trapped, though, and will sound off an alarm spell the moment it opens."

"How do you know?" Haern asked.

"Do you think this is the first building I've broken into that was warded by wizards?" his father asked.

Haern shrugged. Fair enough.

"How do we get out?" he asked instead.

"The third floor; there's another exit to the hidden shaft along the interior. If we move fast enough, we should be out before anyone realizes you're missing."

Haern nodded.

"Lead the way," he said.

Thren turned and dashed up the remaining few steps. They emerged on the first floor of the Stronghold, a room clearly built with defense in mind. A stone barricade was erected just before the large double doors, forcing anyone entering to veer left or right. On either side were perches so men could attack from high ground, and around the corners was another spiked barricade with crossbows permanently bolted to it. A pile of bolts lay on either side, waiting for use. Beside the doors, Haern caught sight of two more young men who lay slumped beside it.

"Come on," Thren whispered. Beside them was another doorway leading to the stairs, and they rushed up them. Haern caught a glimpse of the second floor before they continued up the winding stairs, this a room of wealth and luxury, red carpets and gold trim everywhere. As they passed, Haern swore he heard men carrying on a conversation. He paused only momentarily to ensure they were not alarmed, and ahead of him, Thren beckoned Haern to hurry.

The third floor was a barracks for the youngest members of the Stronghold. Occupying nearly all of the twelve beds in the single open room were boys, some old as twelve, most younger than ten. They all slept; at least, it seemed like they did. Taking a deep breath, Haern hoped his stay in the prison hadn't cost him the coordination to move through such a room without noise.

Wordlessly, Thren pointed out their objective: an ornate painting of the Stronghold, the canvas kept in an enormous silver frame secured to the wall.

Stay silent, Thren mouthed, and Haern glanced to the children. If they woke, if they made a noise, then most likely, the children would die. Thren would let none witness their escape. No matter their future allegiance, no matter the dogma of hatred being drilled into them, the idea still made Haern sick to his stomach.

I will, he mouthed back. *Now lead*.

The beds were to either side of the room, and through the center, Thren walked, crouched over and quiet as a hunting animal in the forest. If he made any noise, it was easily drowned out by the breathing and snoring of the children. After meditating for a moment to force his body to calm down after the battle in the dungeon, Haern followed. The floor was sturdy wood, and unlike other rooms, it had no carpet, an annoyance not lost on Haern. Still, it seemed resistant to his steps, and so long as he moved slowly, there appeared no danger of a creak. The bigger worry was the children. If just one woke needing to relieve himself or shift into a more comfortable position...

It seemed the two worried over the wrong thing. Thren had just reached the painting, and Haern the center of the room, when shouts came from downstairs. They were muffled, distant, but the alarms wouldn't take long to travel up the stairs. Knowing the time for caution was over, Haern quickened his steps, crossing the room at a blistering pace as his father tugged on a corner of the painting, then slid it to the side. The movement made the tiniest of creaks, but the creaks were nothing compared to the growing shouts of alarm.

Move! Thren mouthed before diving into the slender gap revealed behind the painting.

The children were stirring in their beds. No time left, Haern sprinted the last few steps and then leaped feetfirst into the gap. As he slid, he turned, grabbed the corner of the painting, and yanked it shut.

Total darkness bathed him, and letting out a relieved sigh, Haern began to scoot down what appeared to be a slender stone chute. He'd passed by several openings on his climb up, and he figured he was in one of them.

"The tunnel ends abruptly," Thren said from further down, his voice startling in the quiet. "Make haste, but don't be careless."

"Noted," Haern muttered as from the other side of the painting he heard a ruckus growing.

The chute wasn't long, and at its end, Haern found his father waiting for him.

"Ready?" he asked.

"I am," Haern said. "But I'm going first."

Instead of arguing, Thren merely laughed and shifted aside so Haern had room. Reaching out to his right, he felt one of the rungs, grabbed it tight. It felt so similar to when his father had first sent him tumbling down, but if Thren desired to kill him, there were certainly far better ways than breaking into the Stronghold to do it.

Swinging onto the ladder, he began climbing down, rung after rung, as he listened to the Stronghold continue its search for the escaping intruders on the other side of the stones.

"We had little to go on regarding your fate," Thren said as they descended. "I felt they would not kill you if you were captured, nor let you die easily. I'm glad my assumptions were not wrong."

"What of my little fall you sent me on?" Haern asked, unable to keep the bitterness from his voice.

"Clearly, you survived," Thren said. "Spare me your tantrum."

That was it, then? His betrayal was nothing to concern him, his frustrations mere tantrums of a child? Haern rolled his eyes in the darkness. Why had he ever believed it might be otherwise?

When his foot felt no more rungs beneath, Haern took in a deep breath and then leaped blindly to the other side. Sure enough, he rolled into the tunnel he'd come from, and on his stomach, he crawled into the narrowing space. Ignoring the scrapes to his elbows and the cuts to his outfit as he rushed along, he did his best to dismiss the contradiction of his father betraying him on their way in, yet risking his life coming back to rescue him from the dungeon. He reached the end, found the hidden door above him. With only a moment to brace himself, he pushed it open and pulled himself out.

As Thren crawled out behind him, Haern quickly spun to survey his surroundings. In all directions from the Stronghold, he saw men in armor carrying torches, searching in parties of two.

"To the wheat fields," Thren said in a hushed voice as he kicked the door shut to the secret entrance, not bothering to hide it. They sprinted, and when they were halfway there, Haern saw the stalks split and Delysia slip out, urging him onward with a hand. Seeing her there, unharmed, flooded him with relief. The relief did not last long, for his instincts cried out warning, and from the corner of his right eye, he saw a single paladin bedecked in the dark armor of his order riding toward them on a black steed.

No torch, thought Haern, diving out of the way. *Sneaky bastard.*

The dark paladin's sword cleaved where he'd been, the fire around the blade darker than the night itself. Instead of trying to gain distance, Haern flung himself into the fight, knowing he had to strike immediately before the paladin could ride away. His swords cut into the side of the mount, but not enough to score a fatal hit. The man rode on, his sword blocking an attempted thrust from Thren on the other side. The dark paladin looped around, and he cried out warnings to the rest.

"Here!" he shouted, lifting his enormous two-handed sword into the air. "Over here, my brethren!"

"Shit," muttered Thren.

The dark paladin rode toward them, blade still raised, but before coming into range, he suddenly pulled back on the reins.

"You'll suffer for such insolence," said the paladin, and he held his sword in one hand, the other balling into a fist. Violet flame leaked through his fingers, and then the man thrust it outward. Haern crossed his swords and ducked his head, unable to dodge in time. Fire roared, bursting forth in a tremendous cone from the paladin's palm. Turning his face, Haern shifted in a desperate hope to absorb the brunt of it against his side, but before it could burn him, he saw movement, a flash of light.

Delysia stood between him and the dark paladin, hands clasped, red hair fluttering in a silent breeze that swirled about her from all directions. The fire could not touch her, could not even withstand being in her presence. As the dark paladin recoiled with surprise, she reached out with a glowing hand.

"The flames are yours," she said. "Take them."

And then the fire erupted back to life, only this time engulfing the paladin and his horse, consuming them. He opened his mouth in a final, horrific scream matched only by the dying cries of his mount. After but a second, they were both silenced, the heat so intense, the dark paladin was ash and bone before his melting armor hit the ground, landing amid a cloud of all he had once been.

"Come on," Delysia said, turning and offering her hand. Haern took it, and together they fled into the wheat fields, Thren at their heels, as dozens of horses from the Stronghold thundered in chase.

They said nothing as they ran, all concentration on putting one foot in front of the other. Haern felt the toll of his imprisonment wearing on him, his heart pounding and his lungs gasping for each breath. He did everything he knew to ignore the pain, but it didn't take long until Delysia was tugging on his arm to keep him moving. With how tall and tight the wheat grew, he could only see Thren on occasion, trailing alongside them, his head constantly on a swivel. The horses were spreading out, and it'd only be a matter of time before they were spotted.

"Delysia," Haern said, his hand slipping free from hers. Noticing, she stopped, rushed back to him. A glowing hand touched his chest as her body pressed against his.

"Stay strong," she said, and he felt the exhaustion in his body fade as if it had never been. On impulse, he kissed her forehead, then grabbed her hand.

"Stay with me," he said, and they resumed their run, this time with him in the lead. To their right, a paladin burst through the wheat, and Haern dropped to the ground as the horse passed on by. Too close, he knew. Just a matter of time, but they had to run, had to keep gaining distance. Every second that passed, more of the paladins were waking up, throwing on their armor, grabbing their weapons, and rushing out into the night to join the chase. Distance was their friend, delay their enemy.

Another rode on to their left, and when he let out a cry, Haern knew they'd been spotted. To confirm, Thren rejoined their side, shouting orders.

"Surprise is our only hope!" he shouted. "Crouch low, and cut them down as they ride by!"

Between the darkness and the wheat, any rider would have difficulty spotting them, and Haern knew his father was right. In open battle against an armored, horsed rider? Hopeless. But cutting them down as they closed about, keeping them off-balance and confused? Haern dropped to his knees, willing himself into becoming a specter of the fields, a coiled animal ready to strike. At his side, his father did the same as Delysia ducked low, watching intently.

The rider who had first spotted them came back around, still calling for his allies. He rode mere feet to their left, and as he passed, Thren lashed out, thrusting a short sword beneath the man's plate mail and into his ribs. As the man screamed, Thren pulled the blade free and then smacked the horse with the flat edge, sending it bolting away.

Two more came riding in from the other direction, and Haern timed their arrival. Their aim was off, the two clearly not yet having located them, so he knew he'd have his chance. Running while crouched, he shifted aside at the last second, both swords slicing into the legs of the nearest mount. It let out a horrible noise as it crumpled, trapping the rider beneath it as it continued to let out pained screams. Before the other paladin could stop, Haern rushed around to the other side, jammed a blade into the throat of the trapped man, and then sprinted back toward Delysia and Thren. As he did, he saw another paladin veer away, having just barely avoided an ambush by his father.

"It's not enough," Thren said as he joined his side.

"Look," Delysia said, pointing. The paladins had grouped together, nine of them at least, and they circled around them on their horses. They did not close in nor attempt to find them within the vicinity. Haern frowned, none too pleased with the strategy, and then the largest of the riders curled in, riding in a circle just barely within the others. From the feet of his midnight-black mount burst flames, as if its hooves were the center of a bonfire. Around and around it looped as Haern, Thren, and Delysia pressed against each other, back-to-back. The fire grew, its center a deep purple, its outer reaches darker than the night itself.

"Stay with me!" Delysia cried as the fire roared to life, rolling toward them from all sides. The priestess's hands lifted above her head, locked together in prayer as the wheat blackened and collapsed into ash from the fire's passing. Just before they themselves were consumed, Delysia let out a cry, flinging down her arms and grabbing Haern and Thren by the shoulders. He felt a tingling, and then the fire passed over him. His skin was not burned, nor did he feel its heat, yet beneath his feet, ash gathered from the charred wheat.

The spell ended, and circling them were the nine dark paladins. Their cover was gone, as was any surprise, any hiding. Now in the open, Haern lifted his sabers and stood protectively before Delysia.

"Go down fighting," he said. "You don't want to be taken to their dungeons."

"Speak for yourself," Thren said. "The only ones dying this night are our enemies."

The nine dismounted, drawing weapons wreathed in black flame. They stayed close, steadily closing the gap to prevent any hope of them punching through. Among themselves, the paladins gave quick orders, keeping their approach controlled, their eventual assault in perfect unison.

"Listen to me," Thren said, tilting his head toward them, yet keeping his eyes on the dark paladins before him. "If we're to live, you have to hold nothing back. Every bit of your power, every bit of your rage, it must be let free. Unleash death upon them, or we die ourselves."

"I know how to fight," Haern growled.

Thren's eyes flicked to Delysia.

"My words were for her."

Tighter and tighter the circle closed, a wall of swords, axes, and plate mail.

"Our lives or theirs, priestess," Thren whispered. "Make your choice."

With a unified cry, the dark paladins rushed in, and Haern took Thren's advice to heart. Hold nothing back. He knew how to become that animal. He knew how to unleash that power. Harnessing every bit of his anger, frustration, and doubt from his imprisonment, he lunged toward the closest paladins, charging just as they themselves issued the orders to attack. With his back to her, he did not see the brilliant flash of light Delysia cast, but he saw its flare in the eyes of his foes, saw them cry out, blinded. Two at once he fought, slipping through their frantic defenses, twisting his body to avoid being chopped in half from the right shoulder down. His saber found the throat of one, then both blades crashed into the sword of another, batting it three times so quickly, it sounded like a single ring.

And then he was away, racing toward the other side of the circle, crashing right alongside his father into a group of three.

Side by side they fought, blades dancing, perfect mirrors of the other. Thren slammed the sword of one out of position, screaming in pain from the fire that encased the weapon, and then Haern plunged a saber through the armpit of the man. It wasn't deep enough to kill, but the man could press no further. Behind him, Delysia had cast another flare of light, knocking back the other half of the group, but she was exposed and Haern would not let them overwhelm her.

Back to the other side he rushed, and his father joined him. He leaped past Delysia, dropping into a roll to duck beneath the swing of an ax, then coming about to stab at the man's back. He turned to block it, and then Thren slammed into him, smashing him to the ground with both short swords puncturing his face. Haern rushed left, Thren right, each engaging another paladin while they still had some measure of surprise. Their foes held strong, falling back while expertly positioning their blades. Each time their swords made contact with that black fire, Haern felt an ache growing in his hands and at the center of his chest, an ache that would soon leave him in agony from the unholy powers they wielded.

"Us or them!" Thren screamed, suddenly disengaging. He rolled underneath a swing, then kicked into the air so he could intercept two men rushing toward where Delysia stood. "There's no other choice!"

Haern spun, using his cloak to disguise his movements before he too retreated, back to his father's side. The older man was struggling to keep the two at bay, most of his attacks feints to keep the paladins on edge and prevent them from advancing. Haern had a split second to see the pattern his father used, then joined him, following up a feint with a stab of his own. The dark paladin, having also sensed the pattern and therefore ignoring the feint, was unable to position his blade in time to avoid Haern's attack. His saber cut across the man's face, splashing blood through the air as the steel tip scraped against teeth. A kick sent him staggering away, but as always, another stepped up to replace him. The newcomer's thrust might have impaled Haern, but Delysia was there, unleashing an invisible wall of force that sent the man rolling away as if struck in the chest by a boulder.

Every nerve on fire, every reflex ever drilled into him over a lifetime of training pushed to its limits, Haern twisted and turned, blocking one attack, thrusting for another, only to pull away to avoid having his head cut clean off his shoulders. In the back of his mind, he heard a ringing, heard his father screaming.

"Will you let us die, Delysia? Will you let us all die? Let go, damn it, *let go!*"

Too many, they were just too many, too strong, too skilled. Haern unleashed a flurry of attacks on one opponent, then spun right to block the killing thrust of another. One saber each battling a different opponent, he blocked, parried, and waited for one of their burning blades to finally make it through and end it all.

And then Delysia screamed.

It was an unearthly cry, thunderous in power, terrifying in its rage. A white mist rolled in all directions, followed by a shock wave that knocked Haern to his knees. The dark paladins staggered backward, and above Haern's head, a golden blade shimmered into existence, then flew through the air. It cut two at once, slicing them cleanly in half so that they fell in pieces, blood and innards spilling out upon the blasted circle of ash that was their battlefield. A third moved to strike, but then he screamed as his body turned rigid. His mouth opened, and it seemed light shone from his throat and eyes, a light that burned like the sun itself. When he dropped, his eyes were blackened holes, his mouth hanging open to release a trail of white mist that floated to the sky like smoke.

Haern spun, awestruck by what he saw. Delysia hovered a foot above the ground, the irises of her eyes shining a vivid gold. Light lashed off her hands as she turned to the next paladin, cutting like blades through his armor. When the man turned to flee, she crossed her wrists and then flung them downward. Another wave of light, this time shaped like an X, flew through him, cutting into his back. When it hit, the man screamed, then fell to his stomach and did not move.

The last survivors, two dark paladins with great axes wreathed in flame, attempted to assault her at once. Haern thought Thren might try to stop them, but he was nowhere to be found. There was only Delysia, and at their approach, she lifted a single hand. Light grew in her palm, pulsing with silver and gold, and then it shot out in a solid beam that slammed into the first. The man's ax shattered, his armor crunched inward, and then he flew, ribs broken, blood spewing from his mouth. The other swung, but she stepped in, catching his wrist and shoving her other hand against his face.

"Damn you," she whispered, and it seemed those words traveled for miles. The man's body snapped erect, every muscle tight as he screamed and screamed. When Delysia stepped back, releasing his face, it seemed every inch of his flesh became light. It burned, dissolving, becoming a white mist that floated into the air. As his armor hit the ground, only bones remained within, clattering as they hit the ash beneath.

And with that, they were alone, just Haern and Delysia. Leaping to his feet, he rushed to her side, his mouth hanging open as she floated back to the ground. Delysia turned to look his way, the gold slowly vanishing from her eyes, returning to their deep green.

"We need to run," he told her, grabbing her hand. She said nothing, only nodded. Deeper into the wheat they rushed, Haern changing their angle at several intervals to ensure no one might guess their initial direction and follow. Given the miles that stretched out and the chaos of their battlefield, it'd be difficult to locate them until morning should any more be pursuing them.

Haern felt Delysia tug against his hand, and he turned to see her stagger, then collapse to her knees. Fearing her display had weakened her somehow, he grabbed her in his arms, went to lift her back to her feet, but he stopped when he realized she was crying.

"Del?" he said, tilting her chin with his hand so he might look upon her.

"Never again," she said, voice remaining strong despite the many tears that ran down her cheeks. "I never want to be like that again."

He clutched her tighter against him, kissed her forehead.

"I'm sorry," he said. "You saved our lives, but you never should have had to. We shouldn't have come here, shouldn't have ever left Veldaren."

Wiping tears from her face, she kissed his lips once, then pressed her forehead against the side of his cheek.

"Help me up," she whispered.

He did, and hand in hand, they ran from the Stronghold, ran until the morning light began to creep above the cloud-covered horizon.

CHAPTER

25

Haern and Delysia avoided the roads for the first two days they traveled north, reasoning that the paladins of the Stronghold might send riders out in search. The way wasn't difficult, the land mostly flat, the lush grass almost comforting as it brushed against their legs. All the while, they saw no sign of Thren.

"He only told me you two were separated early on," Delysia had explained while they fled through the wheat fields, putting the Stronghold far behind them. "I knew he was lying, but he was just as upset as I was when night came and went without your return. I'm not surprised he betrayed you like he did, but he must have had his reasons, especially for him to risk his life to save you."

"I'm sure he did," Haern had said. "But they'll be his own selfish reasons. I should have known better. I should have seen it coming." She had neither argued nor berated him, instead letting the matter drop. She'd asked what he learned, and he'd told her of what he'd found in Luther's room. None of it made sense, nor did it feel worth their trek, but she voiced no such opinion. For that, he was grateful.

On the third night, they risked building a fire. Haern kept it small, just enough for some heat and comfort. After their evening meal, the two sat side by side, Delysia leaning her head against his shoulder as they both watched the last of the slender twigs and branches burn away.

"With just the two of us, we should be able to make decent time," he said. "Leen isn't too far, and we can stock up on supplies once we arrive."

"What if the paladins have people looking for us there?" she asked.

Haern nudged her in the side.

"Come, now," he said. "Give me some credit. I can disguise myself if need be. Even if they have someone waiting, I'll make sure they have no reason to think it's me. And given the losses they've already suffered, I doubt they'll give us chase."

"You underestimate their thirst for revenge."

Haern chuckled.

"Well, they'll just have to go thirsty. It's a long trek from the Stronghold to Veldaren, and they have no reason to know that's where we're headed."

At the city's mention, Delysia let out a long sigh.

"It'll be good to be home," she said, voice wistful.

"Miss your brother already?" Haern asked, gently pushing his elbow into her side.

"No more than you do. I see the look in your eye. You dream of his pointy yellow hat, don't you? Is that what kept you going in the Stronghold's cells?"

She'd said it with a smile, but the comment struck a nerve that he found difficult to shake off.

"No," he said. "No, Del . . . that was you."

Her own smile faltered, and she fell silent as she pressed her head once more against his side. She was so close, her arms wrapped around his, her red hair brushing the side of his cheek. Ever since his escape from the Stronghold, he'd felt painfully aware of her presence, of how long her eyes lingered on him, of how bright her smile had been at his presence.

"You scared me, you know," she whispered. "I've always trusted you to return, but that place was awful, those men… Their hearts are so black, so terrible."

She was reliving the final combat with the dark paladins, he knew. It seemed so strange to him. Here was a woman with incredible power, yet she had no desire to use it, felt no joy in its embrace. In so many ways, it seemed she was everything he was not. Daily, he had to remind himself to remain humble. Daily, he had to pretend that the familiar thrill of battle, of taking the life of a foe, was something he did not enjoy.

"I was scared, too," he finally admitted as the fire crackled. "The idea of spending years in there, never seeing you again…"

He couldn't continue the line of thought, but he saw the recognition in her, the awkward way she closed her eyes and shifted her face to the side. What was she thinking? He didn't know. But damn it, he was the Watcher of Veldaren. To be this cowardly… to be this unsure…

"Delysia," he whispered, and when she turned, he pressed his lips to hers. Her eyes flared open, and for the briefest moment, she remained still as stone. As he held her close, he felt her relax, felt her lips open the slightest bit to kiss back. Haern tried to be gentle, kissing slowly, banishing her fears and memories in the only way he knew how. His heart hammered in his chest as her fingertips gently pressed the side of his neck, a tentative touch with a trembling hand. Haern had imagined such a moment a thousand times before, but still he felt clumsy, reckless. He held her tighter against him, wishing to banish his own memories, his own confusing, torturous journey with his father.

His right hand was curled about her back, clutching the fabric of her priestly robes. Slowly, he brought it around, across her side, to cup her breast in his palm.

Immediately, he felt her body stiffen in his arms. He kissed again, but there was no response this time, no give to her lips. It was as if her fire had suddenly gone cold. He felt her hand grab his wrist, and she sucked in a gasp of air as she gently pushed him away.

"In time," she whispered, and he could tell she was still short of breath, her heart aflutter. "I'm sorry, Haern. Just...in time."

Haern's mind was a racing mixture of anger, embarrassment, and shame. He kissed her one more time, trying to pretend nothing had happened, that nothing was wrong. Hand free of her grasp, he pulled her close, this time into a hug that she could not object to. As she pressed against him, he felt her grip him tightly, clutching him as she might a piece of driftwood in a storm.

"It's all right," he told her. "And I'm sorry."

She pulled back, kissed him once more on the lips, and then lay down on her bedroll, back to him. Haern stared at her, at her beauty in the red glow of the firelight, and then shook his head in a futile attempt to clear it. Dejected, he lay down in his own bedroll, wondering if she were mad at him. That was quickly answered by her turning to him, arm draping over his chest, face pressed into the side of his neck. She said nothing, but she didn't need to. Haern slid his arm beneath her, holding her against him, and did his best to relax.

The night wore on, and it took her awhile, but at last she slipped into a deep sleep. Sky clear, cicadas singing, Haern did his best to drift off as well. The grass was a soft blanket, the stars above his ceiling. He stared at them as Delysia began to softly snore beside him.

She's worse than Brug, Haern thought, and the remembrance of home made him smile. It'd be good to return to Veldaren, he decided. The streets were a burden, but at least he had family there, a clear purpose. As always, it seemed venturing outside those walls only reminded him how little he knew, how little he could change. Come their return home, tonight would just be something to forget, a mistake to pretend never happened. Closing his eyes, he let his mind begin its drift into sleep, only to be halted by something hard and small striking his cheek. Haern's eyes snapped open, and his heart leaped. There was only one person it could be, and as a second stone bounced against his chest, he looked to see his father standing at the edge of the dying fire's light. He said nothing, only met his gaze before turning and walking away.

Damn it, thought Haern. Just when the night seemed it could get no worse...

Careful not to wake Delysia, he slipped out from his bedroll, buckled his swords to his waist, and then followed.

Several hundred yards to their east was a slender hill, which Haern had positioned between them and the road in hopes of hiding the light of their fire. At the top of it, wind blowing through his hair, stood Thren. His swords remained sheathed, his eyes locked upon the pale moon.

"So, why did you betray me?" Haern asked, stopping at the foot of the hill.

"I had no choice but to go alone," Thren said, not turning to face him. "A man with your abilities, I trusted you to endure whatever might be below. Despite your temporary imprisonment, I was not wrong."

"If you needed to go alone, you might have just asked."

"And what would have been your answer?" Thren asked, cold blue eyes suddenly glaring at him. "Do not pretend you'd have let me visit with Luther without you. I am no fool."

Haern quietly accepted the rebuke. His father was right, of course. Under no circumstances would he have allowed Thren to go alone into the Stronghold. Together, they'd come to visit with Luther, to learn the man's secrets. And now they were solely in Thren's hands, and he would receive only what his father offered.

"What did he tell you?" Haern asked, hoping he might at least glean something. "Did he say why he did what he did?"

Thren's gaze returned to the moon.

"Religious nonsense," he said. "Fate and prophecy and other such things. He thought he was on the side of righteousness, of course. Men like him always do."

There was more his father was hiding; that much was obvious. Haern shifted his weight from foot to foot, trying to think of a way to drag it out of him. The night, which had been pleasant as he lay down beside Delysia, now carried an icy bite upon the steadily growing wind.

"I've traveled with you this far," he argued. "And it was at your suggestion, Thren. Don't betray me like this, not after all your pompous speeches about how I could trust you. What did Luther want? Why send the Sun Guild after us in Veldaren?"

Thren scratched at his face, thinking.

"The Sun Guild was smuggling something into Veldaren for him," he said.

"Smuggling what?"

His father chuckled.

"Remember that wagon full of tiles marked with the symbol of the Sun? Those."

It was the last thing Haern expected. It made no sense. For what reason would a priest desire the heavy stone slabs distributed throughout the city? Was there a trick to them? A trap, perhaps, or a spell he wished to perform in Karak's name?

"So, what he did," Haern said, trying to scrape the slightest bit more of information out of him, for he felt certain his father was still keeping secrets, "he did for Karak?"

A smirk tugged at the side of Thren's face.

"To be honest... I have no idea. Such are the ways of gods and servants. The moment you start letting right and wrong be decided by imaginary whispers in the heads of men, the world becomes a confused, twisted place. The weak think they are strong, the dead in their graves yearn to rise, the strong put chains on their wrists and bow their heads to idols and ideals."

Thren looked to him, half his face in shadow, the other seeming to glow in the moonlight.

"You're one such fool, aren't you?" he asked.

Haern's first instinct was to deny it, to declare his own strength to his father, and the realization nearly made him sick.

"You know nothing of me," he whispered.

"I know you better than you would like to admit. That's what frightens you."

Haern crossed his arms, and he felt his patience wearing thin.

"What do you want from me?" he asked. "Why are you even here?"

Thren sighed and put his back to the moon, framing his outline in silver, his face in darkness.

"I have no more time for games, Watcher. No more patience for it. You stand at a crossroads, and just this once, I'd like you to open your eyes and see the correct path. Fire and death are coming to Veldaren, but we can stop it if we're strong. If you're with me. Luther's future does not have to come to pass."

"If I'm with you?" asked Haern. "Tell me you jest, Thren. Tell me it's all a joke."

"Our *lives* are the joke. Don't you get it? Humorous playthings in the hands of gods. I know the symbol you wear around your neck, and it isn't the salvation you think it is. It's a prison, a shackle weighing you down."

He took a step closer, reached out his hand.

"You are the finest killer I have ever seen," he said, his voice softening, almost pleading. "You are a thing of beauty, and I will not deny your sense of nobility and honor. But you've crafted yourself into something that cannot be maintained. There is a natural order to things, and it is not what you desire. The strong rule the weak, Haern. So it is in the wilds, so it is in our cities. Stop flailing. Stop struggling against the current of the river, the winds of the grasslands, the pull of the earth itself. You don't need gods. You don't need creeds and rules, and you don't need forgiveness to remove the guilt you've been taught to feel. Stand at my side. Cast off the burden on your shoulders, and let go in your heart of those who would drag you into the grave."

The words were razors cutting into him, but Haern tried to stand strong. He looked into the eyes of his father even as his jaw trembled. From the chill, he told himself. From the icy wind.

"You're wrong," he said. "You have to know it. No matter how hard you pretend, I know you're human. I know you grieve for loved ones lost. I know you've watched friend after friend die, and some by your own hand. You've sacrificed *everything*, Thren, and for what? A legacy of fear and bloodshed? A remembrance that will fade in time, fade like all other kings and conquerors? You've clawed and killed and set fire to everything your hands may touch. What has it given you? What worth have you found?"

Haern gestured to grasslands, felt a fire growing in his chest.

"Look around you. You have nothing left. It's just you and I on this little hill. You claim I'm at a crossroads, yet you face the same one. You don't have to go back. You don't have to return to Veldaren and walk down that same road. Our lives, we'll both find them cut short, and we'll both die amid blood and metal, but my hopes are not for this world. My hope is that I will have loved ones to bury me, loved ones I'll wait for, come their own time after. That is my hope, Thren. What is yours?"

Thren descended the hill. His lower jaw trembled, and his eyes were wide. There were tears in them.

"My hope?" asked Thren, standing before Haern so that he towered over him. "My *hope?* My hope is to carve a scar into this damned world that's given me nothing, carve one so deep and so bloody that it never heals. And I'll do it on my own, with my own two hands. No gods, no kings, no priests or prophets. Mine. Of my own body. My own blood. No matter who betrays me, no matter who abandons me. And do you know the difference between your hope and mine? I'll never need to beg, nor surrender, to achieve it."

"I'll stop you," Haern whispered. "You know I must. Don't do this. There's another life waiting for you, if you'd take it, and I promise you it would not be so alone."

Thren reached out and grabbed the front of Haern's tunic, yanking him close. Haern stood firm, matching his father's powerful gaze.

"Alone?" he asked. "That's all we are. Is that how deep the lies are buried in you, that you think otherwise? I know you believe Ashhur is where I'll find some measure of comfort, but you're wrong. When those you love are dead, when you hold one of them bleeding in your arms, console yourself with your prayers. Tell yourself whatever lies you need to put an end to your tears. Truth hurts, Haern. It never heals. Fuck the gods."

Thren pushed him away, and as Haern stepped back, a question came to his lips, one meant only to hurt, and he was unable to stop it.

"Who died in your arms?" he asked, even though he knew the answer. "Whose death left you with so little hope?"

It was Marion, his mother, whose face he had clouded memories of, snippets of stories and half-remembered songs. But clear was the day his father had come home to their safe house, hands bloodied, a prisoner with him bound by rope. His older brother, Randith, had asked for their mother, where she might be.

"Dead" had been his father's only reply, and it was more than Haern would receive now. Thren looked betrayed by the very question, and instead of answering, he drew his swords and held them at his sides.

"Put those away," Haern said. "I won't do this."

"You will," Thren said. "You said you'll stop me, so here I am. Stop me. Put an end to this part of the game. I swear to kill, to murder. I promise you a thousand souls will suffer before I reach my grave. Aren't you Veldaren's Watcher? Aren't you their protector? Prove it. Draw your damn swords and cut off my head."

"No," said Haern. "I won't. Not here and now. Not while there's still a chance."

"A chance of what?" shouted Thren. When Haern did not answer, he swung a blade. Haern flinched, but he remained still, even as the edge cut into the side of his jaw and remained pressed there. Staring down Thren's glare, he refused to give in to the fury growing in his chest, the despair at seeing just how twisted and hurt his father truly was.

"We're all murderers," Thren said, voice cold and quiet. "Some are just better at hiding it than others. Ashhur kills as well as Karak, or did you not see what your priestess did back there?" He pulled away the blade. "I don't want your mercy. One day, neither will you. Mercy cuts deep and will only harm those you love. This cruel world will make sure of it."

Thren sheathed the sword and walked past Haern down the

hill. Haern turned to watch him go, the maelstrom of emotions in his heart rooting him firmly to the ground.

"Why'd you come back?" he asked. "Why not leave me in that dungeon if you resent me so?"

Thren continued without pause, ignoring the question. As if it were beneath him. As if it were obvious.

"Father..." Haern whispered.

Thren hesitated the slightest step at the bottom of the hill, then trudged on. Haern pulled the hood low over his face, felt tears swelling in his eyes, and he let them fall. For a long while, he stood there, watched until his father faded into shadow, became nothing. His chest hurt, and he wished more than anything he'd never come west.

Back at their camp, he removed his belt and placed the swords beside his bedroll. When he sat down, pulling his cloak and hood off his face, Delysia stirred.

"Haern?" she asked. He said nothing, only stared into the ashes of their fire. The priestess sat up, tossed the blanket aside. "Haern, you're bleeding."

"It's nothing," he said.

She put a hand on his face anyway, and he heard her pray. A gentle ringing sounded in his ears. He closed his eyes against a soft glow of light, and then the skin on his cheek tightened. The pain dulled, then faded away completely when she pulled back her hand. Kneeling, she looked at him, a dozen questions unasked on her lips. Haern wanted to answer them, couldn't. But she knew what had happened, at least in some fundamental way. Her fingers brushed hair away from his face, and she kissed where she'd healed him. That single kiss felt far more loving than any other she'd given him that night.

"I'm sorry," she whispered.

"I should have known better."

"It doesn't matter."

"It does," he said, looking away and feeling embarrassed. "I was a fool and apparently the only one who didn't know it."

Delysia put a hand on his cheek, her warm fingers gently pulling him back to look at her.

"You saw hope in your father where even I saw none," she said. "I could never fault you for that."

"It just means I was naïve, Del."

She wrapped an arm around his waist and put her head against his shoulder. Normally, such closeness would have comforted him, but this time he only felt awkward, exposed.

"Better that than the man your father would have you be," she said.

Haern's retort died on his tongue. Kissing the top of her head, he finally returned her embrace.

"You're better than I deserve," he told her.

"And don't you forget it."

He broke from her grasp and lay back down on his bedroll. Delysia joined him, lying on her side with her hand on his chest. Haern put his hand atop hers, clutched her fingers, and closed his eyes tight. The bed of grass beneath him didn't feel quite so comfortable, the ceiling of stars so vast and empty, he dared not look upon it.

He's wrong, he told himself, thinking of all the vile words his father had spoken. *He's wrong; he has to be wrong. We're meant for more than this, for more than living and dying and suffering at the hands of others. We are not alone. We're not.*

Easy words to tell himself.

Hard words to believe.

CHAPTER

26

Tarlak sat with his elbows on his desk, hands holding up his head as he stared at the large map of Veldaren spread out before him. At one time, it'd been color-coded to show the estimated territory of the various guilds, but that was gone now. There was no point. From the castle at the north to the slums in the south, it all belonged to the Sun Guild. Instead, he'd placed little pins to mark the location of their tiles, though by the fiftieth, he'd stopped. As he stared at it with his head pounding and the morning sun rising, he wondered if that had been a mistake.

"Come in," he said when he heard a knock on the door behind him, refusing to turn around. It was either Brug or a person come to kill him, and given his mood, Tarlak didn't feel like spending the effort to address either one.

"Starting early, are we?" asked Brug, and he leaned over Tarlak's shoulder at the map. "Gods, there's a lot of them, aren't there?"

"No kidding," said Tarlak, slumping back in his chair. "I saw five more along the marketplace yesterday; didn't even bother to put them on the map."

"There's another two on Iron Road," Brug said. "Probably added them a day or so ago."

Tarlak glanced over at the bearded man.

"You're sure?" he asked.

Brug nodded, brow furrowed.

"Yeah, I'm sure," he said. "Where do you think I get my metal to make all your little toys? I go there once a week, and trust me, they're new."

Back to the map Tarlak turned, and if he could have glared it into flames, he would have. Technically, he could have burned it with a snap of his fingers, but that'd have involved effort.

"We're missing something," he said. "Something obvious. Why would Muzien be adding in more of those tiles to the Sun Guild? The city's his, and ever since that sickening display at the marketplace, everyone knows it, too. Who else is left to oppose him?"

Brug shrugged.

"The king, maybe? I think the Ash Guild's holding on, too, but they're more hiding than anything else. Victor's not dead yet, either."

"None of them are threats, not anymore," Tarlak insisted. "Besides, you think a few more tiles will change that? There's something to them, and I'm thinking it is time we go and find out."

Brug gestured to his long red bedrobes.

"Now?" he asked.

"Now," Tarlak said, rising from his chair.

"Haven't even eaten breakfast yet," Brug mumbled as he headed for the door to change.

"Suffer for your vocation," Tarlak said, following him. "Besides, I pay you to obey my every whim, not eat."

"So, what's the plan?" Brug asked as they walked down the main road running from the western gates of the city to its center.

"You assume I have one?" Tarlak asked as he kept his eyes open for the tiles. "That's just foolish."

"Well, you're a foolish guy," Brug said. "Any chance we can get something to eat while we're out here?"

"Not until we're done."

"But I don't know what it is we're *doing*."

Tarlak raised an eyebrow his way.

"Well, then," he said. "You'll just have to trust me to tell you when we're done."

Even amid the constant rumble of chatter and those passing by, there was no hiding Brug's groan. Not that Tarlak would argue with him. Even he wasn't entirely sure what he was doing, just playing a hunch. The tiles were important, and more and more, he felt certain it wasn't for serving as a way to mark territory. That left relatively few possibilities for them, and none of them were particularly good.

"Come on," he said. "Let's get somewhere a little quieter and less likely to have a member of the Sun Guild notice our poking and prodding."

They ventured south, past the various workshops, past the large granaries and warehouses, and into the poorer stretches of Veldaren. Tarlak felt eyes upon him, not that he minded. Of course he stood out. He was wearing bright yellow robes, after all. Even without them, his hair and goatee were neatly trimmed, his clothes clean, his skin pale and free of dirt. Under normal circumstances, he'd have a sign floating above his head screaming, "Rob me," but Tarlak knew wizards carried enough mystique, no one would dare harass him. When first setting up his mercenary band, he'd reinforced the matter by turning a few troublesome ruffians into frogs and leaving them in their respective guild territory, their cloaks still tied to their little green bodies. Some men didn't fear death, but life as a frog?

Well, everyone had their limits.

"Getting quiet," Brug said. A few children played down one alley, and stray dogs barked farther up the street. All around were ramshackle homes with heavily locked doors.

"Good enough for me," Tarlak said. "See one of Muzien's tiles lying about?"

"By the corner," Brug said, pointing.

It was at the intersection of a road, a single tile dug into the rough dirt adjacent to the last home on the block. Tarlak knelt before it, analyzing it. It looked like all the others, thick, heavy stone with the four-pointed star carved into its front. His fingers traced along the star, and he racked his mind for any magical symbols or meaning the star might have beyond the guild affiliation. There were none that he knew of, though he made a note to check on it when he returned to the tower. As particular as Muzien was, Tarlak had a feeling he'd stolen it from somewhere to use as his own.

"Receiving any magical revelations?" Brug asked, leaning against the home beside him with his arms crossed.

"Not yet," Tarlak said. "But that's next on the agenda."

Closing his eyes, he put his palm flat on the tile and began murmuring the words to a spell. It was fairly simple, the very first one taught to any student that gained admittance to the Apprentices' Tower governed by the Council of Mages. His eyes changed for a brief moment, accessing a vision spectrum known to very few. Any object that contained a spell or enchantment would shimmer and glow with a multitude of colors, revealing to him its intricate mechanics so he might dispel or activate the magic if necessary. The required incantations finished, he opened his eyes.

The tile was as dim as the dirt it was buried in.

"Huh," said Tarlak, baffled.

"What is it?" Brug asked. "They enchanted?"

"I can't decide if it's good news or bad," Tarlak said, standing. "I was sure they had some sort of arcane effect sneaked into them, but, well... nothing. Far as I can tell, they're plain old regular stone."

"Excellent," Brug said. "We've learned what they're not. I'm willing to call that a good day. Care if I run off to the market and grab me a caraway cake?"

"Sure, go ahead," said Tarlak. "Teach me to try making you work on an empty stomach."

"Work?" asked Brug. "You want me to work, how about this? I'll start scouting out the northern district, tallying up these tiles, where and how many. May not know what it is they're for, but at least we'll know where they all are."

Tarlak scratched at his red goatee, frowning down at the stone tile as if it'd insulted him.

"Sounds like a plan," he said. "Go ahead. I'll start here in the south. Make sure you check the symbol carved into them. You find any that are different in the slightest, I want to know about it."

"Will do," said Brug, who was already walking away with his back to him.

What am I missing? wondered Tarlak. *And what game are you playing, Muzien?*

He'd told Brug he'd work on the south, but his heart wasn't in it yet. The four-pointed star surely had some history to it, and he'd feel more comfortable scouring his personal library for books than wandering around jotting down locations of those stupid tiles. That was more his territory, anyway. After all, what other reason had he hired Brug for other than for grunt work and blacksmithing skill? Surely not his prowess in combat.

Tarlak returned to the main crossroad, then headed west. As he left the city, a wagon was passing through the guard post, and painted in white on the wagon's side was the symbol of the Sun Guild. Tarlak watched the guards wave the driver in without even a cursory glance at his goods.

What did you just let in? Poisons, wines, more of those damn tiles?

Ignoring a childish desire to set the wagon aflame, he continued on to his tower. The weather was fine, the sun high and warm, and so he enjoyed the breeze blowing against him as he crossed the grass. By the time he reached his tower, he was smiling, and he was thinking maybe he should just take a break and relax for a few hours. He couldn't spend his whole life trying to keep track of the underhanded dealings of a city. Snapping his fingers, the door opened for him, and pulling his hat off his head, he moved to step inside, then froze.

Waiting for him, arms crossed and standing beside the hearth, was the giant man with the painted face.

"How did you...?" Tarlak began, mouth dropping open. He had a dozen various alarms cast all across his tower. Should a man try scaling the walls, digging through the floor, breaking down the door, even flying through one of the windows, he'd have known.

"Simple enough," said Ghost. "I walked right in."

Tarlak extended his right hand, palm outward, and shot a bolt of lightning straight for Ghost's chest. The thunder of its casting echoed throughout the lower floor and hurt Tarlak's ears. Amid the flash, Ghost dropped to his knees, and come the return of Tarlak's vision, the man was gone. Tarlak stood there frozen, baffled. Seconds passed, and he heard nothing, saw nothing.

"I'm losing it," Tarlak said, staring at the blackened scorch marks above the fireplace where his bolt had blasted into the stone.

"Not quite."

He whirled, deadly shards of ice growing on his fingertips, but it was too late. A meaty fist greeted him, and then all was darkness and stars.

When Tarlak came to, he lay propped against a wall, hands bound behind his back. His head throbbed, and when he opened his mouth to groan, he tasted the coarse dirt of a gag wedged between his teeth. Vision tilting as if he'd just spun in a circle for several minutes, Tarlak shut his eyes and waited out the distortion. His stomach felt as if he'd eaten a vulture's meal, and as for his fingers, they were tied so tightly, they'd gone numb. A precaution against any spellcasting, he knew. At least Ghost hadn't gone the full distance and just chopped them all off.

"You're awake," he heard Ghost say.

Tarlak opened his eyes, and this time the world did not tilt back and forth. Ghost sat opposite him on a wooden chair. The chair from his study, he realized. To his left was the fireplace, his right the door to the tower, which was now shut. Tarlak wondered how much time had passed. If he'd been out for a few hours, perhaps Brug might return. Even the slightest distraction might be enough for him to pry his hands free…

"I want you to listen carefully," Ghost said, rising from the chair and crossing the carpet. When he reached Tarlak, he knelt down so they might stare eye to eye. At such distance, he could easily see the white paint smeared across the man's face...only it didn't seem like paint anymore. It looked like scarred flesh.

"Your hands are bound, and bound well," Ghost continued. "Now, I know there are some spells you can cast using just your words, but I'm going to risk this. Just ask yourself which will be faster, your tongue or my swords?" The man ripped the gag from Tarlak's mouth. "Trust me, few men who doubted my speed have ever lived."

"It's nice to see you too, Ghost," Tarlak said, and he swallowed. It made his stomach gag, but he needed the taste gone from his mouth. "You're looking as cheery as ever."

Ghost walked back to the chair and sat down. As if to purposefully contradict Tarlak's words, he frowned all the deeper. He said nothing, though, just stared. Tarlak would hardly describe his situation as comfortable, but that stare certainly didn't help matters. So, he did what he normally did when faced with awkward situations: he rambled.

"Sorry about burning you like I did," he said. "Not that I had much choice, since you seemed pretty bent on killing me and Brug. Glad you're all right, though. You nearly killed me and failed, and now I've nearly killed you and failed. So, let's just call this whole thing even. Sound good?"

Ghost's left hand drifted to the sword at his hip, and he gripped the hilt hard enough to whiten his knuckles. For the first time, Tarlak noticed how pale the man's skin had become. He looked unhealthy, there was no denying that, yet the man also had a cold sweat breaking out across his face and neck.

"I have no true desire to kill you," Ghost said, ignoring his earlier rambles.

"That so?" Tarlak asked. "You have a unique way of showing it."

"The first time, you were merely in my way," said Ghost. "A potential interference to my hunt for the Watcher. I'd not dueled a wizard in years, and I must admit, I was eager to test my abilities. You were a worthy foe, so when I say I am glad you survived, you must understand I speak the truth."

"Comforting," said Tarlak, still clueless as to where the conversation was going. "Is that why you gutted Senke, too? He was in the way?"

This seemed to affect Ghost far more than Tarlak expected.

"The Watcher called me a monster afterward," Ghost said. "Do you think that is true?"

"If you're trying to argue you're not, you're going about it a pretty piss-poor way."

Finally, Ghost laughed, leaning back in his chair and running a hand across his bald head.

"I argue nothing," he said. "Monsters. Aren't we all monsters? You wield fire with your bare hands and summon lightning from your palms. Tell me, would men not quake in fear of you should you bring your wrath upon them?"

"Anyone afraid of me will deserve whatever wrath that befalls them," Tarlak said. "I don't kill the innocent."

"Innocent?" Another laugh. "An odd way to call men and women you know nothing about. I doubt anyone would call *you* innocent, Tarlak."

"Is that why you tried to kill us the second time?"

Ghost shook in his chair, and it made Tarlak all the more nervous. Something was terribly wrong with the man. He looked ready to explode, yet at the same time, it seemed he clung to consciousness by a thin thread made solely of pure stubbornness.

"I don't have a *choice*," he said. A smile flashed on his face, vanished. "Not anymore. Right now, it's your life or mine,

Tarlak. Would you blame me for killing you when forced into such a situation?"

"Honestly?" asked Tarlak. "I think you look like a man who doesn't care whatsoever about what I have to say. Nor do you look like a man who can be forced to do anything, not even when threatened with his life. So, if you're going to kill me, please, for the love of Ashhur, just go ahead and kill me."

Ghost stood, and now both hands clutched the hilts of his swords.

"Or we can continue chatting," Tarlak offered.

"All my life," Ghost said, slowly walking toward him. "All my life, I denied being a monster. I embraced people's fear. I painted my face and grinned at their prejudice and unease. That fear was their own failure, not mine. The color of my skin gave them their anger, not my own self. No matter what, because of my skill, my strength, I was free. I was dangerous and proud. But now?"

He drew a sword and placed the edge against Tarlak's neck. Tarlak tensed, and he refused to look away from Ghost's bloodshot eyes.

"And now," said Ghost, "all I can feel is a need to cut your throat. It doesn't matter, my desires, my thoughts. That need is there, an ache, an addiction. I've been *made* into a monster, wizard, and my heart rebels against it with every last vestige of my pride."

"Then fight it," insisted Tarlak. "No one can make you into a monster, Ghost, only show you the way."

The blade quivered at his neck. Ghost's eyes narrowed, his obsidian skin considerably paled. Tarlak could hear his breathing, and he swore he could even hear the hammering of the giant man's heart.

Ghost let out a scream, turned, and drove his sword with all his strength into the floor of the tower. Back to him, the man stood there, shoulders rising and falling as he gasped in air. His hands were clenched into fists, and they trembled.

"The man I killed," Ghost said. "Senke...was he a friend of yours?"

Tarlak swallowed down a sudden knot in his throat.

"Yes," he said. "A good friend."

Ghost turned his head.

"I'm sorry," he said, his eyes firmly locked on the floor. "I long told myself it was because of the job, but it never was. I killed because I could, because I thought it elevated me beyond all others. But when the choice is taken away...when it's still my hands..."

"You're sorry," Tarlak said, and he rose to his feet. His hands were still tied behind him, and he pulled against them as he felt his own rage growing. "You're *sorry?* Good for you, you bastard, but I'm not the one you should be apologizing to. Senke was my friend, but he was a brother to Delysia, and you butchered him like a piece of meat."

Eyes still on the floor, Ghost opened his mouth to speak, but instead, he collapsed to his knees...and then seemed to sink into the very floor. Tarlak's mouth dropped open, baffled by the sight. Letting out a slow groan, Ghost pushed himself back up through it, his feet setting back atop the floor with a heavy thud before he collapsed onto his hands and knees. Boils shimmered across his arms, rising, popping, and vanishing without leaving a trace beyond the faintest of scars.

"Delysia," he said, and he sounded feverish. "She's...she's the priestess that was with you. Your sister?"

"Yes," Tarlak said. "You nearly killed Senke once, but she saved him, brought him back. And then you stabbed him again, except this time, she wasn't there, and you know why? Because *I* made her stay behind. I wish she'd have just blamed me like any normal person, but she never did. Just herself for not ignoring me, for not coming with us. You killed him, and she carried the guilt instead of you. I don't want your damn apology. I just want you out of my life. I want to stop thinking about how if I'd only been stronger, if I'd only turned you to ash before you ran into Leon Connington's mansion..."

His voice trailed off, unable to finish, too angry, too hurt.

"If that's what you want, then so be it," Ghost said. Retrieving his sword, he slipped it into the sheath strapped to his thigh, then slowly rose to his feet. He wobbled, grabbed the doorframe to steady himself. His back was to Tarlak, and he looked over his shoulder to ask his question.

"Where is your sister?"

Tarlak glared at him.

"Why do you care?"

"Because of Senke," he said. The white paint began to run down his neck as if it were melting. "I have to tell her. I have to know."

It made no sense. Why would he even ask? Did Ghost truly think he'd just reveal Delysia's location?

"I won't tell you," he said. "Kill me if you must, but I'm not putting my sister's life in danger."

He'd thought Ghost would be upset or threaten him, but doing the expected appeared to be the last thing the giant man intended.

No, instead, he laughed.

"Threaten?" he asked. "Threaten? Look at me, wizard. Look at the fever in my face. Look at the rot in my flesh. Death comes for me, not your sister. I just want to talk. You say she carries the guilt, so let me absolve her of it. That's all. Can you do that? For her?"

It was insane, Tarlak knew. Absolutely insane. Every part of his mind told him to lie, but deep in his chest, he felt something insisting he speak the truth. Haern would be at her side, and he'd have to trust them to be strong enough to endure whatever it was Ghost had planned.

"She traveled west months ago, toward the Stronghold," he said. "I don't know how long it will be until she returns, but if she does, it'll be by the main road."

"Thank you," Ghost said, swallowing heavily. His eyes closed for a moment, opened again. Blood had pooled in them, washing away the white with red. "Thank you."

With that he was gone, leaving Tarlak standing there by the wall with his hands bound behind his back.

"What in the world did I just do?" he wondered aloud. Hurrying to the stairs, he climbed up to Brug's room, where there were more than enough sharp instruments scattered about the workplace for him to cut into the rope binding his hands. Once they were free and he felt the feeling returning to his fingers with each painful throb of his heartbeat, he looked to the roof and shook his head.

"Keep an eye on her," he said to Ashhur. "Because if something happens because I just told that lunatic where she is, you better be hiding when I enter the golden lands for myself."

CHAPTER

27

Their travel back to Veldaren was somber, despite Delysia's best attempts otherwise. It wasn't as if Haern never laughed or smiled when she joked, or that he did not stay close to her come nightfall. With Thren no longer around, Haern was comfortable enough to remove his hood, and at one of the larger towns, he bought a plain shirt and breeches so he might appear as any other commoner during their walk. But the clothes never seemed to fit just right, and his smile was always temporary, his laugh an ephemeral thing. Whatever joy she'd known in him, it seemed to have left that night he'd spoken with his father.

"Are you all right?" she'd had the courage to ask him only once, after they'd crossed the rivers and into the land of Omn.

"I will be," he said, and she trusted him enough to let the matter remain at that.

Every night, when she closed her eyes to sleep, she prayed that Haern would find a way to move on. And every night, she listened for the quiet footsteps she knew she'd never hear, those of Thren Felhorn sneaking into their camp to do away with the scars of his past. As week followed week, it seemed neither would come to pass.

They bought their rations at the trading towns they came across, ate them in quiet meals, and traveled the miles with comfortable silence. Sometimes, Haern left her to hunt, but not often. Their rations, wrapped cakes, were more than enough to last until the next town, and so long as they foraged whenever they came upon a patch of berries or fruit hanging from low branches, they managed to keep themselves from ever feeling hungry.

"It's my turn this time," Haern said as they prepared to set up camp for the night. "You tend the fire and let me scratch up my arms picking through the thorns."

He referred to a patch of blackberries they'd passed only minutes before, a patch for which Delysia had insisted they sacrifice a few more hours of travel to pick for dinner.

"If you insist," Delysia said, casting her eyes about in search for proper kindling. "I'm better at it than you, though."

"Yes, but you have such delicate baby skin. A single scratch would be a great travesty."

She rolled her eyes, and he laughed.

"Just don't be long," she said. "I'd hate for my pretty little head to start feeling worried during your absence."

He bowed comically low, sweeping an invisible hat off his head while doing so. The simple gesture left her smiling. For the first time in quite awhile, Haern appeared to be himself again. Perhaps because they were so close to home, or he was finally free of his father's gloomy presence, but the reason hardly mattered so long as he was smiling.

Delysia hummed to herself as she collected the slender twigs for the fire. They were not far off the well-traveled road to Veldaren, which was only forty miles away by Haern's estimate, just enough so that when they built their fire, they might have some measure of privacy and safety from anyone who might be prowling about the night with ill intentions. All about were the widely spaced trees of a forest, casting comfortable shade and making it easy pickings for her firewood. The moment was so peaceful, so serene, she felt betrayed by the sound of another person's voice.

"At last. I thought he'd never leave."

The sound of that voice sparked a dozen memories, none of them good. Her heart leaped into her throat, and she turned, a bundle of twigs still in her arms. Standing there in the forest, between her and the road, was a specter from the past who should have been long dead. He towered before her, obsidian skin even darker in the shadows, his painted face seeming to glow. She remembered when he'd bound her while waiting to ambush Haern, how he'd mocked her as Senke bled out before her eyes. The only differences now were that his frame looked lankier, drained, and his face bore thick scars that seemed to meld with the very paint across his face.

"Hello, Delysia," said Ghost.

"Stay back," she said, dropping her bundle and lifting her hands before her. Defensive spells ran through her mind, and she nearly froze trying to pick one. His swords remained sheathed, and he stood there with an arm braced against a tree, supporting his weight. If he was to attack her, he certainly didn't look ready for it.

"I'm not here to . . ." he said, then stopped. It seemed the very words caused him pain. His eyes closed as he grimaced, and she watched his arm sink into the wood of the tree, vanishing as if he were not real, only a memory.

Light shimmered across Delysia's hands as she pulled power from Ashhur into her being. He may not seem ready to attack her, but the man was dangerous and clearly ill. His eyes were bloodshot, and when he pulled his hand from the tree, his skin seemed to shimmer like morning fog atop a lake.

"Haern killed you," she said as he stood there, unmoving. "How did you survive?"

"Not now," Ghost said. His voice was heavy, and so very tired. "I don't have time for that, Delysia. That I'm here...I can hardly believe it, either. It's been so long waiting...so long..."

Delysia looked beyond him to the road, and she wondered how long Haern might be. If only he could come back and find her, perhaps help her subdue Ghost before he drew his blades. As she watched, the giant man took a single step, pushing himself away from the tree. As he did, the skin of his face began to bubble beneath the white paint, and all across his arms she watched burn marks appear without reason.

"Waiting?" she said, trying to stall, to keep the man talking. "Well, you've waited, and here I am. If you have something to say, then say it."

"I'm sorry."

That was it. He said it with such finality, such weight, she found herself speechless. Her head tilted to one side, and she looked at him as if he'd tricked her.

"Sorry?" she asked. "Sorry for what? For murdering my friend?"

Another step.

"Yes," he said. "For causing you pain. I did it out of pride... out of weakness...and it cost me everything. You only wanted to help him, didn't you? I can sense it...That's who you are. Who you've always been. I used to think I was better than that. Stupid. So stupid."

Whatever fear she'd felt of him was long gone. That he was conscious at all appeared a miracle. The burns on his arms were worsening, and she saw several more spreading across his neck. Sweat poured down his face, and his eyes were nearly a solid red from angry veins. Every word he spoke was labored, a clear struggle to remain coherent. She tried to reconcile the wretched sight before her with the cool, confident man that had battled her and her friends with such ease, the man who had stabbed an unaware Senke in the back, yet she could not. The passing years had been unkind to him, to say the least.

"Ghost," she asked. "What's wrong with your body?"

With his left hand, he scratched at the paint on his face, and she saw that it was no longer paint. His skin had assumed the color, and instead of peeling it away, he drew blood that dripped down along his skin in crimson trails. On a hunch, she cast a spell over her eyes, granting her sight into a realm not of magic, not of flesh and stone, but of gods. It seemed all the land darkened, including Ghost before her, but surrounding him, swirling like fire made of shadow, were over a hundred chains. She could see but the faintest hint of his being beneath, imprisoned, condemned.

A curse, she thought. *But for what? And why?*

"I want to know," Ghost said as she ended the spell, the chains vanishing, revealing only the tired, bleeding man. "I mean, I know the answer, but I'm asking anyway, while I still can. Delysia... do you think you could forgive me?"

Delysia swallowed, her mouth and throat suddenly dry.

"For what?" she asked, even though she knew. But she wanted to hear him say it. She wanted to know for sure.

"For killing your friend," he said. "For hurting you, your brother. For enjoying it all. Do you think... do you think you could? I'll die alone and having hurt so many. But you...someone like you...I don't want to die with you hating me."

He was desperate, she saw, lost and hopeless. She had a feeling he would not have been able to explain, even to himself, why he'd come.

"For so long, I had only my brother," Delysia said, her hands curling into fists at her side. "But then Senke joined us. He was part of our family, someone who would listen, who would be there. I loved him, Ghost, and you cut him down...for what? For your pride?"

His eyes remained on the dirt, and he nodded.

"I was the better killer," he said. "That was reason enough."

Blood had begun to drip from the burns, oozing down his arms to his fingers to collect like raindrops.

"You want to hear me say it?" she asked. "You want me to say I forgive you, that I no longer hate you? What then, Ghost? If I say it, if I give you your absolution, then what happens?"

He looked up, and his shoulders sagged, his eyes filling with tears.

"I don't know," he said. "Because I know you'll never say it. So kill me, Delysia. Burn me away and free me of this curse."

He spread his arms out to the side, as if inviting an old friend. Delysia tried to push aside the confusion in her mind, all the hurt memories of Senke, his smile, his laugh, the way he'd bled on their floor while she'd been tied to a chair. The way Tarlak had looked at her when he came back to their home that horrible night, blood all over his yellow robes. The way he'd been unable to answer when she asked if Senke was all right.

"I blamed myself," she said, a knot in her throat. "Did you know that?"

His head hung low, and she heard his labored, raspy breaths.

"Your brother told me," he said. "Now do it. You know what

I am. I'm a monster, Delysia, a horrible fucking monster. I don't even know my own *name* anymore. Whatever it was, it's gone. I'm a ghost, a demon, and there's only one fate for things like me. We burn."

She felt her own tears building, and she looked at the rotting wretch before her, saw a man mired only in misery. She knew the rage she should feel, felt the sorrow, but it wasn't right. It wasn't her. The man wanted to find some sort of cleansing death. Appearing to her, giving her a chance to slay him...it was a gift, the only one he knew to offer. To be so broken, to think the sorrow she'd known could be made pure by the taking of a life...

"I cried my tears long ago," she said. "And no, I don't hate you. You were a broken man long before you came into our lives, and I only pity the life you led that carried you to such a place."

Ghost wiped at his eyes, smearing blood across his white-scarred face.

"My road," he said. "My choices. Don't you dare pity me."

"You wanted my forgiveness, and now you have it. What more can you ask of me, Ghost?"

He tried to answer, but instead, he took several steps backward and clutched at his head. His face was the purest expression of pain Delysia had ever seen. Doubled over, Ghost let out a scream, and his fingers scratched deep grooves into the sides of his neck.

"Not yet," he screamed. "Not yet!"

And then it was over. Ghost stood there, tired, bleeding, but acting as if it'd never happened.

"I was given a task," he said, and he seemed a bit more coherent than before. "Three jobs, that's it. You Eschaton, the Watcher, and Alyssa's faceless woman. Karak wants you dead. That's what they told me."

"Who told you?"

He chuckled, shook his head.

"Doesn't matter. It's simple, so simple. If I didn't kill you, if I failed my task, then my life was the price of my failure."

Ghost drew both his swords, but she remained where she stood, defiant, unafraid. There was no malice in him. No danger, only regret. The giant man fell to his knees, and he stabbed both swords deep into the dirt of the forest. The act done, his entire body racked with shivers, and it seemed he would soon pass out.

"Ghost?" she asked, feeling the first edges of panic tingling up her spine. "Ghost, what are you doing?"

He looked up at her, and for the first time, he smiled.

"I'm *failing*."

Blood dripped from his mouth. His arms were nothing but burned scars, and she saw thin trails of smoke rising into the air. His obsidian skin paled, as if all color within him were draining away. His hands gripped his swords hard enough to turn his knuckles white. Eyes closed against the pain, she watched him as he gasped, waves of agony overwhelming him, striking him down, tensing the muscles in his back and ripping gashes across the front of his neck.

Dying for her, she realized.

She stepped toward him, hand outstretched, palm pressing against the very center of his white face. The heat of his skin was incredible, the paint burning her like fire.

"No," she said, and with her words she released all the power she'd built up inside her. Channeling it through her hand, she poured it into Ghost. She imagined the shadowy chains, and she smashed them. She saw his burns, and she flooded them with light. The color returned to his flesh, his mouth opened to scream. As she watched, the paint upon his face hardened, peeled away, and then fell to the ground like scales. His head snapped back, and it was as if his entire body were smashed with an invisible force. Delysia felt the wretched presence of Karak, and she prayed it away, denying it with every last shred of her being. In her ears she heard a constant ringing, intensifying as her spell reached its end.

She pulled back her hand, and Ghost knelt before her, his eyes wide, mouth open amid his bewilderment. His burns were gone. For the first time ever, she saw his face without the paint, saw how handsome he was. He looked up at her, tears running down his cheeks.

"Delysia," he said, and he reached out a hand.

She reached back, a smile forming on her lips, a smile that died the moment she saw the blur of cloak racing toward Ghost.

"Haern, no!" she screamed, fearing it was already too late.

CHAPTER

28

Picking through the blackberries, Haern felt at peace, and it was almost strange. Veldaren wasn't far away, and though he was eager to return, he also felt a bit of trepidation, and he welcomed the excuse to remain back and add several more hours to their trip. Still, what relief to return to the life he knew. The guilds, the Trifect, their scheming and ruthless games...those he understood. Those he knew how to play. He'd let down his armor around his father, allowed himself to become vulnerable. Hopefully, it'd not happen again.

When he had two handfuls, he knelt down so he might place them on his cloak and wrap it as a basket. Then came the scream.

Haern was racing back to the road before it was ever finished, with no care for the thorns that scratched at his skin or tugged on his clothes. The scream, it had been a man's voice. Delysia was in trouble, perhaps ambushed by thieves or thugs with rape on their mind. Legs pumping, he flew across the road, then cut off toward where they had planned to set up their camp. Reason overcame him at the last moment, and he slowed so he might at least get the jump on whoever might be there.

It was only one man, Haern saw, and so far, Delysia stood unharmed before him. He felt relief, but it was fleeting, for something about the man was horribly familiar. His skin was dark, his head shaved, and as Haern crouched down and slid from tree to tree, he caught glimpses of the man's face...his white, painted face.

Ghost, thought Haern, and he felt his blood chill in his veins.

The man who'd captured Delysia, knocked Tarlak unconscious, stabbed Senke through the stomach. The man who'd finished the job later in Leon Connington's mansion. His friend's murderer...right there, in the forest, kneeling before Delysia. His entire body was covered with burns and blood, and Haern could only guess at whatever road the man had traveled to get there. Last Haern knew, he'd left Ghost for dead. The wounds had been fatal, he knew, surely they had been fatal...

Haern drew his swords. Apparently not. Ghost lived, and whatever he'd told Delysia, it clearly troubled her. His body began to convulse, she reached forward, and then came a burst of light that hurt his eyes, forcing him to look away. Healing, he decided. The man had tracked Delysia down to force her to heal him. Surely no priest of Ashhur in Veldaren would have been foolish enough to do so.

Shifting back, keeping himself low and out of sight, he prepared his attack. He wouldn't make the same mistake again. Ghost was a monster, a vicious killer who'd relished every second of Haern's pain as Senke died before him.

Mercy cuts deep and will only hurt those you love. This cruel world will make sure of that.

Not a mistake he'd make again. When he'd left Ghost, the man had been breathing. This time, this relic, this memory of pain and hate, would die and stay dead. Haern angled himself back around toward Ghost's blind side, with Ghost still on his knees and unaware of his approach. Delysia's eyes were on him too, the woman bent over with her hand outstretched. Haern knew he'd have no better time, and he flew across the forest floor without care for stealth, only speed.

He was almost there when Delysia caught sight of him, and instead of hiding the realization, she opened her mouth and screamed.

"Haern, no!"

Too late to stop himself, but her cry was enough to hesitate, to slow the killing thrust. With speed unreal, Ghost whirled, pulling his swords from the earth to successfully parry the attack. Their blades interlocked, and Haern's momentum slammed them together. He tried to continue, to bowl over the giant man, but Ghost's legs braced, resisting him. With narrowed eyes, the man returned Haern's glare.

"I'm not here for a fight," Ghost said. The very sound of his voice was like razors cutting across Haern's skin.

"I am."

Haern pushed away to gain separation, then slashed for the man's neck. Ghost blocked it easily enough, his superior strength batting away Haern's follow-up strokes as if they were those of a child. The sound of steel rang out, twice, three times, before Haern positioned his weapons high, interlocking them with Ghost's so he could kick at the man's knee from the side. The bigger man sidestepped it, then shoved both swords out to push Haern away.

"There's no need for this," Ghost said, stepping backward, each one matching Haern's steady approach. "Leave me be, Watcher. I've given Delysia my apologies, and she her blessing. After this, I go west, and you'll never see me again. I want nothing to do with you."

"A new life?" Haern said, quickening his steps. Ghost would soon back himself against a tree, and the moment he ran out of room to retreat... "You don't deserve a new life. You want to offer an apology? Stick out your neck, and I'll accept it with my blade."

Ghost's back bumped against the bark of the tree. If he was worried, he didn't show it. Behind them, Delysia shouted for them to stop, but both refused to acknowledge the demand.

"Your friend has given me my life," said Ghost, "and I won't disgrace that gift by letting you take it, Watcher."

A grim smile tucked at the corners of Haern's lips.

"Let me?" he asked, suddenly lunging into an attack. His swords crossed side to side, ringing off of Ghost's expertly positioned blocks. Undaunted, Haern continued weaving his weapons in, feeling like a lumberjack trying to cut down a tree by pummeling it into submission. So far, Ghost showed no signs of countering, so Haern pushed himself on, trying to find the slightest opening for the kill.

"Let me?"

Ghost tried and failed to parry a wide slash aimed for his face. The man ducked backward, striking his head against the bark of the tree. The tip of Haern's saber cut through his cheek, just a thin slice that sprayed a thin jet of blood through the air. Haern looped both weapons around, slamming them down into the X that Ghost had crossed his swords into just prior to the stroke.

"Have you forgotten, Ghost?" Haern asked as he tried to

push through, to close that minute gap between the sharpened edges of his blades and the exposed flesh of his foe's throat. "I was the better fighter. I killed you once, and I'll kill you again."

Despite his efforts, Haern's strength seemed to not bother Ghost in the slightest. Instead, the man grinned, and a bit of life sparkled in his eyes.

"Better?" he asked. "Perhaps then . . . but now? Let us see."

The man flung himself forward, and given his size, his speed, Haern had no choice but to retreat as those swords came slicing in. Left, right, he batted them aside, spun while ducking to avoid having his head cut off his shoulders, then sprinted away to gain space. Six steps later, he dug his heel into the soft earth, pivoted, and flung himself right back into the fight. Again, they crashed together, swords interlocking and pushing aside so neither was impaled. Haern angled himself so his knee struck Ghost's stomach, and the other man likewise slammed his elbow into Haern's cheek. Blood dripping from his teeth, Haern spun away, fighting through a brief wave of dizziness.

"Stop it, both of you!" he heard Delysia shout. Haern again pretended not to hear her, instead rekindling the anger in his breast as Ghost crouched down, anticipating another barrage.

Before he could attack, a flash of light burst between them, blinding in its brightness. Haern let out a cry at the pain, but he refused to be slowed. Rushing forward, he used every bit of his childhood training. He knew how to anticipate an opponent's reaction, how to sense their location by the sound of their feet scraping the dirt. But Ghost was no common foe, no stranger to sightless battles. The world a haze of yellow and white, Haern cut where the larger man should have been, only to have both his swings blocked. Stepping left, he tried sweeping Ghost's feet out from underneath him, but the man was not there. Instead, he'd already fallen back, and through the spots in his vision, Haern watched him weave his swords into a defensive pattern in case he'd pushed onward.

"The better fighter," Ghost said as he halted upon realizing no one chased. "I've learned of you since my release, Watcher. I know what it was you sought to do at the Conningtons' mansion. I fought for coin and my reputation, but you fought for peace; you fought for the love of your friends."

Ghost's face darkened as he crouched down and lifted his swords.

"But now?" he asked.

Without warning, he burst forward. So big, so strong, he was as terrifying as a charging bull. Haern dared not meet him head-on, instead having to constantly leap away. Anything to keep Ghost moving, to keep him from being able to close the distance fully or brace his feet to put all his strength into a swing. Parrying one swing, he leaped back, caught a tree with his shoulder, and then rolled along the ground. Ghost's swords struck dirt, and then Haern was on his feet, bolting forward as his foe's swords sliced through the air where he'd been.

"What is it you fight for now?" Ghost asked. "Pride? Retribution?"

"What does it matter?"

Haern spun around a tree, and when one of Ghost's swords struck the bark, Haern rolled back around it and launched into an offensive. Awkwardly positioned, Ghost had to retreat, violently yanking on the sword to free it in time for a block. Haern kept it up, pushing forward, hammering at Ghost's swords. His hands were a blur, his every nerve on fire. *Overwhelm him*, thought Haern. He had to overwhelm him.

"What does it matter?" asked Ghost, and despite his apparent exhaustion, despite Haern's onslaught, he was grinning. "It's the *only* thing that matters."

One of his steps back suddenly wasn't a retreat at all, but a shift forward. Haern's left-hand blade was easily blocked, the other thrusting too far to the side. Taking advantage of the opening, Ghost kneed Haern in the stomach, then smashed a fist into the side of his neck. Letting out a scream, Haern toppled back, swords raised in a meager defense. Except Ghost did not pursue. Instead, he hovered over him, yelling, mocking him as he paced.

"I was a monster!" he shouted. "I thought you were too, but you fought for something. You bled for others. You're bleeding again, Watcher, so tell me, who's it for?"

Simply breathing hurt, but Haern forced himself to his feet, stumbling backward to gain some space. Ignoring the pain, he stood tall and stared down the giant man. In his mind, he replayed that horrible moment when Senke had lurched forward, a blade piercing his chest. The way the pain had overtaken him. The way the life had left his eyes. Haern needed that rage again. He needed to remember why, no matter the cost, this man must die.

"A monster?" he asked. "Is that what you want? Then raise your swords, Ghost. I'll show you a monster."

Before either could move, Delysia stepped between them, a hand outstretched toward each.

"Enough!" she cried. White light shone from her palms. "This fight ends now, I swear it. Drop your blades. The moment *either of you* moves against the other, I will take your life."

Haern could hardly believe the anger in her eyes. This was the man who'd killed her best friend . . . yet now she'd threaten murder to protect him? He couldn't abide it. He couldn't allow it. This man . . . this Ghost . . . deserved death. Every bone in his body knew it, every pounding of his heart screamed it.

"Get out of the way, Delysia," he said. "This must end; you

have to understand that. I won't let him live. If not now, then tomorrow, or the day after. Even if I have to hunt him down like an animal, he will die."

Opposite him and Delysia, Ghost remained tense, swords raised before his chest. The look on his face was impossible to read. He was waiting for the right moment, Haern decided. Watching for the perfect opening to attack.

"Haern," Delysia said, and he heard the pleading in her voice. Haern tightened the muscles in his legs, preparing for a leap. She wouldn't hurt him. There was no way she'd choose to take his life to protect that monster.

"No," Ghost said, before Haern could lunge. "I won't let you carry that sin, Delysia. That belongs to another."

Ghost launched forward, his speed surprising even Delysia. Haern panicked, convinced the man would kill her, and he raced across the ground as fast as his legs could carry him. As he watched, Ghost collided with Delysia before she could enact a spell. Instead of striking her, the giant man pushed her hands so her beam of light flashed harmlessly into the trees, then shrugged her aside with his elbow. Speed hardly slowing, Ghost continued on, eyes locked on Haern's. Refusing to slow, Haern drew his blades and thrust for the man's chest. He felt the anticipation building in him, the seductive excitement of battle. This was it. This exchange would define them, reveal whose skill was greatest. As his swords closed in, he was already mentally calculating the defenses Ghost would take and how to counter them.

Instead, Ghost spread his arms, ensuring an opening.

Haern's sabers jammed between his ribs, pierced both lungs, and then tore through the flesh of his back. Ghost's body slammed into him, but Haern let out a scream and pushed his legs to remain standing. The other man draped over him, his weight entirely supported, as warm blood poured across Haern's hands, down his wrists, and to the ground below. Lifting his head, Ghost coughed more blood, spewing it across Haern's cloak.

"The better monster," said Ghost with the last of his ragged breath.

In the distance, as if in another world entirely, Haern heard Delysia scream.

Haern shifted so Ghost dropped to his back, the sabers easily sliding out of him. So very still, he lay there, blood dribbling from his lips. From the corner of his eye, Haern saw Delysia rushing toward him, healing light already glowing on her fingertips. He thought of Ghost surviving a second time, stealing away his kill, denying him his retribution.

"No," Haern said, and he lifted a bloody saber and pointed it her way. She froze, the tip hovering inches away from her neck. "He dies."

Delysia met his gaze, and her fury nearly overwhelmed him. Pure stubbornness kept him there as he listened to the wet coughs of Ghost dying. Slowly, the priestess stepped forward, until the tip of Haern's saber pressed against her throat. Ghost's blood dripped upon her, the scarlet startling against the paleness of her flesh and the white of her robes. Not once did her eyes leave his.

"Move," she said. That was it, but her voice carried such authority, Haern trembled. He pulled the weapon back, and he suddenly felt aware of what he'd just done.

"Del," he said. "Del, I'm sorry, I didn't mean to . . ."

But she was already past him, ignoring his words and kneeling down next to Ghost, who had begun convulsing. Despite the miracles she could perform, Haern knew the man was too far gone. Knitting back torn flesh would do nothing for the terrible blood loss Ghost had already suffered, and that ignored the damage to the lungs. It seemed Delysia knew it too, for she did not bother attempting. Instead, she put her forehead against Ghost's, and the man's gaze turned toward her. Amid the convulsions of his body, he tried to say something, but all that came out were dying gasps. Delysia was praying, though Haern could not hear what. Suddenly, she leaned back, and she stared right into Ghost's eyes.

"Lawrence," she said, brushing her fingers across his face. "Your name was Lawrence. You may die, but it won't be nameless."

It seemed an immediate change came over him. Ghost's convulsions stopped, his mouth closed, and with gaze unmoving from Delysia's beautiful face, he slowly let out one last gasp and then lay still. Delysia bowed her head, once more pressing her forehead to his, and then she slowly rose to her feet. Her back was to Haern, her shoulders slumped, her long red hair like a shroud. With Ghost's passing, it seemed the forest had fallen unnaturally quiet.

"He came to me," Delysia said softly. "Came hoping I'd kill him. What have you done, Haern?"

"I took the life of a terrible, loathsome murderer," Haern said, voice rising. "Have you forgotten what he did to you, to Tarlak? That man killed Senke, butchered him like a piece of meat, and then mocked me for it. He called *me* a monster, even as Senke bled out at his feet. That Ghost was alive at all is my fault, and consider this me correcting that error."

She stepped toward him, and when he reached for her arms, she shoved him away.

"He was so close," she said. "So close. How could you? How could you!"

Her fists rained down upon his chest. There was something he was missing, he realized, but he felt too angry to bother, too frustrated to care. Would Delysia have him spare the life of every single thief and murderer he went up against? Would she have him live a secluded life free of his role as the Watcher? When he came back from Angelport, she'd given him her blessing, said she understood the bloodshed.

"I kept you from making a mistake," Haern said as her blows slowed, came to a stop. "That's all. I had to do it. If you spared his life, I'd only take it again. He deserves no better for what he did to me, what he did to *you*."

"I *forgave* him, Haern; don't you get it? Of course he deserved no better. Lawrence was a poor, broken thing on his knees, and I forgave him. But you just couldn't let it go, could you? You couldn't let it go . . ."

"Of course not!" Haern said. "People like him don't change, Delysia. They don't escape their pasts, and they don't magically become better men. Those with blood on them keep it all their lives. He killed our friend, Del, our *family*, or do you not remember?"

"I remember," she said, stepping away from him, her arms crossed over her chest. "I remember when a little boy knelt before me days after helping kill my father."

It was a cold knife she stuck into him.

"This isn't the same," he said, anger growing white-hot in his chest.

"It is. I forgave him, just like I forgave you."

"*He wasn't yours to forgive!*" Haern screamed. "Do you think Senke meant nothing to me? Ghost's life or death, it wasn't in your hands, his hands, Karak's, Ashhur's, no one's hands but mine. *I* left him alive. *I* failed to kill him. That he somehow survived was—"

"A gift?" asked Delysia. Haern froze, and he felt his heart leap into his throat. "Not from the gods, but from you. Is that right, Haern?" Tears began to swell in her eyes, and though she knew her next words would hurt, she said them anyway.

"Your father would be so proud."

The image of her jerking forward, an arrow piercing her chest, flashed before his eyes.

"That's not fair," Haern said, and he felt his face flushing, felt as if his mind were raw. "Don't you dare be that cruel. All my life, I've wanted to be better than that, to be anything other than what he'd have me be. I've clung to Ashhur's teachings, but nightfall in Veldaren is not a place for mercy and forgiveness. It doesn't work, Delysia, you know that; you can't be that naïve."

It was the wrong thing to say, every word, and he knew it the moment they left his lips. Delysia stared at him, and it seemed her entire body had grown rigid. He reached out to her, wanting to hold her, to find some way to tell her that he knew he was being stupid, but she slapped his hand away. He reached again, and she repeated the slap, pointing a finger at him, her green eyes wide, the tears in them long since fallen and gone.

"Don't touch me," she said. "You just…stay away from me for a while."

"Delysia," he said, but what else did he have to say? That he was sorry he'd killed Ghost? But he wasn't, and he wouldn't lie to her. She'd sense it immediately and just distance herself further. The priestess weaved through the trees, heading for the distant path.

"Delysia!"

She paused, and he watched her take in a deep breath before she turned to face him.

"You once told me that as long as I was there for you, as long as I could forgive you, you would endure," she said. "That you'd remember who you were and believe you were still worth saving. You wanted me to be there for you, but I'm not sure I can. If I'm so naïve, if I'm not part of your world, then I can't be the one to help you remember who you are. Someone else has stolen that place from me."

He started toward her, but her glare held him back.

"You have a body to bury," she said, and then she returned to the road, leaving him alone in the silence.

Haern felt his anger bubbling up, overwhelming him, keeping his anguish at bay. Like a statue he stood, watching Delysia until she was gone. At last, he could control himself no longer. Turning to Ghost's corpse, he drew his sword again.

"Why couldn't you stay dead?" he asked it, falling to his knees and plunging the sword into Ghost's unmoving chest. Ripping out the blade, he jammed it in, again and again. "You bastard! You were dead, four years you were dead, so why now?" He beat the corpse with his fist, punctuating his words. "Why...now!"

There was gore all over him, and Haern leaned back, feeling so tired, so very tired.

"I'm not him," he told the quiet forest. "I'm not the same. I've only done what was necessary. I'm better than him, better than he could ever be!"

But there was no one there to argue, no one to call him a liar or believe his words to be true. So, alone Haern stayed, pulling up the soft earth to bury Ghost, using the man's swords to mark his grave. By the time he was done, the night was deep, the cicadas in full rhythm. Hiding from the stars, Haern slept wrapped in his cloak, but even its comfort was meager, for it stank of drying blood.

CHAPTER
29

It was a meeting Alyssa could put off no longer. She went to her room and sat down on the bed beside Nathaniel, who'd been waiting there per her request.

"Is everything all right?" her son asked. Alyssa wrapped the boy in her arms, holding him against her as she struggled for the right words.

"It will be," she said. "I promise, it will be."

That was it; she had nothing more for him, but she'd wanted him close for a moment, to remind herself why she did what she was about to do.

"Go on," she said. "And tell one of the servants to find Lord Victor and show him to my room."

"Yes, Mother," Nathaniel said. He slipped off the bed, and she heard his feet pad across the carpet to the door. It creaked open, he spoke softly to someone, and then silence. Alyssa sat amid it, trying to keep her heart steady.

"Zusa?" she asked. "Are you there?"

Only more silence. Good. She didn't want Zusa near, not for this. That would come later. One struggle at a time.

The door opened, and she heard a man clear his throat.

"Milady?" asked Victor.

"Shut the door," Alyssa said, hands squirming in her lap. Victor had been visiting nearly every day since he'd come with Antonil's help to free her from John and Melody's imprisonment. She now did her best to greet him warmly, but still she felt uncomfortable in his presence. Too much of his true self remained guarded, and what she could glimpse was tainted with frightening zeal.

When the door was shut, she heard his heavy footsteps lead toward her, then pause in the center of her bedroom. He had nowhere to sit, and she knew he would not be presumptuous enough to sit beside her on the bed.

"Matters appear to have settled down significantly," Victor said after clearing his throat. "Muzien has not repeated his spectacle at the marketplace, and what information I can gather shows him carefully guarding anyone who pledges money to him for protection."

"Such a benevolent ruler," Alyssa said, unable to hold back a bitter smile.

"There's some truth to that, sadly," Victor said. "But we know better. His extortions are far from extreme, his greed bearable, because it's not coin he wants. It's power. If we bend our knee to him and offer coin for protection, does it matter if we give one or a thousand, so long as our knee is bent?"

Alyssa shook her head, thinking of how the elf had sneaked into her room. He treated everything like an amusing game, and they were but interchangeable pieces. When Victor had come to her after Melody's death, he'd tentatively suggested paying the protection money Melody had promised. He'd been so nervous, so fearful to offend, it had made Alyssa laugh in his face.

A show of strength meant nothing if she could not back it up. There would be a time to resist the elf, but it wasn't now, with her house in shambles. If she was to make enemies out of an elf who, by all accounts possible, now ruled the entirety of Veldaren, she'd do it when victory could be hers.

"Have you heard any rumblings from John Gandrem?" she asked, trying to push Muzien from her mind and talk on matters more immediate.

"None so far," Victor said, and by his footsteps and moving voice, she could tell he was pacing. "He's still upset, to be sure, but more that you'd question his honor. He really did feel he was doing what was best, but now that Melody is out of the picture, he's willing to let bygones be bygones, you might say."

Alyssa sighed. She'd thought about executing John for his part in everything, but Victor had insisted she hear him out. John had calmly but firmly declared his respect for her and his love of her son. Everything he did, it'd been lawful and just, and had he not ordered his men to stand down come Victor's attack to free her? Given her drastic lack of allies, Alyssa had allowed him to escape without major punishment, though she'd still banished him from ever setting foot inside her home again, as well as promising no further contact with Nathaniel until he came of age. It was a slap on the wrist in her mind, but at least it didn't seem John was actively trying to replace her, nor spreading foul rumors or hateful speech.

"Victor," she said, trying to find the right words. She sensed him straighten up, as if he too sensed the importance of what she sought to say. "After everything that's happened... are you still willing to fight against the guilds?"

Victor cleared his throat before answering.

"I am," he said. "Perhaps not in the way I started, but my resolve has not broken."

Alyssa rose from the bed, and she walked in the direction of his voice, hand outstretched. His hand touched her arm when she neared, as if letting her know of his position, and she then put her fingers against the side of his face. She used it to see him, to remember the blue of his eyes, the strength of his stare. A man who would refuse to allow even death to deny him success. A man fueled by a righteous fury.

"Let me hear you say it," she said. "Tell me Muzien will not destroy us. Tell me you'll have his head on a pike before the gates, along with all others of the damn guilds that have torn our lives apart."

"I swear it," said Victor, and his tone gave her chills. "I swear it on the grave of my parents, swear it on the lives of every single one of my men who's died bringing them to justice. Their time must end."

"And my son," she said, voice softening. "Would you protect him as well?"

It seemed he was beginning to understand what was happening, and he took both her hands in his.

"He's a smart lad, kind and honest," Victor said. "I would be honored to raise him as my own."

Alyssa took in a deep breath. This was it, then. Her decision was made, her heart committed.

"Then I wish to accept your offer of betrothal," she said.

"Wonderful," he said, then after a pause, "Wonderful. Just wonderful."

She wished she could feel the same. Not that she'd expected love and romance to be the reason for a marriage, not since Mark Tullen's death and Arthur Hadfield's betrayal years ago, but this felt less like the joining of equals and more like her attaching herself to a train of horses stampeding down a hill.

"Indeed, truly wonderful," Alyssa said, not bothering to fake any enthusiasm. "I'll contact Terrance and have him begin the preparations for a wedding. I'm sure he'll be in touch with you as well, in regard to any customs or requests..."

"I do have one," he said, interrupting her.

"You do?"

Another hesitation.

"Your...pet. Zusa. I would know just what she is to you and what she will be to me."

Zusa? wondered Alyssa. *What does he mean?*

"I don't understand," she said.

Victor pulled back from her hands yet remained before her, hovering in her mind's eye.

"She has never hidden her disdain for me, and I am no fool to the power she wields. Against my wishes, she murdered your mother. Melody deserved a trial, Alyssa, a chance to explain herself, a chance for us to see if anyone else was pulling the strings behind her strange ascension."

"I understand, but she only..."

"She does what she wishes," Victor said. "Or she does what you command. I must know, Alyssa. Is she a servant? A soldier? Your protector, or something more?"

Alyssa's mind scrambled as she tried to think of the proper answer...or even one that was true. What was Zusa to her?

"Zusa has been with me since the very beginning," she said. "She's the truest friend I have ever known."

Victor's heavy hand fell upon her shoulder, and she sensed him leaning closer, felt the heat of his words lightly brushing her face.

"You don't get to have friends, Alyssa. Not with your position.

Not with your power. If I am to enter your household, it must be as an equal. Zusa may stay, but as a servant, obedient to both your orders and mine. Is that acceptable?"

She knew the answer she had to give, and it put a fire into her stomach. Grabbing the front of Victor's shirt, she yanked him closer, brushing aside his hand from her shoulder.

"If I do this, you best pray to the gods you succeed," she said. "I want Nathaniel to stand atop the graves of the guilds. That's all that matters now, and if you can help me achieve it, I will reward you with everything I have. But if you fail..."

"If I fail, then you may let Zusa herself remove my head and present it to you on a silver platter. Is that acceptable?"

Alyssa fought down a grimace.

"It is," she said.

"Then there is no sense in wasting time," he said, and his footsteps headed toward the door. "I'll send for her while I inform Terrance. You may tell her while I am gone. Make her understand, Alyssa. My request is not so great, not so peculiar. There will be dozens outside our home walls wishing to have me killed. I'd rather know for certain there are none within the walls of our home as well."

The door shut, he was gone, and that was that. No happiness. No celebration, discussion over plans, who would move where, what would happen to the Kane family holdings. Not even a kiss on the cheek, just moving from one business to another.

Her father would have been proud.

The minutes crawled on as Alyssa sat back down on her bed, feeling more nervous than she had in years. She ran words through her mind a hundred times, trying to find something, anything that sounded right. It never did.

The door opened, far quieter than when Victor had come, and then a wrapped hand touched her own.

"You called for me?" Zusa asked.

Alyssa's teeth clenched. She had to say something, anything. Nothing would be right, nothing would work nor convey her frustration and sorrow, so she just said it as plainly as she could.

"I'm marrying Victor," she said.

Zusa's hand on hers tensed, the woman's sudden apprehension immediately apparent.

"Are you sure that is wise?" she asked.

"Wise?" Alyssa laughed. "The wise path is for me to lie down and die, letting Muzien conquer our city, all while praying Nathaniel somehow endures the following chaos. No, it's not wise, but it is what must be done. Another war against the underworld is coming, and I cannot fight it on my own, and neither can Nathaniel. Someone must wield the sword for me, and Victor can be that man."

"I could do it," Zusa said. Her grip on her hand tightened, so much it nearly hurt. "I can lead your mercenaries. I can protect your home. You don't need Victor. You don't need to throw your lot in with that madman."

"You?" Alyssa said, and the words were like fire in her throat. "You have no name. No home. No heritage. You're just one of the monsters in the shadows, Zusa. No mercenaries I hire will show you loyalty. No nobles will accept your power. Victor gives this legitimacy. If he adopts Nathaniel as his own, it gives him a chance of inheriting the Gemcroft fortune without a thousand vultures circling. Nathaniel will come from the Kane family line, a true lordly heritage. No longer a bastard. No longer the shameful seed of the destroyed house of Kull."

"He is *your son*. What legitimacy does he need beyond that?"

"You know better," Alyssa said, and she felt her heart hardening. "Don't pretend you don't see it, that you don't hear it. Nathaniel's my wounded child, the child of a woman most think lost her mind years ago. They don't respect me, and they don't respect him. We're not what this damn world wants. But someone like Victor..."

Zusa rose from the bed, and Alyssa could only imagine her standing before her, fingers curled into fists. Were there tears in her eyes? There were none in her voice...not yet, at least.

"Victor won't give you what you want," she said. "This risk you take..."

"Answer me this, Zusa, and answer it truthfully," Alyssa interrupted. "Do you feel Victor is a danger to my son if we were to marry? Do you think he is a danger to my own life?"

A long pause.

"No," Zusa said. "I think he favors Nathaniel and would treat him as his own son. As for you...betraying you would be beneath him. I think he views himself as more honorable than that."

"Then what else matters, Zusa? Nathaniel will have a father, and more importantly, he'll have a future. Veldaren's gone to shit, and if we're to endure, we need the help of someone like Victor."

"You never needed anyone before. You once flooded the streets with fire and steel, and you were unafraid."

Alyssa remembered those two nights, remembered the pain she'd felt.

"I was turning Veldaren into my own personal funeral pyre," she said. "That wasn't strength. That was recklessness. I can't afford to be so reckless now. Muzien would have my head the moment he sensed betrayal. But if we're patient, if we plan, if we coordinate with Antonil and Victor and my own forces..."

Zusa's hands wrapped around hers. They were soft, and she felt the distinct touch of her unique wrappings about them.

"Please, Alyssa, I beg you," said Zusa. "Don't do this. Don't put yourself at his mercy."

"There's more," Alyssa said, trying to ignore the ache in her friend's words. "If we marry, you must promise to respect and obey Victor as you would myself. That is his only demand."

"Like a servant," Zusa said, and there were finally tears in her voice.

Alyssa hated herself, hated every word she spoke, but what choice did she have?

"Yes. Like a servant."

She'd have given everything to see Zusa's face at that moment, to witness her reaction, to see if the wounds she felt she caused were as deep as she feared.

"As you wish, milady."

Silence stretched out, ended by the slamming of her door. At its sound, Alyssa broke, tears running down her face, a sob escaping through her clenched teeth. It shouldn't have been so hard. It was a simple request, damn it! Zusa was more than a servant, more than a friend, but could she remain so once Alyssa married? Once she slept in Victor's bed, once the holdings of their families merged and Victor took on the Gemcroft name, what then would Zusa be to her? All Zusa had to do was listen, and trust her... but deep in her heart, she knew it unfair to demand that of her friend all while refusing to give her the same trust.

Minutes crawled, and she slowly wiped her face clean. She'd known marrying Victor would be difficult, but she'd never guessed the difficulties would start so soon. As she regained her composure, she heard the door open, and Alyssa turned away, a meager defense against her own indecency.

"Yes?" she asked with a quavering voice.

"It's only me," Victor said. He said it so softly, so gingerly, it made a mockery of the stern, proud man he'd been only moments ago. "Did Zusa take it well?"

She almost told him the betrothal was over. She almost

screamed for him to leave her home, leave her life, to go marching back to his wheat fields and leave Veldaren to burn and die without his help. Things could return to how they had been, just Alyssa and her son, cowering in their home while the Darkhand claimed street after street, always watching, always waiting to see if any would betray his dominance. But just as she would not surrender to Muzien's fear, she refused to surrender to her guilt.

"No," she said, elaborating no further. Victor sat beside her and put a hand on her shoulder, and she nearly laughed at his touch. Here was her future husband, and she felt not the slightest attraction, not the tiniest excitement at having his hand upon her. Only dread and a sickness to her stomach. He tried pulling her close, but she resisted, and thankfully, he did not seem offended.

"I'm sorry," Victor told her. "Perhaps if I talked to her, we might reach an understanding..."

"Give it time first," she said. "Just give us both time."

His hand squeezed, and she allowed him to pull her against his side, allowed him to offer his meager comfort.

"The pain will pass," he told her. "And if she is the friend you believe her to be, she will come around. Remember, there are risk and pain to every grand accomplishment, and I assure you, yours will be grand indeed."

"What accomplishments?" she asked. "Burning down a city to avenge the death of a son who still lived? Losing my sight to a confused, sickly boy? Or being overthrown by my own mother? Which accomplishment of mine will be written into the chronicles of time?"

"Forget your past," he told her. "The future is all that matters. Here in this city, we have an opportunity to rise above our failures, rise so high we will salvage something from this horrid mess. I have dreams for you, Alyssa, dreams you have denied yourself for far too long. With me at your side, you may become what you were always meant to be."

At first, she thought he meant the crushing of the thief guilds, but it felt wrong. He spoke of something else. Something…grander.

"What dreams?" she asked. "What is it you would have me become?"

She felt his breath against her neck, his lips nearing her ear.

"I would make you a queen," he whispered. "Your little son would become a prince and, one day, a king. Tell me, is that not a legacy worth fighting for?"

What he spoke was treason, and ridiculous to even think possible, but something about the way he said it, the way he *believed* it, made her response catch in her throat. Her son… king?

"How?" she dared asked.

"In time," he told her, and he took her hand in his. It was larger than Zusa's, rougher, and she found herself missing the other woman's touch. "But imagine how much better the city would be if you sat on the throne. If someone strong like you, or like me, could look upon the corruption and despair and denounce every last shred of it all. What city could we create? What nation? Think of the legacy we could leave for your son to inherit."

It wasn't a game, and it wasn't a dream. Victor meant it, and he carried such conviction, there must be a way.

"Queen," she whispered, imagining a crown on her head.

"Queen Alyssa," Victor repeated. "And Prince Nathaniel."

King Victor Gemcroft went unspoken, but the name lingered in the air, and she knew it was in Victor's eyes, on his lips, and buried deep in his heart. It was madness. It was insane.

But if it wasn't?

This time, when Victor pulled her close, she settled into him, feigning happiness at his touch, her mind trying to wrap around what it might mean to rule a kingdom. She thought of the armies she might command, the wrongs she could make right. She imagined the pride in her chest as her son ascended to a golden throne while all the lords and nobles who had mocked him behind his back were forced to bend their knees and bow their heads.

Prince Nathaniel Gemcroft...

Such a beautiful name.

CHAPTER

 30

As you wish, milady.

Zusa walked down the quiet street, seeing nothing.

As you wish...

The sun had just begun to set, and in her wrappings, she knew she was a strange sight, yet she could not muster the strength to care. She wasn't even sure how long she'd wandered, aimless, crisscrossing streets, seen by dozens as over an hour crawled by, if not two. But it didn't matter. None of it did. With the sun setting, she was only reminded that come nightfall, she had no home to return to, no waiting bed, no family. Dimly, she thought to go to the Eschaton Mercenaries, but it felt too much like begging, and she had more pride than that. At least, she liked to think she did, but as she passed down yet another nameless street, still lost in her sour mood, she wondered just how much pride she actually had left.

It helped none to see so many tiles bearing the mark of the

Sun. Each one reminded her of how Alyssa had surrendered to their demands. Each one reminded her of how she would trust Victor to keep her safe from them, trust him more than she trusted her. All those years she'd protected her, stayed at her side, loved her...did they mean nothing now? Or perhaps she'd only deluded herself. Could she truly consider herself so important to Alyssa's life if her opinion could be cast aside so easily?

Stop it, she told herself. *Stop moping. Stop wallowing. Think on the task at hand!*

Doing her best to ignore anything but the present day, she knew her immediate need was to find a place to sleep. She had more than enough coin to rent a room in an inn, for several months, even, but the idea left a bad taste in her mouth. A last resort, perhaps, if not her only resort. Still, as she walked, she thought of the only other home she'd known. It was a strange nostalgia coming over her, but to the south of Veldaren she ran, finally feeling a purpose to her footsteps. Yes, there'd been one other home for her, and odd as it seemed, there were still many good memories attached to it.

The home was a simple one, and though large, it lacked any decorations. There were no windows, a single door, the roof flat and the sides a dull brown. It was built right up against the southern wall, not far from the squalor and rows of homeless tents and shanties that occupied much of the wall's length. Zusa walked up to the door, touched the handle. Doing so flooded her with memories, and she paused, trying to decide why she was even there.

She'd been an orphan, given over to the priesthood of Karak when she was but a babe. Growing up in its dark walls, the temple had been her home, at least until her affair with Daverik. Then they'd exiled her from the temple, deeming her unworthy of remaining within the holy ground. Before her was the home she'd been exiled to, along with her other faceless sisters. It was there they'd slept, eaten, and trained, overseen by the eldest of them, a woman named Eliora. Taking a deep breath, Zusa pulled open the door and stepped inside.

It was so familiar, that grand room with the fireplace and shelves full of books outlining the strictest tenets of Karak. The same round rug remained before the fireplace, and as Zusa stepped inside, she thought of the many winters she'd lain upon that rug, watching logs burn as the fire's warmth seeped into her skin. The fireplace still showed signs of use, and she wondered if Daverik's recent rebirth of the faceless had used the place as they always had before. They were all dead now, killed by either her hand or the strange Ghost who had interfered at the last moment to save her.

Zusa walked to the shelves, found a well-worn leather-bound book she'd read many times, *The Lion's Walk*. Flipping it open, she put her fingers on the faded brown pages, felt the crinkled paper as she read the first line aloud.

"Heavy walked the lion, and he made no noise to alert the farmer's daughter who worked the fields that day."

It was a story told fully in symbols and metaphors, setting it far apart from the dry rules and speeches that filled the others. Zusa closed the book, put it back on the shelf. She looked to the other books, thinking of the anger they spewed, the righteous condemnation of nearly everything that it meant to be human. On a whim, she returned to the fireplace and the small flask of oil waiting beside it. One after the other, she tossed books in, doused them with oil, and then lit them with a readied piece of flint. As the books burned, she watched, hoping the fire would give her comfort. It did not. Only *The Lion's Walk* remained by the time she was done.

Now uncomfortably hot from the fire, Zusa moved on to the only other room in the building. In it were four beds, and they still had the same blankets, heavy and dark green. It was as if, even in sleep, Karak wished to smother them and hide their bodies. Zusa sat on the edge of one, hand drifting across the rough fabric. She thought of the times she'd spent with Nava and Eliora, how they'd clung to one another, together fighting against the loneliness that threatened to swallow them all. Never did a day go by that they were not reminded of their failures, their inherent inferiority. It'd been driven into their prayers. It'd been whispered with every bit of cloth they wrapped about their bodies. But come nightfall, there were no priests, no gods, just them and their beds that were always too cold, too small.

"You were always so faithful, Nava," Zusa whispered, thinking of the girl's small hands and beautiful brown eyes. She used to play with her dark hair, which, despite how short she cut it, was still soft and smooth and fun to rustle with her fingers. They once joked about growing out braids and finding a way to tie them so the wrappings still covered them appropriately.

"The priests would never approve," Zusa had told her.

"What does it matter if they never know?" Nava had asked. "They will think I have strange lumps on my head, that is all. If they ask, I'll tell them Karak has cursed me with a great ugliness."

"They think that already," Eliora had said, kneeling before her bed in prayer while the other two sat together, waiting for her to finish. "And they would know the moment you tried. The eyes of priests are always undressing us."

They'd never mentioned braids again.

Zusa stood, already rethinking her plan to use the home as her own. Too many memories, and they all ended the same.

Karak's *mercy* came for them, killing her sisters with the blade of a dark paladin, smothering their happiness with oppression and hate and self-loathing.

"We were beautiful," Zusa breathed aloud, the greatest blasphemy she could think to utter in that place. "Beautiful, pure, and never once in need of the Lion. You gave us nothing but shame."

She started toward the door to leave, then froze. A sound, so soft, but her ears picked it up nonetheless. It was the slightest rattle of wood, but from where? Zusa froze, trying to think. There were only the two rooms, and she'd been in both…

But no, that wasn't right. There was a third, the safe room they were to hide in if guards ever came looking for them for the killings they committed in the name of their glorious Karak. Zusa drew a dagger, and slowly, she stalked toward the far side of the room, to what appeared to be a simple blank wall. She knew that not to be the case, and she readied herself for an attack. All four faceless were dead, but what if there were others she'd not been told of? Or what if Daverik had already recruited more?

Free hand finding the slender groove necessary to open it, she tensed, took in a deep breath, and then yanked open the hidden door leading to the secret hiding room. Her eyes widened, her body froze. In her gut, she felt her insides twist, and in her chest, her heart break.

Within were two girls, and they wore thin black shifts that went underneath the wrappings that were pooled beneath them both on the floor. Both their faces were hidden with white cloths, with only a slit to reveal their eyes. One girl's skin was dark, her eyes brown, curls of black hair peeking out from beneath the cloth, while the other girl looked pale. Her pretty blue eyes stared up at Zusa, wide with fear.

They couldn't be any older than nine.

"Are you one of us?" the darker girl asked, and she pointed toward the wrappings Zusa wore. Zusa swallowed, tried to think of what to say.

"No," she said. "I used to be, but not anymore."

This seemed to make them all the more nervous, and they shrank further back into the safe room. Zusa clutched the doorway with one hand, the hilt of her dagger with the other, needing something to keep them from shaking with her rage.

In the other room, she heard the door open, close.

"Girls?" asked a painfully familiar voice.

"Stay here," Zusa told them, and she pushed the door shut, returning the two to darkness. Racing between the beds, Zusa made sure she was flying by the time Daverik stepped into the bedroom, a loaf of bread in one hand, two apples in the other. The food crashed to the ground as Zusa's knee connected with his stomach, her fist striking his throat to rob him of any words. Her momentum carried them into the other room, and Zusa twisted so she could slam him against the wall beside the fireplace. She drove her dagger into the palm of his left hand, ramming it into the wood of the wall and pinning him there. The other she pressed against his neck.

"How dare you?" she said, voice nearly a snarl.

"I don't under..."

"The girls," she said. "I found them. Are you recruiting them so young now? Or did you fuck them yourself so you could declare them unclean and therefore worthy of your purposes?"

"It wasn't like that," he said, hoarse from the blow she'd given him. "I brought them with me from Mordeina. One of the priests there, he couldn't control himself. They were in danger, so I took them with me. It was to protect them, Zusa, I swear!"

Zusa forced him to look her in the eye.

"Protect them?" she asked. "Tell me...were they whipped?"

He said nothing.

"Stripped naked before their lover?"

Again, nothing.

She smashed her knee into his groin, then slammed his head back against the wood. Holding him by the hair, she pushed her other dagger tighter against the flesh of his throat.

"Damn you," she seethed. "Did you not think to stop them? Did you not think to argue that no man can be seduced by a *nine-year-old?*"

"I did what I could," Daverik said, breathing quickened from the pain. "I swear, I did what I could. You know the laws— Karak's laws—and they don't change."

Such a pathetic excuse, and even worse, she knew he believed it. By bringing them with him to Veldaren, hiding their faces, hiding every stretch of their skin with wrappings, he thought he made them pure. Made them holy.

"You're sick," she said. "Sick, blind, and pathetic."

He looked down at her, and in his eyes, she saw something broken. Something empty.

"What are you going to do?" he asked. "Will you kill me?"

"You think you deserve better?"

With his free hand, Daverik grabbed her wrist, but instead of trying to force her away, he only pushed it harder so that it drew blood when he talked.

"I am but a sinful creature deserving death," he said. "But what I've done, Zusa, even you would have done the same. The prophet is almost here, and the future he brings with him... I've given everything to save us from it."

Zusa leaned closer, so that her lips could brush against his ear. She'd once kissed that man's neck, once let his hands drift about her body, but now she only wanted him to feel the heat of her breath when she spoke.

"The prophet is a *myth*, you damn fool. All you've done, you've done for a lie, and now you're dying for one."

Before he might react, she cut across his throat, slicing it open. His blood spilled upon her. He opened his mouth to speak, but he could not form the words. Holding him aloft, she stared into his eyes as he died. She wanted the last thing he saw on this world to be her face, her eyes, empty of tears, empty of sorrow.

When he was gone, she freed her dagger, returned to the bedroom, and pulled open the door to the hidden room. The two girls were within still, and they'd completed the process so that their tiny little bodies were covered with wrappings. The sight of it brought tears to her eyes where Daverik's death could not.

"Remove the cloth," she told them. "Let me see your face."

They looked to one another, clearly unsure, but with a bloody dagger in her hand and her chest covered with the blood of their master, she was hardly surprised they obeyed. Off came the white cloths, revealing their cherubic faces. Zusa knelt before them, but the first she reached for backed away.

"How long have you been with Daverik?" she asked them.

"Six months," said the pale girl with the blue eyes.

"Then you've been taught to hide, to steal, to survive," Zusa said. "Both of you, you have to understand. What happened, what you've been told...it's not your fault. It was never your fault. Listen to me, I beg of you. There is no salvation for you at the Lion. There is nothing to feel shame over, nothing to condemn you. Your master is dead. Flee. No one will look for you. No one will know you're gone, I promise. Make a life for yourselves; just please, do not return to the temple. Don't let them hide everything wonderful about you. Your face is not sinful. Your hair is a gift, your eyes a temple, your smile a blessing. Let all the world see. Can you do that? Can you? You're beautiful...so beautiful..."

She was crying, she realized, and the two girls stared at her with expressions she could not begin to read. They merely nodded, and when Zusa stepped away, the two ran for the door. Zusa watched them go, and in her gut, she felt certain they would return to the temple. Where else would they go? Here she was, sick and terrified of making a life for herself, and she was a woman grown. Them? Children.

She looked down to her wrappings, the markings of the faceless that she'd carried even after turning her back on Karak. Suddenly, every reason she'd ever used for keeping them rang false. Stupid, cowardly, and petty. She wanted nothing to do with them now. The only meaning they carried was that when those two girls first saw her, they saw what they would one day become.

Taking the bloody knife to her neck, she cut down, into the cloth. Tears still running down her face, she sliced them away, strip after strip. Her movements grew quicker, more rash. Sometimes she cut into herself, and she did not care. She wanted the wrappings gone. Hacking away, she freed herself from them as if they were bonds. Finally naked, she crouched atop the shredded remains, feeling the weight of the day crushing her. Openly, she sobbed, and there was something cleansing to finally letting it all free. She said good-bye to the memories, to her sisters, to every life she'd known before stumbling into Maynard Gemcroft's mansion all those years before.

Slowly, she rose to her feet, and she felt her emotions seeping back under control.

"I'm sorry," she whispered to the ghosts of the women who

had once stayed there. "I'm so sorry, but I will wear them no more. Not even in remembrance of you."

The drawers had no other clothes, which left her with but one choice. She went to Daverik's body and stripped him naked. His trousers were a bit too wide, but she cinched the belt tight enough so they would not fall. Over her neck went the shirt, and she cut at its overly long sleeves with her dagger so they would not interfere. His blood was on it, and she stared down at the stain with a growing detachment. What did it matter, the blood?

"All for a myth," she whispered, chest hollow, eyes wet.

To the growing dark outside she went, but before she did, she grabbed the lone copy of *The Lion's Walk* and tossed it into the fire, let it burn with all the rest.

CHAPTER
31

Into his adulterous city Thren walked, keenly aware she'd abandoned him for another. Night had fallen, and it seemed so strange to see how dead the streets had become. With the gate closed, he'd had to climb the wall, using a hook and rope stashed by his disbanded guild for whenever they needed to smuggle in goods better left unseen by the city guard. Before a lantern-wielding patrol discovered him, he'd paused, overlooking the homes. Even the very feel of the place was different, and he'd wondered just what it was he'd sensed.

Have you changed in my absence? he'd wondered. *Or do you merely hide your head and pray for the Watcher to come save you?*

At the end of the marketplace were several taverns, competing with one another for nightly clientele. The one on the left, the far more ragged-looking place named simply Filled Cup, had always been his former second-in-command's favorite. Assuming he was still alive and Muzien had not killed him.

Pulling his hood lower over his face, Thren pushed open the door and stepped into the lively bustle within.

It seemed tonight was a night for celebration. Men and women filled the seven tables, gathered together with plenty of drink to go around. Three of the tables were singing songs, though each of the songs was different from the others, which made them only compete to see whose song could drown out the others. Flitting through the tables, their assets on clear display, were the whores, smiling, laughing, acting as if each man were the handsomest they'd ever seen...at least until it was clear they had no coin to pay for the privilege. Of the women, all but one wore a simple yellow gem on a cord around their neck, pinned to their blouse, or in a ring on their finger. The gem signified their allegiance to Muzien, as well as who would come to their aid should someone try to skimp on a payment or play too rough in bed.

Of course they are yours, thought Thren as he approached the barkeep. *Once the whores are in your pocket, who would dare refuse you and risk losing such illustrious company?*

"What'll it be?" the barkeep asked him, a hairy man with forearms as big as Thren's head.

"I'm looking for a friend," Thren said. "Name's Martin, ten years my younger. Brown hair, sometimes goes by the name of Softhands."

"Martin Softhands," said the barkeep, nodding. "He only uses that name when trying to impress the ladies. Surprised he didn't name himself Longtongue or Goodfuck for all the good it'd do."

Thren grinned.

"Never let him hear you say that," he said. "He might adopt Goodfuck out of pure amusement. So, do you know where he is?"

The barkeep paused.

"You know I can't tell you that."

Thren reached into his pocket and then dumped out a handful of coins onto the counter.

"A good friend, this Martin," Thren said, and the barkeep snatched up the coins with practiced speed.

"Upstairs, using those deft hands of his, and not on himself."

"Which room?"

For a moment, the barkeep ignored him, instead counting up the coins.

"Room three," said the burly man. "That's the room you just rented from me for the night. Of course, I might have mixed up numbers, and room three's already occupied..."

"The night's busy and the tables loud," Thren said. "Who would blame you for an honest mistake?"

Thren tipped his head in respect, then made his way to the stairs.

There were five rooms in total, small and cramped from what he could see of the lone door that was open. The others were closed, and the telltale sounds of sex came from within.

Animals, thought Thren. He approached room three, marked by deep grooves cut into the front. He tested, found it locked. Sighing, Thren put the slightest weight on it to test its strength, discovered it was held shut by a simple chain at the top. Easy enough. Stepping back, he rammed his foot into the door, snapping the chain and smashing open the door to reveal Martin sitting on the edge of the bed, an older woman on her knees before him with her head in his lap.

"What the fu..."

Martin's voice trailed off, his anger quickly changing to stunned silence. The woman pulled back and rose to her feet, with no care to her modesty, instead reaching for a slender dagger she'd hidden within the folds of her discarded dress.

"He's finished," Thren said to the woman. "Take your clothes and go."

The woman looked back to Martin, who nodded.

"He's right," Martin said. "Go ahead and get out of here, and keep the coin."

"Had no plans on giving it back," she said, and within moments, she had her blouse back on and her skirt replaced. Thren stepped aside so she could leave, then crossed his arms and waited as Martin put on his pants.

"She seems a bit old," Thren said, glancing back over his shoulder as the woman climbed down the stairs.

"Just means she knows what she's doing. I don't like paying for amateurs, and so long as my eyes are closed, every woman is sixteen and slender."

Thren shrugged. Fair enough.

Martin tightened his belt, then walked over to him, bare from the waist up. The man had a rugged look to him, face and neck carrying the scars of his livelihood. Of all those he'd recruited into his guild since the Bloody Kensgold, Martin had been the one most practical and aware of how the city worked. Thren had hoped there'd have been fear at seeing his return, or perhaps optimism at a possible resurgence of the Spider Guild...but instead, Martin just looked annoyed and bored.

"What?" he asked.

That tone...he'd never have used that tone with him before, not while wearing the deep gray of the Spider. Gone for but a few months, yet already his reputation was sinking? It was enough to make Thren want to scream.

"Do I bother you?" Thren asked, and his right hand drifted down to the hilt of his sword. "Or did Muzien bore a hole through your skull when you became part of his Suns?"

Finally, a bit of fear in the man's eyes, a measure of respect. If this was how his second-in-command reacted, well...restoring his Spider Guild to a position of power was going to be harder than he thought.

"Of course not," Martin said, putting on his shirt. "Just... bad timing. So, you're back, I see. I hope you enjoyed your time away from this shithole."

"Pleasant," Thren said. "But also irrelevant. I've come to rebuild, and I need your help to find the others. It's time we call in every last member, and remind them to whom their true allegiance should be."

"Former members," Martin said, walking back to the bed and grabbing a long dagger, which he jammed into his belt. "They've joined the Sun Guild now, all but perhaps a few that died to that Victor bastard. Truth be told, Thren, I'm not sure how you plan on convincing them. This city is Muzien's now, from top to bottom."

"But only in my absence."

Martin laughed.

"You think that matters?"

Thren stepped closer, grabbed Martin by the front of his shirt, and yanked him close.

"I have been here for decades," he said, feeling his temper overwhelming him. "I've watched guilds rise and fall, I've cut off the heads of kings and queens, and I've earned every last bit of respect the scum of this city can muster. I will not be turned away nor insulted. You think my name means nothing? We'll find out, Martin. When I remind them of who I am and what I can do, we'll see if they're willing to throw their lot in with a damn elf over one of their own."

Martin swallowed, clearly worried but still able to meet Thren's stare with his own.

"Have I made myself clear?" Thren asked.

"Perfectly," Martin said.

Thren let him go, and his former most trusted smoothed out his shirt, and just like that, his worry was gone, and he slipped into the role he'd filled for many a year.

"Muzien's kept most of the guilds together, even if unofficially," he said. "Helps with the transition, I'm guessing. Most of those downstairs once wore the gray as well, and that's where we'll start. It'll be tricky though, Thren. One word to Muzien, and it all goes to shit."

"Then we have to make them afraid," Thren said. "More afraid of me than of Muzien."

Martin grinned.

"Is that all?" he asked. "So be it. Find yourself a room, and once I get myself a good night's sleep, I'll start working on the others tomorrow. Now, if you don't mind, I'd like to go find another girl to finish what you interrupted."

Thren stepped out of the room, and he frowned.

"Take care of it yourself. Cheaper that way."

"Not all of us want to build up a fortune like you," Martin said, walking past him to the stairs. "Some of us would rather enjoy the spending."

Thren looked to the empty room, shook his head, and then followed Martin down the stairs.

"Sorry about that," the barkeep said, gesturing Thren over. "Room five's the one open. Five. Hope you don't mind the slipup."

Thren smiled, deciding he liked the man.

"Not at all," he said, heading toward the door. He was too wired to sleep, not yet. The journey had worn on him, but damn, it felt good to begin planning again. It'd be slow, steady work, but strand by strand was how you built a web, not all at once. No doubt a few of his former members would have to die to make the others realize the consequence of denying him and remaining loyal to the Suns. Truth be told, he felt himself looking forward to it.

Out into the night he stepped, breathing in the lingering odors of the marketplace tinged with the scent of alcohol and rotting fruit and bread cast off from earlier in the day. He looked to the stars and tried to tell himself that the city was his, no matter the dozens of tiles marked with the Sun he'd passed on his way there. His city. His home.

As he stared, he saw someone crouching at the edge of a building, watching. Thren grunted, and he pretended not to see. Down the street he walked, aimless, in no hurry. He didn't want to let whoever tailed him realize he'd been spotted, not yet…

The tail was on the rooftop on the right side of the street, so once Thren reached an alley on his left, he suddenly sprinted down it, racing as fast as his legs could carry him. He'd thought it'd be an easy enough task to leave whoever it was behind, but instead, he had to come to a sliding halt before reaching the other side. A man had stepped out, the four-pointed star sewn onto the front of his shirt, the daggers in his hands gleaming in the moonlight. Spinning about, Thren saw the other entrance blocked by two more. Gritting his teeth, he looked skyward, saw three more lurking above him, faces hidden by the hoods of their cloaks.

Damn it, Thren swore. *Someone alerted them, but who? Martin? The barkeep?*

Assuming he lived, Thren knew who the first would be to serve as an example for those who would deny his return.

"Thren Felhorn," said a haunting voice behind him. Slowly, Thren turned, pulled the hood away from his face, and stood tall before his former master.

"It's been a long time, Muzien," Thren said to the elf at the far end of the alley, flanked by two more of his guild. "Have you finally come to greet me?"

Muzien stepped into the alley, eyes like ice, mutilated ears seeming all the more grotesque with the way the moonlight colored them, making the scars seem almost purple.

"It seems I must," said the elf. "For you sneaked into my home and did not think to seek me out."

Your home?

It made Thren want to smack him across the face with a blade, but he kept his temper in check. If there was one thing Muzien knew how to wield as both weapon and shield, it was arrogance.

"It has been my home for far longer," Thren said. "I'd like to think of it as you merely borrowing the place prior to my return."

Muzien smiled, but there was no enjoyment in it. It was a smile Thren recognized all too well from growing up under Muzien's tutelage. It meant the elf was tiring of a game, and when he tired of a game, he didn't stop playing. He simply won it.

"You know you have no more power here," Muzien said. "And I will not pretend otherwise to satisfy your tired pride. This is my city now, Thren, and if you wish to live in it, I will have you bow before me and serve."

Thren glanced back to the rooftops. All three above had crossbows drawn and aimed. Much as he wanted to make a move toward the elf, he knew he'd die before ever getting close, and that wasn't counting the two at his side who would certainly move to block the way.

"Why now?" Thren asked. "I've done everything you asked. You wanted me to come to Veldaren, and I did. You wanted me to create an empire, and I did. Everything you taught me, I used. Every trick and scheme, I performed to the highest of standards. Yet you sent Grayson in to kill me, and now your guild has moved in, crushing everything I built. I was your heir, damn you, so tell me what I did that had you turn on me so."

Muzien approached, and with a wave of his hand, those with him stayed behind. Confidence, Thren knew. Arrogance. No fear of him whatsoever, and if Thren were honest with himself, he knew it was true. Muzien had taught him all he knew of swordplay, and not once had he ever, *ever* won a duel. The elf's face remained cold, passive, but his blue eyes seemed to sparkle with a disgust Thren felt betrayed by. What had he ever done to deserve such emotion?

"You were indeed my heir," Muzien said. "I put my years into you, training you, molding your mind and body. A single breath of mine is worth more than the lifetime of your kind, yet still I devoted it to your betterment, creating an heir worthy of my legacy. A *worthy* heir, Thren. I could name any fool as my successor, but I desired someone who could keep my empire together instead of letting it crumble mere moments after my death. Yet you..."

Muzien gestured about.

"What is your legacy here? Everything you built fell to ashes and dirt, and from what? An interloping lord, a few wealthy merchants, and a mysterious vigilante killer?"

"You belittle my challenges," Thren said.

"Your challenges belittle you! I listened to the excuses. I observed from afar as your war was waged, as the Trifect bled and the guilds consumed one another. At last, I knew I had to come for myself. What did I accomplish in your absence? Domination, Thren. In four months, I have accomplished what you have not in all your years stalking these streets. Four months."

The elf shook his head.

"I know your abilities. I know what you can do, and everything I have done was always within your reach. Something held you back, Thren. What, I cannot guess. I thought I had purged your weaknesses, but some remain. Complacency, in merely ruling a few guilds? Foolishness, in trusting the wrong men? Cowardice, in signing the Watcher's agreement? I'd ask, but truth be told, Thren...I don't care. You are old and unworthy. With Grayson dead, I must begin anew and adopt new heirs to potentially inherit my wealth and power. It won't be you. It cannot be."

"Do you think to insult me?" Thren asked as Muzien turned away. "That I *want* to inherit a single coin after your death? I built everything here on my own, and I will do it again if I must. No matter how certain you are, Muzien, this city will never be yours. I won't allow it. I will leave you with a graveyard of fire and death before I let you pretend to be its god."

Muzien turned back about, his blue eyes seemingly on fire with his rage. Closer he came, towering before him, their faces mere inches apart. So close. So easily could Thren draw a blade, but instead, he met Muzien's gaze and refused to back down.

"*How?*" Muzien asked, full of mockery, that one word defining his entire opinion of Thren and his worth.

Thren gave no answer. He dared not even move. The slightest insult meant death. He would challenge the Darkhand in time, but not yet. Not there...and not alone.

"I thought not," Muzien said. "I'd hoped you could at least loyally serve, despite your faults, until a new heir could be trained. I had even entertained the idea of you helping with the training, but that was my own fault for thinking you could be of any use."

He turned, long coat flapping behind him as he strode away.

"Get out of my city, Thren," Muzien called after, not

bothering to turn around. "The next time we meet, it will end with your head in a bag."

And just like that, they were gone. The Suns at either side of the alley vanished, and when he looked up, the rooftops were clear, only stars looking back. Thren stood there, breathing heavily, doing his best to stay calm. Despite all his years, he'd never once endured such disrespect from his teacher as he had then. Before, Muzien had always believed there was some sort of promise in him and Grayson, something special and worthy of his time. No longer.

"Your city?" Thren whispered. "This isn't your city. It will never be your city, not while I live."

The elf's words repeated in his head, deepening his anger. "How?" Muzien had asked, as if there were no possible way, as if the task were so insurmountable. Thren, a mere human, overthrow the demigod that was Muzien?

But it wasn't impossible. In fact, it was terrifyingly easy.

"Fire and destruction," Thren whispered, echoing the words Luther had spoken just before his death. From underneath his shirt he pulled out Luther's medallion, held the cold metal in his palm.

"My city," he said, remembering the promise he'd made in what felt like ages past. "My city, or ashes."

He could make it come to pass. All the lives and toil of man could come crashing down with a single word, and the medallion was the key, the catalyst. In his hand, the medallion twirled. Life or death, all contained in a single disc of gold. Luther would have him destroy Veldaren to save it. Better in ruin than in the hands of the prophet, the priest had insisted. It was a feeling he understood so well. Better to leave the city in ashes than in Muzien's hands.

But there was still a way to reclaim his city, to bravely stand before a conquering army without fear. A way to defeat the legendary Darkhand and return Veldaren to the rule of the Spider. A way for Thren to prepare his legacy, his heir, as he had always dreamed.

"Aaron," he whispered. "Watcher. Haern. Whoever it is you are...given the choice, the Sun, the Spider, or nothing at all, which would you choose?"

To the night sky he looked, imagined his little boy on his lap, listening to him, adoring him, trusting him above all others. Before the world tore him away. Before gods and priests and little red-haired girls made him believe in a world that would never be.

"Would you join my side to prevent the deaths of thousands, my son?" Thren wondered, but the stars could give him no answer, only silence.

CHAPTER
32

Haern paused before the Eschaton Tower, and he almost didn't go inside. The night was late, and for all he knew, those inside were asleep. It was a nice enough excuse in his head, but as the cicadas droned on, he knew it was a lie. Ever since their fight the day before, he was yet to see Delysia. She'd surely beaten him home, given the time it'd taken him to bury Ghost's body. What might she have told her brother? Everything? Nothing?

On either side of him were long hills covered with flowing grass, and behind the tower was the King's Forest, and either sounded like better places to sleep. Cowardly places, of course, and that was what kept him going, walking up the path, to the door, and inside.

"Was wondering when you'd show up," Tarlak said, stretched out on a couch with a drink in his hand and his feet pointed toward the low fire that burned in the fireplace.

"I had a body to bury," Haern said, and he realized how

absurd a greeting that was. He'd not seen his friend in months, and those were the first words out of his mouth?

"So I heard." Tarlak gestured to the chair opposite him. "Take a seat. It feels like forever since your skulking hood graced my tower."

Haern hadn't even realized he had it on, and he quickly pulled it off as he sat down beside the fire. His swords and pack he put down beside him. He felt awkward, wishing he could just come right out and ask what Tarlak knew but was unable to be so direct. So, instead, he let out a deep sigh and sank into the chair. No matter what, he was indeed home, and it felt good to be there, despite all the awkwardness.

"Did you talk to Delysia?" Haern asked, thinking it about as gentle a way to broach the subject as possible.

"I did," Tarlak said.

Haern tried to read the wizard, but whatever thoughts were behind those green eyes and red goatee were well hidden.

"And?" Haern asked.

Tarlak sat up, and with a sigh he let go of his glass, which hovered in the air for a brief moment before vanishing.

"And I can tell something happened between the two of you," he said. "Though I admit I'm hopeless as to what, because my dear sister is as stubborn as she is beautiful when she wants to be. All she'll tell me is that Ghost showed up, you two fought, and Ghost lost. I don't know if that has something to do with why Delysia was so upset, or something else. My gut says your father's involved, given the only thing good that's ever come out of him is, well, you."

"The months were definitely long," Haern said. He shifted, not liking the way Tarlak was looking at him. "As for Delysia... we had a disagreement; that's all. We'll be fine."

The wizard lifted an eyebrow.

"Are you sure?" he asked.

Haern rubbed his eyes.

"Honestly...I have no clue, Tar. Can we talk about something else? How's life been here in Veldaren?"

Tarlak chuckled.

"If you're hoping for more happy subjects, you're going to be sorely disappointed."

He snapped his fingers, and his glass reappeared, this time full of a white wine. Tarlak took it from the air where it floated, sipped at it.

"Pretty much everything you've ever set up in the city has been eradicated," Tarlak said. "The agreement with the Trifect, the truce between the guilds...it's all gone."

Haern sat frozen in his seat, unable to believe it. Everything he'd worked for, all the blood and sweat and killing, was over? The wizard said it nonchalantly, just no big thing, but Haern felt as if he'd been slapped in the face with a wet rag.

"All gone?" Haern asked. "How is that possible?"

"Well, your absence didn't help matters," Tarlak said. "Nor did Thren's, honestly. The Sun Guild came back with a vengeance, and this time with their leader, Muzien the Darkhand. Every guild that refused to submit to his command, he crushed, one by one. After that, he cowed the king, putting himself safely out of reach of the city guard, and then began working on the Trifect. The elf's a cruel bastard, and what he's done to secure his power is sickening, to say the least."

"Why haven't you stopped him?"

Tarlak frowned.

"I'd say that's *your* job, actually, but you were too busy traipsing west in search of...what was it again? Luther? What did you find out about that, anyway, because Delysia was none too talkative?"

Haern sighed.

"Nothing," he said. "Thren betrayed me when we reached the tower, and he was the only one to speak with Luther. The man was a priest held prisoner at the top of the Stronghold; that's all I know. Beyond that, his task in Veldaren was some plan involving Karak and those stone tiles the Sun Guild's using. I'm sorry, Tar; I really can't offer more than that."

Tarlak downed the rest of the wine, made the cup vanish, and then rose to his feet.

"Glad to know it was all worthwhile," he said. "A priest working for Karak...I never could have guessed that. Meanwhile, Muzien controls every inch of our fair city. We've needed you bad, Haern, but I don't know where to even start. I feel like a war happened right underneath my nose, and something tells me under no circumstances were we the victor."

"I'm sorry," Haern said. "It isn't too late, though. I'll get to the bottom of this; I promise."

"Like you got to the bottom of this whole Luther business?"

"Enough, Tarlak. Quit acting like this is my fault!"

"Will you two kiss and make up already?" Brug said as he emerged from the staircase, his own beer mug in hand. "Gods, I could hear the two of you yammering from my bedroom."

He tipped his head in Haern's direction.

"Good to see you, bud," Brug said, and he grinned. "Now come give me a hug. After months with dealing with just that idiot over there, I could practically kiss you for finally coming home."

Haern felt his face flushing, and embarrassed, he went over and clapped Brug across the shoulder.

"Good to see you, too," Haern said.

"Aye, a happy homecoming," Tarlak said. Haern glared his way, expecting more sarcasm, but it seemed the wizard himself was embarrassed by his earlier outburst.

"It really is good to have you back," Tarlak said. "This city isn't the same without you, and neither is this tower."

Haern pulled away from Brug and retrieved his swords from the chair.

"I've had more than enough time to rest," he said. "Has every guild fallen to Muzien?"

"All but the Ash," Tarlak said. "And I'm not sure if they're still alive."

Haern pulled his hood over his head, feeling the comfortable shadow encasing him.

"Let's hope so. We could use whatever allies we may find."

Haern went to the door, and he saw Tarlak go to stop him, then change his mind.

"Stay safe," Tarlak called after him. "It'd be a damn shame for you die on your first night back home."

Despite his dour mood, Haern chuckled.

"That it would, Tar," he said, shutting the door to the tower behind him.

The walk to the looming walls of the city was a long and familiar one, and Haern felt himself slipping back into the persona he'd carefully crafted. His hood hung low over his face, his cloak disguising his movements, melding him into the darkness. At his sides were his swords, and at least they were a reliable comfort. He knew the fear he carried, the reputation, and as he began to run to close the distance, his troubles drifted away. Just like when he'd come home from the snow-covered northern plains or the distant city of Angelport, there was something comforting about his city's familiarity. The guilds, the Trifect, the cowardly king: he knew them all and they him.

Using disguised handholds he'd had Tarlak magically carve into the side, Haern scaled the wall, slipped across it after a patrol passed on by, and then raced down the steps and to the street below. Home at last, he ran, letting the familiar sights welcome him... only, the sights weren't so familiar. Street after street, he checked for the hidden markings of the Wolf Guild, the scrawled legs of the Spider Guild, even the thick smear of Ash, but they were not there. Along the sides of homes and stalls, and even in the very street, he saw only where they'd been. The symbols had been burned, scraped, and painted over if necessary. No guilds, no colors.

Just the Sun.

"You weren't kidding, Tar," Haern said as he continually scanned the rooftops on either side of him. Surely a scout from one of the guilds would have located him by now. Haern used a window to vault up, and from atop a shop he looked about. No one. The night was calm, and he did not like it. Panic nipped at the edges of his mind. Going into the city, he'd always felt in control, the mad puppeteer holding all the strings, but it seemed his absence had been far too long.

Haern raced along the rooftops, extended his body to leap across the alleys, his legs pounding to keep up speed, his body shifting to adjust his weight as he moved across the consistently uneven terrain. Sometimes he stopped, but each time was only to see the symbol of the Sun, a reminder of the underworld's new king. The truce, his deal with the king... Haern tried not to dwell on it, to let the pounding blood in his veins drown it out, but all he could think of was how his entire legacy, everything he'd killed for, had vanished like a puff of smoke from the end of Tarlak's pipe.

His movements slowed. It seemed there would be no trouble that night, not unless he went looking for it in the various safe houses about the town... and even then he had no guarantee they'd be in use anymore. And with the silence, with the isolation amid the shadows, he could not hide from his thoughts.

You wanted me to be there for you...

Always, he thought. Always, he'd relied on Delysia to understand, to never judge him for the blood on his blades.

...I'm not sure I can...

His foot slipped, and he rolled down a slanted rooftop, gaining his balance only moments before leaping over an alley and crashing along the wood shingles of another.

I can't be the one to help you remember who you are.

Teeth clenched, he tried pushing himself back up, to run with a frenzy and purpose that showed he still ruled the night. Instead, he stumbled again, and when he leaped to the next home, he did not cover the distance necessary. Arms out, he caught the side, felt the shingles dig into his hands. His momentum sent his knees smacking into the side, and he sucked in air to keep his cry down. Pulling himself up, he crouched there, body heaving breaths in and out, as he felt his deadened mind betray him with its cruel remembrance.

Your father would be so proud.

It wasn't the same. It couldn't be. He'd denied him, denied everything his father would have him become. That's why he wore the Wraith's hood...wasn't it? His choices, his killing of Ghost, they all had their reasons. The type of man to treat life as a mere obstacle in the way of his goals...that wasn't him. It couldn't be.

But Delysia was supposed to be there for him, to let him know if he ever stepped foot on his father's path; only, now she was gone, he was alone, and all he had were his memories of the arrow piercing her breast intertwined with the way she'd stared at him with a mixture of horror and rage as he lifted a bloodied saber to ensure she did not heal the dying Ghost.

Slowly, he rose to his feet and looked out across the city. He'd once sworn to never call it *his* city, and he understood the wisdom of that even more clearly. Only a few months gone and it had forgotten him, moving on to new masters, with the Darkhand spreading fear with strength far beyond what he as the Watcher had fostered. There was a way to pull it back to him, he knew. All he had to do was inspire fear above all others, just as he'd once set out to do that night Senke died. But doing so would take him to places far beyond comfort. Onto a path he might recognize all too painfully well.

As he looked, he finally saw another with him on the rooftops, and a familiar face at that. Trying to shove away his troubled thoughts, he carefully made his way there, having to climb down only once to cross a street and then snake back up the side of a home. Sitting with her back against a stone bird atop a modest mansion, Zusa stared into nowhere, head resting on her knuckles.

"A quiet night," Haern said, standing beside her.

"If only all may be this quiet," Zusa said, eyes never shifting. Haern followed her gaze, and in the distance, he saw the Gemcroft mansion, its windows shining by the light of dozens of candles. Around its fences patrolled men with torches, looking like little bugs in the night.

Haern noticed her clothing, loose-fitting pants and a shirt that clearly did not belong to her. There was blood on it, though from no apparent source. Tarlak had said nothing of the Trifect, Haern realized, and he wondered just how well Alyssa had taken Muzien's rise and subsequent dissolution of the Watcher's truce. By the looks of it, not well at all.

"Mind if I join you?" he asked.

She finally looked his way, and he saw the redness of her eyes.

"Yes," she said. "Please."

Haern pushed his cloak aside so he could sit. Looking about, he saw they were very much alone, and he removed his hood as well. Hiding his face from her seemed pointless given their time in Angelport, and honestly, did it matter if someone else saw? Reckless, he knew, but his foul mood made him not care.

"Trouble at the mansion?" he asked, seeing her gaze return to her home.

"In a way," she said. "Alyssa will soon marry Victor Kane, and I fear I will no longer be welcome in their home."

Haern did not bother containing his surprise.

"You've been with Alyssa since the beginning," he said. "How could you not be welcome?"

Zusa rubbed at her eyes, and he heard her sniffle.

"Because staying means obeying that madman as if he were an equal to Alyssa. I can't do it, Haern. I can't pretend to serve him."

Haern almost reached out to her, wishing he could comfort her, but his hand remained at his side.

"I'm sorry," he said instead. "You deserve so much better."

"I deserve nothing," she said. "I have no family line. No money, no land, no reputation or soldiers sworn to my name. No matter how many years I stay at Alyssa's side, I'll always be the strange little woman lurking in the shadows. I'm a priestess hated by the only god she ever worshipped; a bodyguard abandoned by the only woman she ever loved; a stupid girl who killed the only man who ever loved her."

"Stop it," Haern said. "You're more than that, so much more."

She looked to him.

"And you?" she asked. "It's good to see you back, Haern, but I fear you've returned far too late. Will you still prowl the night, even without reason?"

"I'll always have reason."

"And I'll always have reason to protect Alyssa and her son," she said. "But it only means I'm a stubborn fool."

Haern shrugged.

"You're hardly alone in that, either."

Finally, she smiled, and it lit up her face, even if only for the briefest of moments. Zusa shifted so that she sat closer to him, and she leaned her head against his shoulder, her short hair pressing against his neck. Unsure of what to do, Haern slowly put his arm about her, and he felt her relax at his touch.

"I'm so tired, Haern," she said. Her voice was quiet, distant. "I have no home, nowhere to go, no person to be. Have I robbed myself with my devotion? Has my love cheated me of a true life?"

"I pray not," he whispered.

"But you've made it work. I've seen it, the way they care for you at that tower. Who are you, Haern? When the cloak and hood come off, who are you that allows them to love you so?"

He held her tighter against him, imagined Delysia's betrayal, the way she'd struck his hand when he'd reached for her.

"I'm not sure I know anymore."

They fell silent, Zusa in his arms, watching together as the deep night wore on. When she finally pulled away, a look was in her eyes, and he could not discern it.

"Forgive me," she said.

And then she kissed him. His entire body froze, but she pressed herself against him, put her hands on his neck. They were so soft, so controlled, yet when he kissed back, he felt them dig into his skin with a strength bordering on desperation.

"Zusa," he said, pushing her away, his scrambled mind trying to regain control.

"Don't misunderstand this," Zusa said as she unhooked his cloak and spread it out behind him on the rooftop. "A man and woman needing comfort. That's all this is. Can you give me that?"

She put a hand on his chest, slipped it underneath his shirt to touch his skin.

"Please," she said, and he saw a fragile honesty so rarely allowed upon her face. To reject her would break it, perhaps forever. She'd endure, he knew, but it'd be alone. Delysia's face flashed in his mind, and he thought of his fumbling attempt to caress her. Her rejection had been the kindest possible, but it'd still left him feeling ashamed, foolish, lost. *In time*, she'd whispered. But now he saw only her tears, felt only her anger and betrayal as Ghost died at his feet. She might come to forgive him...but would she ever love him? Would there be enough time in the world for that wound to heal? He didn't know. He didn't want to know.

A man and a woman needing comfort. Zusa was the one ready to break, the sorrow naked on her face, but as Haern reached out, he felt his need for comfort just as terrible. His hand looped behind Zusa's neck, and pulled her close so he could kiss her again. Her hands were on him, and she breathed in his kisses as if afraid each one would be the last. Off went his shirt, as did hers, and she took his hands and placed them upon her breasts before forcing him onto his back, her lips returning to his. Even now, she needed to be in control, Haern sensed, but he let her, feeling swept away and refusing to do anything that might dare stop it. Another long moment later, she pulled up, her breathing heavy, the last of her clothes quickly removed. Haern stared at her in the moonlight, beautiful, naked, body so strong, eyes so dark.

Zusa leaned back so she could pull away his pants, then climbed atop him. One more kiss, and then she guided him inside, body curled into him, her forehead pressed against his.

She moved slowly at first, fingers digging into his shoulders, and he reacted only in concert. His hands drifted down her sides until he held her waist, keeping her against him, almost fearing she might leave. The way she clutched his body, he knew she felt the same.

Haern leaned his head back, and above him, Zusa moved faster and faster. Her strong legs were unrelenting, and she closed her eyes and tilted her neck so that her short hair covered her face. For some reason, it made the moment all the more private and her all the more vulnerable. There was no denying her sorrow, her despair, but her pleasure was a mask across it, and that was one thing Haern could understand. Finally, he took control, pulling her against him, moving beneath her so that she could remain wrapped in his arms. Her lips flitted across his neck, everything even slower now, but it was enough.

His body tensed, his arms a vise, her moans in his ear, and then he let go. Slowly, he exhaled, and he felt her body go limp atop him. Still he held her, fearful of the moment when her warmth would leave him, when all the world would come crashing back in. Her face remained pressed against his neck, his skin wet from tears he didn't realize she'd cried.

"Can you stay with me?" she asked.

"I will."

His voice sounded so far away. Wishing for the right words yet not finding them, he clutched her thin frame tightly to his body, felt her shudder.

"I'm sorry," she said, just as when they first started. She pulled off him, reached for his cloak, and then curled it about her so she could lie with her head on his chest and her eyes closed.

"It'll be all right," he whispered as she nestled against him. A sigh escaped her lips, content enough that he allowed himself to believe the lie he spoke. Her breathing steadied, and he put his arms around her, holding her close.

Happiness, he thought. *At least one night of happiness.*

It was only then he leaned back, closed his eyes, and let his own tears fall.

CHAPTER

33

Pelarak, high priest of Karak's faithful, rose from his bed at the sound of knocking. He grabbed his deep black robe from a hook on the wall, slid it over his thin body, and then opened the door to his room.

"What is it?" he asked another of the priests, a handsome, clean-shaven man named Essau.

"Grim tidings," Essau said, bowing his head low. "I fear Daverik has been murdered."

"Murdered?" said Pelarak. "How?"

In answer, Essau stepped aside, revealing two little girls standing in the dimly lit hall. The very sight of them was a prick to the back of his neck. Kneeling before them, he offered them his hands, yet they shied away, afraid.

"Lesha, Jayda, you have no reason to fear me," he told them. "I am Karak's most faithful, and so long as you are faithful too, then I am your fiercest protector in all the land."

Lesha, the darker-skinned of the two, crossed her hands behind her back and looked to the floor. All her body but her face was covered with dark black and purple wrappings, and through the white cloth covering the gap, he saw that she was crying.

"What is the matter?" he asked. "Is it true? Did someone kill your master?"

"With a dagger," Lesha said. "She told us not to come here. She said..."

The girl's voice trailed off as Jayda elbowed her in the side. Together, they stood there, bowed, silent, and clearly afraid.

"Who is she?" Pelarak asked.

Jayda was the one to meet his eye this time.

"She used to be one of us," she said. "But not anymore."

Zusa, thought Pelarak, and the priest felt a familiar fire burn in his stomach. Would they never be free of that horrible woman? Pelarak stood, ran a hand through his gray hair. Now Daverik was dead, along with four others he'd trained, leaving just these two. The question was... what were they to do with them?

"Wake the rest of the elders," Pelarak told Essau. "I would have us pray before the altar."

"Can it not wait until morning?"

Pelarak put a hand on little Jayda's shoulder, felt her tremble at his touch.

"No, it cannot."

Down the hall he led the girls, back to the main worship chamber. Before the rows of pews towered the great statue of Karak, with purple fire burning in braziers at his beloved god's feet, fires that would never dwindle or fade. They, like Karak, were eternal. Pelarak ordered the girls to kneel at the altar, which was still wet with the blood from that nightfall's sacrifice. They crossed their hands in prayer, quiet and obedient, and it made the priest smile. No doubt they were troubled, scarred by witnessing Daverik's death and now adrift with an uncertain future, but their souls must have been loyal, for in prayer before the statue of the Lion, they were calm, they were at peace. The same could not always be said of kings and wise men.

"Do not cease your prayers," Pelarak whispered to them. "No matter what you hear, what my fellows discuss, never cease."

They both nodded, eyes closed, never looking up.

The door left of the altar, which led to the various barracks and dungeons of the temple, opened, and out stepped Essau.

"They'll be here shortly," he said, standing beside Pelarak as they overlooked the statue. He gestured to the two girls. "I'm not sure I understand the need for haste. They're members of the faceless, now and forever. Are we to choose another teacher?"

Pelarak crossed his arms, fingers digging into the thick, rough fabric of his robe. He'd never been pleased with the faceless, viewing it as an unpleasant necessity at best, a poor punishment at worst. When Eliora and Nava had died and Zusa gone rogue, he'd been content to consider the matter dead. But then had come Daverik, along with the backing of several prominent priests in Mordeina, all insisting it be started up anew. Against such pressure, he could not back down, especially since dogma was on their side. But that didn't mean he had to like it, nor did he have to honor it . . . not if it went against Karak's wishes.

"Our temples have played games," he said. "And these poor girls have been caught in the middle. You ask what we are to do with them, and it is a question we must receive an answer to. But I will not consult books, nor tally votes among our elders. No, Essau, we will call for the voice of the Lion before we resort to lesser, imperfect measures."

In groups of two and three came the rest of the elders, until all seven were there with Pelarak and Essau. They lingered about, speaking softly with one another. Still did Jayda and Lesha remain in prayer like proper students. Pelarak knelt beside each of them, putting his hands on their backs and closing his eyes so he might pray with them.

From the mouths of children, he prayed. *May there be no other wisdom but yours.*

With that, he stood, turned to address the various elders.

"I know the hour is late, but I believe we cannot delay," Pelarak began, "for one of our own, Daverik, has been killed by the hand of our most shameful failure, the woman Zusa. These two, Jayda and Lesha, have come to us, for they are without home and master."

"They cannot stay here," the oldest of them all said, a pock-marked man named Geas. "It has been temple law since time immemorial. The faceless are not allowed to dwell within the holy ground."

"Not so immemorial," Pelarak said, turning to face Geas. "For we have writings from Theron the Wise, who first created the order, and he never decreed any sort of banishment."

"But even Theron ordered them to eat and sleep separate from the rest," Geas argued. "And in time, Karak imparted us wisdom as to the proper way of dealing with the greatest of betrayers."

Pelarak struggled to keep his eyes from rolling. The greatest of betrayers? Before him were two girls, neither older than ten. He knew how they'd been taken, defiled by one of the priests in Mordeina. He'd received word that they'd removed the man's genitals to ensure it never happening again, yet still they'd sent the two with Daverik, demanding they be made members of the faceless. There were a dozen punishments they could have been given instead, down to a mere few nights of fasting and prayer, but no, to Veldaren they'd come. Now they were his problem, and Karak damn it, he wanted the faceless buried and forgotten, not continuing on for decades because of these two young girls, their only fault merely being mice in front of a depraved snake.

"Our high priest did not bring us together to discuss dogma," Essau said, preventing any further argument. "This matter must be settled once and for all."

"The faceless have always been a stain upon our orders," Pelarak said, addressing Geas in particular. "Already we have rules and punishments for those in our ranks who forfeit their shame to their sexual desires, and it is those we should abide by. I say we declare Jayda and Lesha free of the title, free of the wrappings, and introduce them back into the fold, where they may be raised as priestesses."

"What you suggest is heresy!" said another of the elders.

"Perhaps," Pelarak said. "But let us discover for ourselves. Let us hear the voice of the Lion decree their fates."

"Karak will give you no answer," Geas insisted. "Not when the answer is already known."

"If we hear silence, then we will debate come the morning," Pelarak said. "For now, prepare the candles and the knife. We have work to do."

The ritual was one they'd all performed dozens of times, and they began their work in earnest. Perhaps it was out of duty, or faith, or merely wanting to go back to bed, but they arranged the candles in several concentric circles about the altar, as well as fetching the other required components, with record speed. As Pelarak watched, the ceremonial knife in hand, Essau slid over to him, back to the others as he murmured.

"You know Karak does not like to involve himself with our discussions of dogma," said the priest. "It is beneath him."

"Perhaps," Pelarak said, eyeing the two girls. "But you've felt it, haven't you? Karak's presence...it's heavier upon our city. Something approaches, some moment or crossroads...and I think tonight, he will answer."

Essau glanced to the others, frowned.

"I pray you are right, because those two won't stay in this temple otherwise."

The circles made, the candle lit, the girls bowing before the great statue of Karak, all was completed as Pelarak took the knife and stepped through the ring of priests that stood with their arms raised to the ceiling. His mouth suddenly dry, he knelt and took a silver bowl from the feet of the statue and placed it before the two girls on the altar. He saw Jayda's eyes flick open just a moment, widening at the sight of the bowl. She'd be the first, Pelarak decided.

"We seek the voice of the Lion in a world that has known only silence," Pelarak said, reaching out and taking Jayda's hand in his.

"*Karak, hear our prayer,*" echoed the rest of the priests.

With his free hand, Pelarak tilted Jayda's face up with his finger, and she opened her soft blue eyes. Fear lingered in them, but she was strong, she was brave. He smiled, knowing she would make him proud.

"The pain is ephemeral," he told her. "The blood is full of power, yet so easily replaced. Cry out to Karak. Cry out for his voice, his words, his wisdom and glory. Can you do this?"

Jayda's lips trembled, but she bobbed her head up and down.

"I can," she said.

"*Karak, hear our prayer.*"

Pelarak put the knife to the palm of her hand, edge against the dark wrappings.

"Close your eyes," he said.

She did, tight as she could. Taking in a deep breath, Pelarak offered his own plea for guidance. With a single smooth movement, he cut across the little girl's palm, opening up a streak of red that quickly flowed across her revealed pale skin. Grabbing her wrist, he held her hand over the bowl, let the blood drip down as she screamed out in pain.

"Karak, hear our prayer."

He held her, firm, unmoving, and despite her tears, despite the constant flow of blood, she did not fight him. Instead, she closed her eyes and prayed with an earnestness that made him all the more furious at the man who had dared defile one so young, so full of faith.

"Please, Karak," she prayed through her sobs, "I'm sorry, so sorry."

When the bottom of the bowl was completely covered, Pelarak pulled her away, taking a cloth set beside the bowl and pressing it into her palm. Gently, he let her hold her wounded hand against her chest, and heart heavy, he turned to Lesha.

"Your hand," he told her.

The knife cut across her dark skin, and she screamed, even louder than Jayda.

"Karak, hear our prayer."

"We stand before you humbled and unworthy," Pelarak said when the bowl was filled, both girls kneeling with heads bowed, cut hands bleeding into cloths pressed against their bodies. "We stand, we pray, we beg that your voice guide us. These two, what are we to do with them? Are they to remain faceless, or shall we welcome them back into the fold?"

He took the bowl as all around him, the priests echoed his prayer, begging Karak to answer. The candles flickered, shimmered a rainbow of colors before becoming deep violet. The room bathed in its glow, the statue of Karak towering above, Pelarak took the bowl and lifted it high.

"Let us hear the roar of the Lion!" he cried, and he flung the blood across the statue. The red splashed upon the stone breast-plate, the armored greaves, the feet, the hands. Pelarak held the bowl in one hand, the blood dripping down beside him to the floor, as he stared into the eyes of his god. In the sudden silence, they heard only the sniffles of the two girls. Pelarak waited, tense, yearning for Karak to answer. He'd staked his reputation on this, as well as the fates of Jayda and Lesha.

Nothing but sniffles.

"The Lion is not with us," Geas said.

The eyes of the statue flared red, the violet flames surged, and Geas had but a moment to gasp before the fire of the candles leaped from the wicks and poured down his throat. They robbed him of sound, of breath, and as Pelarak watched in stunned silence, the old priest collapsed and died. Pelarak's mouth hung open, his mind reeling, unsure how to react.

From all four corners of the room came a chilling wind, and in its howl, the two girls' sobs grew louder, more terrified. As the other priests fell to their knees, begging Karak for mercy, Pelarak flung himself between Jayda and Lesha, and he pulled them about to face him. Their eyes were open but rolled back into their heads as they shook. It seemed to be a seizure, but still they cried, and then those cries became something differ-ent, something more.

"This city trembles," Jayda said, her voice firm and con-trolled despite the shaking of her body. "It aches, it pleads, but it will not know peace."

Pelarak clutched her to him, trying to keep her still. Her head lolled back, and when she spoke again, Lesha echoed her words.

"All will burn," they said. "This city, this land, this nation, this world. All will burn."

Suddenly, their arguments over the faceless felt so petty, so simple, and mired in worthless dogma and pointless tradition. The very temple seemed to shake with the violence of their vision, the statue above shimmering with a horrible power.

Fear the power of the gods, Pelarak thought, a line from a sermon he'd once delivered. *We are but dust to the divine, and we will never be enough to withstand their presence.*

"Karak, my god," Pelarak whispered as the other priests wailed, fearing the temple would collapse upon them. "Tell us your wisdom; tell us what we are to do."

The girls spoke in unison, but as they did, the priest realized the words were not for him, nor intended for any of them. They'd dared thrust themselves into a world beyond understanding, one of visions and power eternal, and now they must pay the price.

"Nathaniel," the girls whispered, softer now, gentler. "You must understand. The only hope is in my prophet's return..."

On the floor of the hallway, Nathaniel writhed, but he could see it no longer nor feel the carpet against his skin nor hear the cries of servants gathering about him. Instead, his vision was dominated by fire and destruction overwhelming the city of Veldaren. Nathaniel stood just outside the wall, naked and pale, as he watched fire spread as if guided by invisible hands.

Nathaniel, spoke a voice, one Nathaniel recognized as clearly as he recognized the voice of his own mother. It was deep, frightening, carrying authority no mere human could ever possess.

"You must understand," Nathaniel heard himself whisper,

echoing Karak's voice. There was no thought to this, no ability to resist. "The only hope is in my prophet's return..."

Someone cried for a priest, but the words came as if from a thousand miles away. His feet lifted off the ground, the world shifting away from him, and then Nathaniel was soaring over the tops of buildings, watching them all shake and crumble. Roar after roar shook his bones, as if enormous lions had taken up residence within the city. Desperately, Nathaniel prayed for it to end, yet he was denied such a blessing. The city was ash. A pair of red eyes watched it from afar, and he felt their cold pleasure in witnessing the destruction.

While immersed in the fire, he'd felt intense heat on his skin, yet now he felt a chill as wind blew in from the west. With its arrival, the night sky covered with clouds, and thorough darkness overcame the land. Standing amid it, Nathaniel felt intense loneliness and despair. The city was gone. Everything was dust, and within the wreckage, he knew he was but one of a thousand charred corpses. The vision was so hopeless, the darkness so complete, he didn't understand the point in showing it to him.

And then Karak spoke.

You can save them, Nathaniel, said the cold voice of an imprisoned god. *You can save them all.*

The vision shifted, and the shadowy form with the red eyes was before him, arms crossed, body hidden by a black robe. The man said nothing, but as Nathaniel's sight widened, he saw that the city of Veldaren stood once more.

This is my prophet, whom I love, Karak whispered. *You are not meant to fear him, my child. You are to* embrace *him. Melody's heart was true, but she was fooled by the traitor priest, Luther, who would tear down my beloved city, destroying it with fire and destruction. But there is still hope. There is a way to spare*

*this land, save its people, and bring about true order. It is you,
Nathaniel. You will be the boy who opened the way, if you would
only listen and obey.*

People's hands were on his body, but again, he felt them like
one feels a waking limb. At that moment, he was lost in the
presence of another, grand and powerful, overwhelming him,
suffocating him. But within it he sensed the hope Karak spoke
of. Within it, he knew he could make a difference. So, he whispered the words that ended the vision, sent it crashing down
with only the promise of a future answer.

"Tell me what to do."

EPILOGUE

Are you all right?" Tarlak asked his sister, who was yet to leave her spot by the fire on the lowest floor of their tower.

"I'll be fine," she said, sipping from a clay cup filled with steaming broth from a boiled beef bone. Her eyes remained locked on the dwindling flames. Seeing this, Tarlak snapped his fingers, surging the fire back to life. There'd be no cold chill for his little sister, not on her first night back from Ker.

"Sure, eventually we'll all be fine," he said, crouching opposite her on the rug. He took her hands, squeezed them until she finally looked his way. "But perhaps it'd help to talk about it anyway."

Delysia pulled his hands up so she could kiss the tops of them, then pushed him away.

"You're a jester in a world of serious men. Having you around is enough to help, Tar."

"Just as long as I keep dancing, eh?"

She smiled.

"If that's how you see it, then yes."

He stood, bowed low before her.

"Then dance I will. But first, I have business in Veldaren. Care to come with?"

"Take Brug," she said, settling back down into her chair. "I haven't finished my broth yet."

"A fine excuse. Since you've just come home from a lengthy, arduous journey, I will let it slide for now." He walked over to the stairs, cupped his hands in front of his face. "Come on down, Brug; we have work to do."

It took a few more yells, but finally, Tarlak had the man ready to go. The stars twinkling above them, Tarlak led the way as they walked back to the city.

"Not sure why this couldn't wait until morning," Brug grumbled.

"Bit of fresh night air will do you good, Brug." He gestured to the silver moon above, the swaying grass that seemed almost blue in the midnight glow. "Take in the beauty of nature, and then tell me, where else would you rather be?"

"In my bed, asleep."

Tarlak chuckled.

"Me, too," he said. He pointed ahead, to where the great walls of Veldaren loomed. "But something Haern said finally gave me an idea about those damn tiles of Muzien's."

"And what's that?"

"I had the right idea, but the wrong source. It's the gods, Brug. Things are never as simple as they seem once the gods get involved, especially that psychotic undead-worshipping Lion-humper we lovingly call 'Karak.'"

"Fascinating. Would still rather be sleeping."

"The sun went down barely thirty minutes ago. Quit your whining."

The road flattened out, the grass dead and the dirt faded and smooth from the daily wear of wagons and horses. Higher and higher the walls seemed as they approached the city, and Tarlak stared at them, wondering about those within.

"Think Haern's doing all right in there?" Brug asked, as if reading his mind.

"I hope so," he said.

"It's just...you know, him and Del, they ain't seemed the same since."

"Whatever it is, it's between them. For now, let's keep our minds on the task at hand and let the scum of Veldaren worry about Haern's return home."

They passed through the gates of the city, and once inside, Tarlak steered them directly south, keeping close to the wall. The streets were quiet, but they were often quiet at night since Muzien's takeover. All squabbles over territory, all back deals and smuggling of goods...it took place during the day now. What need did the Darkhand have for the cover of night? He feared no one, no guards, no kings, no other guilds. The city was his, and Tarlak felt himself hoping Haern's return would give him a nasty dose of humility. Despite his warnings earlier, he'd never bet against his friend. The Watcher had his reputation for a reason, after all.

"So, where is it we're going?" asked Brug.

"Somewhere quiet and isolated," Tarlak said. "Just in case things go horribly wrong, of course."

Brug gave him a rather rude, displeased look, but Tarlak just grinned at it and continued on. Over the past weeks, they'd drawn up an extensive map of the location of all of Muzien's tiles. Brug had called it both pointless and wasteful, but Tarlak's gut kept insisting it'd pay off eventually, even if he had no clue how. But then Haern had mentioned Luther's supposed connection to the tiles, and suddenly, Tarlak had a feeling he knew what he'd been missing all those times before. So, now they went to one of the many tiles he'd marked, in a quiet little street that dead-ended at the western wall.

"Here we are," Tarlak said, stopping in the center of the street, where the tile was buried mere feet away from the wall. It looked like all the others, with no special markings or engravings, just the same symbol of the sun. Brug stood beside him, arms crossed over his chest, as he watched Tarlak kneel.

"I thought you already tried this," Brug said.

"Not quite," said Tarlak. Closing his eyes, he began repeating a spell he'd memorized over the past hour. While before he'd used a simple spell all young magic-users learned, this one was far more demanding. It wasn't the world of magic he wanted to see, that shadowy place of the arcane. Instead, it was a different type of magic, that of priests and paladins and necromancers. He sought power tied to the deities themselves and to view its markings. A wave of dizziness came over him as he finished the last phrase of the spell, and he felt a bit of power leave his chest. Taking in a deep breath, he opened his eyes to view the tile.

It shimmered red in the darkness, and swirling about it were three long chains composed of intricate runes he couldn't begin to decipher. They dipped into the very earth, then came back out, always in constant motion, while the red glow pulsed as if tied to a distant heartbeat. The very sight of it filled Tarlak's throat with bile, and he had to force himself to remain calm.

"Brug," he said. "I want you to get away from me, all right?"

"What's going on?" asked his friend.

Tarlak looked to either side of him, saw the dilapidated homes.

"Check both of them," he said. "If there's anyone inside, make them leave."

Brug nodded, and he kept whatever questions he wanted to ask silent. Tarlak turned his attention back to the tile. Despite the ache to his head, he focused harder, and within the pulsing he saw what could only be described as thin pieces of string intertwined with the runes, each a slightly different hue of red. That was how he could decipher the magic's purpose, he knew, what all it could do if activated. Because that was the one thing he was certain of, that the magic contained within the tile was being held back.

"Both empty," Brug said a few moments later.

"Good," Tarlak said.

He swallowed, then clapped his hands together.

"All right," he said. "Let's do this."

He could undo the strings, he knew, slowly untangling them as well as breaking the spinning runes, but it was no different from undoing a particularly insidious knot. If he didn't know how, or didn't know the exact details of the spell, then he would accomplish nothing at best, or harm himself at worst. Removing any curse was a tricky matter—same with any skillful enchantment (which the tile clearly had).

But *activating* the magic...

"Here goes," he whispered. Safely undoing a knot was one thing. Chopping it in half with a sword was another. With but a thought, he pulsed magic into the tile, putting whatever spell was buried in its center into motion.

The runes vanished, and for a moment, all was silent. Tarlak's skin tingled with anticipation. This was it, the true purpose of the tiles, the reason for their very existence. In its center he watched a tiny black spot appear, crackling with white lightning. It shimmered, then vanished. The tile cracked, its center rimmed with fire, and then Tarlak had the briefest moment to react before the shock wave hit him. As a great roar shook his being, he crossed his arms, enacting a protection spell out of pure instinct. The ground trembled beneath him, and then suddenly, he was flying through the air. When he landed, he rolled, and all the while, he heard nothing but a constant ringing. When he came to a stop, Brug was hovering over him, his mouth moving but producing no words. It was only when the ringing faded that Brug's voice finally returned.

"...all right, Tar?"

Instead of answering, Tarlak pushed himself up to a sitting position, and with his mouth hanging open, he stared at where the tile had once been. In its place was a gaping crater, and fire burned within it, the flames a deep violet. On either side, the homes were shattered, the roofs collapsed in and the wood already aflame. Even the great stone wall, which had surrounded the city since the day Karak himself built it, was cracked, with large portions having collapsed and layering the surrounding area beneath with debris.

"My god, Tar," Brug said, staring with his mouth hanging open. "What did you do?"

"What it was meant to do," Tarlak said, viewing the wreckage while feeling dazed and lost. Another large chunk of the wall collapsed, the rumble deafening, as was the sound of the stone breaking upon the road, sending pieces rolling in all directions.

"One tile," Brug said, and he sounded as horrified as Tarlak felt. "How many throughout the city are there?"

"As of last count?" asked Tarlak as all around people flooded out of their homes to see what was the matter. He didn't know whether to laugh or cry as he thought of all their planning, their little map detailing the tiles' locations. Not a single street unmarked. Not a man or woman safe. He put a hand on Brug's shoulder and slowly stood as dust and stone fell.

"Over three hundred and twenty-seven."

For once, Brug was speechless. Tarlak watched the strange purple flames dwindle down to nothing in the crater, and he let out a sigh.

"Brug," he said. "We're fucked."

A NOTE FROM THE AUTHOR

Well, it feels like it's been ages since I got to write one of these and *not* have it be about the various tweaks and changes I made to my self-published version. So, instead, I get to discuss legitimately new stuff, the first new Haern book I've written in over a year. Shocking concept, eh?

Going into this one, I had a few specific goals in mind, direct attempts to counter either things I failed to adequately deal with earlier or areas I just felt I had not given near the attention they deserved. The first, and most important to me, was Haern and Delysia's relationship. I wanted to establish her better as a character, as well as how she and Haern complemented one another. And then on the other side, Haern and Zusa... there were more than a few asking me what happened with them, particularly after the chemistry they showed in *A Dance of Mirrors*. Well, hopefully, this book has done both (obviously, I have more to do still in book six, but hey, one book at a time).

The other big part, and one that clearly dominated much of this book, was Haern and his father. There'd be no more relegating Thren to the background, no more leaving it ambiguous as to why he tolerated his son's nighttime adventures. This was their attempt to recruit each other, and honestly, that chapter where they just savaged each other near the end was the most difficult one to write in this entire book. No others were even close. I've never wanted Thren to be a simple cardboard-cutout villain, and between this and the Cloak and Spider collection, I'd like to believe I've at least elevated him to a three-dimensional cardboard cutout.

To those of you who've read the Paladins, I hope you enjoyed Luther's little moment to shine, as well as his callback to his final meeting with Jerico. To those of you who have *not* read my Paladins books, I did everything I could to fill you in without spoiling the previous adventures. I do my best to include events and characters from other series yet, at the same time, try never to leave anyone in the dark if they haven't read them. As usual, I hope I succeeded, and if not, I hope you forgive me for the failed attempt.

So, what's next? Well, I'm stupidly excited about Muzien the Darkhand. One thing I've realized I've lacked over the course of the first four books was any sort of consistent villain. It was Thren in one book, then Ghost, then the Wraith, and finally, a whole mess of people like Grayson and the Bloodcrafts in book four. It lent more of an episodic feel to the series, which honestly isn't a bad thing, but I really, really like my villains. With Muzien, I finally have someone I can set up for more than a single book. Not only that, I have someone who can legitimately look at my hero and smirk.

Of course, that's not to say Muzien will be the only villain in book six. Is there such a thing as bad guy overload? Because I might be getting close...

Oh, and speaking of Ghost...yeah, he was totally dead in

the self-published edition (there goes my earlier excitement about not discussing self-pub editions). No excuses, no possibilities; I left him butchered and bleeding and with his internal organs as an eviscerated goo. But! There's advantages to going over every single book and changing whatever I feel like for the Orbit relaunch. In case you never read the redone *A Dance of Blades*, I made sure Ghost actually survived Haern's thrashing, and had them speak a quick bit of dialogue to establish that yes, Ghost is still breathing. He's in bad shape, and anyone can expect him to die shortly, but the last thing I wanted to do was cheat. So he survived, he vanished, and now I got to bring him back in. Every chapter with him was a ton of fun, and yes, I got the idea to bring him back while re-editing *Blades*. Consider it a weakness of mine. Dead people tend not to stay dead, not when I think there's more fun to be had (Half-Orc fans in particular are rolling their eyes at me right now, I'm certain).

So, was bringing back Ghost worth it? I think so. I got to finish the character arc that was only hinted at with his initial scenes with Calan, as well as take the overall direction of his return in a way that hopefully no one saw coming. Obviously, you all will be the final judge of that.

All that's left now is to put a nice bow on everything I've built. This book in particular was one that daunted me for quite some time, and I actually put it off to write the sixth Half-Orc book instead, solely as a way to stall. Having it finished is stupidly rewarding. The next book, though? *A Dance of Chaos* has been stewing in my head for quite some time, and I've been rubbing my hands in anticipation for so many scenes. The showdown with Muzien? The assault on Veldaren? The climactic confrontation between Haern and his father? Oh, yes. This will be fun.

And to those of you who have read *The Weight of Blood*...

yes, it is *that* battle that's approaching. I've always wondered where the heck Haern and the Eschaton were when it happened.

Time to show just that.

Thanks to all of you for sticking with me, putting up with my little idiosyncrasies, and this overall transition from self-publishing to Orbit's guiding hand. I hope it's all been worth it, and that this book, and the next, will be worthy of Haern's shadowy legacy.

David Dalglish
October 31, 2013

extras

www.orbitbooks.net

about the author

David Dalglish currently lives in rural Missouri with his wife, Samantha, and daughters Morgan and Katherine. He graduated from Missouri Southern State University in 2006 with a degree in mathematics and currently spends his free time teaching his children the timeless wisdom of Mario jumping on a turtle shell.

Find out more about David Dalglish and other Orbit authors by registering for the free monthly newsletter at www.orbitbooks.net.

if you enjoyed
A DANCE OF GHOSTS

look out for

A DANCE OF CHAOS
Book Six of Shadowdance

also by

David Dalglish

Prologue

Into the secluded shrine below Palace Thyne walked Muzien Ordoth, and he was pleased to see he was not alone. He'd feared the high priest of Celestia would be afraid to meet with him in such a clandestine manner, or even worse, deem such a meeting beneath him. They met in a place long forgotten, accessible only through ancient tunnels cut into the granite beneath the palace. The shrine itself was lit with forever-burning torches that produced no smoke, their yellow light reflecting off the emerald walls.

"You should have been here before me, kneeling in prayer to our goddess," said Varen Dultha, rising from his knees before the statuette of Celestia that rested atop an oaken altar. When he turned, his smug distaste tested the limits of Muzien's patience and control. "But then again, you've never been much for prayers and worship, have you?"

"I do not appreciate having my faith questioned," Muzien said. "My loyalty to the goddess has not wavered once over this past decade."

"I find that hard to believe," Varen said. "Living among humans? Trading with them? Keeping many in your employ? The goddess commanded us to watch over them, guide them, and remain neutral in their affairs if they would not listen. Pray tell me, how you were doing *Celestia's* work there in Mordeina?"

Muzien took in a deep breath, then slowly let it out. He needed to remain calm and not let his regular disagreements with the high priest get in the way of all he'd done. In the secret records of their people, he would have himself placed as the savior of their city, perhaps their entire race. What did a few insults to his pride matter compared to that? But before he answered, he walked past

Varen and put a hand atop the nude statuette. It was of their goddess, arms raised above her head, mouth open. Carefully carved to represent the delicate nature of balance, she could have been bound and in pain or finding pleasure in freedom. Often, it was the viewer's mood that was reflected back, a subtle point Muzien wished more elves would understand. Above the statuette, carved into the emerald and filled with gold, was a four-pointed star, the fabled form Celestia had taken when coming down to speak with the brother gods before their war thousands of years ago. It was as symbolic as it was historical, for that same star often represented the sun, showcasing the duality of the goddess, of her watchful eye in both day and night.

After whispering a prayer for guidance, all while fully aware Varen impatiently watched, Muzien crossed his arms over his chest and met the stare of the priest. Varen was slender, even for an elf, his long hair so white it approached silver. He was young, though, nearly as young as Muzien. The two had risen in power together over the last century, but it had been Varen who won the position of high priest, the youngest ever to have done so. The wound to Muzien's ego had taken years to heal, the bleeding only halting when he'd realized there were far better ways to protect his people than from within the isolated halls of their temples.

"I do Celestia's work by protecting her people," Muzien said.

"Are her people in danger?"

Muzien's jaw clenched tight, grinding his teeth.

"You're no fool, Varen," he said. "The humans' view of us has worsened drastically over the past twenty years. They fear us now, that fear bordering on the insane. In their cities, men and women preach hatred toward us, a hatred so primal and raw no peaceful solution will ever suffice."

Varen's eyes narrowed.

"Is that why you've pulled me down to this forgotten place?" he asked. "To insult my diplomats before they may even have the chance to speak a word?"

Muzien shook his head. Conflict between the races was growing; everyone could see that. Over the past year, as a way to counter this, Varen had championed an initiative to send dozens of trained diplomats to permanently live in Mordeina, the capital city of the human nation of Mordan. But Muzien had beaten them there by a decade, and he knew the futility of such an attempt. His voice went unheard during the debates, for he had no time for such things. He had a war to prevent.

"Your diplomats will be made to wait at the gates," Muzien said, stepping closer to Varen. "After a week or so, they'll be allowed in, only to be met with vicious crowds. They'll be cursed at, spat at. Little boys and girls will hurl stones at their heads. Whatever home you think they'll stay in will be burned to the ground. Should they go to speak with the king, they will be denied nine times out of ten, and whatever audience they find will be brief and spent listening to the king inform us of our failures and deviousness. This anger they feel, it is a sickness, without base or merit or reason. It's founded on one thing, Varen: fear."

"If all this is as you say," asked Varen, "then how have you lived there so long?"

"Because I *want* them to fear me."

Muzien could feel the conversation slipping away from him, so before the priest could respond, he pressed on, letting his anger fuel his words.

"Listen well, Varen," he said. "You know war is coming, as sure as the rising sun. It is only a matter of time before the humans raise their banners and descend upon our forests. They'll burn every tree to ash if they must to satisfy their bloodlust. If we don't do something to prevent it, our people will suffer terribly."

For once, that smug look faded, revealing a very tired, frustrated Varen.

"Of course I know it," he said. "But too many consider the humans as curiosities to be ignored, not feared. They see the borders of our forests as impenetrable. To even convince them to permanently station diplomats in Mordeina took more effort than you can imagine. Damn it, Muzien, it is easier for me to find an elf *eager* for war than one who will accept mankind as a legitimate danger."

Muzien reached out, put a hand on Varen's shoulder. He tried to remember a time when he'd considered the elf a childhood friend.

It felt like a different life and a gulf of blood and coin lay between them.

"There's still hope," Muzien said, and he felt his heart speeding up. This was it, the culmination of his plan. "In Mordeina, I have formed a guild of men and women loyal to my name. They're bound by greed and ambition, and for that alone, they are both predictable and reliable. I've dipped my fingers into every bit of trade, particularly the vices their kings and queens have declared illegal. The price was dear, Varen, and I have spilled more blood than I wish to ever see again in my lifetime, but I would gladly pay it a hundred times over if it means the safety of our people."

"I don't understand," said Varen. "How does a guild of humans spare us from a potential war?"

"By bringing the war to them. A minor noble from the southern nation of Ker has made repeated claims that he could conquer all of Mordan, usually under the guise of some bloated family history…a noble that is firmly in my pocket. I've secretly contacted mercenary bands from all across Mordeina and Ker, drawing them south to join him. Should he march upon Mordeina and place it under siege, my guild will sabotage the defenses, overthrowing that wretched Baedan family line that has ruled Mordan for far too long."

As Varen listened, his pale face somehow steadily grew paler.

"You would incite a rebellion against their king?" he said when Muzien finished. "Even worse, you would have us explicitly responsible? Should the humans hear…"

"They won't," Muzien insisted. "I've used my guild's connections for every step of the plan, protecting our people from blame. When the fighting begins, it will be sudden, chaotic. We'll position the various mercenary groups all across Mordeina. At my word, they'll begin burning villages to the ground. The combination of chaos and surprise will prevent the king from properly mustering his troops, and that's when my puppet noble marches on Mordeina. The plan will succeed, Varen; I promise you."

Varen looked away, to the statuette of the goddess. Putting a hand atop it, he closed his eyes, shook his head.

"What is it you want from me?" he asked. "If you didn't need help, you'd have already put this plan into motion, consequences be damned."

Muzien felt relief sweep through him. If Varen was ready to consider the cost, then the hardest part was over.

"My guild's trade network is extensive, and it has grown rapidly over the past few years, but it is still not enough to pay for an entire army's worth of mercenaries. I need the coffers of the priesthood opened to me. With it, I can establish a puppet king loyal to my desires. Even if we fail, we'll plunge the human nations into chaos that will take years to recover from. All I ask is that you trust me."

"Why come to me?"

"Because what we do must be kept between just us. The fewer who know, the safer we are. You control the coffers, and you alone. I bring before you a plan to save our people; now all you must do is give me the word to begin."

Varen opened his eyes, and his hand fell from the statuette.

"That coin is tithed to us so we may build statues and temples to our goddess," he said. "It is given to us so we may feed any who may go hungry and clothe those who would go naked otherwise. Come the midsummer festival, when we rejoice in the love of our maker, it is those tithes that pay for every instrument, every singer, every baker. And you would have me spend it on mercenaries to slaughter entire villages in the vain hope of replacing one human king for another?"

"I do what must be done," Muzien said, his temper flaring.

"And I do what the goddess says is right! The humans are flawed, but they hold as much capacity for good as they do evil. We will reason with them, Muzien. We will find ways to make them listen to us, to show we are not their enemy, and we'll do it without becoming the monsters they already think we are."

Varen moved to walk past Muzien, and fighting off the beginnings of panic, Muzien stepped in his way and put a hand on his chest to halt him.

"This is a mistake," he said. "Before us is a threat, and it must be met with force, not delusions of peace! I do the goddess's work, restoring a balance so horribly broken that only the most desperate of paths will save us. How can you not see that?"

The high priest grabbed his wrist and pushed it aside.

"Those years in Mordeina have corrupted you," Varen said. "And what I see is a sad shadow of my former friend. Conquest through coin? Death before peace? Celestia's blessing is not on your hands, Muzien. You're more human than elf now."

The words were a knife directly to his heart, and he felt his whole body tremble with growing rage. Reaching back, he put his hand on the statuette of the goddess, felt the cold stone against his skin.

"Varen," he said as the priest headed for the door.

"Yes?" asked Varen, turning about.

Muzien struck him across the head with the statuette, a corner of the square base crunching into his temple. Varen let out a single cry before dropping to the ground, his entire body limp. When he landed, he splayed awkwardly, the back of his head smacking the hard stone with an audible crack. Dropping the statuette, Muzien stood there in the middle of the shrine, feeling panic nipping at the corners of his mind.

"Her will," he said to the body. "I did her will, always her will, yet you'd turn on me? You'd have my ten years of living among those wretched humans be for nothing? *Nothing!*"

He kicked Varen in the side, but there was no reaction. Blood continued to spill out across the emerald floor, taking on a purplish hue. Trying to fight down the panic, Muzien scrambled for ideas. There had to be a way to make his plan work. There had to be a way to salvage the situation. But everything involved coin he didn't have, and with Varen dead, there was little chance for him to obtain any wealth from his brethren.

Turning, he let his eyes fall upon the statuette, which lay on its side, the bottom of it still stained with the priest's blood.

"I did this for you," Muzien said, voice dropping to a whisper as he fell to one knee and reached out to take it. "Tell me what to do, my goddess. My actions were just; I know it with all my heart. Please, tell me how to save our people."

The fingers of his left hand closed about the goddess's legs, and he bowed his head, eyes closed. He prayed for a voice, a sign, a whisper of wind in his ear confirming all he'd done…but instead, he only felt pain. It grew steadily, burning, charring, but he refused to relent. Varen was wrong. Celestia would not abandon him so. She would not betray him. But why did his hand burn? Why did the pain sear into him, and why must he now be screaming?

At last, he could stand no more. The statuette dropped to the ground, and when he opened his eyes, he saw the briefest of glow fading from the stone. As for his hand, he held it shaking before him, saw the blackened remains through the blur of his tears. His skin was charred, and with every twitch of his fingers, fresh pain shot up his arm.

"No," Muzien whispered, tears falling. "No, damn it, no!"

Slowly, he stood, his chest suddenly feeling hollow as Varen's words echoed in his mind.

You're more human than elf now.

More human? Then so be it. Drawing a knife from his pocket, he walked to the altar where the statuette had first rested and then dropped to one knee.

"If you would deny me, then I deny you as well," he said as he took the sharpened edge to the tip of his left ear. "If you would rebuke my attempts to save your people, then let them all burn."

He cut into the ear, removing the curled tip that set him apart from the men and women he'd walked among throughout the city of Mordeina. As the blood ran down his neck, he took the knife to the other ear. After two quick breaths, he cut it as well. Rising back to his feet, he sheathed his knife and clutched the bloody stumps of cartilage tightly in his darkened hand.

"If I am more human than elf, then let me become the greatest at being human," he swore to the heavens. "Their love of coin, their lust for power, their hearts ruled by pride and slave to ambition… everything they cherish shall now be my god, my only god. I need no other."

With that, he kissed the burned flesh of his hand, felt the heat of it on his lips, and then exited the hidden shrine. The severed tips of his ears he left atop the altar, just beneath the four-pointed star.

His final sacrifice to Celestia.

His first to a new god of blood and coin.

if you enjoyed
A DANCE OF SHADOWS

look out for

BLOOD SONG
Book One of Raven's Shadow

by

Anthony Ryan

Verniers' Account

He had many names. Although yet to reach his thirtieth year, history had seen fit to bestow upon him titles aplenty: Sword of the Realm to the mad king who sent him to plague us, the Young Hawk to the men who followed him through the trials of war, Darkblade to his Cumbraelin enemies and, as I was to learn much later, Beral Shak Ur to the enigmatic tribes of the Great Northern Forest – the Shadow of the Raven.

But my people knew him by only one name and it was this that sang in my head continually the morning they brought him to the docks: Hope Killer. Soon you will die and I will see it. Hope Killer.

Although he was certainly taller than most men, I was surprised to find that, contrary to the tales I had heard, he was no giant, and whilst his features were strong they could hardly be called handsome. His frame was muscular but not possessed of the massive thews described so vividly by the storytellers. The only aspect of his appearance to match his legend was his eyes: black as jet and piercing as a hawk's. They said his eyes could strip a man's soul bare, that no secret could be hidden if he met your gaze. I had never believed it but seeing him now, I could see why others would.

The prisoner was accompanied by a full company of the Imperial Guard, riding in close escort, lances ready, hard eyes scanning the watching crowd for trouble. The crowd, however, were silent. They stopped to stare at him as he rode through, but there were no shouts, no insults or missiles hurled. I recalled that they knew this man, for a brief time he had ruled their city and commanded a foreign army within its walls, yet I saw no hate in their faces, no desire for vengeance. Mostly they seemed curious. Why was he here? Why was he alive at all?

The company reined in on the wharf, the prisoner dismounting to be led to the waiting vessel. I put my notes away and rose from my resting place atop a spice barrel, nodding at the captain. 'Honour to you, sir.'

The captain, a veteran Guards officer with a pale scar running along his jawline and the ebony skin of the southern Empire, returned the nod with practised formality. 'Lord Verniers.'

'I trust you had an untroubled journey?'

The captain shrugged. 'A few threats here and there. Had to crack a few heads in Jesseria, the locals wanted to hang the Hope Killer's carcass from their temple spire.'

I bridled at the disloyalty. The Emperor's Edict had been read in all towns through which the prisoner would travel, its meaning plain: no harm will come to the Hope Killer. 'The Emperor will hear of it,' I said.

'As you wish, but it was a small matter.' He turned to the prisoner. 'Lord Verniers, I present the Imperial prisoner Vaelin Al Sorna.'

I nodded formally to the tall man, the name a steady refrain in my head. Hope Killer, Hope Killer . . . 'Honour to you, sir,' I forced the greeting out.

His black eyes met mine for a second, piercing, enquiring. For a moment I wondered if the more outlandish stories were true, if there was magic in the gaze of this savage. Could he truly strip the truth from a man's soul? Since the war, stories had abounded of the Hope Killer's mysterious powers. He could talk to animals, command the Nameless and shape the weather to his will. His steel was tempered with the blood of fallen enemies and would never break in battle. And worst of all, he and his people worshipped the dead, communing with the shades of their forebears to conjure forth all manner of foulness. I gave little credence to such folly, reasoning that if the Northmen's magics were so powerful, how had they contrived to suffer such a crushing defeat at our hands?

'My lord.' Vaelin Al Sorna's voice was harsh and thickly accented, his Alpiran had been learned in a dungeon and his tones were no doubt coarsened by years of shouting above the clash of weapons and screams of the fallen to win victory in a hundred battles, one of which had cost me my closest friend and the future of this Empire.

I turned to the captain. 'Why is he shackled? The Emperor ordered he be treated with respect.'

'The people didn't like seeing him riding unfettered,' the captain explained. 'The prisoner suggested we shackle him to avoid trouble.' He moved to Al Sorna and unlocked the restraints. The big man massaged his wrists with scarred hands.

'My lord!' A shout from the crowd. I turned to see a portly man in a white robe hurrying towards us, face wet with unaccustomed exertion. 'A moment, please!'

The captain's hand inched closer to his sabre but Al Sorna was unconcerned, smiling as the portly man approached. 'Governor Aruan.'

The portly man halted, wiping sweat from his face with a lace scarf. In his left hand he carried a long bundle wrapped in cloth. He nodded at the captain and myself but addressed himself to the prisoner. 'My lord. I never thought to see you again. Are you well?'

'I am, Governor. And you?'

The portly man spread his right hand, lace scarf dangling from his thumb, jewelled rings on every finger. 'Governor no longer. Merely a poor merchant these days. Trade is not what it was, but we make our way.'

'Lord Verniers.' Vaelin Al Sorna gestured at me. 'This is Holus Nester Aruan, former Governor of the City of Linesh.'

'Honoured Sir.' Aruan greeted me with a short bow.

'Honoured Sir,' I replied formally. So this was the man from whom the Hope Killer had seized the city. Aruan's failure to take his own life in dishonour had been widely remarked upon in the aftermath of the war but the Emperor (Gods preserve him in his wisdom and mercy) had granted clemency in light of the extraordinary circumstances of the Hope Killer's occupation. Clemency, however, had not extended to a continuance of his Governorship.

Aruan turned back to Al Sorna. 'It pleases me to find you well. I wrote to the Emperor begging mercy.'

'I know, your letter was read at my trial.'

I knew from the trial records that Aruan's letter, written at no small risk to his life, had formed part of the evidence describing curiously uncharacteristic acts of generosity and mercy by the Hope Killer during the war. The Emperor had listened patiently to it all before ruling that the prisoner was on trial for his crimes, not his virtues.

'Your daughter is well?' the prisoner asked Aruan.

'Very, she weds this summer. A feckless son of a shipbuilder, but what can a poor father do? Thanks to you, at least she is alive to break my heart.'

'I am glad. About the wedding, not your broken heart. I can offer no gift except my best wishes.'

'Actually, my lord, I come with a gift of my own.'

Aruan lifted the long, cloth-covered bundle in both hands, presenting it to the Hope Killer with a strangely grave expression. 'I hear you will have need of this again soon.'

There was a definite hesitation in the Northman's demeanour before he reached out to take the bundle, undoing the ties with his scarred hands. The cloth came away to reveal a sword of unfamiliar design, the scabbard-clad blade was a yard or so in the length and straight, unlike the curved sabres favoured by Alpiran soldiery. A single tine arched around the hilt to form a guard and the only ornamentation to the weapon was a plain steel pommel. The hilt and the scabbard bore many small nicks and scratches that spoke of years of hard use. This was no ceremonial weapon and I realised with a sickening rush that it was his sword. The sword he had carried to our shores. The sword that made him the Hope Killer.

'You kept that?' I sputtered at Aruan, appalled.

The portly man's expression grew cold as he turned to me. 'My honour demanded no less, my lord.'

'My thanks,' Al Sorna said, before any further outrage could spill from my lips. He hefted the sword and I saw the Guard Captain stiffen as Al Sorna drew the blade an inch or so from the scabbard, testing the edge with his thumb. 'Still sharp.'

'It's been well cared for. Oiled and sharpened regularly. I also have another small token.' Aruan extended his hand. In his palm sat a single ruby, a well-cut stone of medium weight, no doubt one of the more valued gems in the family collection. I knew the story behind Aruan's gratitude, but his evident regard for this savage and the sickening presence of the sword still irked me greatly.

Al Sorna seemed at a loss, shaking his head. 'Governor, I cannot . . .'

I moved closer, speaking softly. 'He does you a greater honour than you deserve, Northman. Refusing will insult him and dishonour you.'

He flicked his black eyes over me briefly before smiling at Aruan, 'I cannot refuse such generosity.' He took the gem. 'I'll keep it always.'

'I hope not,' Aruan responded with a laugh. 'A man only keeps a jewel when he has no need to sell it.'

'You there!' A voice came from the vessel moored a short distance along the quay, a sizeable Meldenean galley, the number of oars and the width of the hull showing it to be a freighter rather than one of their fabled warships. A stocky man with an extensive black beard, marked as the captain by the red scarf on his head, was waving from the bow. 'Bring the Hope Killer aboard, you Alpiran dogs!' he shouted with customary Meldenean civility. 'Any more dithering and we'll miss the tide.'

'Our passage to the Islands awaits,' I told the prisoner, gathering my possessions. 'We'd best avoid the ire of our captain.'

'So it's true then,' Aruan said. 'You go to the Islands to fight for the lady?' I found myself disliking the tone in his voice, it sounded uncomfortably like awe.

'It's true.' He clasped hands briefly with Aruan and nodded at the captain of his guard before turning to me. 'My lord. Shall we?'

'You may be one of the first in line to lick your Emperor's feet, scribbler' – the ship's captain stabbed a finger into my chest – 'but this ship is my kingdom. You berth here or you can spend the voyage roped to the mainmast.'

He had shown us to our quarters, a curtained-off section of the hold near the prow of the ship. The hold stank of brine, bilge water and the intermingled odour of the cargo, a sickly, cloying mélange of fruit, dried fish and the myriad spices for which the Empire was famous. It was all I could do to keep from gagging.

'I am Lord Verniers Alishe Someren, Imperial Chronicler, First of the Learned and honoured servant of the Emperor,' I responded, the handkerchief over my mouth muffling my words somewhat. 'I am emissary to the Ship Lords and official escort to the Imperial prisoner. You will treat me with respect, pirate, or I'll have twenty guardsmen aboard in a trice to flog you in front of your crew.'

The captain leaned closer; incredibly his breath smelt worse than the hold. 'Then I'll have twenty-one bodies to feed to the orcas when we leave the harbour, scribbler.'

Al Sorna prodded one of the bedrolls on the deck with his foot and glanced around briefly. 'This'll do. We'll need food and water.'

I bristled. 'You seriously suggest we sleep in this rat-hole? It's disgusting.'

'You should try a dungeon. Plenty of rats there too.' He turned to the captain. 'The water barrel is on the foredeck?'

The captain ran a stubby finger through the mass of his beard, *contemplating the tall man, no doubt wondering if he was being mocked and calculating if he could kill him if he had to. They have a saying on the northern Alpiran coast: turn your back on a cobra but never a Meldenean. 'So you're the one who's going to cross swords with the Shield? They're offering twenty to one against you in Ildera. Think I should risk a copper on you? The Shield is the keenest blade in the Islands, can slice a fly in half with a sabre.'*

'Such renown does him credit.' Vaelin Al Sorna smiled. 'The water barrel?'

'It's there. You can have one gourd a day each, no more. My crew won't go short for the likes of you two. You can get food from the galley, if you don't mind eating with scum like us.'

'No doubt I've eaten with worse. If you need an extra man at the oars, I am at your disposal.'

'Rowed before have you?'

'Once.'

The captain grunted, 'We'll manage.' He turned to go, muttering over his shoulder, 'We sail within the hour, stay out of the way until we clear the harbour.'

'Island savage!' I fumed, unpacking my belongings, laying out my quills and ink. I checked there were no rats lurking under my bedroll before sitting down to compose a letter to the Emperor. I intended to let him know the full extent of this insult. 'He'll find no berth in an Alpiran harbour again, mark you.'

Vaelin Al Sorna sat down, resting his back against the hull. 'You speak my language?' he asked, slipping into the Northern tongue.

'I study languages,' I replied in kind. 'I can speak the seven major tongues of the Empire fluently and communicate in five more.'

'Impressive. Do you know the Seordah language?'

I looked up from my parchment. 'Seordah?'

'The Seordah Sil of the Great Northern Forest. You've heard of them?'

'My knowledge of northern savages is far from comprehensive. As yet I see little reason to complete it.'

'For a learned man you seem happy with your ignorance.'

'I feel I speak for my entire nation when I say I wish we had all remained in ignorance of you.'

He tilted his head, studying me. 'That's hate in your voice.'

I ignored him, my quill moving rapidly over the parchment, setting out the formal opening for Imperial correspondence.

'You knew him, didn't you?' Vaelin Al Sorna went on.

My quill stopped. I refused to meet his eye.

'You knew the Hope.'

I put my quill aside and rose. Suddenly the stench of the hold and the proximity of this savage were unbearable. 'Yes, I knew him,' I grated. 'I knew him to be the best of us. I knew he would be the greatest Emperor this land has ever seen. But that's not the reason for my hate, Northman. I hate you because I knew the Hope as my friend, and you killed him.'

I stalked away, climbing the steps to the main deck, wishing for the first time in my life that I could be a warrior, that my arms were thick with muscle and my heart hard as stone, that I could wield a sword and take bloody vengeance. But such things were beyond me. My body was trim but not strong, my wits quick but not ruthless. I was no warrior. So there would be no vengeance for me. All I could do for my friend was witness the death of his killer and write the formal end to his story for the pleasure of my Emperor and the eternal truth of our archive.

I stayed on the deck for hours, leaning on the rail, watching the green-tinged waters of the north Alpiran coast deepen into the blue of the inner Erinean Sea as the ship's bosun beat the drum for the oarsmen and our journey began. Once clear of the coast the captain ordered the mainsail unfurled and our speed increased, the sharp prow of the vessel cutting through the gentle swell, the figurehead, a traditional Meldenean carving of the winged serpent, one of their innumerable sea gods, dipping its many-toothed head amidst a haze of spume. The oarsmen rowed for two hours before the bosun called a rest and they shipped oars, trooping off to their meal. The day watch stayed on deck, running the rigging and undertaking the never-ending chores of ship life. A few favoured me with a customary glare or two, but none attempted to converse, a mercy for which I was grateful.

We were several leagues from the harbour when they came into view, black fins knifing through the swell, heralded by a cheerful shout from the crow's nest. 'Orcas!'

I couldn't tell how many there were, they moved too fast and too fluidly through the sea, occasionally breaking the surface to spout a cloud of steam before diving below. It was only when they came closer that I fully realised their size, over twenty feet from nose to tail. I had seen dolphins before in the southern seas, silvery, playful creatures that could be taught simple tricks. These were different, their size and the dark, flickering shadows they traced through the water seemed ominous to me, threatening shades of nature's indifferent cruelty. My shipmates clearly felt differently, yelling greetings from the rigging as if hailing old friends. Even the captain's habitual scowl seemed to have softened somewhat.

One of the orcas broke the surface in a spectacular display of foam, twisting in midair before crashing into the sea with a boom that shook the ship. The Meldeneans roared their appreciation. Oh Seliesen, I thought. The poem you would have written to honour such a sight.

'They think of them as sacred.' I turned to find that the Hope Killer had joined me at the rail. 'They say when a Meldenean dies at sea the orcas will carry his spirit to the endless ocean beyond the edge of the world.'

'Superstition,' I sniffed.

'Your people have their gods, do they not?'

'My people do, I do not. Gods are a myth, a comforting story for children.'

'Such words would make you welcome in my homeland.'

'We are not in your homeland, Northman. Nor would I ever wish to be.'

Another orca rose from the sea, rising fully ten feet into the air before plunging back down. 'It's strange,' Al Sorna mused. 'When our ships came across this sea the orcas ignored them and made only for the Meldeneans. Perhaps they share the same belief.'

'Perhaps,' I said. 'Or perhaps they appreciate a free meal.' I nodded at the prow, where the captain was throwing salmon into the sea, the orcas swooping on them faster than I could follow.

'Why are you here, Lord Verniers?' Al Sorna asked. 'Why did the Emperor send you? You're no gaoler.'

'The Emperor graciously consented to my request to witness your upcoming duel. And to accompany the Lady Emeren home of course.'

'You came to see me die.'

'I came to write an account of this event for the Imperial Archive. I am the Imperial Chronicler after all.'

'So they told me. Gerish, my gaoler, was a great admirer of your history

of the war with my people, considered it the finest work in Alpiran litera-
ture. He knew a lot for a man who spends his life in a dungeon. He would
sit outside my cell for hours reading out page after page, especially the
battles, he liked those.'

'Accurate research is the key to the historian's art.'

'Then it's a pity you got it so wrong.'

Once again I found myself wishing for a warrior's strength. 'Wrong?'

'Very.'

'I see. Perhaps if you work your savage's brain, you could tell me which
sections were so very wrong.'

'Oh, you got the small things right, mostly. Except you said my
command was the Legion of the Wolf. In fact it was the Thirty-fifth
Regiment of Foot, known amongst the Realm Guard as the Wolfrunners.'

'I'll be sure to rush out a revised edition on my return to
the capital,' I said dryly.

He closed his eyes, remembering. '"King Janus's invasion of the northern
coast was but the first step in pursuance of his greater ambition, the
annexation of the entire Empire."'

It was a verbatim recitation. I was impressed by his memory, but was
damned if I'd say so. 'A simple statement of fact. You came here to steal
the Empire. Janus was a madman to think such a scheme could succeed.'

Al Sorna shook his head. 'We came for the northern coastal ports.
Janus wanted the trade routes through the Erinean. And he was no
madman. He was old and desperate, but not mad.'

I was surprised at the sympathy evident in his voice; Janus was the
great betrayer after all, it was part of the Hope Killer's legend. 'And how
do you know the man's mind so well?'

'He told me.'

'Told you?' I laughed. 'I wrote a thousand letters of enquiry to every
ambassador and Realm official I could think of. The few who bothered
to reply all agreed on one thing: Janus never confided his plans to anyone,
not even his family.'

'And yet you claim he wanted to conquer your whole Empire.'

'A reasonable deduction based on the available evidence.'

'Reasonable, maybe, but wrong. Janus had a king's heart, hard and
cold when he needed it to be. But he wasn't greedy and he was no dreamer.
He knew the Realm could never muster the men and treasure needed to

conquer your Empire. We came for the ports. He said it was the only way we could secure our future.'

'Why would he confide such intelligence to you?'

'We had . . . an arrangement. He told me many things he would tell no other. Some of his commands required an explanation before I would obey them. But sometimes I think he just needed to talk to someone. Even kings get lonely.'

I felt a curious sense of seduction; the Northman knew I hungered for the information he could give me. My respect for him grew, as did my dislike. He was using me, he wanted me to write the story he had to tell. Quite why I had no idea. I knew it was something to do with Janus and the duel he would fight in the Islands. Perhaps he needed to unburden himself before his end, leave a legacy of truth so he would be known to history as more than just the Hope Killer. A final attempt to redeem both his spirit and that of his dead king.

I let the silence string out, watching the orcas until they had eaten their fill of free fish and departed to the east. Finally, as the sun began to dip towards the horizon and the shadows grew long, I said, 'So tell me.'

CONTINUE THE ADVENTURE

For exclusive news, giveaways and more join us on the official Shadowdance Facebook page.